BELLA WAXMAN

The Enigma

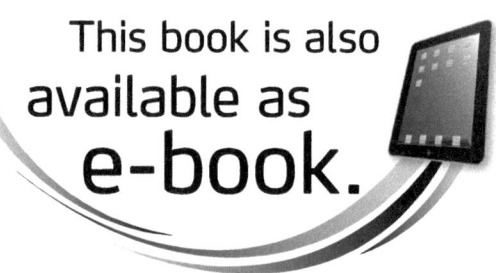

www.novum-publishing.co.uk

All rights of distribution, including film, radio, television, photomechanical reproduction, sound carrier, electronic media and reprint in extracts, are reserved.

Printed in the European Union, using environmentally-friendly, chlorine-free and acid-free paper.

© 2016 novum publishing

ISBN 978-3-99048-298-8
Editor: Arun Natarajan
Cover photo:
Lars Zahner | Dreamstime.com
Cover design, layout & typesetting:
novum publishing

www.novum-publishing.co.uk

A Dedication

This book is dedicated initially to Sister Denise, OSB, whom I knew for only a short while but with whom I spent lovely hours exchanging tales and experiences, comparing ours with the unfortunate lives of other women. Denise, who had had such a hard life growing up in Maine was sadly taken from all her friends in 2007 when a car driven by a drunken young man ploughed into the one in which she and two of her companions were traveling in Richmond, VA. Unfortunately they were all killed.

I think of Denise every time I re-read the many little cards she gave me or slipped under my door when I lived with her community for a few months in Virginia, USA, in 2006.

In addition to the dedication to Denise, this book is for all those unsung heroes who get on with their lives after experiencing tremendous struggles with their gender. Many commit suicide in order to rid themselves of the extreme pain, discrimination, and often violence against them. Many are successful and change without much antagonism from others. Some are attacked by violent bigots and left maimed for life, while others, like Claire in this story, are attacked verbally, especially by family members who refuse to accept change. So this story is dedicated to all those who have struggled in one form or another with their gender identity, especially the members of 'Edinburgh TransWomen,' a community group based in Edinburgh, Scotland, of women who share similar stories of their past lives.

Bella Waxman

It is obvious from the start of our lives that boys are led to believe that their lives are more worthwhile than their sisters"; mothers favor sons over daughters, daughters learn to defer to brothers, sons model themselves on their father. Little boys learn, by osmosis if not by explicit lessons, that the world is fashioned to suit the male of our species, and that they are entitled to any advantage given to them.

Burton, Betty (2004) *Josephine and Harriet.* HarperCollins, London, UK.

The Enigma

While this story is essentially a work of fiction, characters and some events in the novel have been based to some extent upon those experienced by a number of women I have known and who have shared their stories with me. In many ways therefore, it is somewhat biographical. While I have obtained permission to use the experiences of others, I have been careful to change personal and place names. Nevertheless, many events portrayed in this novel tend to be based on true happenings.

I have relied also on my own experiences of places, individuals and events, especially with parents and siblings, to build up a story that is both factual and at the same time a work of fiction. Some events may have been related due to the detail being in the public domain, but others are imaginary even if they might bear the name of places which exist somewhere, on any continent. In such cases, a place name in this story may not bear any resemblance to the actual town or place which is so named.

Many of the stories attributed to the main character Claire Wilson, are based on her life experiences. The only friends, who know of her past apart from her family, are all supportive of her bravery to follow her dream. Toward the end of the book and into its sequel, *The Nymph* outlines colleagues who walked away from her to leave her almost destitute. As for her family, with only a few exceptions, they have discriminated against her. Of those around her today, no one knows of her past and as a result she lives a peaceful life. When Claire and I saw on ABC 7.30 (Australia) in February 2014 a program which outlined the life and struggles of Lieutenant Colonel Catherine (Cate) McGregor of the Australian Army, who had gone through a similar gender change, it was very painful for her. She realized that if someone was identified in the public media as a notable person in their own right, then a gender change was big news. For Claire, and many of those women and men who are simply ordinary folk who have undergone a similar change of gender, there is no publicity, no public acknowledgement of their struggles and they simply blend into society without "a bang or a whimper" (Victor Hugo).

It happened again when Claire watched Cate McGregor, now described as a transgendered RAAF Officer, address the National Press Club of Australia one lunchtime in April 2015. She had matured as a woman and spoke eloquently, though at times with obvious melancholy in her voice, but there was universal acceptance of those in her audience. She described how everyone, from the Prime Minister downward, had accepted her almost universally. Hearing this, Claire became somewhat morose, being so conscious of many in her family and former work colleagues, who opposed her. Claire has over the years had some family members, especially in the USA and the UK come out publicly to support her, but by and large she has found that when people know she was transgendered, the more they reject her, no matter how beautiful she might have become in the process.

Bella Waxman 2015

Prologue
2002

Claire and her fiancé Harvey had been to visit Sharon Nixon, a woman with whom she had previously shared what some might say was an intimate life. Harvey had suggested he meet Sharon after Claire had started to tell him her story. At first Harvey told her that he really didn't want to know the gory details as he would make his own mind up, in his own time and in his own way. On that particular evening, at his home in Cleveland, just south of Brisbane, she had given him the bare essentials when he said: "Look Claire, I don't really want to know any more. As far as I am concerned you are a woman whom I have fallen in love with and that is enough for me. To be quite honest, I wouldn't have known anyway, so let's leave it at that, shall we?" This from a man who, upon meeting her for the first time at a picnic shelter in Yamba, on the NSW Northern Coast, had presented her with his business card and a color photograph of himself wearing a dark blue blazer, shirt and tie. Claire was to discover later that this was an unusual way of dressing for Harvey, who normally passed his days in a Hawaiian brightly-colored shirt and a pair of pale colored shorts.

Now as they drove away from Sharon's home in Elgindale in Harvey's Mercedes, without turning to look at her he commented: "To be quite honest Claire, now that I have met Sharon face to face, I would have said that she is much older than you, not the other way around." Claire had to smile to herself as Sharon was five years her junior and Harvey was also her junior too, by ten years. It seemed that at sixty-two Claire was constantly being told that she looked as though she was in her forties. Even friends in her local women's service club took her for a much younger woman. It was assumed that she might have been perhaps a fan of the late Elvis Presley because of the age she was perceived to be. But Claire certainly wasn't an Elvis fan and never had been. In actual fact she had been raised on the music of Victor Sylvester and his Ballroom Orchestra, as she loved ballroom dancing. In fact, at one stage in her teens she had been a member of a ballroom dancing group in the city of Aireborough in Yorkshire.

Harvey continued, "You know Claire, had I not known any different, I would have said that Sharon might have had a gender change as she has masculine qualities." Claire was shocked, as she had known Sharon intimately. Harvey, with a broad smile spreading across his face, chuckled to himself. He did like to make outlandish statements. That was Harvey. On her part, she simply smiled to herself as she knew both her own story and Sharon's too. But as Harvey was not really interested in any information that was in his own words "secret women's business," his brain turned off as Claire, his fiancée, opened her mouth to make comment.

According to Harvey, she was supposed to take great interest in his "pastimes," like his golfing, his fishing, his crabbing and his other interests, all his needs and desires. There was the time when they were traveling into Brisbane one morning, when he suddenly exclaimed: "Did you see that truck?"

"What truck darling?" Claire stared at Harvey as they drove along the highway in his Mercedes.

"The one we just passed. Don't you ever take note of what we see?"

"Yes darling I do, but I am not interested in trucks."

"Why?"

"Because I'm just not! Women tend not to look at things that men look at, just as you constantly remind me that certain things are in your own words, 'secret women's business'."

"But this is different Claire. That is the model of truck I need to carry my golf clubs, my crab pots and my fishing rods. After we are married we can sell your Hyundai and we'll then have enough money to buy a truck like that one we just passed." Claire went hot and cold in rapid succession. There was no thought that Harvey might sell his Mercedes of course. No, that wouldn't do.

As they were engaged to be married, her needs had to become subservient to Harvey's needs and desires.

"Oh so, it is my money you want, is it?"

"No! Don't put it like that Claire."

"What other way am I to put it. You want us to get married so you can sell my car which is bought and paid for, just so you can indulge in one of your cravings. No darling that is not going to happen. I am definitely not going to sell my yellow Hyundai. Perish the thought."

Harvey went into a deep sulk, and did not come out of it for the rest of the day. Claire presumed that it had been his intention all along to indulge his cravings at her expense. So she had to put her foot down firmly, and now was the time.

Harvey had even gone to the extent of deciding where they were to be married. It was to be in Brisbane's Anglican Cathedral and attended by his cronies in a movement he called the Knights of St Jerome in which he was apparently known as a squire, prior to becoming a full knight. He was going to ask the bishop to marry them too. Claire was not consulted. She was merely a woman and was obliged to follow the lead of the man in everything. That was what it so often said in the Bible, and that was Harvey's belief. To her, such outdated beliefs stemmed from one disgruntled and extremely bigoted man called Sha'ul of Tarsus, known by Christians as St Paul. She found it difficult to believe that after almost two millennia, people believed such ancient garbage.

As for Harvey, it came to a head one day when, through her tears, Claire cried that he never took her anywhere, unless it was to a free luncheon. In fact the second time they had dated, it was at a small restaurant on Queensland's Gold Coast, near Surfers' Paradise, and he actually admitted, nudged by some pointed questions from her, that he had won two free tickets for a meal by answering a question on a local radio program. That was Harvey, anything for free. So this time he had promised to take Claire out to lunch, followed at her insistence that they go for a long walk on the beach. All was fixed for a particular day.

Claire had already booked an appointment at a beauty salon in Cleveland to have her usual three-weekly acrylic nail refill while Harvey admitted he had a meeting with his psychiatrist. Yes, she knew that alarm bells should have rung loudly in her head at this news but she supposed she must have had blinkers on at the time. She was certainly not aware that he consulted a psychiatrist. But don't lots of folk have a psychiatrist, even if she didn't? Well, perhaps Claire might have done a few years earlier, but that was for some other reason, which will be explained later as her story unfolds.

Claire had given Harvey a particular time to collect her from the salon but he turned up half an hour early expecting her to be waiting for him with shiny red nails. When the nail technician told him to come back in a half hour he sulked and told Claire to be at his Mercedes around the corner when the assistant had finished.

An hour and a half later, after she had been sitting in the hot sun near his car for at least an hour or more, he calmly strode up, unlocked the doors and climbed into the driver seat. His dearly beloved was expected to step forward, open the passenger door herself and sit down, close the door and act as though nothing untoward had happened. Harvey then sped off as though he was in an enormous hurry. They had only traveled about a kilometer when his mouth opened, "Oh by the way, I'm playing golf this afternoon."

"But darling what about the magazines you were planning to take to the Seamen's Mission, and then our lunch and walk on the beach?"

"What lunch and walk on the beach?"

"You said we would have a nice lunch out and then after dropping the magazines off at the mission, we would go for a stroll along the beach."

"Did I?"

"Yes you did."

"When was that?"

"Last evening after I complained you never took me anywhere and then again this morning before we drove off."

"I don't remember."

"Well, you did, so there."

"Well, I've changed my mind. I am playing golf this afternoon." Claire really didn't know what to say as she was so shocked at his change of mind, ignoring what to her were the exciting plans they had made the previous evening.

They drove back to Harvey's blond-brick residence in silence, Claire fuming inside, wondering if he could see the steam coming out of her ears, as her face slowly changed from normal to hot and flustered. Back at his house, trying to hide her anger, she asked, while trying desperately to keep a cool countenance: "Shall I make you some lunch darling?"

"No, don't bother. I will get some lunch at the club."

With that he went back into the garage, threw his golf clubs into the car's trunk and reversed out of the driveway. The electrically operated garage doors slowly descended leaving Claire, his beloved future wife, staring into nothingness. All she had in front of her was a black fog, accompanied by a deepening silence.

Why was I putting up with this treatment? Claire had to ask herself. Was she so desperate for a guy like Harvey that she would put up with anything he verbally threw at her? They had previously split up for six months to see how they both felt. Claire had suggested the separation following her discovery that he was secretly dating oriental girls through the Internet, causing her to blow up over the issue. She had told him in no uncertain terms that if they were to be married, then she had to be the only one he was to date. So, after he departed for his golf club, Claire decided to have a look on his computer to see if he still had photos of a selection of Chinese girls on his screen saver. Thankfully, he hadn't, but she was still suspicious, so she looked through his folders. *Ahah, you bastard, got you.* She mouthed softly, but with venom in her voice. What he had done was to sideline the portraits which had previously been on his screen saver to store them in a new folder. So, Harvey was obviously still online dating. Hmm!

That does it, She said to herself, closing his machine down and then walking defiantly back into the kitchen. What was she to do? Moving into the bedroom she methodically packed her case and carried it to the front door in readiness for loading into the back of her bright yellow Hyundai. But then, turning sideways saw her car, still under the side awning of the house and the gates were locked. Harvey had driven her car in the previous evening prior to his intention to mow the grass at the front of the house, which as it happened, he then forgot to do, instead staying glued to the television, watching the cricket. *Typical man,* she thought.

Claire went into the garage and spying her blue metal tool box, which he had taken from her shed in Elgindale; she found what she had been advised was 'a shifter' and was able to undo the hex-headed screws on the gate lock. *Yey! What a clever girl,* Claire thought to herself. She drove out her car and replaced the screws on the lock, putting her case and the toolbox into the back of the Hyundai.

However, driving off in so much anger she had cleanly forgot to check the washing machine, to see if she had left any laundry behind. Crying all the way to Grafton, it was almost evening when she took a room in a cheap motel on Pacific Highway, bought a burger and fries from McDonald's and cried herself to sleep. Clearly she had fallen for a nut case and no mistake. Or, was he typical of many men, full of their own importance and to Hell with interfering women?

Driving back up to the Tablelands the next morning, Claire decided that as she had already sold her beautiful pre-Federation cottage, she would find a new home on the coast as it was certainly cooler than in the New England during the summer months. How she arrived home she really didn't know as she started thinking of her enigmatic and often traumatic past. Why had one particular guy told her that she was a parasite on society and should have been drowned at birth like an unwanted kitten? Why did people turn against her when they knew or had been told of her past? Certainly Claire had many friends whom she had not told and they remained loyal. Even a couple of her older friends, who had known her for many years, had stayed loyal. So why was she a victim of her birth? Why were some people, especially many of her relatives, so cruel and brutal in their condemnation of her? Claire appeared to be no different to other women, having the same physical and emotional characteristics, so why was she attacked from time to time by those who knew of her past?

As she once again recalled her former life, so many events brought tears to her eyes, together with tremendous heartache and melancholy. But here, right now, her story begins again, so that folk might understand why women like her are sometimes victimized. Is it any wonder that Claire describes her life as an exploding enigma?

1

1940

Claire's mother, Olivia Wilson (née Levine) had always imagined her first born would be a girl. Olivia's sister-in-law, Deborah, who had married elder brother Jeremy, had given birth a few months earlier to June; the first girl of her Levine generation, and Olivia hoped with all her heart that she also might give birth to a girl. Her older sister Elaine had had a boy to Norrie Stevens, so Olivia thought it was definitely time for another girl to be born into the Levine clan.

On the other hand, Milton, Olivias husband, was expecting the new baby to be a boy. Kate, the wife of his older brother Clive, had given birth to Kirsty eight months earlier, and Daphne, the wife of Milton's brother Sandy, had given birth to Coralee, about the same time. So the next generation of the Wilsons, should, by rights, be a boy one presumed. But Milt, as most people called him, not only presumed, but claimed that he, like many pseudo-macho misogynists, full of his own capabilities as a self-proclaimed full-bloodied male would have a son, and no mistake. *'A man's a man for a' that'* the majestic Scots bard had written. Men who sired female babies, in Milt's opinion were less than full-blown men – more on the side of the 'poofters' he detested, than real men like himself, although he did not exactly refer to his brothers in those terms. On Claire's part, with a man like that as a father, she was to experience so much of his character growing up in Micklegate. Known as 'Micky' to most of its residents, it was an outer suburb of the city of Aireborough in Yorkshire.

So, Claire was born in the winter of 1940. In her later childhood and teenage years she always imagined it snowing on her birthday, whether this was wishful thinking on her part or not, she never could recall. You see, Claire certainly had no recollection as to whether it was snowing when she was born, irrespective of her feeling that it did. But no one ever told her, so maybe it was indeed a figment of what might later be described by some members of the family, as her wild romantic imagination. Nevertheless, as Claire grew up in 'Micky' she developed a fascination for the cold white stuff and would spend hours glued to the French door in the dining room looking up at the sky, as the flakes floated gently down to settle on the back garden. It was as though the sky was falling apart and covering the earth with its flakey residue. She was mesmerized.

Many years later, in fact, well into her womanhood Claire had been standing next to a window at Cousin Olivia's house (yes she was named after Claire's mother) in Detroit, Michigan, looking up at snowflakes falling when Olivia commented with a puzzled expression on her somewhat rotund face: "You really have a fascination for snow, don't you, Claire?"

"I suppose I do really. As a little girl I was fascinated by the snow and spent hours staring at the sky, watching individual snowflakes to see where each one landed." So, to some degree, the die had been set. *Me and snow went together like crackers and cheese, or plums and custard*, Claire presumed. It was a given.

But, like all babies upon being born, she supposed she might have slept most of the time, as it takes a lot out of a baby coming into the world. Although Claire was not to know it at the time, she was born a few months into the earth shattering event which was to be known as the Second World War, or World War II, depending on which side of the Atlantic Ocean one lived. All she had recollection of in her first few months was looking up out of her gorgeous soft-brown eyes at her mum, as she enjoyed refreshments every few hours between sleeps. One supposes like most babies she may have cried too, in fact it was most likely that she did. But Claire was to have no recollection of any of this and no one ever told her of anything that hinted at her being fond of crying. In all honesty, she could not remember her mum or anyone else for that matter, saying that she was a good or a bad baby. Not that it matters today in the 21st century, as she tried to recall how her life on this planet began, linking bits and pieces together as one might a 1000-piece 'advanced-level' jigsaw.

There were a few things Claire did remember though. For example she distinctly remembered sitting in her baby carriage, looking out over the cover which was navy blue, with a silver woven design running around the edge. She also remembered being in her cot looking through the white bars. Milton, her dad, was in the habit of telling folk that in order to go to sleep the child would ask him to: "holy hand!" – Her babyish way of asking him to hold her hand. As Claire grew up, she listened to this joke of his over and over again, which somehow made her feel inferior, portraying her as a somewhat effeminate character which her father despised in all males. But then lots of folk remember little things like this. So in that way Claire supposed she was no different to other kids. Or was she?

In 1940, it was not uncommon for women in Yorkshire to give birth at home, and this was true for Olivia Wilson, but under the supervision of the local midwife, Nurse Middleton. Claire's birth was in that category as she was born in her parent's front bedroom. Their house was in a street called Sandy Peth, off Hawkhill Drive, Micklegate, which is today a major suburb of Aireborough. Her parents, Milton Stanley Wilson and Olivia Eliza Wilson (née Levine) had bought the house new in 1938 when Olivia worked as a shorthand typist in the city center and Milton was a draftsman in the drawing office of Burnley Aircraft, which had a factory in Overton Road. Olivia had attended Our Lady's College, a High School for Roman Catholic girls, just off Woodthorpe Lane, past the Brotherton Tower of Aireborough University. In her senior year, however, Olivia had left Our Lady's to attend a course on shorthand and typing at Clark's College, which was later, to become a high school. Olivia told Claire about this many years later when she passed an entrance exam to attend that very same school.

Claire's father Milton, known as Milt by his brothers and friends, was born in Casterley to James William Wilson and Penny Wilson, who had herself been born in the nearby village of

Monk Farley as Penelope Stanley. James Wilson had been a coal miner but had received local, relatively minor, fame as a musician, playing cornet in the Casterley Prize Silver Band. Claire used to think that her granddad had played cornet in his colliery band, but later discovered in a book she bought in Casterley itself that her paternal grandfather played in the town band instead.

Olivia, Claire's mum, had been born to Wilhelm Louis Levine of Micklebrough and Marjory 'Porty' Levine. That nickname was short for Porterhouse, named after a close friend of the family. Nanna Levine, had been born in Sunderland as Marjory Porterhouse Jackson, but as Wilhelm had been transferred from Micklebrough to the southern English port of Chatham because of his work with the Navy, Marjory gave birth to Olivia when they were renting a house in Fosterham, Kent.

At the start of World War II, Micklegate was regarded by its residents as an outer village of Aireborough. In fact Claire's parents, the Wilsons, always believed it might have been outside the Aireborough boundary as her mum and dad added *near Aireborough* as part of the return address on the backs of envelopes. But, and this was an exciting 'but' in Claire's view, Aireborough Corporation trams traveled right up to Micklegate from Wingate via City Square. In fact, the trams terminated opposite the Regal Cinema, in front of Alfie Guy's greengrocery shop, and where Billy Sharpe used to sell newspapers inside the opening of the dark-green-painted wooden tram shelter opposite Mr Guy's shop.

Billy's voice was quite sonorous when he announced the headlines of the *Yorkshire Post*, the *Yorkshire Evening Post* or the *Yorkshire Evening News*. The *Yorkshire Evening Post* always came out like *Air'n Poe*. To Claire's mind this was a foreign language. Growing up she could never, for the life of her, understand how newspaper vendors mispronounced the names of the papers they were selling. However, Billy only seemed to sell papers at the terminus in the winter and spring, as one year when the Wilsons were on holiday in Scarborough, they not only saw Billy but actually greeted him as he was selling newspapers on the sea front. You see, the Wilsons were in the habit of going for their summer holidays the first two weeks in August, like so many folks did at that time. The first Monday in August was marked on the calendar as 'Bank Holiday Monday'. But let's backtrack a little.

The house in which Claire was born was described as "a half-pebble-dashed semi-detached residence." She recalled once seeing a bill of sale for the house and thought she saw that the price was £830 plus extras which totaled £65. According to her dad, the 'extras' had been charged because he decided when the house was being built, to move two walls a fraction, and typical of Milton, he had knocked them down one evening, so that they had to be rebuilt. He had left a note on the door telling the builders that he wanted the wall moved "another foot to the rear." That was the reason why he had to pay extra. Of course, by 2010 standards, the cost of the same desirable residence or 'des res', might have been around £185,000 or even more. The price of progress, one presumes.

The Wilson's 'des res' was described as part-pebble-dashed because the upper storey on the outside was rendered and pebbles thrown into the wet cement before it dried. Claire could never forget this as she and her mum were forever sweeping up the pebbles that fell down every winter, especially after a heavy frost. Sweeping up the residue at the base of the walls in the spring was testimony to the unsuitability of that type of rendering for the Yorkshire climate. But then she later saw many houses in Scotland with this type of external wall rendering, and wasn't the Scottish climate worse than that in Yorkshire in winter?

The front door of the Wilson residence was very beautiful in Claire's eyes. It had colored lead lights in the upper panel, depicting a sunset, with rising or setting suns in each lower corner. Later, possibly in the early 1950s, her dad welded up some new tubular metal gates at "the works" in Starfield and he made them in a design which mimicked the rising sun motif on the front door. Claire always remembered the color of the finished gates – maroon; because it happened to be the same color as the base of the rocking horse her dad had made for her one Christmas, as a present from "Father Christmas."

Their semi-detached house, or duplex, was built on a site which gently sloped down from the footpath and so while the front garden began at ground level near the bullnose-topped brick wall, her dad had created a level lawn which was separated from the house by a low wall made from thin slabs of sandstone, which to Claire's horror became a haven for woodlice, which she was later to refer to in Australia as *slaters*. If one of those critters landed on her she would run about in all directions to get rid of it, jumping up and down in the process. Her pet hate then, and even into adulthood, was anything 'creepy crawly' such as woodlice, earwigs and spiders. Oh yes, and moths, which would fly into her bedroom in autumn and plague the life out of her until she managed to corner them, and put them back through the open window before closing it. Claire recalled that on one occasion, sitting up in bed reading with her back to the bed head, a large moth must have flown through the window unannounced. The next thing she remembered was something crawling up her back inside her pajama top. Screaming blue murder she ripped off her jacket and pummeled the poor unsuspecting creature to death. It had obviously been so disorientated to find itself flapping around in the dark crevasse between her skin and the fabric, to its ultimate demise. Needless to say there was little of the moth left after her brutal onslaught. Olivia had dashed into Claire's bedroom when she heard the scream, thinking the worst had happened, only to find her child in the late stages of performing the annihilation of a poor unsuspecting creature of the night.

But getting back to the plot; the front garden of the Wilson's house in Sandy Peth, comprised a small lawn with the corners cut off at an angle, and in the center of the lawn was a circular bed with a standard tea rose. The surrounding borders had such varieties of plants as golden rod, red-hot poker, lupin, perennial cornflower, antirrhinum, and daisies and in summer blue lobelia and white alyssum, which Milton and Olivia always planted at the front of every border in late spring. The thing Claire didn't like was finding earwigs inside the antirrhinums, or snapdragons as they called them. Milton pronounced these blooms *aunty-rye-nums* and he made fun of Claire's American Aunt Diane many years later when she pronounced them as *anti-ri-nums*. But then Claire's dad was always in the habit of making fun of people, especially our star girl, or whatever she was at the time.

The front door of the Wilson house was set back slightly from the front wall alignment by a curved wall. There was a concrete canopy over the front entrance, which also had side windows with 'rising sun' leaded lights too. Dividing the front step from the driveway was a narrow piece of earth in which Milton had planted a yellow privet hedge. Minor detail perhaps, but Claire could never forget how things looked as she was growing up. Her bedroom window was above the concrete canopy mentioned. So what we are trying to do here is to paint a picture so that the reader may be able to imagine Claire's world at that time. She saw things through the eyes of a child. The main point is that she had a bedroom at the front of the house and her window faced the street, above the front door. Oh yes, the driveway to their house was separated in those days from the Rooney's driveway next door by a fence, not that the neighbors had a car of course, compared to the Wilson family which did.

As children, Claire and her brothers called their neighbors Aunty Margaret and Uncle Henry. Living with them in the same house was Miss Scotia, whom the Wilson kids referred to as Aunty Edna, and Edwin Scotia, whom Claire referred to as "Uncle Eddy." Olivia told Claire that "Aunty" Edna and "Uncle" Edwin were the younger brother and sister of Aunty Margaret. Uncle Eddy used to wear a brown bowler hat and Claire thought him exceedingly smart. Uncle Henry, she recalled, was a plasterer and often arrived home from his jobs in white dungarees covered with plaster dust. As a toddler Claire was constantly being reminded of the times she would knock on the Rooney's scullery door and ask: "Is Uncle Eddy coming out to play?"

Claire was constantly reminded by her dad of one particular story: The Rooney's had had a ladder propped up against their side wall as Eddy had been in the act of painting the surround of the windows to the stair landing and the toilet, both of which were directly above the scullery door. According to Milton's version of events, while Eddy was messing around in their shed for something or other, a wee child wandered around the end of the dividing fence and when Eddy came out, he was to see Claire up six steps of the ladder shouting: "Bush, wanna bush." According to Claire's father, she had wanted to help with the house painting.

This story was often one of the highlights of conversation by Milton and Olivia when entertaining the few visitors that graced the Wilson's home, when the guests showed an interest in the children and their antics, much to Claire's embarrassment. It was like a cracked gramophone record, always the same story, time and time again. Dah di dah dah! Ho hum! Claire was not amused.

The Wilson house had two door openings to the driveway; one of these gave access to the space under the staircase, and was referred to as "the coalhouse." This was a good place to hide when the Wilson kids were playing hide and seek. The key was always left in the door so that they had ready access when they needed to fill up the coal scuttle. This brings us to one of Danny's tricks – but wait…

As Claire was growing up, like most children she was afraid of thunder and lightning. When it thundered, her mum would try to quieten her by saying that the noise was only the coalman delivering bags of coal into the coalhouse. But Claire became wise to that explanation and would hide under the table whenever the noise came down from the sky.

One time, when the children were playing hide and seek in the yard, Claire had hidden in the coalhouse. Her darling brother Danny (with tongue in cheek), after realizing she was inside, locked the door from the outside and put the key in his trouser pocket. It was not until a few minutes later that Olivia heard her eldest child screaming blue murder, together with a constant banging of a tiny hand on wood. She realized what had happened. Of course, Danny pretended he knew nothing about the eldest being locked in, until Olivia asked him to empty his pockets. Upon opening the coalhouse door, Claire was told not to be such 'a big baby' for crying, while Danny was merely told not to do it again. But as Danny could not be trusted, he did it again on a number of other occasions.

The door next to the coalhouse door, separated from it by a small window with a fresh air section at the top covered in metal gauze, was the door to the scullery; a word that seems to have gone out of fashion nowadays in favor of the word 'kitchen'. The scullery was in actual fact quite small and apart from having a gas stove, which today might be referred to as a gas cooker, it had a copper boiler in the corner, in which all the dirty clothes had to be boiled and washed. Next to the boiler was a wooden draining board which sloped into what was known as a Belfast Sink. This was an oblong heavy porcelain sink in which the "wee bairns," as Nanna Levine called them, were bathed every night before bed. Opposite the gas stove was a wooden table covered with an oil cloth and above which were two shelves for the pots and pans. At the end of this table was a cupboard the center of which opened up to what was called 'the cubby hole' through which plates of food could be passed into the dining room next door. This was certainly a modern kitchen by post-war standards.

Milton's garage at the end of the driveway was framed and clad in timber, with outward opening timber doors, painted a shade between grass green and bottle green. Between this garage and the Rooney's gray-painted garden shed, was a space wide enough for little children to squeeze into as a hidey-hole. Into this area Olivia, and Margaret from next door, were in the habit of laying down their clothes props, out of the way of mischievous little children. In those days revolving clothes hoists, the likes of which Claire was to discover many years later in Australia, had not been invented, along with many things taken for granted today.

During the war, a small bin was placed at the entrance to the long clothes prop space and into it, after every cooked meal, went the cauliflower stalks, the potato and carrot peelings and left-over bits of bread. In fact, any food that the Wilsons and the Rooney's thought might be edible to a pig would go into 'the pig bin'. It was emptied each week by someone who obviously distributed the contents to local pig farmers. The Wilson children had been told about pigs because, as Milton constantly reminded them, pigs gave them their Sunday bacon. But of course during the war; and for six years afterward, bacon was rationed, as was most food. But people had to manage as times were hard.

In summer months, the back garden of the Wilson residence was a picture, as Olivia and Milton planted lots of annual bedding plants and perennials. Like the borders at the front, the back borders were also edged in blue lobelia and white alyssum, planted alternatively. Behind these varieties were petunias, salvias, beds of pansies, Sweet-Williams and in the middle of the large border between the Rooney's and the Wilson's back gardens were yet more red hot pokers, golden rod, perennial cornflower and lupins. Claire's favorite flowers were the Sweet-Williams as they had the most gorgeous perfume of all. But she particularly liked the long stems of the various colored lupin flowers. These became a long-lasting memory throughout the rest of her life, especially when she became a brief resident of Prince Edward Island, Canada in her sixties, where lupins and golden rod seemed to be indigenous to the province.

The dining room was the main room at the back of the house, but the Wilson's regular babysitter Moira Fogarty, who lived across the street; referred to it as 'the house' as that was the name her Irish family had given their back room. A glazed door with side windows, which the Wilsons referred to as 'the French window' gave them a picturesque view of their back garden. In winter, Claire loved to stand at the French door looking out, becoming entranced as she watched the snow falling. She did wonder if she would ever get tired of watching snow falling. In later years in Scotland, Canada and America, and even on the tablelands in Australia from time to time, Claire was always so excited when snow began to fall.

The French door opened outward over a concrete step, across an area of grass, to yet another concrete step which in many ways was to prove quite disastrous for a certain little person. That was the time Danny and Claire had taken a couple of burlap sacks from the garage and stepping into them thought they would have a sack race on the back lawn. Olivia was watching them through the scullery window and witnessed the two children step into the sacks before Danny shouted "Go" and raced off toward the other end before Claire was fully into her sack. Danny fell down a few times which gave her the opportunity to pass him as she headed for the narrow end of the lawn. "I beat you" Claire shouted and carried on.

Danny was not happy about this and shouted, "But you cheated when you passed me."

"That's the whole idea silly." Claire answered, as she jumped onto the adjacent crazy paving but then tripped. Mum saw her fall and dashed out of the scullery. Claire's head cracked on the edge of the concrete step. There was blood everywhere and Olivia carried Claire inside and up to the kitchen sink. There she bathed her little child's huge cut and swelling, before she took her up to bed. The swelling was reduced by cold compresses and by the next morning Claire was just left with the pain, which Doctor Kelly said would heal in time.

When Milton arrived home from work, Olivia blamed him for his uneven paving but all he said was that all boys had to take the rough and tumble of playing and dismissed the incident, more importantly wanting to know when his dinner would be ready. A few weeks later, Milton finished replacing the grass in the area outside the French window, by laying yet more crazy paving leading toward the offending concrete step. Then he completed the lower crazy paving path that curved its way to the back of the garden. This ended under an archway in a trellising fence. In the border between the Stewart's and the Wilson's back garden was a crab apple tree and Olivia, assisted by Claire of course, made the most gorgeous yummy jelly from those tiny yellow apples. Claire's job as Olivia's assistant was the stirring and pulping. "A great little helper" she was often described.

At the far end of the lawn was a rockery, under which was the air-raid shelter. At the high side of the rockery and stretching across the garden, was the trellising fence mentioned previously, over which Milton had been trying to train climbing roses. The archway in the trellising led down yet another two concrete steps, to the vegetable garden, the center piece of which was his pride and joy – the greenhouse, in which Milton grew his prize tomatoes. But let's get back to the beginning, instead of munching on her dad's yummy tomatoes.

2

Boy or Girl?

What has not been related to the reader as yet is the occasion of Claire's birth – an event which was to open up a somewhat heated problem for her parents and a total enigma to her life in general. Nurse Middleton, the midwife who lived further down Sandy Peth, after cleaning up the newly born noticed that something was amiss, so different to the many others she had delivered during her long career. Her facial expression took on a surprise of its own, emitting in her frustration a high-pitched throaty squeal. Nanna Levine was apparently there too; for assistance when and where necessary. Marjory Levine, Olivia's mum, looked at Nurse Middleton: "What's the matter?" she feebly and perhaps somewhat nervously asked.

"Well, Mrs Levine, there appears to be a slight problem and I will have to see what Dr Kelly says before I can give you a proper answer one way or the other."

Olivia was by now very sleepy but was lucid enough to make a comment: "Is my baby ill, or something?" She began showed the signs of total exhaustion after giving birth to her first child, and it was already half past two in the morning. But it was obvious that something was not quite right. Her husband, according to Olivia's version of events that night, was fast asleep and snoring in the next room and was not aware of the problem, if indeed there was one.

"Well, to be quite truthful Mrs Wilson, I don't honestly know whether you have a boy or a girl."

"What?" Nanna Levine almost jumped out of her skin at this statement, demanding to see what Nurse Middleton was looking at.

"What on God's earth do you mean, nurse?" queried Olivia, becoming quite scared that she might be losing her fist born, her precious daughter.

"Well, just look at this," pointing to the baby's lower regions. "There appears to be evidence of both sexes."

Marjory Levine and her daughter took a look and gasped. "Holy God!"

Nurse Middleton continued, "Look I know you're more shocked than I am but let's leave it at that for now shall we, until Dr Kelly gets here in the morning. I will call him just before his surgery opens." She became increasingly flustered as she re-wrapped the new infant up again.

Olivia was to relate the events many years later, telling Claire that she was faint with shock and sunk back into her pillows, tears streaming down her flustered countenance. Marjory held her hand and stroked her hair as Nurse Middleton laid the baby in the crib at the side of the bed, tucking Claire in securely. Olivia initially fell into a somewhat erratic sleep. Her mother, seeing her daughter drifting off to sleep, moved across to the basket chair in the corner of the room to try to get some sleep herself.

These were the days before mobile cellular phones were even thought of, let alone available, so Nurse Middleton had no other recourse than to phone Dr Kelly the following morning on her heavy black plastic phone back in her own home down Sandy Peth.

Olivia, allowing the sedative she had been given to make her sleepy, floated in a deep sleep and her mother Marjory decided not to tell Milton of their potential problem before he went to work the next morning.

Why alarm him before Dr Kelly has had a look, she sensibly mused. Both Olivia and Marjory knew that Milton would raise the roof when he was told of the problem. Claire's dad had a violent temper when provoked, and the women did not want to stoke his ire and get his blood boiling before Dr Kelly had been consulted. The family physician would know what to do, so everyone had better try to get some rest before the 'mucky stuff' hits the fan. By three O'clock Olivia was sleeping soundly and by the look on her exhausted face – at peace to the world. Her mum Marjory, after a brief spell in the basket chair had decided to lay down on the settee in the front sitting room, which had been made up into a bed for her.

When Milton awoke to his alarm clock at 5 O'clock, the first thing he thought of was to walk into the main bedroom to see if his wife had given birth. He would have wanted to have been there, but knew from tradition that the birthing room was not a place for men. Nervously he poked his head around the door to see what the score was, only to see his wife fast asleep with the *Nite-lite* still burning, and judging by the bundle wrapped up in its cot, it was obvious that his 'son' was sleeping too. *Bloody marvelous*, he thought, *just wait 'til I tell Mam and the fellows at work.* He would buy Olivia a bunch of flowers to bring home with him after work, providing he could find someone selling them, at this time of year in the middle of winter. *Maybe one of the shops near Oakwood Clock might have some.* He left full of the joys of spring, even if it was only late February.

Dr Kelly came over to address the Wilson's problem around lunchtime. After a general check-up he then concentrated on the area between Claire's legs, the opposite end of what appeared to be a rather sweet and docile baby girl. As the doctor inspected her genital region, he pondered over his options. He had been requested by the Levine family to perform their customary and traditional circumcision on all their male offspring, but right now he was puzzled by what he saw. The crux of the matter was that Olivia's first child had been born with both genders, what might be termed 'hermaphrodite' according to the very brief lectures on the subject, he had attended at medical school. Somehow the Wilson's child had been born with what looked like a very tiny penis, if it was that at all, and what could be described as the early signs of a vagina. He gave instructions to Nurse Middleton that no decision could be made with certainty for some time as genitalia could take years to develop fully. But he would consult his colleagues at Aireborough General Infirmary in the meantime.

Olivia was presented with Dr Kelly's verdict by Nurse Middleton after Dr Kelly had left to drive back to his surgery in Arkroyd Road. The verdict was that Olivia's baby had definitely been born with both female and male genitalia. The district nurse gave Olivia and Marjory Levine the information Dr Kelly had given her, that things should be left as they were for the time being until he could consult his colleagues at the Infirmary. Nothing more could be done for now and Nurse Middleton advised her agitated patient to continue to sleep off her ordeal. Baby Claire had already slurped through her third meal of the day and was asleep in the cot over by the window.

In the meantime, Milton had been able to get the news to his mother, Penelope Mariner, through a neighbor who had a telephone. He told the neighbor to tell his mum that she had her first grandson. Such news was greeted with excitement and it quickly spread to every member of the Wilson family, especially gloating over the news to his brothers Clive and Sandy, whose wives could only provide them with daughters. Milton didn't contact any member of his wife's family as he considered them less important than his own, so it was left to Marjory Levine, to pass the news on to her family, Olivia's brothers and sisters, and a great aunt in Sunderland.

Milton could hardly wait to get home after work. War time was such that they were in the middle of making design alterations to parts of the airplanes that they produced at the factory. However, home time came at last and Milt dashed out, to drive his little Ford Eight to his mum's house in Darley Avenue, off York Road. She was all smiles and hugs, explaining that his stepfather Henry Mariner had had to go down the pit that morning and would not be back for another hour. She suggested that Milt take Olivia some flowers and after a few minutes was able to furnish him with a bunch, of rather bedraggled early snowdrops and crocuses from a neighbor's garden, wrapped up in yesterdays *Yorkshire Evening News*.

Milton was so excited driving home. So much so that when he reached Number Eight Sandy Peth he threw back the gates of the driveway with a flourish before letting his Ford roll down to a stop outside the scullery door. Opening the door, he was met by his mother-in-law, Marjory Levine, who was cooking some tea for them all. He pushed her aside and confidently strode down the hall, turned an abrupt left and flew up the stairs two at a time. Olivia was breast-feeding her beautiful baby daughter as he burst through the door wearing a grin from ear to ear. "Hello love, I didn't wake you this morning when I went out at half past five. I saw you were sleeping and crept across to see William asleep too, so I left you both to sleep on. Well done love, here are some flowers mam sent for you."

Olivia laid the half-dead flowers on the other side of the bed and, pointing a finger to her left cheek, demanded a kiss from her husband. Then she asked him to sit next to her on the bed: "Is everything all right love?" Milt asked, realizing that his wife had not said much while he had been ranting on.

"Well, husband, there is a slight problem."

"A problem, how can there be a problem, William looks alright to me?"

"William? What's with 'William' all of a sudden?" Olivia asked him pointedly.

"Because that's the name I have given our son."

"Well, you had better sit down while I outline the problem."

By this time Milton's smile had turned to a frown as he sat on the quilt covering the double bed. "Go on then, what's the problem?"

"Well, according to Dr Kelly, our baby is neither a boy nor a girl."

"What? You're joking. That's bloody impossible. He's having you on love. That is a complete and utter impossibility." He stared at Olivia as she stared back at him in all seriousness. "Go on; tell me it's only a joke. It has to be. That is absolutely bloody crazy. It just isn't possible."

"Sorry love, it is no joke."

Milton stood up looking very angry. "I'm telling you Olivia, it has to be a huge joke as it is physically impossible." Milton stared Olivia in the face, his mind racing as the news gradually filtered into his mind. "There is no such thing as a baby being born with two sex parts Olivia, it simply cannot happen. A baby has to be either one or t'other; either a boy or a girl. God doesn't make mistakes. Let's have a look, I'll tell you what his gender is."

"Just wait a minute love until she finishes feeding."

"What did you bloody say – She... SHE? You must be out of your tiny mind Olivia. We are not, and I repeat NOT, going to have another bloody girl in the Wilson family. I want a boy, not a shitty girl. A girl would be absolutely useless. No it has to be a boy! Let me have a look. Forget the stupid feeding because I want to have a look – NOW." With that he wrenched Olivia's hands off 'his son' and laid the baby on the bed between them. "Take the stinky nappy off him so I can see for myself. I'm not going to touch that scabby thing. That's your job."

Olivia did as she was bid as by now she was getting frightened of Milt's attitude. Getting more and more agitated Milton pushed her hands off 'his son' and stared. "Bloody Hell! It can't be true. It can't be true! He's a poofter." Milton went red in the face.

"Dr Kelly says..." started Olivia.

"Dr Bloody Kelly, what the hell does he know? We have to take the baby to the Infirmary for a specialist to do something. I'll get time off work and take you tomorrow, or the day after, whenever I can get time off. I'm telling you now Olivia, I'm not going to have a poofter in this family. I would be the laughing stock of the whole Wilson family not to mention my workmates."

"Hold on Milt, you didn't let me finish what the doctor said." Olivia tried to explain as Milt looked up at the ceiling, saliva creeping out of the corner of his mouth.

"Go on then," he said looking at her again with squinting eyes, "but I know what I am going to do. Go on..."

"Well, he says that when this happens, the baby is termed a hermaphrodite."

"A what? A bloody 'hermaphrodite'? How am I going to tell my family that? They'll laugh me to Kingdom Come. I've already told them I have a son, and that's that. I'll make sure he is male and not female, I can tell you that for bloody certain." He blabbered, by now the saliva dripping onto the quilt. Olivia, staring at her husband, thought he was about to have a seizure.

"Milt will you please listen to me. Dr Kelly says that he wants to consult his colleagues at the Infirmary to see what to do, but for now we have to do nothing. We can do nothing to change the situation anyway, what's done's done."

Milton pointed his finger at his chest, "Not in my bloody book it isn't woman. But we'll see what he has to say in a couple of days but I'll tell you something for nothing, I am not having a shitty girl in this house. I can tell you that for a start. As far as I'm concerned that's a boy even if he might look like a poofter," pointing to the new addition to the family, back feeding on her mother's other breast. Milt added, almost as an afterthought, "That thing will be a boy by the time I'm done with him, if it's the last thing I do."

Milton quickly turned away as he went for the door handle. Turning around at the door he pointed a finger at his wife: "I am really disappointed in you Olivia. I thought you would provide me with a boy, not a bloody poofter. Something will have to be done. I'm not having this shame forced on me." With that he stormed out.

Olivia was really scared and exasperated at Milt's attitude but decided to keep her feelings to herself. The truth of the matter was that her husband was now performing like a petty tyrant, as though it was only him that faced the problem. If her baby was intersex, maybe it was on Milton's side of the family, not hers. In later life, this situation proved to be the case. In fact Milton himself was to show abnormal tendencies from time to time. But no matter what Olivia said, he would overrule her as usual. Stating that he was the head of the family and what he said was what had to be done.

3

The Truth of the Matter

Two days later, Dr Kelly called at the Wilson's after his morning surgery, while Nurse Middleton was there on her rounds. The doctor told Olivia that he had made an appointment for her and her husband to take the baby to the General Infirmary for an inspection on Wednesday of the following week and he would abide by the specialists' prognosis. So when Milton came home from work, Olivia imparted this news. Her red-faced husband on the other hand, was hardly listening. His face set as hard as a rock.

"I have had to tell all the family that we have a son and we will call him James William Wilson, after my dad and granddad."

"But what if she turns out to be a girl?" Mum asked.

Milton went as red as a beetroot, almost spitting out his words: "I've told you Olivia, there isn't going to be any more bloody girls in our family. If my poncey brothers aren't man-enough to breed boys, then I am."

"Oh Milt, why do you have to take that attitude. You can't change nature."

"We'll see about that. We'll take my son to the hospital as our quack doctor says and they'll do something, just you see. I'll make damn sure they do, as if it turns out to be a bloody girl or a poofter, you know what you and IT can do don't you?" By this time Milton was frothing at the corners of his mouth as he usually did when his anger was aroused: "I'll find someone else to give me a boy, just you see if I don't." With that he stormed out of the bedroom.

Olivia was dumbstruck. Was this the real Milton? Had she married an out-and-out bigot? She already knew that he had fixed ideas on so many things, but was this going too far? Once again she withdrew within herself. She knew when Milt went into one of his stick-in-a-mud moods, there was no changing him. But his hard words did have her worried. They really hurt. What if her baby was in reality a girl but with some complication to be sorted? Would Milton abandon her? Was he really serious about finding someone else? Olivia's nerves started playing up and she became very tetchy about her future with Milton. Maybe all would be well after all. *Jesus, Mary and Joseph would sort things out*, she thought. She would pray to *The Holy Family* for the problem to be sorted. Heavenly intervention was the answer. She did think of speaking to one of the priests but on reflection, especially when she and Milton did not attend Mass on a regular basis, decided against that idea. Prior to giving birth Olivia had the distinct feeling that she was carrying a baby girl inside her, and the feeling was so very strong that she struggled with the raw medical truth of the matter in now accepting that her baby might be a boy. She had already decided that her baby's name would be *Claire*, a name harping back to her great grandmother's roots in Donegal, Ireland. Tears welled up again in her eyes as she wondered what the future held for her baby daughter and herself.

The following Wednesday Milton had been allowed to have some time off work to take his wife and 'his son' to the Infirmary. He had told his drawing office manager that it was a minor problem which would be sorted out at the Infirmary. Dr Kelly arrived at the hospital before the Wilsons and was waiting for them near the reception desk. Mr and Mrs Wilson were advised to sit in the waiting area until the specialists were ready for them. But it wasn't long before they were called and ushered down the corridor into a private consulting room. A nurse asked if she could take baby and reluctantly Olivia handed Claire, her precious daughter, nervously into the outstretched arms of the nurse. "Could you both wait outside please, there are chairs there to sit on?" said the nurse. Milton refused to sit down, preferring to walk back and forth, looking for all-the-world like he was plotting something. The atmosphere was tense and it was a struggle for Olivia to get any response from her agitated husband.

After about three quarters of an hour had elapsed two doctors accompanied by Dr Kelly, the Wilson family's own medical practitioner, came out to invite Olivia and Milton back into the consulting room. It was suggested that they be seated. Olivia sat but Milton preferred to stand and stare at the men in white coats.

"Well, Mr & Mrs Wilson. Our diagnosis is that your baby is definitely a hermaphrodite, one born between two genders, what some specialists are already referring to as intersex. But there is not at the moment sufficient genitalia showing to confirm one way or the other how she or he will develop in later years. I have to admit that from the rare cases of which we know, the greater probability is that your baby will be basically female but with the genitalia of both genders. What we suggest is that you take baby home and consult Dr Kelly every month from now on, and he will keep us posted on her progress."

With the specialists referring to their baby as a 'she' Milton's face became a very noticeable shade of purple, his nose seeming to throb in front of his yet darker cheeks. Olivia related the events to Claire many years later that she thought her husband might explode.

"But we have to have the baby Christened in our local Catholic church as soon as possible in case she dies and goes to 'Limbo'. So what name are we going to have her christened with, a girl's name or a boy's name?" Olivia questioned.

By this time Milton was absolutely fuming, on the verge of exploding into tiny fragments. He was literally just about at the end of his patience. It required much strength for him to keep his nerves in tact to stay quiet, not wanting to embarrass himself in front of others, especially in front of these 'so-called' professionals. In later years, Claire was to experience her dad's contempt for those who were academically and medically superior. He was to tell her in her teens that he was worth far more to the world than any university-trained graduate, constantly repeating his well-known belief that University-trained men were of little use to society at all, compared to him and other businessmen. He paid no regard to women in any shape or form, as they were God's gift to men to bear their children and look after their homes and provide tasty food. This turned out to be Claire's father, a born misogynist.

Olivia's question was answered by the main specialist, Dr Phillips, "Well, in that case Mrs Wilson might I suggest you choose a name that can be either male or female, there is a fair choice I believe? Although the problem is extremely rare, you are not the first parents in the world to face this dilemma you know. Yes the condition does occur from time to time, but rarely in this country. Generally as the child grows, the genitals develop and we then can tell more or less exactly what gender the child is. But we have to be patient. It will all turn out right in the end, just you see. But it would be wrong of me not to advise you that many babies born this way have tended to die in infancy, either after a few months or as little children. I am sorry to have to warn you of this but take heart as there have been a few cases in Germany, Switzerland and the USA where after some minor surgery, a child can live fairly normally in whatever gender they are meant to be naturally."

The specialist decided to explain a little more to reinforce the opinion of himself and his colleagues. Looking at Olivia directly, as her husband was taking no notice of what was being said, the specialist explained further, "Hugh Hampton Young, an American specialist published a book three years ago called *Genital Abnormalities, Hermaphroditism, and Related Adrenal Diseases* and this is a useful guide for us right now. This was the first American treatise on the surgical treatment of intersexuality. You see Doctor Young was the founder and editor of the Journal of Urology, and the founder and director of Johns Hopkins' Brady Urological Institute, which is a research and clinical facility devoted to the study of genitourinary problems. His book gives us case histories, with detailed illustrations and photographs, of 43 people who were born with the same abnormality as your little girl." He turned and saw Milton's face, "Sorry, I mean baby." The specialist swallowed hard and turning back to face Olivia, continued: "Dr Young's research and findings are a uniquely important historical source, and one which illuminates the ideas, assumptions, and practices of one of the most prestigious practitioners of medico-sexual decision-making in the United States in the inter-war period. So you see Mr & Mrs Wilson, we are slowly getting to know more about this abnormality and your baby could easily become one of the British cases on which research may be based."

Milton had had more than enough. Listening to this jumped up, so-called 'specialist' he just wanted to get out of the hospital as soon as possible. His brain could not take any more of this man's drivel. How dare this idiot tell him that his son was a freak, a bloody poncey freak, and suggest he be used as a guinea pig in their experiments. No way was this going to happen. There had to be a way so that he could keep his sanity and his Wilson pride. While he was deep in thought and becoming more and more agitated over the situation, the specialist held out his hand but Milton, ignoring him, ushered Olivia out of the door and back down the corridor to the front entrance.

The nurse who had been in attendance began running after the Wilsons but the specialist called her back, shaking his head from side to side. "I don't envy that couple Julia. With that man's attitude I suspect their baby is set for a turbulent life as she grows up. Or it may end up being murdered or in utter frustration terminate her own life. The diagnosis is not good. Not good at all with a father like that."

In the street Milton opened the passenger door of his black Ford Eight and then slammed it shut when Olivia was sitting down holding her precious baby, and went around to the driver's side. By this time he had not said a word but stared straight ahead as though he was in a trance. He drove his car back to Micklegate in silence and after arriving at the family home in Sandy Peth, he let Olivia and 'his son' out of the car, and excusing himself, he drove off back to work, without another word.

"Cooee. Are'ya home love?" Came the voice of Marg from next door. "I'll bet you could do with a cup of tea, couldn't you?"

Coming out of her shock, Olivia turned to see Margaret Rooney looking around the door. "Oh yes Marg. Come in. I'd love a cup of tea."

"No worries love, just you stay there and I'll mek yer one." A few minutes later Marg came in with some cups and saucers on a tray and another plate with some buttered scones she had baked that morning. She placed it down on the big table and went back into the kitchen, reappearing with a pot of tea, which she placed on a trivet in the hearth. "Now then love, I know you want to speak your mind, so why don't you tell me what's gone wrong, 'cos I know summat's up, hey?"

Olivia slowly came out of her shell and cried. "Oh Marg, what are we going to do?"

"What do you mean love, it was alright at the hospital wasn't it?"

By this time Olivia had dried her eyes on an already sodden hanky, and explained more of their dilemma. The Rooney's had been brought up to date by her after the birth but obviously there was more to tell. "Well, it has been confirmed that my beautiful and precious baby daughter, which Milt is adamant is his son, has been born intersexed. We have been advised to give her, or him, or it, a name that can be either a boy's name or a girl's. Milt will have none of it and refuses to have a daughter, thinking he is not a real man if he can't have a son. In fact Milt has already chosen the names for HIS son – James William."

Margaret listened without commenting but then said: "Look love, it will all come right in the end, you see if it don't."

"Well, the specialists at the Infirmary seemed to think so but Milt can't wait. He refuses to wait. The specialist told us about some research that has been going on in the USA where they have records of some children born in a similar way as Claire. Oops! Sorry Marg. I have always thought of my baby as Claire since before she was born, or he was born." Shaking her head and crying again, "Oh I don't know Marg, I am so confused." Olivia shook her head from side to side as the tears welled up in her eyes again, eventually breaking loose to roll down her soft flushed cheeks.

As she had been speaking, Olivia had lain Claire down to sleep in her pram in the hallway, so obviously the baby knew nothing of any of this, only to be told the story when she reached her teens. Marg was very understanding and put her arm around Olivia's shoulder to comfort her. They finished their tea and Olivia said, "That's the gist of everything Marg. You can't change nature can you?"

"No, love, I agree with you. You can't. But what has Milton got to say about it all, is he his usual self, you know all knowing and, I have to say this love, a bit of a bigot?"

"Well, he refuses to believe that the baby could possibly turn out to be a girl. He has been dead set on having a boy from the word go; even when I first knew I was pregnant last year. He doesn't speak to me about it anymore. It is 'my son this' and 'my son that' as though he was chatting to himself, and he gets me so scared, I hardly know what to say for the best as he shouts at me to make his views heard."

"Look love you take my advice, and just let things rest a while. Don't push him too hard or he will flip right over. Just enjoy your baby and everything will come right in the end. You'll see if I am not right."

The big problem was that Olivia had set her heart on having a daughter, and Milton had set his sights on having a son, especially to niggle two of his brothers whose wives had already given birth to daughters. Milton had made up his mind that their baby was a boy, and his decision had to be accepted, whether his wife or anyone else for that matter, liked it or not.

4
The Christening

The next afternoon, there were visitors – Nanna Levine and Olivia's sisters; Elaine and Irma. They "goo-gooed" over the new baby in her pram as lots of women tend to do, talking about clothes and food, and all the matters that new mothers talked about in these times of hardship. Elaine had already given birth to the first boy in his Levine generation, except that Elaine's family name was now Stevens, so her son was already christened George Bernard Stevens in St John's parish church on Harrogate Road, Alwoodley.

"So what have you decided to finally call the baby love?" Nanna Levine asked her daughter.

"Well, I had always imagined me giving birth to a beautiful baby girl and I would call her Claire, my favorite Irish saint's name, and named after granddad's aunty in Donegal. I would have had her christened Claire Anne at St Brigid's. But Milt insists that 'his son' shall be christened James William. He won't even consider that 'his son' might actually be a girl."

"Well love, we know what Milton is like so just let things settle down. You don't have to have the baby christened just yet anyway."

"No, but I don't want to leave it too long. I don't want her dying and going to Limbo with all the other little babies. We have to make an appointment with the parish priest Father Cordingley soon. Milt says he will fix everything."

"Olivia, we know that things will work out, so try not to worry too much."

Nanna Levine and Olivia's sisters left, after washing up the tea things for her, and she was left on her own to think things through. Just sitting, looking at her beautiful baby daughter sleeping peacefully beside her. Olivia was really worried and slipped into a somnolent world, dreaming of a perfect life in which nothing had gone wrong with the birth. She was shocked out of her dreamlike state by her husband's voice: "I'm home Olivia." Milt shouted through the scullery door. "What's for tea, I'm starving?"

"Sorry Milton love, I've had a house full of people all day today and haven't been able to do a lot. Do you mind if we have fish and chips for tea, I mean it is Friday after all?"

"No love that's fine with me. You know I love Yorkshire fish and chips any time. Good Yorkshire food that is. Best fish and chips in the world."

"Well, could you walk around to Mrs Coe's and get some love before the queue really starts, while I do the bread and butter and some tea? Just get fish and chips once and an extra fish, as I won't be able to eat a lot."

"No, I'll get fish and chips twice, as I am so hungry with my news that I'll eat all the chips you can't eat." With that he walked out the door.

So, while Milton walked up the path and around the corner to Mrs Coe's, Olivia cut some bread, buttered it, cut the slices into triangles and put them on a plate. She set the table in the dining room while Claire slept peacefully. By the time Milton returned with some steaming crispy battered fish and chips, with scraps, from Mrs Coe's, the tea was mashing in the pot on its trivet by the fire, and the dining room was warm and cozy.

As they started to eat, Milt could hardly wait to voice his news. "Oh, by the way, I called at the Presbytery on my way home and I've booked Father Cordingley for the Baptism. It is fixed for the beginning of April, on a Sunday afternoon. I thought everyone could come here after the service if it isn't too much for you love?"

"Well, thanks for telling me husband of mine, it's very good of you to let your wife know when her baby is to be christened." Olivia was furious over her husband's superior attitude as usual, making decisions without even consulting her. In truth she was absolutely livid, but tried to hide her steaming emotions.

Milton went on: "Don't be like that love, it has to be done doesn't it, if you want our son to be christened a Catholic?"

"Well, yes, but I wish you had consulted me first instead of deciding what you want as usual."

"Oh, so we are on our 'la-di-dah' high horse again, are we?" His temper being quick to flare up as was his wont. He pushed his plate of half-eaten fish and chips away from him in a gesture of abandonment, and folded his arms.

"No, don't be like that Milt. But you always decide things to suit yourself and I am rarely consulted until after it is done. You should be more considerate."

"Oh, so I'm not considerate now, am I? I married you, didn't I?"

"You know what I mean Milton."

"No, I bloody well don't know what you mean. I get blamed for organizing things and blamed for letting things slide, what do you want. Eh?" Staring at his wife intently he continued, "Come on make your mind up you lazy bitch. Well? What is it to be? Do you want our bloody son Baptized or don't you?" With that outburst Milton had done it again; he had put his wife Olivia down, just like he always did. She could only go along with him or there would be no peace in the house. They seemed to argue a lot more nowadays and all she wanted was peace.

"Yes love. I want the baby christened. I will have to get some cards sent out and arrange for a Christening Tea here as you have decided." Milt walked out the scullery door and into the back garden, which he was slowly working on.

Over the next couple of weeks, Olivia bought some christening cards at Premier Press in Station Road and after filling in everyone's names addressed them, asked Milt if he could post them on his way to work. "No. You post them Olivia, when am I going to get time to go to a bloody post office. Eh? I've an important job to do in this stinking war as if you've forgotten. No, that's your job. That's a woman's job. That sort of thing's not a man's job."

"Well, can you give me some money for the stamps please and some extra to buy the food for the Christening Tea?"

"Why? Can't you make do from the housekeeping I give you, eh?"

"No love, you only give me enough to budget for our weekly food and the insurance. There's never much left over to buy anything extra."

With that Milt put his hand into his pocket and fished out a wad of pound and ten shilling notes, peeling off a brown *Tenner*. "Will that be enough?"

Olivia tried to count up some costs in her head… "I'm not sure. Maybe a little more perhaps?"

"Well, come on how much do you need, I'm not made of money you know. I have to earn this instead of sitting on my backside all day like you do." He took a half-crown from his trouser pocket and added that to the notes. "There now you'll have to make do with that." He walked out of the room and went into the garden, down to his new greenhouse.

The Sunday afternoon booked for the christening soon came around and Father Cordingley saw the family arrive from his living room window in the presbytery. He went out of the front door which looked over the vegetable garden, turned right and right again to walk down the concrete ramp to the school yard. He was wearing his usual black soutane, comprising cassock and shoulder cape, and wore his black biretta on his rapidly balding head. He approached the Wilson and Levine clans as they walked around the front of the school toward him. "Welcome everyone to St Brigid's. Please follow me."

The parish priest walked around the side of one of the school's air-raid shelters and led the family toward the building extension at the back of the school. This housed the church sanctuary and sacristies. He unlocked the glazed door and bade everyone enter and sit down. For Sunday mass, the screen separating two classrooms from the sanctuary would normally have been open, creating a nave out of the space so formed; but as there was no evening Mass, the screens had been closed ready for classes on the following day. On the walls of each of the two classrooms hung the 'Stations of the Cross' depicting in carved relief the various stages of Christ's journey to Calvary. The little children saw these somewhat gruesome carvings each day as they sat in the classrooms for their lessons.

Father Cordingley went into the priest's sacristy to vest for the Christening while two altar boys flitted around lighting candles and pouring some water into the carved wooden baptismal font with its brass center. Everyone waited as the parish priest came out of the sacristy wearing over his cassock a white cotta with lace sleeves and a deep lace hem. He wore a stole in the color of the day, around his neck and was still wearing his black biretta. Milton's brothers Sandy and Clive apparently started sniggering on seeing a man wearing lace. They had been raised as Baptists and even now as low-church Anglicans were not used to seeing a grown man wearing lace. Roman Catholic vestments looked very un-English to them. The Roman Catholic religion was to them a foreign religion, not English. Perhaps fine for the many Irish and some Italians who lived around them, but definitely not English.

The christening service commenced in the traditional way with some simple Latin prayers until they came to the naming. Father Cordingley said he had been advised that the child would be known as James William Wilson. Olivia went as white as a sheet and swayed to one side as Nanna Levine and her daughters looked at her. Irma, thinking Olivia was about to faint, stepped forward and put her arm around her elder sister as support. The baby's godfather, Wilhelm Louis Levine, and godmother Irma Levine then repeated the prayers in English after the priest had said them in Latin. Olivia was strongly of the opinion that if the Church christened her baby with a boy's name, it was a *fait accompli*; she had lost the daughter she had hoped and prayed for. The specialists had effectively been put in their place by her husband Milton, so what use was there in objecting to anything anymore. Milton had decided what he wanted as usual, and organized it behind her back? Her wishes were of no importance to him. *Didn't her marriage vow state that she had to 'obey' him as her husband?*

The Christening over, everyone either drove or walked around past the Police Station and in front of the cobblers' shop and Mr Guy's grocery store, across the tram track to the Regal Cinema and along to Sandy Peth. There, the Wilson's neighbors, the Rooney's, had laid a lovely table with sandwiches, buns and cake, and after borrowing another kettle to put on the gas ring, there was soon lashings of boiling water to make some tea. As Milt was a teetotaller, not touching any alcohol until a few years later, Olivia's elder brother Wilhelm produced a quarter-bottle of Whisky "to toast the baby's health." Milton didn't approve; his Baptist upbringing seeing alcohol as coming from Satan. Olivia's Roman Catholic family was obviously not thoroughly English to him but he had to make allowances. He knew they weren't Irish or Italian but had not the inclination to think any further of Olivia's ancestry. It was many years later that Claire discovered that the Levine's had originally been German Jewish, converted to Lutheranism. The Roman Catholic faith had entered the Levine history when an ancestor in Sunderland had wanted to marry a second time after Claire's great grandmother had died. The woman was a Roman Catholic and the priest said that he would allow her to marry her intended if he and the children by his first marriage all converted to Catholicism. This was par for the course in those days, the Roman Catholic Church believing, as it does even today, that it is the only true church established by Jesus Christ. In Claire's later life, she discovered that this was not historically correct but in the 19th and 20th centuries the Church, 'the True Church' had to come first in everything.

5
The Mutilation

Over the next few months, the new baby was inspected and probed every month until one day Dr Kelly announced that she was to be admitted into the Infirmary for an operation. Olivia asked what that was for and he told her that as her husband had made up his mind that the child should be a boy, having had the child registered as such and being confirmed by baptism into the Roman Catholic religion, then some adjustment to the baby's genitals had to be made. Olivia was horrified, as once again, she had not been consulted. Apart from running off with her baby daughter to God knows where, she was thoroughly stuck. Dr Kelly had added that it was normal in such cases to re-form the male organ on a baby so that the female genitals could develop as normal as possible. But in this case, Milton had insisted that Olivia's precious baby daughter should be a boy and so basically, Claire's tiny vagina and labia had to be sewn up to allow the gonads space to develop and the enlarged clitoris develop into a penis. Whatever might happen to Claire's genitals later, as a result of the mutilation was not of an immediate concern. It was all so very simple to one particular man, Milton Wilson. He wanted a son and his decision was final.

Two weeks later Olivia and her mother caught a tram from Micklegate terminus down into City Square and then took a short walk to the Infirmary. Olivia carried her daughter inside the building and after giving her name to reception, a nurse came out to take them through to a consulting room. Presently a surgeon arrived to announce what they were going to do.

In 1940, it was the considered opinion of some psychiatrists that the real gender of a child born in such circumstances, after appropriate surgery to remove or sew up certain parts, developed through nurturing and lifestyle. In this the major players were the parents, and a child was likely to grow up normally if given the right nurturing. It was considered that a child afflicted with a gender abnormality could easily be brought into line through normal parenting. Boys were to be raised as boys, with guns, footballs and manly things, and girls to be raised as girls with dolls, pretty things and the ways of women. The theory was that if Olivia and Milton raised and nurtured their new baby as a boy, then she would turn out and act like a boy. In Claire's case, it was naturally assumed that being raised as a boy would solve the problem of what was between her legs at birth. A child brought up liking dolls and teddies, loved dressing up and singing, dancing, painting and music would be a girl. On the other hand, a child reared on Meccano, dinky toys, trains, guns, fighting, cars and machinery, rugby, soccer and cricket would be a boy. All of which was pure assumption on behalf of the psychiatrists, without much foundation. But in 1940 in the UK, gender psychiatry had become experimentation to some degree as there was little research to fall back on. This attitude persisted for many years until specialists in the USA and Switzerland started to expand their research, publishing their findings, amid much opposition by those who thought traditionally, especially Christian fundamentalists. It was Harry Benjamin who carried out some of the most interesting research a few years after, but there were still many psychiatrists who believed him to be wrong. It was not to be until the turn of the 21st century that real scientific research proved that all previous beliefs and understanding were wrong. The subject was eventually to become an enormously complicated set of scientific experiments.

   Back at the Infirmary, however, the surgeons had decided that as the misshaped clitoris could become a penis, if they sewed up the vulva, it would all heal into place. They already knew that the human body sorted itself out in time. Many years later Claire researched the type of information that would have been available to psychiatrists and surgeons in 1940 and it was at best extremely basic. In today's terms the information available to them could only take account of clinical tests made in the 1930s in Switzerland and in the USA. It would not be until after the 1960s that real research and clinical tests began to be available on a scale which might be used as guidelines to the average physician. In a nut shell, gender surgery was extremely primitive at the commencement of World War II.

It was Dr Jorge Daaboul, who had been Director of Pediatric Endocrinology at the Children's Hospital of Oakland, CA, who was to deliver a key talk to the American Association for History of Medicine's annual conference in Bethesda in May 2000. In *Does the Study of History Affect Clinical Practice? Intersex as a Case Study: The Physician's View*, Dr. Daaboul said that contemporary medical practice is based upon an implicit, and unexamined, assumption that intersexed individuals could not possibly live normal lives as intersexed individuals; the only chance for happiness and psychological well-being is the establishment of a secure male or female gender identity. There was simply no precedent for intersexed individuals living as normal people in our society.

As Dr Daaboul and other specialists believed, and taught, the problem with society throughout this period, and still applicable today, was that the medical world and society in general saw gender as being of either male or female. It was not until the 1960s that babies born with Claire's condition were assumed to be essentially female. Fifty years later, even this assumption was to be proved incorrect. But in 1940, having a vulva but with an oversized clitoris/penis meant that if the latter was reduced in size and the vulva left intact, the likelihood was that the child would more than likely grow up as a normal female. But the developing war with Germany was becoming a far more serious concern, and the medical profession had far more important decisions to make than the perceived gender of a tiny baby.

It appears, according to a later discovery by a specialist surgeon, that in 1940 all the surgeon had done was to sew up what he saw as perhaps a vagina, and to expose an over-enlarged clitoris and some tissue that may develop into gonads. To him it was all he could do, not knowing that the child would in later years go through a thorough examination which indicated that Claire did not even have a prostate gland. What the medical world did not realize at the time was that the appearance of genitalia was only one sign of a child's gender. The child would, in all probability, not survive for many years anyway, so the simplest solution was perhaps the best option. At this stage, there were no rules and regulations as to what should be done. Some babies born with a similar problem had died and others had ended up in mental institutions, such as the asylum at Menston near Aireborough. In more advanced cases, it was decided that electric shock treatment to the brain would cure each patient of the thoughts of the opposite gender. That it never worked was of no concern, leaving many patients dead as a result of such barbaric treatment was of no concern either, their deaths going unrecorded. Society did not need to know about such abnormalities.

In Claire's case, she was to be somewhat of an experience for her mum, but a closed book for her dad. As far as the latter was concerned, he had a son and that was the end of the matter – no arguments. Olivia was extremely distraught over the issue as she could see her daughter in the new baby. Milton dug in his heels and his word was final, his wife Olivia had no choice in the matter. If his son did show any signs of femininity then he would drive it out lock stock and barrel.

It was not until Claire was fourteen, when she and her mother Olivia were in the middle of one of their occasional "mother and daughter" chats, that the truth was revealed. Rained off from school sports, Claire was doing her art homework on the dining room table. By this time Olivia knew without a shadow of doubt that her teenager was her daughter and told her that had her birth been straight forward, then she would have been called Claire Anne. Little did Olivia know at that time that her teenager would one day come out of her shell to become the daughter she had always wanted, but for her that event was not to be until after she had passed away – or murdered. But that was a story for the future.

In those days it was still common practice to dress all babies alike in romper suits and pretty dresses for best, and this was how baby Claire, or William to her father, started her early years. She was pretty baby girl but given the name of a boy and registered by her father as male.

Big mistake Mr Wilson! Big, big mistake!

6
Siblings

In July 1942, two years after Claire was born, her brother Danny arrived on the scene and as per family tradition, was baptized into the Roman Catholic religion as Daniel Lester Wilson. There were no problems with his birth; *thank the Lord for that*, relatives had whispered to each other at the Christening. Danny was subjected to circumcision in accordance with the Levine heritage, and he grew into a healthy fair-headed boy, full of mischief. There was a rumor that circulated for many years that Danny had been born a twin to another that had died. However, it was generally considered that the rumor could not have been true as if it were, especially where a Roman Catholic child might have been born, the deceased would have been given a name and a suitable burial, as the baby would have been considered to have a 'soul'. Claire was taught at St Brigid's school a few years later that if a baby died before it was baptized, it would go to a secret place in the sky called 'Limbo'. If it was baptized it could go to Heaven but babies who weren't baptized could not be admitted to the ethereal place called 'Heaven'. She didn't think the babies suffered in Limbo, *not like the men who went to 'Purgatory' which is where people went if they died without receiving what were known as 'the last rites',* whatever they were. It was all so confusing and quite often she wished the nuns hadn't told them anything. However, as there was no funeral for a supposed twin to her brother Danny, Claire felt convinced that there had not been another baby alongside him in her mother's tummy, or from wherever babies came? The general opinion, therefore, was that the rumor was untrue.

Around this time Milton came home one day with a dog and said that his name was 'Jock' because he was what was popularly known as a 'Scotty' dog. It was later felt that Claire's father had been feeling left out of the family, his wife spending all her time on the children, that he himself was in need of some companionship. However, Milton was not used to having a dog around the place and neither of the parents in the habit of looking after a dog. Consequently, Jock escaped whenever he could to run back to where he used to live, with a family on the Gipton Wood Estate. Three times, the police had to ring Milton to explain that his dog was in the Gipton Wood Police Station and would he please collect him as soon as possible.

In November 1944, Olivia gave birth to her third child, Gerald, who was given the middle name after Milton himself. Apparently, there was an old Wilson tradition in naming the boys of the family after famous people, in this case after the poet John Milton. Gerald, or as Claire used to call him – *Gerry*. He was her baby, at least that was how she saw him. She distinctly remembered being called into the front bedroom after his birth and having been seated on a chair in the right hand corner by the window, was told that this was 'his' new baby brother. She was very excited as she held him in her arms. He was so cuddly and smelled lovely, like all babies.

Claire started primary school in January 1945, a few weeks before her fifth birthday. Her mother Olivia had taken her to St Brigid's Primary School in Station Road, Micklegate, in the previous December and she remembered standing at the right hand side of Mrs Donatello's desk looking into a fish tank, in which a Christmas crib had been set up. Because of her dad having registered her as a boy instead of a girl, however, she was dressed as a boy, but at that age she was not aware of the implications of her predicament. But she did remember starting school, and especially having to drink a small bottle of milk every morning and to rest every afternoon, with her head laid across folded arms on the desk top. Being at school was a busy job, so the kids needed their afternoon nap after all.

Those were the days when children had to write on slate boards with chalk, not on paper or in books as today. When the children started to learn to write, they were each given a wooden-framed slate board, which had a writing surface of either green Westmorland or blue-gray Welsh slate. Claire didn't like the Welsh slate as the chalk didn't write as well as on the green one. Using chalk on the blue slates, it often squeaked, which was not only an annoyance to Mrs Donatello but gave great delight to the boys as they liked the scratchy noise, trying to make their chalk squeak all the more – all at the same time. But the children really had no choice in the selection and took whatever slate they were given, even though there was the inevitable grumble and snide remark.

Some mornings all the children had to attend a school gathering called 'Mass'. The central folding partition between Miss Comerford's and Miss Seaford's classrooms was folded back as were the rear screens, and there before the assembled throng was what was called 'the sanctuary' with its altar and six very high brass candlesticks reflecting the lights above to make them glisten brightly. So arranged, the classrooms had instantly become 'a church'. At each side of the sanctuary there were rooms which were the priest's sacristy to the left and the altar server's sacristy to the right, where the flowers were also arranged for the highly polished brass vases.

To the tiny kindergarten children in Mrs Donatello's class, Claire's class in fact, 'the Mass' was something strange. They didn't really know what it was except that it was in a language they could not understand and 'Mass' was something they had to attend or they would go to 'Hell'. Catholic children were told that in Hell they would be burned alive as a punishment for not attending 'Mass'. Hell was a scary place for the children and it certainly kept them in line. When Fr Cordingley, the parish priest, visited each classroom from time to time, always before the lunch break, he stressed that if the pupils didn't attend Mass on a Sunday, they would be committing a mortal sin and if they died after it, they would not go to Heaven but straight to the fires of Hell. Not a nice prospect for little children. So, after telling her mummy and daddy all this, much to her Dad's amusement, it had been decided to ask Moira Fogarty who lived across the road with her parents and brothers Kelvin and Terry, to take 'their son' to Mass with her each Sunday. As it happened, Moira became their regular babysitter.

Claire remembered being presented with a Christmas present from her godmother, Aunty Irma, of a tiny book called *My First Mass Book* which had a red cloth binding. The book took children through various sections of the Mass in word and pictures. It wasn't until Milton was to pass away in 1998 that Claire once again found the little book in her possession after over 50 years. It appears somehow, that in the intervening period of time, it had placed itself among her father's possessions. After his death, her step mother discovered a suitcase under the bed in their spare bedroom, and *My First Mass Book* was among the few books and papers she found there, together with some rosary beads and an old Protestant Bible with its hard covers ripped off. When the little Mass book came back into Claire's possession she could not resist browsing through its pages, full of wax crayon scribblings and written claims that her brother Danny had over the book. Musing on the tiny book's content, as a grown woman, Claire saw it in a totally different light – Roman Catholic propaganda. It illustrated a man, supposedly the mythical 'Jesus Christ' dressed as though he was a Catholic priest wearing Roman vestments. It also had illustrations of priests celebrating 'Holy Mass' and all of them looked like monks, each figure with tonsured head. But as 'a wee bairn', according to her Nanna Levine, as bemused as kindergarten children often are, all this sailed over her head and she accepted whatever was placed before her as verbatim. The Church wouldn't brainwash little children who knew no better – would they?

The air-raid shelter behind the rockery at the bottom of the garden, had been excavated and built by Milton in brick and concrete, and the green-painted entry shutters allowed access to its deep steps leading down into a mysterious world. Often Claire would stand under the trellis archway at the side of the air-raid shelter and look ahead of her at her Dad's greenhouse, his pride and joy. She could taste its rich harvest of tomatoes and cucumbers just by looking through its murky algae-covered windows. Claire loved to stand near her father as he tended his precious tomato plants, and quite often in season, he would take a small tomato which had ripened early and presented it to her as a special gift. These were the most delicious fruits she had ever tasted, apart from the crab apples from the tree adjacent to next door's fence. Even today, Claire savors the tangy taste of a freshly picked red tomato, and of course, she always grows them in her garden where the climate allows.

The aforementioned crab apple tree became one of the symbols of Claire's growing up. Even though she may have occasionally picked one of the tiny fruits to munch, the big day always came around when Olivia wanted to make some crab apple jelly. Claire helped gather a large basinful of fruit from time to time so that her mother could boil the harvest with some sugar and then, pour the residue into a calico bag. This was then tied with string and hung over a pan so that the contents of the bag could filter through the fabric. Left behind was a mess of skins, softened cores and pips which went into the pig bin. The liquid in the pan would quickly turn to jelly after mum added some lemon juice and other bits and pieces; and hey presto, they had a few jars of their favorite jam, which they called 'crab apple jelly'. This was the best Claire had ever tasted, and as most of their children's snacks comprised bread and jam, in times of hardship, it often became a complete meal for her siblings and herself. The taste of the sweet jelly became etched into her subconscious, along with the scones, buns and cakes her mum used to make; not forgetting the 'baps' and 'oven-bottoms'.

7

Teddy Bears Picnic

Prior to Christmas 1946, Mrs Donatello trained her kindies to perform their first concert. The children were too young to appear in the annual school pantomime with the big girls and boys, so they practiced it in their own classroom. The concert was to be *The Teddy Bears Picnic.* Various mums had made the main costumes and the rest were dug out of the school's costume cupboard in the staffroom, situated at the other end of the long corridor where the big boys' and big girls' classes were located. Except that the really 'really' big boys, who Claire saw as men, had a prefabricated concrete classroom at the side of the front playground.

Most of the kindies had parts as either teddy bears or rabbits. Claire wanted to be a teddy bear but drew the short straw when decisions were being made by Mrs Donatello. Instead, she had to be content with being a brown rabbit.

The children practiced the songs every day for two weeks, especially the main song, which Claire knew off by heart as they had a gramophone record of the song at home. She never forgot the words and to this day she still recalls the day of their class concert.

If you go down in the woods today
You're sure of a big surprise.
If you go down in the woods today
You'd better go in disguise.
For every bear that ever there was
Will gather there for certain because
Today's the day the teddy bears have their picnic.

Every teddy bear who's been good
Is sure of a treat today.
There's lots of marvelous things to eat
And wonderful games to play.
Beneath the trees, where nobody sees,
They'll hide and seek as long as they please.
'Cause that's the way the teddy bears have their picnic.

The chorus line was:

Picnic time for teddy bears.
The little teddy bears are having a lovely time today.
Watch them, catch them unawares
And see them picnic on their holiday.
See them gaily gad about.
They love to play and shout, they never have any cares.
At six o'clock their mummies and daddies
Will take them home to bed
Because they're tired little teddy bears.

If you go down in the woods today
You'd better not go alone.
It's lovely down in the woods today
But safer to stay at home.
For every bear that ever there was
Will gather there together because
Today's the day the teddy bears have their picnic.
Today's the day the teddy bears have their picnic.

The day came for the concert and those children who were to perform had been told to ask their mums to provide them with a small jar of cold cream. The children had not been told why they needed the cold-cream, but they dutifully pestered their mums to provide them with the essential product. Claire was no different and clutched the precious jar of Pond's Cold Cream which her mum had gently placed in her tiny hand, with an instruction not to drop it or lose it, and certainly not to show it to her father. On arrival at school the children held out their tiny possessions only to be told by Mrs Donatello that the cold cream wasn't needed just at that moment. The problem was that no one actually told any of them when or how to use it; or even what it was for.

The concert was to be held on a Friday afternoon and at lunchtime. Claire had not been successful in trying to persuade either her mum or dad to visit the school to watch her, so she wandered back to school with a heavy and sad heart. To her dad, she was supposed to be attending school to learn 'Reading, Riting and Rithmetic', not 'bloody' play acting. He was not happy about it at all.

In Miss Bonar's adjacent classroom, the kindies dressed for their concert. Their faces had been made up for the pantomime with red rosy cheeks and red lips. The whiskers were sewn into the costumes around the opening for the face so they didn't need extra lines drawing on their faces. The children were all so eager and excited to show off their little play and fidgeted, skipped and moved around in anticipation, as little children do. Even today with tears almost welling in her eyes, Claire still enjoys watching children performing their little hearts out with so much enthusiasm and excitement.

Getting ready had been just as much fun as performing. However, one funny incident she finds it hard not to smile about even today. That was when one of the rather 'weight impaired' little boys in her class found a lipstick laid on one of the desks. He knew what it was for as he had watched his mummy apply it many times. He decided that he really did need more lipstick on his lips than the smear which one of the ladies had applied for him. No one took any notice until his task was almost complete, when one of the other girls saw the result and shrieked:

"Mrs Donatello. Mrs Donatello, look what Kevin has done." She pointed at him and everyone laughed. Their teacher asked one of the helpers to wipe his widely smeared red mouth, and the boy was duly smacked, the helper refusing to apply any more to his lips. He was in total disgrace. That was naughty Kevin Mulcahy. VERY naughty Kevin! Always very naughty!

A number of parents had arrived to watch their little darlings perform and clapped eagerly to all the songs and actions. So everyone, parents, siblings and performers enjoyed the afternoon thoroughly. Judging by the clapping of the parents and the beaming smiles of 'the artistes', the concert was judged to have been a great success. Claire especially, loved singing the theme song *Teddy Bears Picnic*, the signature tune of the performance. It was a happy time for all of the kindies, except Claire was sad that neither her mum nor her dad had bothered to make the effort to go and see her in what was to be her first public performance. She was, however, not the only pupil whose parents had stayed away. Many of the children lived in what they called 'corporation houses', estates of houses owned by Aireborough Corporation, and many parents could not take time off to attend their children's schools, unless the events were in the evening. Claire's situation appeared to be for the same reason. She realized many years later that her dad lived for his work, and expected his wife to drop everything to support him, despite the fact that she had to look after the two smallest children too. In a nutshell, Claire's parents did not seem to feel the event important enough to make any effort to attend. In her mum's case, she had both Danny and Gerry to look after, although she managed well enough to go shopping with them in the pram, Gerry tucked under the blanket and Danny dangling his legs under the pram handle.

After the concert, the children wandered off home, still clutching their precious jars of cold cream, Claire's as yet unopened. She could not understand why some of the older boys walking along the same streets that she walked along, were pointing and laughing at her. That was, until she reached Mr Guy's grocery shop near the tram terminus. Claire had developed a fascination for looking in shop windows even at that young age, and as she passed Mr Guy's, she looked through the window only to see her mother buying something at the counter. Excitedly she ran to the door and opened it with its usual 'ping' and approached her mum. With great excitement she started to tell her all about the concert. Olivia turned to look at her and shrieked. Mocking her, she had Mr Guy and the other customers laughing. This was a huge humiliation after the excitement of Claire's performance. It appears that when Olivia took one look at Claire's face, alarm was written all over it. "Come on, let's get you home and cleaned up before Daddy sees you."

She was not to know at the time, and no one ever explained it to her, that her dad had some fixation against any man or boy wearing make-up. Readers should be reminded here, that from being registered at birth as a boy instead of a girl, Claire was dressed as a boy and had been forced to live the life of a boy called William, much to her later consternation. What people did not know was that she had been born with a congenital defect as a hermaphrodite, having parts of both sexes, and where, at the insistence of her obstinate father, the female genitals had been surgically mutilated. However, this did not change the conviction she had of herself as a girl, a situation that grew in time to become a major psychological enigma. It was to become a permanent scar on her life for many years, and a worry as to how to change things for the better.

From Mr Guy's grocery counter Olivia's intention was to rush 'William' home, wheeling Danny and Gerald in the pram, and then upstairs into the bathroom before Milton arrived home from work. However, it was a Friday and oftentimes Milton's factory would close early for the weekend, even though he often went into work on the Saturday morning. It happened to be Claire's bad luck to find that her father was already at home ready to greet his wife and sons. But, horror of horrors, as Olivia opened the scullery door Milton glared at 'his son' and commanded his wife to: "Get that poofter stuff off his bloody face right this minute." He went red with rage and stormed back into the dining room to sit supposedly reading the *Yorkshire Evening Post* but not concentrating on any article on which he tried to focus. He was seething with rage, reacting to an inbuilt revulsion of anything related to 'poofters'. It brought memories back to him of Claire's birth and he decided that he must make sure that 'his son' was never to come face to face again with anything that girls might have, or do. Olivia had to be made to reinforce this.

In the bathroom Claire's mother tried to get the lipstick off her lips and cheeks with a face washer, which they used to call 'a flannel' in Yorkshire in those days. Together with soap and water Olivia scrubbed Claire's face until it was red raw. Her delicate skin revolted to the treatment and her mother's efforts, and the exercise was to psychologically dampen further her rapidly waning artiste's exuberance. In truth, she did not know what she had done wrong as Olivia scrubbed away without words.

Later in her life as she looked back on this event, without any knowledge of the consequences, it seemed to transgress some unwritten code. Her dad's ire obviously confirmed. But from such an event, followed by subsequent experiences regarding her father's anger over 'his son's' femininity, she was to undergo severe chastisement, ridicule and discrimination at the hands of her father during her formative years. She began to notice more and more his comments and snide remarks about people born with disfigurements and/or abnormalities. It became painfully obvious to her that 'his son' had some of the characteristics which fuelled her father's attitude. But as for detail, at that young age, although she was dressed as a boy daily and her name on the class register was down as 'William Wilson', she still felt like a girl and was, unaware of the genital differences between males and females. She could not fathom any tangible answer to the giggles she was experiencing from others around her.

One day as she left St Brigid's to walk home, a boy walked up to her and accompanied her as she walked. "Why are you different?" He had asked her.

"I don't know what you mean."

"Well, you aren't like the rest of us. You even speak differently, sometimes like a girl."

"I still don't know what you mean." She blurted, really becoming quite frustrated at this boy's assertions.

"Well, you don't run like we do and when you throw a ball you do it differently to us boys." He was staring her in the face.

"I think you're a girl dressed as a boy. I'm going to tell the teacher." Claire was just about to tell him that she thought she was a girl but he ran off.

But back at home, after the class performance she retreated to her bedroom. After Olivia had descended downstairs to the kitchen to prepare the evening meal of finnan haddock, a type of fish Claire wasn't exactly keen on, she sat in front of her dressing table mirror, nursing a very sore face. She opened the jar of 'cold cream' and applied some to her face. She reasoned rightly or wrongly that as it was called 'cold' cream, it might do her some good right at that moment. It did. The coolness of the cream brought about a pleasure which was indescribable. It was soft and cold and soothed her red lips and cheeks and she then realized in her childish understanding that *Pond's Cold Cream* was for soothing sore skin.

Down in the dining room when Olivia announced that dinner was on the table, the rawness of Claire's face was still in evidence and she was ragged by her dad and brothers throughout the meal. The latter individuals, especially Danny, sniggered and continuously pointed his finger at her. She really could not understand what all the fuss was about. Some people in the world around her were not very nice at all and fond of making fun of others.

8

Beauty

It would be toward the latter part of 1948 when Claire was chosen to take a lead in the school pantomime. Her class teacher Sister Mary Rose had asked Olivia through a note Claire had to take home, if 'William – her son' could sing. The result of this was that Claire's mother took time out of her busy schedule to visit St Brigid's one afternoon in order to collect 'her son', and to speak to Sister Mary Rose personally. Olivia willingly offered the news that 'William' had a lovely sweet voice. So Claire was chosen to take the part of a shopkeeper in a sketch about a toy store, in which, after closing time, the toys came to life. She had to wear a new boy's suit that her Uncle Andy had made for her from a bolt of cheap cloth he had managed to obtain without rationing coupons from Montague Burtons, the Aireborough-based men's garment manufacturers and outfitters, where Andy worked. The suit, made from a reddish brown material had short pants, which Claire thought made her look silly, and a jacket in a matching fabric. The problem was that when she saw what the other girls were wearing, she was almost struck dumb. The ones from her class were to dress up as chorus girls with sailors hats on, bearing the names of famous movie screen actresses on the front band. She would have given all her possessions to change places with any of them.

Claire thought the best part in the sketch was that of the Fairy Queen, played by the head girl whom the other children called 'Aunty Ada' as she seemed to act older than her real age of fourteen. 'Aunty Ada' was taller than the rest of the girls and in the playground she could easily demand a following to skip with her and her gang. Quite often Claire, as 'William', used to skip with the other girls when there was a long rope into which a number of them could skip aside each other. But if the boys saw her they would point and laugh and call her *a sissy*. Sometimes, however, when there were no boys present, Claire would run and jump into the line of other girls skipping over the swinging rope, especially when there were two ropes alternating. She always considered it fun to be able to jump in and out to the tunes that they used to sing. For Claire, it was wonderful to play with the other girls instead of the cruel and stupid boys.

She was so keen on skipping that she told her mum that she was going to ask *Father Christmas* for a really good skipping rope with ball bearings which allowed the rope to spin and not form knots. Apparently Olivia mentioned it to Milton, who blew his top at the idea. A skipping rope was for girls, not boys. But, it was Olivia who in the end succeeded in persuading Milton to acquiesce. To him, at least at the outset of their argument, it was girls who skipped; while boys did boxing. As he was trying to rear 'William' as a boy in the hope that 'he' would turn out to be one, Milton was against anything that smacked of feminine ways. But Claire's mum, cleverer and wiser than her dad, suggested that even boxers skipped and in this she won over Milton. So much so that the idea was no longer Olivia's but his. As Claire unwrapped the present on Christmas morning her father piped up immediately: "We thought Father Christmas should bring you a skipping rope like the one used by boxers; to keep you fit, and make you into a strong boy." *Yeah, big deal Dad! Big deal!*

Milton also justified Claire's choice of knitting as a hobby by convincing himself that as sailors had to knit and darn their own socks, it was okay for 'his son' to knit. It was Olivia who taught her and Claire enjoyed joining the girls' class next door to Miss Comerford's when it came to craft time. She would traipse out with the other girls to sit at Miss Seaford's desk to knit a scarf. The problem was that the boys laughed at her when she chose to use the colors of dark blue and white. She was ragged by them because those were the colors of Hull Kingston Rovers and not Aireborough United which used a paler blue with yellow and white. Years later, in her teens when she explained to her mother that she would like to start doing some embroidery, her dad finally acquiesced by attempting to sew himself a badge onto his blazer pocket. The trouble was that he was 'all fingers and thumbs' like most men seem to be, and had to let Olivia take over his task. Claire always had the impression he had chosen to embroider a badge as in his mind, he was trying to justify her love of embroidery. It was years later however, that Claire was to take it up as a serious hobby and even turn it into a small craft business in Australia.

In many ways, at school Claire was regarded as insignificant and often felt alienated, easily melting into the school's red brick walls. It was during play time outside, especially in frosty weather that she started coughing up phlegm. She would sit in the playground with her back against the classroom wall, and cough her little head off until she was successful in getting the nasty green-yellow stuff out of her throat. Years later she reasoned, rightly or wrongly, that it had been caused by her mum's smoking. Claire hated the smell of the horrid things her mum stuck in her mouth and then after setting fire to them with a smelly match, sucked in the smoke before blowing it out of her mouth and nose. As a result of her mum's addiction, everyone else around her had to breath the acrid smoke that surround her head most of the time. But the Wilson children had no choice as their mother had become hooked on inhaling the harmful chemicals in the cigarettes, a compulsive drug.

It was a saving that in the summer Claire had her own bedroom, which during the colder months was simply a freezing box-room over the staircase. So Claire now felt that she should be able to choose her own toothpaste as she was getting bigger. As a result, 'Father Christmas' had placed a tin of *Gibb's Dentifrice* in her Christmas stocking. The stocking was pinned to the fireplace mantle-shelf alongside those of her brothers. Claire liked the 'dentifrice' so much that she begged Olivia to buy another tin each time the previous one had been used up. The 'paste' comprised a solid cake of compressed pink-colored powder in a flat tin. Claire loved putting water on her toothbrush and then swirling it around the cake so that the brush was full of froth before putting it into her mouth. She was growing up and by that time she had had to have some teeth removed as her jaw was too small.

Traveling on the tram from Micklegate to the Shaftesbury Cinema on the corner of York Road and Harehills Lane, she then had to walk up to the school dental clinic further up from the movie theater. She hated going there like most of the children, as her first visit turned out to become a constant nightmare.

Claire had had to have a tooth removed from both sides of her bottom jaw, and as she sat in the dentist's chair a nurse put a clip on her nose and a rubber mask over her mouth and administered a gas that put her to sleep. When she came back to consciousness, not only did she feel really sick, but her mouth was full of blood and it hurt so much. The nurse led her into a side room with a large bath in the center and Claire had to stand at its side together with other children, all of whom had had similar extractions. They had to swill out their mouths with warm water from a special faucet and then spit the blooded residue into the bath. The image of this process stayed with Claire for years and put her off going to the dentist. She remembered receiving cards at St Brigid's from time to time which stated that she was due to attend the dental clinic and had been booked for an appointment on a particular day. But when she became wise to this she used to tear up the cards and flush them down the first toilet bowl she came to in the school yard. She would have been about eight years of age at this time. The way the system worked was most unsatisfactory and it put her off dentists for many a long day.

A few years later, when Claire had to visit a private dentist in Arkroyd Road, in the end unit of shops almost opposite the Cooperative Store, she would shake in her shoes with fright. Mr Ormond was a heavy smoker and she hated his nicotine-stained fingers being placed in her mouth. It was bad enough having a mother who smoked, but to have a dentist who did this also, was just too much. Smoking was a filthy stinky habit. Claire could not understand why adults would want to suck such horrid smelly smoke into their lungs. Surely it was not healthy?

She had been pleading with mummy and daddy for some months to buy her a pet rabbit. Eventually her wishes were realized when, on her ninth birthday, she was able to cuddle her *Beauty*, an 'English Butterfly' rabbit. The most beautiful rabbit she had ever seen in her short life, hence her choice of the name. Beauty was basically white with black markings and black ears. The rabbit hutch was a really desirable residence made from a large wooden blanket box, in which Claire's dad had fitted a wooden divider with an access hole, through which Beauty could squeeze. Looking from the front, the left hand side was her bedroom, in which Claire devotedly laid fresh straw, wood shavings or shredded paper every few days, and the right hand section of the hutch was Beauty's living/dining room.

Every day, Claire would take her pet some tea leaves added to some porridge oats, together with some carrot peelings, cabbage stalks and the outer leaves of a large lettuce. To heck with putting them in the 'pig bin', Claire would then scour her dad's greenhouse for any fallen tomatoes for her pet too. Beauty had fresh water and often a whole carrot which was 'going spare'. In spring, when the leaves started to form on the trees and the grass started growing again, Claire would roam the streets looking for dandelion leaves growing on the grass verges and between cracks in the concrete edgings, in the convinced belief that these succulent leaves had to be a special treat for her floppy-eared friend. Claire thought of Beauty and her as devoted friends, loving each other to distraction.

The rabbit hutch was supported on the old cast iron stand on which Olivia's *Singer* sewing machine had previously stood. When Milton cut the lawns, Claire would make sure that Beauty had the pick of the fresh grass clippings. In summer, she loved to take her beautiful little friend out of her 'residence' and let the furry bunny sit on the back lawn next to her. Beauty seemed to just love to hop around her mistress, munching as she hopped. Sometimes, especially if no one was looking, Claire would pick some red and black currants from bushes that had been planted by her dad in the back garden near his greenhouse. But Claire could only pick them when the roses on the trellising were in full leaf as then she was shielded from view by the greenery and thought no one would notice a few currants missing.

Unfortunately, this was not the case as Olivia had noticed a lot of bare stalks on which berries should have been growing, and she confronted 'William': "Have you been picking currents off the black and red current bushes?"

Claire had to admit to her *faux pas* and was soundly berated, being reminded that as the War had only recently ended, the shortages they all faced meant that the fruit was for the use of the family, not a pet rabbit. But, from time to time, she had to later admit, she still sneaked a few currants to add to Beauty's rolled oat and tea leaf mix. This was a special treat for her pet and Claire was sure Beauty appreciated it with the special love they obviously had for each other.

One of the games she used to love in summer was to play 'house' on their back lawn. If Olivia was not using the wooden clothes horse Claire would ask to borrow it and cover it with a gray government-war-issue blanket. She would take out her teddies and *Mumfy*, a blue cuddly elephant with over-large ears and a long trunk, and pretend to have afternoon tea with them and read them stories from her books. Claire had already become an avid reader as books took her into other worlds, whether real or imaginary.

The books she had acquired by this time were Christmas or birthday presents from relatives, and she treasured every one of them. One of her favorite was a poetry book called *Sketches of Natural History, or Songs of Animal Life by Mary Howitt* and this book is still in her possession, albeit having been scribbled in by her extremely annoying brother Danny. Claire loved Mary Howitt's poetry and could let the hours drift by of a Sunday afternoon quite easily, looking at the sketches in the book, reading Mary's poetry and dreaming of the animals, with herself among them.

9

New Friends

One strange thing Claire had noticed after a few years had been that while she had not been allowed to have dolls, her youngest brother Gerald was allowed to have them. At the time she couldn't understand this. But with hindsight, she later reasoned that as Gerry was the youngest child of the family, remaining baby-like for many years, he was spoiled terribly and could do no wrong. Later Claire wondered if her mother treated him like a girl as she had lost her real daughter through Claire's mutilation at Milton's intervention a few years previously.

Even Claire's favorite teddy was stolen by Danny on *Guy Fawkes Night* one November Fifth. Danny's intention apparently had been to make the teddy his 'Guy' on the street bonfire. He had sneaked into her bedroom and taken *Bunty*, her only teddy, off the pillow on the bed.

Standing next to the bonfire talking to some other girls, Claire didn't notice what Danny was doing, until she saw him reach over the bonfire with a furry toy on the end of a long stick. There was a noose around the neck of what appeared to be a teddy bear, and Danny hooked it over a stake standing in the middle of the slowly rising flames. She felt sick in her stomach and excusing herself from her company, she ran inside and up to her bedroom. Looking at her bed head she was mortified as she saw the pillow devoid of her precious Bunty. Danny had obviously crept into her room, taken the teddy and rushed out to the bonfire without anyone noticing. *The little Devil,* Claire said to herself as she dashed back outside. "Mummy, Danny has been in my bedroom and stolen Bunty and he has put it on the bonfire as a guy," she cried in total exasperation.

"Don't worry dear, we can always get you another one."

"But that was my only teddy, my Bunty. Danny is a thief."

"Now then William, don't go making wild accusations. Danny probably thought you were too big to be having a teddy bear at your age. Don't make a scene in front of our neighbors. We'll sort it out later."

It was never sorted out. Claire was the one accused of having a teddy bear at nine years of age, and told that "he – William" should be setting a good example to 'his' brothers instead of getting all worked up over it.

Thankfully, she still had Mumfy, her cuddly blue elephant which Danny somehow did not see sitting on the dressing table. Olivia then developed the habit of telling her that she was 'a big boy' and should not be so babyish over the loss of Bunty. But Claire didn't let things rest until her father became involved and supported Danny and Gerry in their making fun of her. Danny started calling her a little girl and would add to these accusations by putting his tongue out at her and pushing her shoulder with his hand. Then Gerry started calling her names too and kicking her. If she retaliated and pushed Danny back, Claire was the one accused of starting it all, not her brothers. This was not fair. Whenever they did that, or whenever her parents sided with her brothers over similar incidents she would retire to her bedroom, her sanctuary. She was able to calm down in her own space, but it didn't stop her hating her brothers, and often times her parents too.

The usual spate of children's illnesses spread through the streets and schools of Aireborough, and Claire was not at first affected by them. The reason was that as soon as her brothers started with the early signs of an illness, she was 'farmed off' to either of her grandparents or to a favorite aunt and uncle. One particular week in 1949 as her brothers came down with chicken pox, Claire was sent to live with her Uncle Andy and Aunty Lorna for a couple of weeks while her brothers suffered the worst stage of the illness. At Andy and Lorna's flat, Claire's bed was a mattress laid on the floor under their bedroom window which looked over Arkroyd Road. Her Aunt Lorna and Uncle Andy lived in a one-bedroom flat in a large house on the corner of Arkroyd Road and the street that led up to the Parish Church. Their flat was not far from Dr Kelly's surgery which, at that age Claire already knew so well. Lorna's kitchen and main living room were on the side looking into Church Street, opposite Batty's Garage and the window in the other wall looked down onto Arkroyd Road. This road continued out into the countryside as Barnbow Lane as it led past the Royal Ordinance Factory where they made tanks for the British Army. The road then made its way up to square pond, where many of the Micklegate children caught *tiddlers* and tadpoles.

Claire always thought it strange that her Uncle Andy and Aunty Lorna had to walk across a staircase landing shared by other tenants, to get from their bedroom to the living room. Many years later as an Australian, Claire traveled back to the UK and living in Aireborough for a time she took a bus from the city center to Micklegate. Walking down Arkroyd Road in her hiking gear, the building she described previously as 'flats' had been converted into the office of a realtor; in English parlance referred to as an 'estate agent' or 'chartered surveyor'. On that return to the suburb of her birth she was to see Arkroyd Road as a dirty, disheveled street with no soul left. In the days of her childhood, it was a wonderful hub of excitement to her as she had gotten to know all the shops and some of the shopkeepers. Her later visit was to become a big disappointment to her.

At some stage Claire had become friends with Mungo Ryan who lived with his parents and grandma on the corner of Hawkhill Drive and Hawkhill Crescent, a distance of literally two house blocks and a road junction from the Wilson house in Sandy Peth. Mungo had been crippled with polio, an illness which left him in a really bad state. Having no strength in his legs, he had been fitted with calipers when he was eventually released from hospital. What Claire hated was that other children at St Brigid's poked fun at him because he had to wear calipers. They did this with all children who were different through no fault of their own. She discovered that children at Roman Catholic schools were no different to those at non-Catholic schools, all poking fun at those who were different from them. She had thought that because they were good little Catholics they would be a cut above the Protestant children but sadly they were no better or worse.

Claire not only felt sorry for Mungo but found that she seemed to have a natural inclination to befriend him and others with disabilities, those who had problems, both of a physical or mental nature. Having become a friend of Mungo she was constantly invited to his house after school, when they would sit on the floor of the Ryan's front room and chat, looking at some of his toys and the wooden figures his dad had made for him. She especially liked the dinosaurs Mungo's dad had carved, as they were so lifelike. Mr Ryan was very clever, compared to Claire's dad who always seemed to be at his precious 'works' or gardening, or doing something else, always wearing his suit, collar and tie. Milton was often seen as a veritable 'stick-in-the-mud' by those who lived life a little more dangerously.

Olivia and Milton didn't like Claire going to Mungo's house after school and often made snide remarks at meal times, about her being friends with a cripple. On more than one occasion Olivia had asked her why she never invited Mungo to their house. How was Claire to explain? In essence she found the question quite embarrassing as the real reason she did not invite any other children to play was because her parents never seemed to stop arguing and shouting at each other. Claire's answer to questions of this nature was to tell fibs, that Mungo couldn't visit the Wilson's home because of his legs, and his grandma wanted him home. Her brothers didn't invite other children home for the same reason. Her parents; Olivia and Milton, always seemed to be at each other's throats. Her mother would ask: "Why don't you have 'normal' friends? You know, boys who don't have something wrong with them? It might be alright having Mungo as one of your friends but you should play with other boys, so you will grow up big and strong."

"But the other children at school make fun of those with something wrong with them. I don't think that's right."

"But why should you of all children become their friend?"

"Why not mummy?"

"Because people will laugh at us and think there is something wrong with our family and you in particular."

"But Mungo has no other friend except me and I like being his friend."

"Well, don't tell daddy about this or he will get angry."

Claire knew very well what her mum meant. Her dad's attitude was strange to other people. As she grew up she was to realize that he seemed to have an inferiority complex and making fun of others, or criticizing them, appeared to be his way of boosting his confidence.

But Claire was really happy being friends with those who might have some physical or facial disfigurement or speech impediment. No one else seemed to like them, but she could see nothing wrong with them. This attitude was to stay with her throughout her life. She did wonder if it might have been that subconsciously she herself had been born with an abnormality. A geneticist, whom she was to have as her general practitioner many years into adulthood, was to remark that this was a distinct possibility.

On one particular occasion Claire was invited to Mungo's birthday party and the thing she really remembered of it was seeing a pretty relative of his. Bronwyn wore a dress which flared out from the waist, especially when she did a twirl. Claire was insanely jealous of her and would have willingly swapped places with her for whatever she demanded. Bronwyn's dress had been made of a printed fabric on which the flowers were of a poppy-pink, slightly larger than ones on the dresses the girls were supposed to wear at St Brigid's. Except that Claire was not allowed to wear the girl's uniform as she had been registered as a boy, much to her frustration. Bronwyn's dress had puffed sleeves and a pink ribbon around her waist tied at the back with a bow. She was wearing ankle socks too, with lace around the tops, and some gorgeous patent black buckled sandals. Bronwyn's hair had been curled for the party and she was wearing a pink bow in it.

If Claire's envious looks could have killed her, then she would have truly dropped dead on the spot. But Claire was conscious of others staring at her as though they could read her unkind thoughts, and quickly turned her gaze elsewhere.

Claire was so overwrought by her thoughts that by this time in her early life she was old enough to confess her jealousy to a priest. But what could she say to Father Corcoran, who seemed to have become her regular confessor? Boys were not supposed to be jealous of girls even though she knew she was a girl herself. But with all the ridicule she had to endure, she did not want more of the same from the priest. So she disguised her sin as being jealous of "another boy" because of the way he dressed or spoke. Even though she had been given absolution from the priest, she still felt as though she was breaking all the rules, even if she couldn't help herself.

It was about that time too that Claire became friendly with another girl in her class, Annette Sharples. Annette's dad was the head librarian at Micklegate Public Library next to the police station at the end of Farm Road, opposite Mr Bernie Friedman's Pharmacy. But the Wilsons, as usual, poured scorn on any relationship 'their son' developed. One particular time Claire had been in bed with measles and as she was slowly recovering, her class friend Annette had pushed a small hand-made *Get Well* card for her through the letterbox on the Wilson's front door, with its rising sun stained glass. With the card was a note from Annette saying that she missed Claire at school and hoped that she would be better soon. As 'William' was never allowed private mail, Claire's parents opened the envelope and unknown to her at the time; they had both read it with great amusement. Olivia and Milton had finished their usual salad lunch when the envelope was delivered, and shortly afterward Olivia went up to Claire's bedroom to tell 'William' that 'he' had received a letter and card. With Milton standing behind his wife, both of them grinning like the proverbial Cheshire cat of *Looking Glass* fame, Olivia handed Claire the envelope: "This came for you."

Claire took the envelope and noticed that it had obviously been opened. She managed to squeak: "Oh! It's already been opened."

"Yes, well, we didn't know who it was for," was Olivia's pathetic answer.

"But it has my name on the envelope, doesn't it? Why would you think it was for you?"

"Now don't be cheeky young man. Don't you dare speak to us in that tone."

It all seemed somewhat ridiculous as the writing on the envelope was obviously not from an adult. Claire laid the envelope to the side of her on the eiderdown, seething with annoyance. "Aren't you going to open it," Olivia asked, standing there by the door with arms folded.

"No, I will look at it later when I am on my own."

"But whoever it is might need a reply."

"No I don't think so."

"Is she nice?" Olivia asked, after a short pause.

"Who?"

"Annette, whoever she is."

Claire knew then by her mother's admission that her parents had opened the letter and read it, so she turned away from their gaze onto her other side. She felt humiliated at their attempt to control her life, even at that age. When her mum brought up something for her to eat at teatime, she asked: "Daddy wondered what Annette's father does for a living. Does he work in a factory or down the pit?"

"What? Why should he work in a factory or down the pit?"

"Well, as most of the children at St Brigid's seem to be Irish and live in a Corporation house, your daddy thought your friend's family might not be as well off as we are."

"Mummy, as if that matters. No he's been to university and is very clever. He is the head librarian at Micklegate Library. Is that a problem?"

"No, I just thought I would ask."

"Why? Is it important what her father does?"

"Not particularly, but your daddy doesn't want you mixing with people of a lower class."

"Annette is in my class."

"I didn't mean that," Olivia replied. "It's just that we don't want you mixing with people who live on one of the Corporation estates."

"Why not?"

"Well, they are not nice people. Although some might be all right, I suppose," she added as an afterthought as she walked out of the bedroom.

Claire didn't really understand what her parents were getting at. She could see no difference between people who lived in Council or Corporation houses, and those who lived in private houses like theirs, even if it was merely semi-detached. It was not until a number of years later she came to see her parents as 'snobs'. She knew her dad and two of his brothers, had worked in a factory at some stage in their lives, and her granddad Mariner, whom her father appeared to despise, worked 'down the pit'. So what was the big problem? Was she being denied friendships because of their father's employment? This didn't seem right to her and it began to shape her obscure view of the dreaded British class system.

Throughout her early formative years this view was constantly being stretched to its limits by her father who, while coming from a coalmining family, liked to place himself above that of most of his acquaintances. There were two examples Claire noted, often with amusement. The first was her dad's constant reminder as they drove through the main street of Tullminster past two breweries. Brothers Sam and John Smith had separate breweries and their individual building complexes were within walking distance of each other, both behind high metal gates emblazoned with their respective names. While Milton claimed that he was a teetotaller who didn't drink alcohol, he always mentioned to his children that the particular brewery which they happened to be passing, either Sam or John Smiths, was where their granddad Levine got his medicine from. Olivia was furious with him for telling the children such a 'big fib', especially as he was belittling her father, the children's grandfather. All this was Milton's way of criticizing his father-in-law for drinking beer. What

Milton hadn't realized was that Claire knew that her granddad Levine preferred *Newcastle Brown Ale*, not John or Sam Smith's.

The second instance of Milton's deliberate 'fibs' to his children was when they drove past the huge entrance archway to Harewood House, on the road to Harrogate. Every single time their dad would say to them: "Your Aunty Mary lives through there," as he jabbed his finger in the air pointing toward the very ornate gates.

"No, she doesn't. Don't confuse them Milt," came Olivia's comment as she stabbed her finger into his arm, albeit with a smile across her face.

"Yes she does. She's done well for herself our Mary has."

At St Brigid's, Claire would then announce to her classmates that they had an Aunty Mary who lived in Harewood House. Whether the other children believed her or not, she could never remember. Certainly when her teacher heard the story, she glared at her pupil as though she was trying to put herself above the other children, many of whom were Irish.

10

A Naughty Word

Late one afternoon, prior to sitting down for the family's evening meal, Claire's parents were surprised when she announced that she wanted to join the children's section at Micklegate Public Library. She had never seen either of them read a book, as her mum seemed to read women's magazines most of the time, passed on to her after someone else had finished with them. Milton always read the *Yorkshire Post,* which he brought home from 'the works' with him, and they had the *Yorkshire Evening Post* delivered through their front door letter slot in the late afternoon. So the great and devastating news that 'their son' wanted to read books, must have been somewhat of a great shock to them. In the back bedroom, where Claire's brothers slept, and where she was forced to sleep during the colder months, there was a shelf in a display cabinet which held a handful of books, which later had been transferred to a shelf in an old radio-record player in the sitting room. Claire had read the two novels among them, *Nurse Iris* and *Her Saddest Blessing,* the latter of which had been presented to Granddad Wilson for good attendance at a Sunday school in 1899, by the Casterley School Board. That was according to a label stuck inside the front cover. She found this rather strange as these books were obviously written for women or girls, certainly not men or boys. Among the other books was a rather heavy tome about the French Revolution, possibly bought by her dad when he lived and worked in Marseilles in the south of France way back in 1932. The other volumes comprised a set of dark blue-bound engineering books which Milton had to study when he was at night school or when he undertook a course in engineering through the International Correspondence School, studying in the evenings.

"Why do you want to join the Library?" Olivia asked.

"Well, to read books," Claire uttered, thinking her mother's question thoroughly ridiculous. She was totally baffled at her mum's lack of understanding and knowledge.

"What for?" Olivia asked.

"Because I like reading mummy," Claire answered quite truthfully and in all innocence, not wanting in any way to show the growing contempt she was developing for her parents' lack of understanding.

"I don't see why you want to read books from the library child; we have some perfectly good books upstairs."

"Mummy, there are only two novels among them and I have already read those."

"What do you want to read novels for? They will only give you fancy ideas."

"Oh mummy, you don't understand." With that she stormed off to her bedroom.

"Don't you take that attitude with me young man," Olivia shouted after her.

"Your daddy and I know what's best for you."

Oh yeah, big deal! Claire muttered under her breath as she climbed the stairs. "Anyway, I am not a young man, I am a girl."

"What did you say William?"

"Nothing mummy – nothing!"

When Olivia told Milton he followed it up with no more words of criticism, only to make up his mind to order Arthur Mee's *Children's Newspaper* to be delivered along with the comics they had delivered each week. In Milton's opinion, if 'his son' wanted knowledge then all 'he' needed was *The Children's Newspaper*. It was news suitable for all boys; technical matters, world news suitable for children and topics for study. Olivia's *Women's Weekly* magazines, together with *Woman's Day* always finished up under Claire's bed nevertheless, and the stories and articles in them were of far more interest to her than boring boy's stories. The comics that her parents had delivered each week always seemed to end up under Milton's side of their bed as he was the one who ended up reading them. He had told Olivia to order *Hotspur* for 'William' but Claire could not understand why, as she didn't read it. How could she explain that it was a boy's periodical and that she would have preferred to read *Girl*? But then she began to realize that for some mysterious reason, her parents, and especially her dad, constantly stressed that she should be reading boy's stories. Claire was only interested in girl's stories but how could she tell them without her father hitting her as he often did, especially after she appeared to commit some mysterious offense.

Claire did actually wonder if her mother was deliberately testing her. Her mum had always made sure that her hair was cut short like her dad's. It was not until years later, reminiscing through her early life, that she wondered if they were convinced that if her hair was cut short, she would become the boy that her dad wanted her to be.

A few years earlier than this, when she was old enough to have her hair cut professionally, Olivia had made an appointment for 'William' to have 'his' hair cut at her own hairdresser's salon near St Brigid's. The owner of the salon, who obviously knew Olivia, took charge of the situation and had Claire sit near the window and proceeded to cut her hair while she sat in a high chair with a pretty flowered cloth around her shoulders. The appointment had been made to coincide with her leaving school one afternoon and she had been able to slip away from her classmates without much notice. But Claire had not reckoned on the ridicule that some of the boys in her class might shower on her through the glass as she sat in full view of everyone that passed by. "Hey look everyone, there a little girl called William having her hair done," said the first one.

"Doesn't she look pretty sitting there among all those ladies," commented another.

The hairdresser banged on the window to shoo off the boys and after a few moments they left. Claire's face was beetroot red by this time and the hairdresser noticed. "Don't take any notice of them William, they're a common lot."

The next morning of course it started again in the playground. "Here's girly William. Did the hairdresser perm your hair for you little girl?" They all laughed and poked their fingers at her. Annette saw them and was walking over to see what it was all about, but the bell sounded and further humiliation was saved. The duty teacher stood on the entrance step and was ringing the hand bell furiously. But Claire was not to be let off so lightly as at playtime, she was ragged some more and had to sneak into the cloakroom to escape their jibes.

As has already been hinted, Claire didn't like her hair being cut in the first place but this event was ridicule at its highest level and she was mortified. That fateful day, after her hair had been trimmed, she arrived home with tears streaming down her cheeks and her mother asked what the problem was. When Claire tried to tell her however, her mum got the wrong idea and thought 'William' didn't like having 'his' hair cut at her hairdressers, which was only part of the problem. Claire tried to explain that it was the humiliation of being sat in full view of passers-by and being laughed at by her classmates, plus the fact that she didn't like short hair. Olivia wasn't listening. She thought 'their eldest son' was growing up into the boy that Milton wanted and decided in future to make an appointment at a man's barber. How could Claire tell her parents that she was a girl?

At that stage in her young life, the comics that were delivered were *Radio Fun* and then after Milton had made a television in 1961 – which is another story – *TV Fun* was delivered in addition. Other comics the children were expected to read were the *Dandy*, the *Beano* and *Knockout*. The *Children's Newspaper* had some interesting articles in it and Milton insisted 'his son' sit between his legs in his armchair when he found time to put the *Yorkshire Evening Post* down. He would read stories aloud to her, as if she was not capable of reading them herself. What she didn't like was the way her dad seemed to fondle her. It made her feel creepy. Later in her teens, she realized that her "daddy" had been trying to put boy's thoughts into her head. Her mother was to tell her later that it was the technique the gender specialist had recommended after she was mutilated as a baby. That particular "specialist" believed that boys and girls took upon themselves their true gender when they were nurtured into it by their surroundings and family. Scientific research into gender dysphoria was to prove many years later, that this assumption was totally erroneous.

Irrespective of her general repugnance at having to read the *Children's Newspaper*, Claire was interested in some of the stories and reports in it, but these were the ones which helped her with school projects. Especially around this time she took an interest in astronomy, as she would spend hours each evening looking at the stars through a telescope which she had found in one of the cupboards in the back bedroom.

Finally Claire was allowed to join the children's section of Micklegate Public Library, her parents having eventually signed the parental consent form. It was a real eye opener for her as she was able to choose her own books without her parent's interference, although they did ask what she had borrowed each time.

The first book Claire selected from the children's section was a book on how to write and speak Chinese. This was in addition to the first of her usual books by Enid Blyton and the classics of *Robinson Crusoe, Little Women, Masterman Ready,* and stories about explorers in foreign lands. When she first joined the library and answered her mum's question on what books she had borrowed, Olivia mockingly laughed at the selection. "What possessed you to take out a book on Chinese, child?" to which Claire innocently replied:

"Why not? I would like to learn Chinese."

"I don't see why you want to learn Chinese. We don't have any Oriental people in Aireborough." Claire was later to prove her mother very much wrong on this point.

When Olivia told her husband on his return from 'the works' that 'William' had borrowed a book on learning Chinese, he laughed and then a smirk spread across his face. "He must be barmy. Stark, staring bonkers in fact." Milton didn't have a good word to say about anyone who wasn't English, especially "the slit-eyed, yellow-skinned natives from China." To Milton, people who lived in Africa, South America or the Orient were ignorant savages.

Once again, Claire always seemed to do the wrong things in the eyes of her parents. But as far as that first book was concerned, she still remembered the first Chinese characters learned. So it was not altogether a waste of time. Consequently, as a result of joining Micklegate Public Library, she became an avid book reader, a situation that her whole family seemed to frown upon and mock from time to time. But speaking of doing the wrong thing, one day she really learned a hard lesson and paid for it dearly for a many a long day.

A number of children from St Brigid's, including Claire, walked home after school on the same route, around past the police station, along Micklegate Road by the tram tracks, across to the start of Hawkhill Drive and turned into Sandy Peth. It was on one of these occasions that she found herself walking along with one particular boy, admittedly one who lived on the Starfield Estate, one of the dreaded Corporation or Council estates, which according to her parents, was a bad area. The boy in question was chalking a particular four-letter word beginning with the letter 'F' on the multi-faceted concrete columns of the gas street lights at the side of the road. Claire had been watching him for a while and asked him what he was writing. He told her that it was a special new word he had learned from his older brother that showed just how grown up he was. Consequently he broke his chalk in two and offering her half, encouraging her to write the same word on the lamp posts on the other side of the street while he wrote on those on the side where he was standing. Thinking that this might convince her father that she was not the 'sissy' he was in the habit of accusing her, Claire took up the challenge. What she had not anticipated however, and had not been aware of at the time, was that one of their neighbors, a particularly sneaky woman who lived a few doors down Sandy Peth, had been watching her. So, when Claire arrived home somewhat later than usual, her mum grabbed her arm quite violently and while slapping her across the face a few times and shaking her, Olivia blurted in extreme anger. "You dirty, filthy little boy!"

"Wha…Wha…What have I done?" Claire cried, thoroughly shattered at such treatment from her mum.

"You have been writing filthy dirty words on the lamp posts haven't you, you mucky little boy? That's what you have been doing – and don't deny it either as Mrs Harrison down the street saw you."

"I didn't know it was a dirty word," Claire sobbed. "A boy was walking home with me and he said it was a new word. I didn't know it was naughty."

"Well, it is. Just wait 'til your daddy hears about this."

Just then Milton happened to walk in the back door, from 'the works', which at that stage in its business development was merely a few sheds in a farm yard. "What's he gone and done now?" he asked, while Olivia was still hanging onto Claire's arm with a wounding grip.

"He's only been writing filthy words on the lamp posts, that's what he's been doing."

"He's done what?" Milton, staring at 'his son' with fury, shouted at 'him' and grabbed 'his' other arm. Claire could not escape. She was trapped, and trembled with such great fear she thought she might pass out. Her dad was becoming angrier with every breath he sucked in. Olivia told him that 'his son' had been seen writing the dreaded 'F' word.

"Come with me," he said as he dragged Claire into the front room and closed the door. "I'll teach you right from wrong yet," he blurted with utter fury as he slapped her across her already smarting and swollen face, time and time again.

Claire was in so much pain that more slapping hardly registered. But her heart was breaking with what her parents were doing to her, apart from the justifiable hatred she now felt for the boy who had encouraged her to write the obviously offensive word. By the time her father had finished strapping her across her bare buttocks with a leather belt, which he kept hidden down the back of a cushion, she felt she was literally black-and-blue and was sent up to her bedroom, not only in total disgrace but without any tea. Claire was told to get into bed and not another peep had to come from her until the morning. She cried herself to sleep as usual, bemoaning the day she was born. In later years such treatment of a child of her impressionable age, would have been construed as cruelty and her parents justifiably reprimanded. But in those days, they were in the right and Claire was in the wrong.

The next morning the growing hatred she had felt for her parents the previous evening still persisted and she refused to speak to them as she devoured her porridge. From this time onward, she had to be more than careful not to antagonize her dad because he had a worse temper than her mum. Claire could not understand why he beat her when she never once experienced him doing the same to her brothers. But as she was in ignorance at the time, she never linked the beatings and chastisement with the congenital defect with which she was born.

At this stage in Claire's young life she knew she was different but didn't know why. She knew she was a girl but was treated as a boy. From time to time she felt that she was trapped in the gender that people saw with their own eyes, but when she looked into her dressing table mirror she saw only a girl, not a boy.

11

Royalty

But life was not all doom and gloom as there were times when Claire seemed to do the right things for a change and she hoped that her parents might have forgiven her the one or two transgressions in which she had unfortunately and unwittingly, allowed herself to indulge. Nevertheless, it was good to be away from her mum and dad from time to time and she loved spending time with both sets of grandparents.

Nanna and Granddad Levine lived in Kelmscott Grove in Minton, which was within walking distance from the Wilson's home in Sandy Peth, and Claire often spent weekends with them and went to Mass with her granddad. Nanna Levine didn't attend as she was a Methodist, Claire was later told. Her grandmother, described as a 'Geordie' by her dad, stayed home to cook the Sunday roast. It was always a treat to have Sunday lunch at her nanna and granddad Levine's as her grandmother made Yorkshire puddings in bun tins, compared to Olivia who made them in large pie tins. In the Wilson home they always started a meal with a large Yorkshire pudding covered in mouthwatering onion gravy. Olivia gave Claire, Danny and Gerry half a pudding each as they could not eat a whole one, with the puddings being so large. In this, Olivia had to do what her husband wanted, exactly as his mother and grandmother had done – that is, to provide large plate-size Yorkshire's. But at the Levine's they had one or two small Yorkshire puddings on the side of each main dinner plate with the rest of the roast dinner. To Claire, this was a real treat and to some degree a novelty, because at her nanna Mariner's down York Road, they always had a large Yorkshire pudding with onion gravy before they had even started the Sunday dinner.

After Claire and Granddad Levine returned to her grandparents' house in Minton after Mass at St Brigid's in Station Road, a half-hour walk from their bungalow in Kelmscott Grove, he always sat on the back step drinking a pint of beer. Newcastle Brown Ale was his favorite, as although he had been born in Micklebrough; his parents were from Sunderland, which was where Nanna Levine had been born. Back a couple of generations, the Levine's had migrated from Germany to Sunderland, as Claire's great-great-grandfather had secured a job as an engineer in the North East mines. She was later to discover that the family name of her ancestors in Germany had been *Levinstein*, but after they had settled in Sunderland, the name had had to be changed due to British hostility to anyone with a German-sounding name. So it was shortened to the more prosaic English-sounding *Levine*. Her great-great-nanna had been born in Durham, to parents who had been transported from Donegal in Ireland, by the British. Claire didn't know all this at the time but it was many years later, as an adult living in Australia, that she received a copy of the *Levinstein* family tree showing that her mother's ancestry was German Lutheran, not always Roman Catholic as she had believed it to be. After further research too, Claire was to discover that her ancestors in the Rhineland had been Jewish before being forcibly converted to Christianity. *Levinstein* was a German variation of the Hebrew name of *Levi*. Some members of the wider *Levinstein* family, who also had migrated to England from Germany, had changed their name to *Levison*. Claire was later to meet some Polish people with the family name of *Levinski*, which she gathered had been yet another spelling variation.

If she stayed at her nanna Levine's on a Sunday night, when Claire was on holiday from school, she would help her nanna with the washing the next morning. Nanna Levine changed the sheets on the beds, the towels from the bathroom and even changed the tablecloth on Monday mornings, come hail or come shine. She washed them in a huge wooden tub lined with metal sheets and Claire loved to beat the clothes with what was called a 'posser'. This was a long stick on the end of which was an upside down bowl made of copper, with holes in it. As she pushed it into the clothes, it would make a 'squelch' as the water squished through the holes. That was her special word for it – *squelching*. She could not understand how, when she pushed the posser up and down on the clothes it sucked the dirt out of them, but it did. When Nanna considered that the clothes and linens had been thoroughly 'squelched' she would swill them in cold water in a nearby Belfast-style sink, and then into a bucket from which she would then attempt to feed them through the 'mangle'. This was a set of three rollers at one end of the tub and when the sheets, towels or clothes were fed through two of the rollers and then back through the other roller, more water came out of the various items. The squeezed sheets and whatever else had been washed were then placed in a wicker basket ready to be taken outside and hung on a line stretched between two posts in the back garden. Marjory Levine liked it when Claire was there as the wicker basket became rather heavy and it was good to have 'William', whom she was convinced, was her daughter's precious 'Claire', hold the handle at the other end. Claire used to love helping to wash clothes this way, it was so much fun.

When recalling her washday antics with Nanna Levine and the wash tub, Claire always remembered the times when her granddad had dug up a few potatoes for the midday meal, because they were washed in the very same tub. One day her uncle Gerald came in the back door and seeing the washed potatoes in the tub, he had taken one and was actually eating a raw potato as Claire approached. She was aghast, her mouth dropping open in absolute amazement. She could hardly speak as she was so dumbfounded. How anyone could eat a raw potato she thought disgusting and horrible. As she stared at uncle Gerald, she dare not ask him what it tasted like, as it was obviously just another of his 'showing off' tricks. Maybe because Gerald could see the girl in 'William', he was showing off in front of her as at this time in his life he would only have been in his late teens.

While recalling those years, Claire remembered her mum making her first appointment with a men's barber and not at the salon of the ladies hairdresser she had previously visited. She remembered her mother calling into Mr Marvin's, a gentleman's barber, who had a shop in a parade on Micklegate Road. A very reluctant 'William' was dragged along, protesting that 'he' did not want 'his' hair cutting. Mr Marvin took control and sat Claire on a wooden board which he placed across the arms of his barber's chair, draped a cloth around her shoulders and tucked the top end into the collar of her school shirt. While he attempted to cut her hair, Claire continued her protests. Olivia, sitting on a chair near the doorway, felt she had to constantly apologize to Mr Marvin for 'her son's' rudeness. On the way home after the ordeal, Olivia explained to Claire that Daddy wanted her to have her hair cut regularly as long hair was for girls and short hair was for boys. It was not until Claire was in her thirties that longer hair for men was to be in vogue, to her complete delight. Letting her hair grow naturally did not come for many years after that, but in this regard she was to eventually achieve happiness, at a price – life or death as far as she was concerned.

One day, Great-aunt Muriel arrived from Sunderland to stay overnight with Claire's nanna and granddad. Great-aunt Muriel, her granddad's sister, had apparently married into Sunderland's Curran family, highly successful automobile dealers. Claire apparently regarded her great aunt in a similar vein to how she saw 'royalty' because she seemed to have bearing and poise. She was her granddad's sister who had traveled on the train all the way down from Sunderland – and she was a Levine too.

One day great aunt Muriel and Claire's nanna walked to her parents' house in Sandy Peth to see Olivia and her family. Claire was told not to get under the feet of Great-aunt Muriel as she was an old lady, but after tea had been served and consumed, Claire was invited to walk back to Nanna Levine's bungalow to stay overnight. All she could remember was walking past the Traveler's Rest pub at the end of Arkroyd Road opposite the National Bank, with Great-aunt Muriel holding her hand. It was as though she was holding the hand of Queen Mary.

While Claire's uncle Gerald had joined the Royal Air Force, he was apparently too young to have fought in the Second World

War. Nevertheless, he was called up for National Service after the end of the war and she remembers him arriving at her grandparent's home after being demobbed in 1948. Claire was sleeping in the same double bed as her godmother, Aunty Irma, and they were both awakened during the early hours of the morning with a gentle tapping on the window, which got louder and louder. Claire screamed in fright as she imagined it to be the 'bogeyman' come to get her, and pulled herself further under the bedclothes. Irma had heard the commotion in the yard and was up in a flash to waken her parents. It was a few minutes later when Claire heard voices in the living room. Gingerly, yet inquisitively, she climbed out of bed and crept into the hallway. Recognizing the voice of her uncle Gerald, she shot through the door screaming: "Uncle Gerald, Uncle Gerald" leaping up into his open arms. She loved her uncle as they used to do things together when he was home on leave. She especially loved to sit and listen to him playing their upright piano in the front parlor. Apparently, Gerald could not read music but had taught himself to play the piano, telling Claire that he played by ear. She could not understand this as he played with his hands, not with his ears. How very strange!

At the back of her Levine grandparents' home in Kelmscott Grove was a field. At some stage Claire remembered her grandparents having a white Billy goat tethered there. Why they kept it she could never fathom out as it certainly wasn't able to give them milk. All it did was eat the grass and weeds while it was on a chain to stop it wandering. Claire would often walk through the back gate and up through the field when she had been asked to go to the shops for her nanna. But years later when she visited the area, she noticed that houses had been built in the field and her earlier memories popped like burst balloons.

12

End of the War

At the end of World War II, the Mariners, Claire's other grandparents, lived down York Road in a terrace house in Darley Avenue. When she wasn't staying with Nanna and Granddad Levine she would stay with Nanna and Granddad Mariner. These grandparents were totally different to her Levine grandparents, mainly because of their accent and lifestyle. In a nutshell, apart from the former having County Durham accents, they were possibly better educated. Nanna Levine had been born Marjory Porterhouse Jackson in Sunderland so had an accent which was very much similar to the 'Geordie' accent of Newcastle, but not quite as broad. Granddad Levine was born Wilhelm Percy Levine in Micklebrough and his accent, according to Claire's ignorant dad was 'Geordie', which of course it wasn't as he wasn't born in Newcastle. But her granddad Levine claimed to be a proud Yorkshireman as Micklebrough was then on the Yorkshire side of the border with County Durham.

On the other side of Claire's family, Nanna Mariner was born Penelope 'Penny' Stanley in Monk Farley near Casterley and had been married to Milton's father James William Wilson, a coalminer of Casterley. Her granddad Wilson had died when Milton, her dad, was in his teens and his mum had then re-married, much to his disgust and the reason he decided to leave home. Nevertheless, Claire's nanna took no notice of her self-opinionated son and married another coalminer, Henry Mariner of Methley. As a result, Milton refused to speak to his mother for a number of years.

As the Wilson children were growing up in Micklegate, Claire's brothers and she were constantly chastised by their dad for referring to step-grandfather Mariner as 'granddad'. Their father had tried to drill it into his offspring that Henry Mariner was not their granddad at all and that they should call him 'Uncle Henry'. This was difficult for the children and they continued to call him 'granddad' despite their dad's orders. Not to do so seemed to hurt granddad Mariner. In their children's world, apart from Granddad Levine, they knew no other than Granddad Mariner.

Strangely enough, Milton's grandmother was still alive and she visited them in Micklegate every so often, but she normally lived with their great-aunt Letty in Barnsley. Claire and her brothers knew their great grandmother as granny Wilson, and Claire always remembered her swinging back and forth in a carved rocking chair in the corner of their sitting room at Sandy Peth, knitting socks and gloves. Granny Wilson always wore black and Claire remembered holding her in the same awe as she did her great-aunt Muriel, both having in her mind the same stature of the King's mother, Queen Mary.

The Mariner's house in Darley Avenue was referred to in real estate terms as a through-terrace house as it had a front door in one street and a kitchen door into a back street. That was where the houses had their washing lines hanging between the houses on a permanent basis. The front door from Darley Avenue led into the Front Room or Parlor, while the room which was used more than that, was the kitchen-cum-dining room, and this was at the back of the house. The kitchen or scullery, as Nanna Mariner mainly called it, boasted a large black-leaded cooking range with a boiler, all set into a wide chimney breast. The back street was where, at the end of World War II, there was a huge bonfire to celebrate its end. At another time, the residents of the houses that faced into the back lane also celebrated the end of the war with a party. The food for this was spread out on long trestle tables covered with white bed sheets, the tables being joined end to end down the middle of the street. Overhead were lines of red, white and blue pennants hanging from the washing lines stretched across the street from the upper windows of the houses. It was a jolly occasion, more especially for the children, as apart from the sandwiches provided; they had cake and jelly, lots of it too. Claire was fortunate to have been staying with Nanna and Granddad Mariner when the party was held.

But at other times she was told to be careful when playing out in the back street with the other children as down at the end, toward East End Park, there were three older boys. These boys used to have most of the neighborhood children shaking in their boots as everyone was scared of them. Quite often the boys, called the Gray Boys, as their family name was apparently 'Gray', would chase other children, boys and girls alike but especially the latter, back to where they lived. It was as though the Gray Boys owned the street. The other children had no choice in the matter and had to rely on their mums and dads to shout at the boys, often in very colorful language.

Quite often a man selling Granelli's Italian ice cream would arrive at the end of the street. The front of his bicycle had a front cart attached and it had a large tub of ice cream set within it. The Italian would ring a hand bell to announce that he had arrived and just about all the children living in 'the Darley's' would take basins and jugs down to him to fill up with ice cream. He would park his bike near the grass verge just at the end of the terraced streets, and nearby was a playground where some of the kids played in the summer evenings. Claire only went there with her granddad as her nanna said it was dangerous for her to be there on her own. It was a real treat for them all when the ice cream man arrived, especially having the freshly made ice cream to consume with some pieces of fresh fruit, especially strawberries in the summer.

Granddad Mariner kept pigeons in a special shed on his allotment alongside East End Park, in an area devoted to community gardens. She loved to watch the pigeons return after a long flight from some mysterious place that her granddad had sent them on a train. Apparently, it was quite customary for coal miners to have pigeons, but to Claire it was part of who her granddad was. She loved walking down to the Park with him, holding his hand, and then when he watched her playing on the swings, the roundabout, the longboat, the slides and the seesaw, he sat with a happy smile across his whiskery face. There was almost always another girl or boy to partner with on the longboat or seesaw.

Because of these children's facilities so close, it was a highlight for Claire to be offered the opportunity to stay with her paternal grandparents, as there were no similar facilities close to the Wilson house in Sandy Peth. In addition to this joy in her life, her nanna always seemed to be cooking, and the smells in and emanating from, the kitchen were mouth watering. The smell was especially so wonderful after Claire had been on a walk down at the allotments with her granddad. She didn't notice until a few years later that her brothers Danny and Gerry hardly ever stayed with any of their grandparents. Claire could never fathom out why this was so but assumed it was because she was somehow different to her brothers and a loner. Her brothers were 'a pair of scallywags' from what she remembered hearing.

Claire often went with nanna Mariner when she went shopping along York Road, to the stores opposite Dalton's Corn Flake factory. One day however, she was in absolute agony as her nanna took her to the doctor's. What had happened was that her nanna had been ironing and the hot flat iron had fallen off its mat on the table and onto Claire's right foot. She screamed blue murder with excruciating pain, and her nanna decided to take her along to the doctor who had a surgery at the end of the short parade of shops. On that occasion she had no broken bones but her nanna was instructed to apply cold compresses to the foot until the swelling subsided. She then had to apply some soothing cream to help the skin to return to normal.

Another event Claire remembered was when Nanna and Granddad Mariner took her to a concert at the Star Cinema in Torre Road. Today, all this area has been re-developed due to York Road having been widened and divided into what the English call a 'dual-carriageway'. The new divided highway splits the whole district in two and the only way to get across the road is to find a nearby intersection, a footbridge or a set of traffic lights. The Star Cinema is still standing but it is now used as a Bingo Club. In 1946 it was a theater/and cinema with a wide stage.

On the particular afternoon in Claire's memory, the performers on stage were members of the armed forces. To her, the soldiers, sailors and RAF men and women presented so much talent to entertain a very appreciative audience. She particularly remembered a xylophonist who was playing what she called a 'plinky-plonk'. Claire was so taken with this instrument that in her early twenties she was to take a special interest in the modern jazz of pianist and xylophonist Lionel Hampton, buying any new gramophone record featuring his music. Even today, in the 21st century, Claire's personal choice of music in her large collection of CDs, apart from the classics, still includes instrumentalists playing 'vibes'.

Granddad Mariner bought Claire her first spinning top and whip. He called the whip's leather cord a 'band' as that was the word he had used as a boy in Kingston-upon-Hull, in the East Riding of Yorkshire. She was told many years later that Granddad Mariner was born in Kingston-upon-Hull, which was situated at the mouth of the River Humber.

Before the children began spinning their tops, they would chalk different designs on the upper surfaces with colored chalks, so that when they were spinning they looked pretty. Claire often used to take her two tops, one large and one a little smaller, to the huge area of smooth tarmac in front of the Regal Cinema across the road from the Micklegate tram terminus. It was a popular meeting place for many of the girls, and by this time she knew without doubt that she was definitely of that number and not the boy that she was supposed to be – being dressed, to her disgust, in boy's clothes. The girls would spin their tops and have a simply great time, spending far longer than their mothers had allowed them. To start a top spinning, Claire would wrap the 'band' as her granddad called it, around the top and then place it under her right heel with the metal tip of the top facing downward. Then she would pull the whip sideways so that the 'band' spun the wooden top and she would whip it constantly to keep it turning fast. It was a knack she had learned from lots of practice.

As Claire grew older, she pestered her parents, who would tell Father Christmas of course, that she would like some roller skates. The older children used to meet in front of the Regal Cinema to skate on its vast area of smooth tarmac. Milton seemed to have no problem in buying her some roller skates as he was under the impression that it was a game that only boys played. It was of course, in Milton's eyes, far too dangerous for girls. How wrong he was! Had he taken time out to walk around to the Regal he would have witnessed both girls and boys skating in front of the cinema. But in particular, he would have noticed that most of the skaters were girls. The times the children met were some of the most important social events of their week. It was Claire's joy to be with other girls of her own age and interests.

13

In Trouble Again

Claire's dad had a black Ford Eight car during the war but afterward he changed this for a Morris Ten, which was luxury after the Ford. But when he started his factory in 1945, among some farm buildings in Starfield, he upgraded to a Morris Twelve. It seemed that the Wilson's were going up in the world. Often on a Monday evening Milton would take Olivia out for a drink. But while Gerald was still a baby, and Danny only a couple of years older than him, it mostly fell to Claire's godmother, Aunty Irma to babysit the children when their parents went out to a country pub. Often Irma would have her best friend, Florrie Byrnes sit with her, both women in their early twenties. But it was in Australia, many years later, that Irma, as Claire's godmother, told her of one specific occasion that had remained a secret. Irma told her that when her brothers and she were supposed to have been fast asleep, Claire appeared at the dining room door when the two young women were sitting knitting and chatting. Claire apparently pushed open the door and walked into the room wearing some of Olivia's clothes and shoes: "Look Aunty Irma, don't I look beautiful?"

Irma said her and her friend's jaws dropped in amazement. "Get those bloody things off before your mam comes back or she'll tan your backside."

Claire immediately hung her head and went into a sulk, not understanding why she was being chastised. Was it not normal for girls to dress up in their mummy's clothes sometimes? The child had reluctantly gone upstairs again and put the clothes back where she had found them and then climbed back into bed sobbing. Her aunty Irma came up a few minutes later and walked into her bedroom. "What possessed you to do that, you naughty boy."

"I'm not a boy, I'm a girl." Claire answered.

"You had better not let your daddy hear you say that or he'll murder you. You are a boy, so you had better get used to it and behave like other boys. Now get to sleep or your mam and dad will thrash you."

Lying in bed; as the poor girl saw herself, Claire cried herself to sleep not understanding why people couldn't see that she was a girl. On the other hand, Irma took Olivia on one side when they came back from the pub, and told her everything. "Well, love, there are things about William's gender that keep coming out. I never told you the full story about the birth, and I don't think our mam has told you either. Perhaps another time, as I don't want Milt hearing me telling you. He is very tetchy about those things."

With that, Irma and Florrie were taken back to the Levine's home in nearby Minton in Milt's new Morris.

Despite Irma's threat about Claire's mum thrashing her for dressing up in her clothes, from this time on she was to continue to wear her mum's clothes when the occasions were safe, but the understanding of her enigmatic dysphoria began to take on horrendous proportions.

Claire knew without a shadow of doubt that she was a girl. She just knew it in her deepest being. She would constantly lay awake night after night toying with her problem. Was there some unwritten code that she was not allowed to be a girl? How did other people know how she felt inside her own body and brain? Why did people, especially her parents, keep telling her she was a boy and that she should take example from other boys? Every night Claire prayed that God would change her into a proper girl by the time she woke up. She knew herself to be growing up with a girl's natural needs, wants and desires; she loved dressing up in her mummy's clothes like other girls did, but she had to do so in secret, as she was convinced that she would have been murdered if anyone was to find out. Claire was therefore forced to keep her feminine side under lock and key in a secret compartment of her brain, mainly it seems so that she did not incur the anger and ridicule of her often violent father.

If Jesus could perform the one miracle Claire's heart desired, then the world would take on new meaning for her. She dreamed of being a famous musician, a ballerina or fashion model and would cry herself to sleep trying to make herself dream about it. It was like living in another world. A world where there were no restrictions on who she was, or how she acted. But would this dream ever be fulfilled? What did the future hold for this little child?

There were times when Claire was able to forget her gender dysphoria, and become excited about other things. One such occasion was a visit to Overton Park with the other children from St Brigid's Roman Catholic Primary school, to a medieval pageant on the cricket arena. As the children sat entranced on Soldiers Hill looking down onto the spectacle, they watched spellbound as knights in shining armor, on horses decked out with armor too, engaged in a joust against each other across a dividing barrier. Each knight looked the part wearing a colorful scapular on top of his armor. Claire was always to remember a particularly liking for a knight wearing black and yellow. For some reason at that stage in her life, she liked those colors and cheered on her champion, her knight in shining armor.

The memory of this event was to return many years later, when she had been taken to a similar joust at a Renaissance Festival at Holly, Michigan, by her cousin Claudine and husband Jackson. On that occasion, she was to cheer for the knight wearing black and emerald green. The rest of the audience cheered on the knight wearing red and yellow. Claire refused to follow the crowd, she had her own priorities and the cheering crowd did not persuade her to change her mind.

The event that Claire attended in Aireborough was the annual *Children's Day*, always celebrated at Overton Park and there were boys and girls from many schools showing off their skills in racing, vaulting, waving ribbons, throwing balls between each other in team races and so on. All looking quite impressive, as at 'Briggers', the colloquial name the children used for St Brigid's, they didn't appear to do anything like that. Maybe the big girls' class might have done something like it at some stage, but the younger ones never did anything as exciting, apart from walking in church parades and processions behind the priests and altar boys. This was the extent of the parish's activities, apart from once or twice at the most, being taken to the local park by one of the nuns, for a game of boring old football.

Claire began to feel that she must have been seen as 'somewhat girly' by her dad especially, judging by his occasional comments. In Olivia's eyes she may have been seen as the daughter she had always wanted, but who had been taken away from her at birth. So it was in 1949 that Olivia started training her in the ways of a good shopper. Claire was to pick up some grocery items from Mr Guy's shop opposite the tram terminus, and then some bread from the baker's shop down Micklegate Road. The latter job she liked best as the smell of the newly baked bread was wonderful when it was taken fresh from the ovens. She felt so pleased with herself if she managed to be given a warm loaf, as then her mum would know that she had managed to obtain a fresh one. Sometimes she was often given a miniature loaf by one of the assistants. Apparently these were made for children like herself. Claire remembers that some of the miniature loaves had the brand *Hovis* baked into the side of the bread. On such occasions Claire would slowly walk back home up Sandy Peth devouring the warm *Hovis* with delight.

What she didn't like were the times her mother gave her a small note to give to Mr Guy personally. She gradually found out what the note said, *Two Woodbines please and wrap them up and place them on top of the shopping.* Olivia was a smoker and the drug had taken over her mental ability to think straight, unless she had puffs on what Claire thought were 'filthy cigarettes'. Milton gave Olivia sufficient money each week for the essential groceries and the weekly payment for the household insurance, the daily papers and comics. So, as Milton was a non-smoker and a very strict misogynist, the only time Olivia could smoke was while Milton was at work or when it was dark and she could sneak out of the scullery door for a quick drag on one of her *Woodbines*. When Claire eventually realized what the little wrapping contained, laid on top of the groceries, she refused to touch it. She saw that smoking was filthy and somewhat contagious. As she grew into her teen years, she stopped hugging her mum as the smell of the cigarettes in her mum's hair and on her clothes made her sick. Olivia tried to hide the smell on her breath by buying a few 'mint imperials', but Claire then started to associate that type of minted candy with smokers, and disliked it too.

On Friday lunchtimes it was her job to collect fish and chips from Mrs Coe's in Micklegate Road, just further up the cottages from Mr Guy's. Well-endowed Mrs Coe knew Claire and it was always good to have some scraps added to the "fish and chips four times," which was her constant order. She was told to order 'four-times' instead of 'five-times' as Olivia used to divide up two fishes and chips between the three children. With lashes of malt vinegar and salt, they were the best fish and chips in the whole world. *Coe's Fisheries* was to become a landmark in Micklegate over succeeding years, and the reputation was well deserved. On Claire's visit to Micklegate in 2012, she noticed that *Coe's Fisheries* was still thriving as an enterprise in the same place as before, albeit in refurbished premises, and possibly under new management.

However, one Friday lunchtime there was disaster. As Claire walked back home with the family's fish and chips she dawdled as usual, daydreaming, but this time poking her index finger into the underside of the newspaper wrapping where it was slightly soggy due to dripping fat. She removed one chip after another and ate them without thought as to the consequences. As if this were not bad enough, in her dream-like state she slipped through the horizontal wires of the fence at the side of the tram track, and walked along the tracks before crossing over to the other side. Unfortunately for her, neighbor Mrs Harrison from down Sandy Peth, who always seemed to report any of Claire's misdemeanors to Olivia, had been watching and she went ahead to warn Olivia. By the time the child arrived home, Claire's dad was there too. His feet were stomping the floor as he demanded his lunch. Consequently, on her arrival back home she was grabbed, shaken, shouted at and slapped across the face for walking alongside the tram tracks. To crown it all, when her mum opened the wrapping to find nowhere near as many chips as there should have been, and the hole through which they had obviously been extracted, Claire, or rather 'William', was again shouted at, slapped and pushed out of the way of everyone, as though she was a total nuisance. Consequently, that lunchtime she received no chips and only a miniscule piece of fish. Her two little brothers were given more than her, their big sister, as she saw herself. They were 'good little boys'. She was bad. This was her punishment for day-dreaming. But this was only part of Claire's problem as she so often lived in a different world – a girl's world.

But the shopping duties still had to be born in sufferance. Olivia explained that she was far too busy to do everything, and so Claire had to start earning her keep. Apart from helping to hang out the sheets when she was on holiday from school, she also washed dishes and swept the kitchen floor when her mother instructed her to do so. At one stage Claire got so fed-up with doing the dishes, she drew up a roster and added the names of her brothers' to it. But when she called them to wash the dishes according to the roster, they refused to help in the kitchen appealing to their dad that it was women's work, not for boys or men. To Claire, her brothers were certainly little children who should have helped, but it was Claire who was ridiculed. This time it was for helping her mum with 'women's work' in the kitchen. She just couldn't leave her mother to do everything while her dad and brothers sat in front of the TV without a care in the world.

Claire remembered this many years later when she was engaged to Harvey in Brisbane, Qld. During that period, she would cook an evening meal and then wash the dishes, while he believed he had earned the right as a man to sit in comfort, drink his can of beer and watch TV. Sure enough, that was Harvey. Cooking and washing the dishes afterward were in his estimation, 'woman's work'. Her fiancé was just like Claire's dad had been – jobs for women and jobs for men. She wondered how many men were in fact like this.

14

The Ballet Shoes

Claire loved going out, especially to visit her grandparents, aunts and uncles, and cousins, so much so that she seemed to spend a whole weekend at either of her grandparents' homes. In particular, she thought perhaps she liked nanna Levine's best as it was more countrified, especially with the open field and the tethered Billy-goat at the back of their bungalow. Nanna and Granddad Mariner lived in a house among rows and rows of other terraced houses and it often seemed quite claustrophobic in such surroundings. In contrast to this, at nanna and granddad Levine's, they had a large garden full of vegetables, and she loved helping gather potatoes, cabbages, rhubarb, carrots and even lettuce and radishes. The front garden with its concrete birdbath in the middle of some crazy paving, always somehow seemed gray as the sun rarely shone on that side, languishing in the shadow of the house.

When she was really little, Claire had found more interest in the footpath outside the garden gate. It was there that she often spent ages cutting out the bright green moss from between the concrete paving slabs with a sharp stick. She would rearrange the moss to make it look like a miniature lawn; as though it belonged to 'the little people' she had heard the Irish children at St Brigid's talk about. Maybe there were such tiny people and maybe they would like a little garden to play in, with a green swathe of moss? After a while she would hear her nanna calling her and her imagination evaporated like mist.

Claire also loved to visit Aunty Elaine and Uncle Norbert's house in Sandhill Crescent, Alwoodley. With her cousin George they would walk in the field at the back of their house, pretending the two of them were on a long trek to some dangerous and mysterious tribal land. In the back garden of the Stevens' house there was a small pond which always had a fascination for Claire. George and she often went for a walk to a nearby larger pond to collect frog spawn to put in George's garden pond. Both of them were in wonderment when the tiny tadpoles began to hatch. Those were happy times as the children chatted far into the night fighting sleep.

Milton's elder brother Clive and his wife Katherine lived in Harrogate in a first floor flat at the bottom of Cold Bath Road, around the corner from the Stray. The latter comprised huge swathes of mown grass stretching from the Wetherton Road to the Aireborough Road. Claire used to love visiting her cousins Kirsty and Sarah as she could relate to them as girls, better than to her brothers Danny and Gerry. When the parents went out for a drink to a local public house in the evening, Kirsty, Sarah, Danny, Gerry and Claire would while away the time playing 'Mummies and Daddies', looking through Kate's stamp collection or playing 'Snap'. A number of years later Kirsty gave Claire her album of used postage stamps, and absorbing the collection into her own, it used to give Claire endless pleasure throughout childhood and into adulthood. It brought back so many memories for her but when she was forced to sell it in Melbourne, Victoria, many years later it almost broke her heart due to all the memories the stamps had evoked.

One Saturday lunchtime, after Milton had been to his precious 'works' he drove Olivia and the children up to Harrogate where they were to watch Kirsty and members of her ballet school perform in the Royal Hall. Of course, as Milton thought ballet was for 'poofters' he didn't want his brother Clive to think he was less than a man if he attended with his family, so he and Clive took Danny and Gerry for a walk around the stray to watch a rugby match being played by one of the local amateur teams. The boys had been persuaded not to attend the ballet performance after constantly experiencing their dad's attitude and ridicule of anything feminine. Claire of course, was by this stage beyond ridicule and felt so privileged to watch her dear cousin dance in their annual performance.

One scene, Claire remembered distinctly, opened with some of the older girls wearing pretty tutus, standing and actually balancing, on very large rubber balls. The girls performed 'dances' on the stage while precariously teetering on these rather awkward inflatable spheres and Claire's heart was in her mouth hoping they did not make mistakes or fall off. But the inevitable did happen, when one of the girls missed her place in the line and, rocking backward and forward rolled all over the stage teetering on her ball. Everyone in the audience was shocked for a second or two, as Claire was too. Then everyone realized that it was all part of the act, to add a little excitement to the show, and laughter soon replaced the initial surprise. In Claire's case, her heart quietly slid from her mouth back into its normal place as she breathed a sigh of relief and started to laugh with the rest of the audience. Her problem was that as she loved ballet, and would have loved to become a ballerina, she imagined herself on the stage with the other girls and even blushed in her dreams that night as her mind re-lived the experience.

Another evening when the Wilson's had been at Uncle Clive and Aunty Katherine's flat, Kirsty showed Claire her new *Bloch's* ballet shoes which her parents had bought her and she was eager to try them on. But Kirsty explained that the shoes had been selected specifically to fit her feet and it was not appropriate for Claire to try them on. However, seeing her cousin's eagerness slip into disappointment so rapidly, Kirsty offered to give her a pair of her old ballet shoes. Claire could hardly believe her good fortune and was in heaven over this, having her very own ballet shoes was like a dream come true. That evening before getting into bed, after trying on the shoes, she practiced a few steps before carefully pinning the somewhat scuffed and faded pink ballet shoes from their ribbons, on the wall near her dressing table.

A few days later Olivia walked into Claire's bedroom, as usual unannounced, and as soon as she saw the ballet shoes hanging there she pointed a waving finger at them: "Where did you get those from?"

"Kirsty gave them to me."

"Why did she do that?"

"Because she knows I love ballet."

"You'd better take them down before your daddy sees them."

"Why should I? That's not fair, it's my room."

"Well, just don't let Daddy see them, or hear you talk about ballet or anything about dancing as he is likely to murder you." With that Olivia stormed out of 'her son's' bedroom. Claire stood there dumbfounded. What was wrong with her dad? It wasn't so much that he had funny ideas, but he always seemed to be taking his anger out on her, and not on her brothers.

It was not until later, that Claire learned of her dad's hatred of ballet as 'poofy'. All male ballet dancers he regarded as not real men but 'poofter-boys'. Sometimes he called them 'poncey-boys'. This explained why, when ballet came on television, he would get out of his chair and change the channel. "We're not having that poncey stuff on" he would say.

"Why?" came back Claire's answer.

"Because I say so and that's why. I decide what we will watch, not you or anyone else in this family."

She had learned not to argue with her dad as any backchat she gave him seemed to be written in black indelible ink in his mind. Her opinions were of no consequence. She was 'a nobody', and 'absolutely useless'. Danny and Gerry often reminded her of this as the children were growing up. The constant reminder that she was 'useless' began to hurt her pride. No matter how good she was at anything, she was always 'useless' to her father and brothers.

15

The 11+ Exam

Early in 1951, a selected number of children, the 'Clever-clogs', in Mr Lynch's class at St Brigid's, and this included Claire, were advised that they were due to sit for what was known in the UK at the time as the *Eleven-Plus Exam*. This was a test devised and implemented in 1944 under a Conservative 'government education initiative' known as the *Butler Education Act* to weed out the children who were more deserving, to attend a selected number of high schools and colleges. Claire, one of the top achievers in her class, but listed as 'William Wilson' on the class register, was among the chosen ones to take the exam. What she, and the other children at St Brigid's were not told, was that places at Roman Catholic colleges and high schools were very limited as the Church had not anticipated the huge growth in the Catholic population due to immigration. For Roman Catholic children in Aireborough there were two colleges for girls, Mount St Maria's College and Our Lady's College, and St Edwin's for the boys, the latter run by the Jesuits.

The small group of boys with which Claire had been grouped had to travel to St Edwin's College one Saturday morning and, sitting at rows of desks in a huge classroom with a high ceiling, they had to complete the dreaded examination paper. This was supervised by a priest wearing a black gown, who sat at a desk raised above the main floor on a dais reading a book. Claire didn't personally think the paper was all that difficult to complete and sat back in anticipation of a good mark. It was true that there were some awkward questions in the paper, but over-all she felt that she had given of her best The following week the same group of boys were again loaded into a bus to be taken to Overton High School where they had to sit for another examination. As Claire was unfortunately listed as a boy, she was obliged to follow protocol and attend. Again she thought the exam paper reasonable and did her best as usual. She did not discover, and had not been informed at the time, that the session held at Overton High School was the 'official' 11+ exam, which they had to complete according to government regulations. The exam paper they had previously completed at St Edwin's was not the 'official' exam, but simply an entrance exam to that particular religious institution. As the children from St Brigid's were Roman Catholic, the Church insisted that children selected to take the *Eleven-Plus Exam* also had to take one of their own exams in addition to the one at the 'Protestant' school. In the scholarship class of Mr Lynch at St Brigid's, Claire had always been in the top stream of those in the class. In later years Claire looked back on two rather curly-edged copies of two of her term results, and on the first of these she had been placed 5th in class and the following term the next report showed that she had been placed 6th in class. Aware of this information at the time, Claire reckoned that, even though she was always nervous when taking exams, as a pupil she could not have been too bad. She reckoned that if her class was allocated two places at each of Mount St Maria's and Our Lady's, and four at St Edwin's, making a total of eight available places, then coming fifth and then sixth, would certainly secure her a place at one of the Catholic colleges.

The exams they had taken were to decide whether or not the selected pupils from St Brigid's Roman Catholic Primary School were mentally and educationally suitable to attend one of the high schools, according to the government regulations. As mentioned earlier, Roman Catholic children had to take two exams, an official one in the State system and an additional one in the Catholic Church's educational program. Claire was later to be told by her father, that she had easily passed the 11+ exam which she sat at Overton High School with an 85% percentage mark, but because she attended a Roman Catholic primary school, her Church would not allow her to attend a Protestant high school – she was only allowed to attend a Catholic school. In the examination she had taken at St Edwin's College, her dad told her later that her mark had been 78%. He had been advised of this when he complained to the principal of the College that 'William' had not been offered a place there. In reply, the principal told him that as they had very few places on offer, even though 'his son' had achieved a very good pass mark, he literally did not have enough desk spaces to house one extra deserving pupil, no matter whether Milton offered money to ease the application through the process or not. Milton had, of course, offered money to the principal but it was to no avail. Apparently there were four others from St Brigid's with marks slightly higher than Claire's; Michael Sanderson, Alec O'Shaunessy, Ian Macbain and Sean Leach, and they were the ones who had been selected to attend St Eddie's. But where did this leave Claire? In her mind she was a girl and should have been offered a place at either Mount St Maria's or Our Lady's College. As a result she envied the girls who were selected to attend the two Roman Catholic girls' high schools, which took two girls each from St Brigid's. Claire's marks in the 'official' 11+ exam had been higher than the marks that two of the other girls had achieved, so had she been registered as a girl, she would have easily been offered a place at either of the two Catholic girl's colleges. Our Lady' College was where her mum had attended a number of years earlier. In Claire's mind she had seen herself attending Mount St Maria's for no other reason than she liked their uniform. Their hats were dark blue with a ribbon of dark blue with stripes of white. But her dreams were shattered and no longer a reality. She had to square up to this with extreme pain, and even years later she recollected the fateful morning when the head sister announced the results.

That morning Sister Bernard had entered Mr Lynch's class to announce the results of those who had passed the 11+ Exam to go to St Edwin's, Mount St Maria's or Our Lady's College, Claire felt decidedly sick in her stomach. Not hearing her name in the list, she was convinced that there was some mistake and asked Mr Lynch if she could go see Sister Bernard in her office. The head sister was a rather large, tall yet somewhat rotund woman, and perhaps unfairly described as 'fat' by many of the parishioners at St Brigid's. She was an institution in her own right as she wielded a thick black cane with a silver top. According to many of the older boys, she was not averse to using it on them for even the slightest misdemeanor. Claire gingerly knocked on sister's door. "Come," was the usual reply. 'William' peeped around the door. "Come in child, don't stand there dithering. What do you want?"

Claire blurted out very nervously that her name was not mentioned when Sister had a few minutes earlier visited Mr Lynch's class. Claire asked her if there had been a mistake and her name left off the list for some reason. "Child, I don't make mistakes," was her curt reply. "What is your name?" She looked at the list again, which was right in front of her. "If your name is not on this list then you will be staying here at St Brigid's for the duration of your education. That is one of the facts of life child, so you had better get used to it. You will not be going to high school and will receive your continued education here in Mr Ward's class."

"But Sister…" Claire attempted to ask a question.

"You may go back to your classroom now boy." Sister Bernard had no warmth or sympathy for this bright pupil, who it seemed with hindsight, was a victim of the inadequacy of the Roman Catholic school system. Claire felt that of the eight places allotted to pupils of St Brigid's to attend high school, she should have been among them. She went hot and cold right at that moment and thought she was going to throw up in front of their head sister. Her heart was by this time dragging on the floor, held by a slim thread from one of her feet. Claire was dismissed with a wave of Sister Bernard's hand, "Go."

Back in Mr Lynch's classroom Claire sat down in her chair, but after a brief interlude of trepidation she started shaking with fear and, having wet her panties, begged Mr Lynch to let her go home early, which he did, seeing how badly the results had affected this bright pupil. Not wanting to belabor the point too finely, Claire reckoned that she should have been allowed to attend one of the high schools, but the Roman Catholic Church put its huge prejudicial foot down and forbade her. To Claire at this young age, it was total discrimination. She knew she had passed the exam to attend Overton High School so why couldn't she go? But there again, Sister Bernard had stressed to them that Roman Catholic children went to Catholic schools and Protestant children went to Protestant schools, and the situation was that all State and Protestant schools in general were classed as 'non-Catholic' by the Church. Sister Bernard had sternly reminded her as a pupil of St Brigid's that she was a Catholic, and therefore she could not attend any other school other than one run by the Church. Claire could not for the life of her, understand why there were 'Catholic' schools and 'non-Catholic' schools. If the rest were 'Protestant' schools, why wasn't St Brigid's school classed as a 'non-Protestant' school? In her developing child's brain her Church was obviously superior so she had to toe the line, so to speak. End of story! Or was it?

As Claire nervously cried the bad news to her mum and dad at lunch time, they were surprisingly very sympathetic as they knew 'William' to be a bright child. They told Claire not to worry as she was not going to spend the next four years rotting away at St Brigid's to end up working in a factory or a shop. Her dad said he would look into the matter and rang the headmaster of St Edwin's College to be given the news that was outlined previously. As a result, Milton entered 'William's' name to take the entrance exam at a private high school called Clark's College. This school, while previously having concentrated on commercial subjects and her mum and even Aunt Diane had apparently attended classes in the commercial section some years earlier, had branched out into general education and was now taking non-commercial pupils. To make sure that 'William' was well up to their standard, Milton had arranged for 'his son' to attend tuition prior to the exam, with a private teacher called Mrs Dillon, who lived in Gledhow. Claire had to attend sessions with Mrs Dillon two evenings a week. To find the Dillon's house she had to catch a bus to Overton High School and then walk down a couple of streets. This was the first time Claire discovered that everyone's house had a different odor. Certainly she could not mistake Mrs Dillon's house with her husband's stale pipe tobacco smell. Yuk!

Accordingly, the time to sit the entrance exam for Clark's College came around and as usual Claire did her very best, certainly no worse or better than the exams she had taken previously at the other two schools. The results of the exam came out fairly quickly and were sent to the head sister at St Brigid's. It was one late school morning, during the children's "religious instruction" class, that Sister Bernard entered Mr Lynch's classroom and read from a list those children who had passed the entrance examinations to a number of Protestant high schools. Barbara Halloran had passed for Thorsby High School, Malcolm Toohey for Aireborough Central High School and two for Clark's College. Claire's name was mentioned as William Wilson, and also to attend was Michael Dawson. Sister Bernard stressed to the children that while they were to attend non-Catholic schools, irrespective of the fact that they may have a few Catholic children on their register, the children whose names had just been announced were in grave danger of losing their 'Holy Faith'. It was therefore essential that they continued to attend mass every Sunday and to partake of the sacraments regularly. They also had to attend special classes run by the parish clergy for all children who attended non-Catholic schools. They had been warned.

Claire's mind, however, had stopped listening to this propaganda, as she could hardly wait to run home at lunch time to tell her parents that she was to go to Clark's College. The following day Olivia and Milton received a letter from Mr Frank Ward, the principal of Clark's College, giving them the result of the examination 'their son' had taken, in which 'he' had achieved a mark of 92%, enclosing lists of the uniform and items needed for the first term. Olivia handed Claire the list of requirements and she was in her second heaven.

On the sheets of paper with great excitement Claire read down the items they had to wear: a long-sleeved white blouse; a school tie (green with yellow and white stripes); a bottle green gym slip; white ankle socks; black or brown shoes; and even bottle-green knickers. That was the winter uniform for the lower girls. The summer uniform allowed for three dresses each in a white or cream material with small flowers printed on them. The material from which the dresses could be made, plus the patterns, could be obtained from the official school uniform suppliers. Rawliffe's in Boar Lane also sold completed garments for those mothers who could not sew. Claire was not aware of the list of items on the boy's uniform list on the other side of the sheet.

Olivia must have been watching 'William' excitedly reading the requirements for girls and leaned down to whisper in Claire's ear, "no love, that's the wrong side of the paper. Can't you see it says 'girl's uniform' at the top?" Claire, with tears welling in her pleading eyes, stared at her mum. Consternation was written all over her young face. Olivia for once had concern for the child that should have been her precious daughter. But her husband had intervened and the baby was subsequently registered as a boy. Olivia remembered one of the specialists at the Infirmary making the comment that according to the limited research available, often babies with the Intersex condition tended to be girls. Milton had refused to entertain a girl in his family as that would have made him less than a full man. That was Milton's prejudice and she had to live with losing the daughter she so desperately had wanted.

Olivia brought her mind to the present and Claire had a rude awakening when her mother took the sheet of paper from her and turned it over. "That is the list for the boys" pointing to the obverse of the sheet Claire had been reading from. She reminding Claire by her somewhat fateful facial expression that she would have to wear the boy's uniform: white or gray shirt; gray trousers; the school tie; and a bottle green or gray pullover, with or without green and yellow edging to the 'V' neck.

By this time Claire's mind had turned off as she thought the boy's uniform so boring. In addition to what her mother had read out, she had to be provided with either a plain green blazer, on the front pocket of which was emblazoned the school badge; or a striped blazer in the school colors, green with vertical stripes of yellow and white. This was not good news for Claire as she wasn't looking forward to wearing a boys' uniform, even though she had been forced to wear a boy's white shirt and gray short pants at St Brigid's. Claire knew that she was a girl and was devastated that she had to conform to society's rules that if she was registered as a boy at birth, then she had to act like, and become a boy. She had no choice in the matter. Those were the expectations of society, not hers.

16

Glass in her Face

When Claire began attending Clark's College in September 1951, she was placed in the upper stream of children of her age, and she threw herself wholeheartedly into her studies. She had been specifically reminded by the priests and nuns at St Brigid's, that the high school she was to attend was a non-Catholic school, a 'Protestant' one, not approved for the education and spiritual welfare of Catholic children. All she knew was that it was different. Claire was to remark to some of her friends at Mass the following Sunday morning that the other children didn't look any different from Catholics, but according to Sister Bernard they were very different, because Protestants would not go to Heaven, whereas Catholics would. It was announced from the pulpit in the notices at the end of Mass that those children who were now attending non-Catholic schools should attend the special religious classes to be held that afternoon from 3 pm to 4.30 pm in Miss Latimer's classroom in St Brigid's school next door to the new church.

Consequently, Claire duly attended the class only to find two other girls there and no boys. She knew that Michael Dawson's parents didn't attend Mass, and even her's didn't, so she was not surprised that Michael's presence was missing. The priest, Fr Corcoran reminded them of their duty to God to attend Mass every Sunday without fail, and to go to confession on the Saturday before. He went through the program they would be following based on the Catholic Catechism, and reminded them that they were mixing with children who were not of their Holy Catholic Faith and to be on guard as the Devil would try to lead them into sin. He reminded the class that if they had any problems regarding their understanding of anything they were learning; to speak to him or one of the other priests. With hindsight, this was the start of their extended indoctrination by the Church of Rome into its belief system. The Catholic Catechism was the standard guide to all matters of faith and morals and this was what they would be using in the first part of the course. Claire remembered the slim but tiny red booklet from Mrs Donatello's class at St Brigid's Primary School, but this larger version had a blue cover compared to the previous version. She would never forget the first question – "Who made you?" The answer in the little red book had been 'God made me', whereas she already knew that her mummy had made her. God was an old man who sat on a golden throne on a cloud in the sky and he made everything: the grass, the cows and sheep, the hens and ducks and the sun, the earth and stars in the night sky too. He was a marvelous God, but he must have been tired of making everything to be sitting on a throne in the sky all the time. Claire had also been confused when she heard the nuns and the priests talking of Jesus as God. Jesus had been born a baby, so how could he also be God? And how could a man give birth to a baby? Only women gave birth to babies didn't they? Something just didn't seem to add up.

The priests told them that Catholics would go to Heaven, where God lived with his son Jesus Christ and a Holy Ghost which strangely was often shown as a white dove in pictures. It was in her late teens that she began to wonder again how an old white-haired man could give birth. But maybe Our Lady had some involvement? Claire didn't really understand as it was all too complicated. She approached Fr Corcoran and asked why Protestants didn't go to Heaven, because she was already making friends with some of them at high school, and she liked them. He told her they would only go to Heaven if they became Catholics, because if they were taught about our Holy Roman Catholic Faith and ignored it, then they would go to Hell for turning away from the One True Faith when it was staring them in the face. As a result of this Claire saw her fellow classmates as different to her. As a Catholic, she was special and the way the Church taught its followers, they were often led to distrust their Protestant neighbors and friends. It was all so simple, Catholics would go straight to Heaven to be with the Jesus God when they died, but the Protestants would go to Hell. So why didn't God make everyone into Catholics so that they could all go to Heaven? This was all very confusing to an eleven-year-old.

Well into her retirement many years later, Claire was confronted by a similar situation, except this time taught by another religion. While visiting Yorkshire from Australia, she had been having her nails done at a salon in Aireborough when the technician told her that according to the tiny son of one of her Muslim customers, she would be going to Hell. The boy had asked her if she was Jewish, and when she told him that she wasn't, he asked if she believed in Allah. She shook her head and the little rascal told her to her face that she would go to Hell when she died as only those who believe in Allah, through his prophet Mohammed would go to Heaven. All non-Muslims were infidels and would go to Hell. *Out of the mouth of babes* Claire thought. How similar that little boy's beliefs were to what she had been taught at his age.

At the end of the first term at Clark's College Claire was placed 6th in class in the exams. This was par for the course to her parents, following her last term results at St Brigid's. Her dad reminded her however that he expected lots of improvement. He stressed that he was not paying for her to attend a private high school for the good of his health. He wanted to see better results. Especially he wanted her to take an interest in rugby and cricket, as these sports made real men out of boys. This was not fair as in Claire's mind those were rough sports for the boys. Girls could not be expected to excel at those sports, but then she had to try to put her real gender to the back of her mind to please her father. This was going to be very hard, very hard indeed. How could she get rid of the thoughts in her mind that she was a girl, until at least something happened to make her into a normal girl, if that was possible?

One of the biggest problems for her was when her class met early Thursday mornings for their weekly swimming lesson at Cookridge Street Swimming Baths. After their names had been checked on the class register while they stood in line outside the lower doors to the large swimming bath, they were ushered through the lower street doors directly into the swimming hall. Boys changing cubicles were to the left and girls to the right. Claire blushed bright pink wondering how was she going to survive this ordeal. She was actually petrified of water as her brother Danny had pushed her into the water at Scarborough's South Bay pool a few years earlier. Had it not been for Milton seeing bubbles spewing from her mouth under the water, she would not be alive to tell the story. Thankfully, her dad had been trained in resuscitation in the St John's Ambulance Association during World War II, so after dragging her onto the pool side he administered the technique he had learned. Otherwise, thanks to her brother Danny, she may have been drowned. This was yet another of Danny's mean pranks, he constantly played on people, especially Claire. What that particular prank did to her was to make her petrified of water, hence her fear of going swimming.

With her heart in her mouth, through a crack in the door of a toilet cubicle, Claire would watch the boys use the urinal stalls, followed by a quick rinse under the shower prior to leaving the sanctity of the ablution block for the main pool. Claire decided to stay in the toilet while the others swam and only when she heard the other children climbing out of the pool she went to the shower and doused her bathing costume with water as though she had been swimming. Then she would walk out of the toilets and nonchalantly go back to her changing cubicle to change back into the boy's uniform she hated so much. This procedure she carried out for a couple of weeks until her sports mistress Miss Coatridge called her over to whisper that she was on to her. She realized that Claire had a problem and wanted to help. Looking straight into her pupil's teary eyes she asked: "What's the problem William?"

"I'm scared of water."

"Why is that?"

"Because my brother Danny pushed me into a swimming pool a few years ago and I would have drowned had dad not rescued me."

"I see. That was a terrible thing to do. But would you like to be able to swim if you could get over your fear of water?"

"Oh yes, I would Miss, as it would show my father that I was as good as all the others. He keeps telling me that I am useless, and my brothers make fun of me because of this."

"Well, then love, next week you and I will start you off learning to swim. There will be no problems and you will be quite safe. Would you like that?"

Claire nodded her assent, yet with much apprehension.

The following week she was guided by Miss Coatridge and her assistant Miss Brown in between their duties to the rest of the class. They were so kind and understanding of Claire's situation. Her first lesson was to hold on to the side of the pool and learn how to kick her legs for the breast stroke. Then she had to hold onto a long pole while Miss Brown let her kick her way from the middle of the pool to the side. Miss Brown promised that she would not let her sink under the water, and she was true to her word. Claire's confidence in her instructors was building up. The next week she was taught the arm movements and was held up with a rope while she tried to swim from the middle of the pool to the edge. All this was successful, but then she had to swim on her own, unaided. This was the hard part as she was so scared of swallowing water, which to her was akin to drowning. So Claire worked out that if she held her breath while swimming, she would not swallow water, and after a few attempts this worked. Slowly, holding her breath she gained the confidence she needed to see that she could keep her head above the water and was able to breathe through her nose at least. By using this technique, Claire was able to swim across the width of the pool. Watching her, Miss Coatridge suggested Miss Brown teach their pupil how to breathe through her mouth too while swimming. This was difficult but she survived the training sessions.

Having swum the width of the pool Claire now attempted to swim the length and found it much easier than she had previously imagined. Doing this for the exam at the end of the first term, she was awarded a quarter-mile certificate for her efforts.

Surely her dad would be proud of her now? But there was still one problem – fear! Anything she could do to avoid getting into the water was still an ordeal and one day she told Miss Coatridge that a few strands of hair were always dropping over her eyes as she swam. She looked 'William' in the face, and taking a bobby pin from her own hair, in a kindly way pinned up the stray strands of 'his' hair. The boys laughed at her and called her names; "Girly, girly," they muttered softly until Miss Coatridge said: "That's enough of that."

But here was ridicule rearing its ugly head once again, and her fear of it returned. Nevertheless, she persevered and began to swim more and more each week in their swimming sessions.

Claire's determination to fight the fear she had grown up with, plus the ridicule of her fellow pupils, helped her swim lengths of the pool equivalent to half a mile. With much perseverance at the end of the school year, corresponding to her being second in class, she received her mile certificate. This was a major achievement for her considering that when she started school she was dreadfully frightened of water. In contrast to that, her brother Danny who attended St Edwin's College could not swim one stroke when he left school, and never learned to swim ever in his whole life. Yet, he was the main one of her two brothers who laughed at her. He was indeed a bully.

Danny had become a pain in her life ever since he pushed a grandmother clock onto her, cutting her face to shreds. Claire could not recall when it happened but he had sneaked into her bedroom one day while she was working at something on her dressing table. He snuck up to the foot of her bed, climbed the end frame, and put his hand behind the grandmother clock which Milton had placed there, supposedly for safe keeping. Claire had a feeling that her dad didn't like its chime or maybe it was broken. Nevertheless, it stood against the wall by the window at the foot of her bed. The next thing she knew was that she could see nothing but red and her face hurt in a million places. Claire screamed for her mum and before she knew it, there she was picking her up and carrying her downstairs. She placed a towel over her head to try to stem the blood oozing from many places where pieces of glass protruded through the skin, and hurriedly walked along Arkroyd Road to Dr Kelly's surgery. Danny claimed of course that he had done nothing to cause the clock face to shatter over Claire's face. Oh no, butter wouldn't melt in his mouth. He would say that wouldn't he? Anything to avert the blame to someone or something else.

Carefully, the doctor removed the glass chards and splinters from Claire's face and prescribed a sedative powder for her. Her anxious mother was to put her to bed immediately she arrived back home. Olivia was in a state of shock over the incident, and Marge from next door, who had been looking after Danny and Gerry while Olivia had taken 'William' to the doctor's surgery, came in with the boys. "Will he be alright Olivia?"

"Dr Kelly says he will, but he has told me to put him to bed after taking this sedative." She showed Mrs Rooney the wrapped powder. "He says to keep Danny away from William until the trauma has passed."

But the 'trauma' was never to go away as Claire had to live the rest of her life with scars on her face as a constant reminder. She would always remember Danny for his mischief and his nasty remarks. Even in her retirement, sitting in front of the mirror at the make-up bench in her bedroom, she often stroked the scars still noticeable on her cheek, under her nose and above her left eye. She cursed Danny. What a horrid little boy he had been, and in later life she was to discover to her chagrin that he hadn't changed over the years. Danny was still a bully.

17

Camping

In 1951 some boys from St Brigid's church tried to persuade Claire to join the parish scout troop. She was more interested in joining the Girl Guide Company that was attached to the Methodist Church in Arkroyd Road, but knew that that desire was impossible. In the first place she was a Catholic and it was forbidden to join anything Protestant, and in the second place she was supposed to be a boy and she would not be allowed to step out of the gender roll she was forced onto her at birth. But, if her father would allow her to join St Brigid's Scouts, it would be a way of getting out of the house and away from the constant ridicule and criticism she had to face day after day.

She was being encouraged to join the scouts by Billy Corcoran who lived down the street in Hawkhill Avenue. Her dad however, was against 'his son' joining anything outside the home where he couldn't keep an eye on 'him'. Milton seemed to regard 'William' as having a frail constitution and unsuitable for anything strenuous like the scouts. But Milton must have given it more thought, possibly remembering the words of the specialists at her birth, that boys should be reared as boys, and girls as girls. Baden Powell, the founder of the Scout movement, had been a soldier and he had established his movement to give boys the training they needed as young men of the future. Previous to learning this, Claire's dad had considered the scouts as 'namby-pamby' boys, but on reflection if 'William' was to mix with them, it might make 'him' more 'boyish' than what appeared to be evident. This thought had not occurred to Claire however, as all she saw in the Scouts was learning skills which she might need at some stage in the future. Also it appeared to Milton that he might be able to get some respite one evening a week from looking at his poofter son. It was not as though 'William' spent the evenings in his company, far from it. Claire did her school homework either on the dressing table in her bedroom or on a board laid over the chair arms in the sitting room. All this while listening to classical music on the radiogram, and then spending the rest of her time drawing and painting.

Subsequently, permission was given for Claire to join St Brigid's Scouts and she was picked to join Swift patrol under Peter Stead as patrol leader. She supposes she could have been regarded as a model scout in many ways, as she obeyed instructions and was willing to learn. Consequently, she quickly earned the tenderfoot badge, the Second Class Badge and interest badges such as designer, cook and first aid. In addition to the normal badges of the Boy Scout Association, the Roman Catholic Church had created a badge called 'the Kiro Badge' which was gained through knowledge of Church matters. This was to be worn on the left breast pocket and was in different colors to show the grade achieved. Claire remembered that one of the tests was to make a model of an altar.

Although Milton had allowed her to join the scouts under sufferance, she was not allowed to go camping. That was completely out of the question. She never thought at the time but later wondered if her dad didn't want her gender dysphoria being discovered and bring shame on him. Another of the restrictions her dad put on her scout activity was that she should not go hiking on her own. This was the reason she never gained the First Class Badge as that entailed planning a hike and carrying it out. Ultimately, Milton relinquished his previous feelings and condescendingly allowed Claire to attend one summer camp near Scarborough, only because her parents and brothers were themselves on holiday in the town itself during the same period.

Father Moxon was the designated scoutmaster, although he didn't wear a scout uniform, and he had taken them to Scorby Farm in a truck, called a 'lorry' in England. Another leader had driven the truck while Father Moxon followed in his car. In those days, it was quite an accepted thing for scouts and guides to be seen sitting in the backs of trucks going to camp. Today this would be regarded as highly dangerous.

Soon after the troop's arrival at the farm on the Yorkshire coast, the scouts quickly erected their bell-shaped tents, borrowed from the Methodist Guides, at the far end of a large field. The farmer had agreed to provide the scouts with bread, milk and potatoes at cost.

On the second day Claire's patrol fenced off the kitchen area and made a table out of some rough wooden planks which had been available, having learned how to lash poles together with various types of knots and lashings. By this time, Claire had taken over from Peter Stead as Swift patrol leader, even though she had not gained the First Class badge. Claire was regarded as the best cook among them because she had gained the cooks proficiency badge, and she busied herself into setting up the week's menu. On the second afternoon, as the rain had stopped, some of the boys decided to walk into the nearest village and invited Claire to join them. In the quaint village shop they purchased a large can of pineapple rings and some cream biscuits, the variety which have two biscuits stuck together, supposedly with a layer of sweet sickly cream.

That night, in the Swift's patrol tent, the occupants passed the time away by telling ghost stories until close to midnight. The skies outside were full of rain and slowly they discovered to their chagrin that their ex-army bell tent leaked, with water running down the seams. Nevertheless, they all dined on slices of pineapple and cream biscuits to their hearts content, more perhaps to their stomach's content. After the lamp was extinguished they all laid in their 'beds' to sleep, breathing in the acrid fumes from the kerosene. Claire lay inside her sheet and blanket which was wrapped up in the form of a sleeping bag. But her 'pallias', a mattress stuffed with straw from the farm, was unfortunately positioned under one of the tent seams as there was no other place available. Consequently, all night long she heard 'drip, drip, drip' as the rainwater ran down the seam above her, landing somewhere she knew not. The answer to that conundrum would be solved the next morning.

The scouts had to attend Mass every day in camp as Fr Moxon had to say Mass as part of his priestly obligations. He had set up his tent with a fly-sheet over the doorway and this acted as a cover over the folding table he used as a temporary altar. The scouts sat or squatted outside to watch the priest celebrate Mass under cover from the overcast sky.

Claire was not feeling very well and begged to be let out of attending Mass, much to Fr Moxon's annoyance. She told him of her stomach pains and in not feeling very well. All she wanted to do was sleep. At the end of Mass, Fr Moxon walked across to her tent to see her, and observing her soggy bed on the ground sheet, decided to move her to his own camp bed, which was raised off the ground on a folding wooden frame. Claire slept fitfully during the morning and over lunchtime, and in the middle of the afternoon she actually felt worse. It was pretty obvious to the priest that Claire had caught a heavy cold. Later in the afternoon she asked Father Moxon it he could please phone her father in nearby Scarborough, and ask him to drive out to collect her in his car? The priest could see the sense in this request and walked across the paddock to the farmhouse, asking if he may use their phone for an emergency.

Mrs Silverwing, the landlady of the boarding house, where the Wilsons stayed in Scarborough, took the call in her hallway and when Claire's parents arrived back from their chalet overlooking the south bay pool, she gave them the alarming news. Apparently Milton's first comment to Olivia was, "I told you so. I didn't think he would like camping. This just proves my point. He is turning out to be just another namby-pamby." Olivia was not so sure that this was the reason.

Milton drove to the farm at tea time, as the assistant cook was making some corned beef hash for the evening meal. By this time Claire was wrapped up in as many sweaters and shirts as she could find to keep warm, and was led off to her father's car, parked near the farm gate. As he drove into Scarborough Milton commented: "So you don't like camping eh? I didn't think you would."

Claire was quiet for a few seconds and then replied, "No, it isn't that I don't like camping, I've caught a cold from having water drip onto me all night, that's all."

"Oh, yes?" he quizzed, looking very skeptical, letting a self-righteous smirk spread across his face. "When you joined the scouts, I didn't think you would be strong enough to go camping."

"That has nothing to do with it. I've simply caught a cold."

"Well, we'll have to put you to bed back at Mrs Silverwing's won't we, and see how you are in the morning, If you improve I'll take you back to camp if you want."

Claire made no comment, so back at the boarding house she was bundled into the large bed that her brothers slept in, and she slept right through until the next morning, much to the annoyance of Danny and Gerry who had to sleep at the other end of the bed, with their feet at each side of Claire's pillow. Gerald was especially annoyed as once again 'William' appeared to have put one over him. He saw himself as the favorite in the family, believing that he should be given first in everything, especially all the attention. Claire's father still saw her as his 'namby-pamby' son, and that she was obviously not suited to the outdoor life with her tender 'girly' constitution. Her cold came on with a vengeance and she didn't start to recover until it was time to drive back to Aireborough on the Saturday morning.

It was during the time in bed that, between sleeping, Claire began to seriously look at her relationship with her dad. She was literally scared to death of him, not only due to his attitude toward her since she was younger but also because of his hot temper which often led to violence. She had noticed that quite often he took it out on her mum by shouting at her, and calling her names which Claire did not consider very nice. She knew that he had been arrested once for failing to pay a traffic fine and she knew that he had been in a fight on more than one occasion, as one time he had been admitted to Aireborough Infirmary after receiving some injury from his opponent and then crashing his motor bike, which was his leisure vehicle aside from his Morris Twelve.

But Claire began to worry about her dad's attitude to other people, often denigrating them for some reason or other. If today's laws on vilification existed when she was younger, she was certain her father would have ended up in court. He was to show his true colors against anyone non-English almost every day and that made Claire wonder about his bigotry. On one occasion she wanted to get his opinion on Jews as there was a high population of them in Aireborough. After listening to his very biased answer, she accused him of being anti-Semitic, although she could not remember using that specific term. In reply he said that he knew many 'Jew-boys' as Milton called them He did business with them, which instantly registered with Claire as her father's use of the term 'Jew-boys' was a name typically used by many of those who didn't like Jews. She already knew that he did not do business with any Jewish companies, as he once let slip in a conversation with Olivia that he wanted nothing to do with the Jews. Attending high school with many Jewish boys and girls, Claire got to know who was who in the Aireborough Jewish community, and her dad never mentioned anyone in business who had a Jewish name. A few years later she discovered a similar attitude of his to people of African ethnic origin. Her dad showed up his ignorance one day when he mentioned one man he had interviewed. His comment to Olivia during their evening meal was that the man was "the best of the bunch that turned up for an interview." Over the meal Milton laughed about the interview and exaggerated the man's accent as though he was from one of the southern states of the USA. He joked about the man and claimed that he called Milton 'honey-child'. Claire actually met the man a few years later and he had a typical Aireborough accent, not American. She began to realize that her dad liked to romanticize his experiences in order to poke fun at people. She didn't like this and wondered what her dad said about her behind her back. Not surprisingly, she was to discover various comments of her father over the years, many of them from the lips of her brothers.

18

The Crystal Set

During the first term of 1952, Claire worked extremely hard at high school and came top of her class, beating Betty Holbrook who came second. The facts were that Claire was good at Latin, and had come top of the class in that subject, and in addition she had been able to speak some French prior to attending Clark's College. Unfortunately, some of her 'French' often comprised swear words taught by her father, remembered from his days living in Bandol while working in Marseilles. Nevertheless, she came top in that subject too. She had always been placed top in Art and English, and had good grades in her other subjects, but sport was another matter. Her dad had suggested she take more of an interest in rugby as he and his brother Clive had played for Kippax Rugby Union Club in their earlier days. In truth, Claire hated all boys' sports as they were far too rough. The only slight exception was gymnastics, in which she excelled to some extent, culminating in her being chosen as a member of the upper school gymnastics team for the final two years of her secondary education.

Because she had been placed top in class and had achieved good marks in just about most subjects, at the end of term her parents had decided to attend the school open day and were presented with a glowing report of 'their son's' work from her class teacher Miss Penelope Hudson, whom the students were in the habit of calling 'Loppy' behind her back. This was the only time at Clark's College when Claire's parents ever visited the school. Her dad didn't appear to take a lot of interest in her education as she had no interest in the usual boy's subjects and she appeared to be turning out to be what Milton referred to as a book worm and not a popular sporty-type. She later wondered if her dad had been trying to mold her into himself as he was not good at school but had seemed to excel at sports, at one stage in his twenties being a coach to the local Baptist boys club in Casterley.

Claire's art however was becoming more adventurous, giving great attention and study to the works of artists in the Cubist school. Her dad did not know from whom in his family 'his son' had inherited 'his' writing talents, even though 'William's' artistic talent had emanated from himself, or so he thought. Staring at her art displayed on the walls of the school corridors, Milton considered her art weird, even 'potty', and her writing was unnatural. There was no basis for her talent in his family. But then Claire's dad spent most of his 'thinking' time and energy in his factory, which was always referred to as 'the works'. He didn't read books, never sketched or painted and wondered where 'William' had gained 'his' skills, if they were skills at all. To Milton, it could not have come from Olivia's family as they were all useless individuals in his opinion.

Claire had the secret feeling that she was certainly not turning out the way her dad had wanted. At their home in Sandy Peth, on the wall of the sitting room there was a framed ink sketch of Chichester Market Cross, which she thought was rather well executed in black ink. Her dad claimed he had drawn this when he was a draftsman and had even signed it in his memorable sloping hand. But as there was no other work of his in evidence and he no longer sketched anything, she wondered if he had really done the etching that he claimed was his. As a result, the visit to her high school by Milton and Olivia was to be the last the staff ever saw of Mr & Mrs Wilson. Claire's parents appeared to lose interest in her education until a number of years after she had left high school. On the other hand, when her younger brothers passed their 11+ exam to St Edwin's College, her dad appeared to switch interest to his 'real' sons. They were not as academically gifted as Claire appeared to be, but they struggled through nevertheless.

Most Saturday afternoons, Claire was forced to travel with the family to watch one or both of her brothers playing soccer.

To her it was thoroughly boring, watching a game in which she had not the slightest bit of interest. As a result, Claire would always take a book to read or a sketch pad, or some of her homework, sitting in the back seat of the car while her mum and dad were on the field sidelines cheering on Danny or Gerry.

On each Saturday morning Milton went to 'the works', leaving her free to earn some pocket money by shopping for her mum and a number of neighbors at their end of the street. The money earned was saved to hopefully one day buy a passage on a boat to America to join her grandparents, whom she missed very much. In this regard, Claire had drawn a map of the North Atlantic showing the British Isles in the east and North America in the west and a spaghetti-like *zig-zag* line all over the Atlantic, divided up into sections each denoting £1 saved for the fare. The bubble burst one day however when her mother walked into her room unannounced, and saw the chart. "What's this?" She asked very pointedly.

"I am saving up to go to America."

Rather than ask further questions of Claire and receive answers that were likely to be pretty obvious, bearing in mind she was fully aware how Milton had been treating 'William' for years, all she said was "Don't let your daddy see it." With that she walked out.

When Claire went back to school after the summer break in 1953, the students had to move up a class and she was mortified to find that she had been placed in the 'B' stream instead of the 'A' stream. She objected to this with venom in her heart as she had been right at the top of the 'A' stream in her first couple of years. She obtained permission of her new class teacher to visit the administration office, to hopefully see the principal. Claire stormed out of the classroom like an angry steamship. She explained to Mr Ward's secretary that she had always achieved great results in her previous two years, even to coming top and then second in the class, compared to another pupil who had also come to Clark's College from St Brigid's Roman Catholic Primary. The secretary asked who that was and Claire had to admit that she was thinking of Michael Dawson, the son of a bookmaker, a man who took bets at the racecourses. The secretary said she would look into the matter and get back to her. Later that morning the new teacher had a note handed to her, which in effect said "William Wilson had been wrongly placed in her class and that he had to move up to 3A". As it happened, Michael Dawson was moved down to 3B. Despite this, Michael still became a school captain for South House, but from this time until they left high school he hated Claire's guts. 'William' had been originally placed in East House, headed by Mr Moody, the geography master, but was never to be given any other duties other than that of class prefect. On one occasion she was to be deprived of a gymnastics badge because she turned up to one morning session with gym shoes that could have done with another coat of whitening. Olivia normally checked all the sports things of her children to see what needed washing. While the sports shoes of Danny and Gerry were black, those of Claire were white and Olivia oftentimes whitened her shoes for her. But our bright student could only blame herself for not having enough responsibility in the matter. In truth, she was beginning to lose interest in lots of things, especially her school work.

Psychologically, Claire was embroiled in an internal struggle with herself, not unlike many teenagers. Who was she? Obviously God wasn't interested in her any longer as he would have changed her to a proper girl before now. Every night in bed she constantly cried her heart out for some sort of Divine intervention, or for God to take her dysphoria, her enigma away.

By this age, masquerading as a boy, Claire was still being forced by her parents to wear gray short trousers and she felt silly as all the boys in her class, and even the lower class, all wore long pants. It wasn't so much that she wanted to dress like the boys in particular, but that she was fed up with ridicule, people laughing at her. Having had to endure this from her father and brothers for a number of years, often over the slightest little remark or event, her life had become a constant stream of jibes, if not about her gender imbalance then about the way she did or said things. But Claire didn't expect ridicule at high school. That may have been going too far. Nevertheless, it did happen, but along different lines to that smeared on her by her family.

One day, during the holidays, Claire was casually chatting to some youth whose name she could not quite recall, standing on the footpath outside the funeral director's house on the corner of Hawkhill Drive and Micklegate Road. She had been on her way home after doing some shopping for her mother when two girls had come up to talk to the boy to whom she had been speaking. Noticeably Claire found herself totally sidelined by all three of them as though she was simply invisible. Trying to put a finer point on the incident, they seemed to ignore her because she looked like a 'little boy' wearing short pants. Her biggest problem however was her intense jealousy of the two girls who at the time were wearing such pretty summer dresses. Claire could have cried there and then because although she had been reared as a boy, in her own perception she was truly a girl, feeling trapped in a cage. That night in bed, her crying was more intense as she tried to sleep. By the time her mum and dad entered their bedroom, Claire was still sobbing and Olivia walked into her tiny bedroom to see what she was crying about. Of course, Claire could not tell her and her mother told her to stop being silly, to be 'a big boy' instead of a little baby and to get to sleep. Maybe, Claire thought later, her mum really did understand and had some inkling as to what 'William' may have being crying about and that was why her mum had said to stop being silly. But Claire couldn't help it and burying her head further into the down pillow she sobbed herself to sleep. Crying bitterly had become a nightly affair. Her gender dysphoria was becoming exceptionally acute and she didn't know what to do. It was as though she was stuck in a time warp. Silently she was screaming for help, and the old man, sitting on his gold throne in the sky wasn't helping her one little bit.

That year the Wilsons took their usual two weeks annual holiday at Mrs Silverwing's boarding house in Scarborough at the beginning of August. One of Claire's recollections was walking past Peasholm Park toward the theater where artists such as Norman Evans, Nat Jackley, Albert Modley and occasionally Arthur Askey often appeared during the summer season. As she walked with her parents and brothers past a particular garden bed on the outer edge of the park, Claire was overwhelmed by the beautiful array of flowers planted there by staff of the council's gardens department. "Look mummy, aren't those flowers pretty?" She pointed to some beautiful specimens. To this spontaneous proclamation of 'his son' Milton erupted:

"Oh, so we have 'pretty flowers' now, do we little girl?" He laughed loudly along with Danny and Gerry at what he had said and they made such fun of Claire that Olivia told them to leave her alone. In truth Claire was thoroughly sick and tired of her dad always running her down in front of her brothers.

One year her parents decided on a change of venue for their annual holiday and stayed at a boarding house in Blackpool. One particular day while waiting for her parents to appear at the front door, Danny and Gerry were standing in the street shouting at some boys on the street corner. Then out of the blue the boys charged toward her brothers waving their fists. Claire was standing near the gate behind the garden wall of the boarding house, and her brothers ran quickly past, knocking her aside in their retreat into the front garden. At that moment Milton and Olivia walked out of the front door. The local boys ran away when they saw Milton and Olivia. Claire's dad asked her brothers what was going on. Gerry piped up first: "Those boys were going to fight us," he blurted.

Dad turned to 'William' and asked: "And where were you?"

It was Gerry who spoke first: "He just stood there and did nothing."

Claire's father turned to her and slapped her across the face, telling her not to be such a wimp and that she should have gone out to fight the boys. The real issue here was that she had done nothing to deserve this assault and saw it as yet another instance of the unfairness metered out to her in her formative years. Milton seemed to use every occasion to belittle 'William' in front of Danny and Gerry. Consequently, Claire was getting extremely angry at being blamed for every little thing mishap. But what could she do? If she complained, she would have been told "grow up and be a man". To Claire this was out of the question. A total impossibility!

Back home in Sandy Peth, in her box-room of a bedroom, she existed on her own away from the rest of the family. It was her retreat away from her mum and dad and her brothers. It was in so many ways a haven, where she could be on her own, almost at peace in her own private world. Nevertheless, in reality Claire knew she had to engage with other people outside her walls, her family included, even if from time to time they appeared to be antagonistic and hostile toward her. Somehow, given a choice, she really would have liked to be part of the world, to have a normal existence, as she felt she was being torn apart. That being so, one Christmas she asked her parents if she could have a crystal-set as her main present. This produced a look of amusement from her mum, but her dad took it that 'his son' was at last growing up as a boy, as only boys chose crystal sets, not girls. To her dad her request might have been some sort of confirmation that his nurturing of her as a boy was working.

On the other hand, Claire saw her request as something totally different. She needed to feel part of the world outside of the home, and as tiny transistor radios had not yet been invented, her only way of listening to music while she was in bed was to have a crystal-set. Basically, the one her dad bought for her looked like a small cream-colored plastic box, almost like a miniature radio of about 10 cm wide by 7 cm high and 7 cm deep. On the front was a small black dial which controlled the frequency band. The pick-up signal was from a springy coil of wire, the end of which was free to be moved over a silvery piece of rock – the crystal. One moved the dial with a small knob which twisted the wire over the face of the crystal to obtain a good reception. There was a knob for volume too, and a connection to an external antenna. Claire led the wire antenna out through the upper opening of her bedroom window, to let it dangle over the concrete front door canopy. On the side of the set was a pick-up point into which she plugged in the jack for the headphones. These were not the lightweight type in use today, but like those worn by army radiographers of the time, large and bulky.

With practice Claire was able to pick up some of her favorite modern jazz programs from America, or some classical music, which she equally adored. Listening to the music when her head touched the pillow sent her to sleep. But when she awoke the next morning it was quite obvious that her mum had entered her bedroom before she herself had gone to bed, as the headphones were laid on their side on the chair at the side of the bed. The chair was placed there each night as the room was too small to fit a normal bedside table next to where she slept.

19

Slapped Across the Face Again

Another year about this time, Claire, having to live as 'William Wilson', had been asked, along with other Catholic scouts, to serve as a messenger to the priests, brothers and nuns, at a Religious Vocations Exhibition. It was held in the grounds of a Roman Catholic school, which no longer exists, on Torre Road, just down from the tram depot. The exhibition comprised a number of interconnected huge marquees in which many religious orders and the diocesan clergy all vied for potential candidates to the priestly or religious life. Claire was absolutely fascinated to see so many religious orders at the wonderful stands, and during a break of running messages and fetching sandwiches for nuns, monks, brothers and priests she was given time to wander around to view the exhibits herself.

Although they were all interesting, some more than others of course, she was especially taken with the stand of the *Sisters of the Cross and Passion*, whom she was later told were more commonly referred to as the 'Passionist Sisters'. But how could she approach them? A girl who looked and dressed like a boy scout should be taking an interest in men's religious orders, not those for women, shouldn't she? This was a huge dilemma for Claire. That night in bed, her cries were over this particular problem, as she really would have liked to become a nun. If nothing else but to get away from her parents and to soak herself in a woman's religious order. Being with others of her real gender was becoming so important to her.

The next morning Claire wore her scout uniform again and after breakfast caught a tram down York Road to the stop nearest the depot and then walked down Torre Road. As on the previous day, after running errands for the religious orders all morning she was allowed free time and chose to visit the stand manned by the Passionist Fathers. She spoke to a lay-brother who seemed to be in charge of the stand during the lunch period and he wrote down her name as 'William' and address in a book, for the attention of the vocations director. Back on her duties, she became so busy she forgot about her visit to the Passionists, and it was back to school the following day.

The daily struggle with her gender at that stage in her life was really bad, as has already been stressed. Claire knew without a shadow of doubt that she was female but her body was showing signs of being male and it revolted her. When she went to bed she used to wrap her scout neckerchief around her bust and tuck some rolled up socks on top of her nipples. Sometimes she would stick adhesive tape around her bust hoping that by morning there might be just the slightest swelling. Unfortunately, what Claire earnestly prayed for didn't happen. The disgusting piece of flesh between her legs caused her the biggest headache as it grew bigger when she thought of herself as a woman, which not surprisingly, was most of the time. She worked out that if she cut a piece of card to the right shape, she could put it down the front of her panties to try to disguise the horrid swelling. When she was in bed or even in the bath she would tuck the 'thing' under her as though it didn't exist. Going to sleep she would lick her lips and imagine it was lipstick she was wearing.

Claire's first orgasm came one Sunday afternoon when she was kneeling on the floor leaning over her bed. On a large board resting on top of the quilt she was designing clothes on tracing paper over photos of some of the models she found in her mum's magazines. Claire suddenly felt a wave of extreme pleasure running through her body, and let the feeling take its course. She didn't understand what was happening to her but it was wonderful nevertheless. She was in a dream world and the experience seemed to take an age. Gradually, however, it subsided and she knelt on the floor looking at what she had been doing, her designs scattered all over the board. Surprisingly, her panties were wet, so she changed them, and hid the wet ones under the bed.

From that time on, having orgasms often happened when she had nice thoughts about being a young woman, especially imagining herself dressed to go to a ball, wearing a pretty gown and feeling so wonderful. She used to cut out photos of her head from those she had of herself, and often placed them on the models in various women's magazines, as though she were that model.

In her bedroom Claire lived the life of a young woman and hated to go downstairs to join the family, as they so often made fun of her and she could not understand why. Her mother's constant question when she went downstairs was, "What were you doing in your bedroom?" *What a silly question*, Claire thought.

Sometimes she would say she was studying; sometimes drawing; and sometimes writing. In the case of the latter she had a follow up answer ready but always her mum's question would then be: "Well, what were you writing about?"

Sometimes she would say she was doing her homework but her mother would then add, "You should do your homework down here where we can see you. We don't like you being upstairs all the time."

Early one Sunday evening after attending the second Mass of the day followed by Benediction, together with some of her friends, she wandered across the school playground to the classrooms where they held their usual church social. The screen between Miss Comerford's and Miss Seaford's classrooms was drawn back to create a large space for dancing. One of the adults had sprinkled balls of chalk on the floor to make the boards suitable for ballroom dancing. At the time Claire was friendly with Therese Gawler and Pauline Mullins and they experimented with the newest types of modern dancing, until one of the priests in attendance told them off. The parish clergy were the arbiters of what was bad and good in the parish. Modern dancing apparently was sinful, whatever that meant. Even ballroom dancing was suspect to one priest and he made them all stand away from each other while dancing, instead of touching.

That fateful evening, however, Claire arrived home about 9.30 pm to find her parents and brothers sitting watching *Sun-*

day Night at the London Palladium on the black and white 30-cm TV her dad had made. She asked Gerald to budge up on the sofa, much to his annoyance, and she squeezed into the available space he had created with reluctance. Normally she would excuse herself and go upstairs to bed but after the constant criticisms that have already been mentioned, she decided to stay downstairs with them and watch the TV show.

Onto the stage of the *London Palladium* came three African-American singers. Claire sat spell-bound as these guys were not only beautiful singers but most gorgeous looking and she was really taken with their performance. When the audience clapped, Claire was so overwhelmed she clapped with them. That was her big mistake, one which she later found difficult to forget when thinking about the relationship she experienced with her father. "Oh, aren't they handsome," Claire exclaimed.

Milton swung around slowly, glaring at her with fury in his eyes. Rising out of his armchair he stepped toward her and slapped her across the face with extreme vengeance. "I've had just about enough of you," he said. "Those people are not like us, they are like cats and dogs to us. They cannot be handsome as you seem to think – they are like animals, a totally different species to us."

Claire was dumfounded for a few seconds, simply staring at him. She could not believe that this man was her biological father as his views were so alien to hers. She was humiliated once again in front of her brothers, especially when her dad had slapped her hard across the face. Claire was stunned and it took her a few seconds to realize what he had done. "No they are not. They are human beings like us. They just have a different color skin, that's all."

"No, you are wrong as usual, they are nothing like us. They are an inferior species to us, like animals are. I am very disappointed in you William. You are not turning out the way I had hoped. If your comments are anything like those of your friends at St Brigid's, then I forbid you to go to any more church socials." With that he went back to his armchair and sat down, fuming, yet feigning to watch the television.

On Claire's part, shock gradually took over her feelings and after a few seconds she eventually stood up, walked out of the room and climbed the stairs to her tiny bedroom. She went in, closed the door, and sat before her dressing table, ruminating over the situation. Olivia barged through the door without knocking: "How dare you say such wicked things to your daddy?"

"Me? He is the one who says wicked things about other people, not me." Through innocent eyes she looked up. Her mother hadn't heard what Claire had said and continued:

"Why do you have to do that to your daddy?"

"Me? He said those nasty things and then hit me across the face. That was not a nice thing to do."

"Well, you asked for it saying those wicked things. I suggest you try to see things from his point of view in future." Her mother still wasn't listening to anything she said.

"What I said is not wicked as you well know mummy, and as for seeing the world through his eyes, that is totally impossible. He is an absolute bigot. His rhetoric is totally outrageous, totally without any form of caring, and I am surprised you take his viewpoint."

"How dare you speak to me like that, using dirty language? I am his wife and he is the head of this household – and don't you forget it. If that is what the education at that non-Catholic school has done for you then the sooner we take you away from their influence the better. You're still not too big to get spanked on your bottom like when you were little."

"Just let him try it, 'cos if he does, I will walk out."

"Huh, you won't get very far without any pocket money." With that she stormed out. Whether Olivia told Milton what 'William' had hinted to her about leaving home, Claire had no idea, except that for a few days he did not speak to her or even look at her when she was at the dining table.

But Olivia did have a point. Claire had no other way of making money until she left high school. What she earned from neighbors for shopping for them on a Saturday morning and during school holidays, added to the money she earned for delivering evening papers for Redmond's in Church Lane, was miniscule. Added to which, delivering meat for Mr Walters the Butcher on Micklegate Parade certainly didn't amount to much, possibly no more than three shillings a week, thirty pence in today's currency, but possibly equaling £3 in value. Not much money to live on if she was to leave home. There had to be another way to achieve some semblance of equilibrium with her father.

20

The Truth is Revealed

The same year, the Wilsons once again went to stay at Mrs Silverwing's in Scarborough for their August Bank Holiday. It was there that another embarrassing event happened. Oh yes, yet another disturbing event.

Olivia and Milton were in the habit of going out for their usual evening drink with Milton's business partner Gordon Hogben and his wife Gwyneth. Daniel, Gerald and Claire had been tucked into bed before their parents left, Mrs Silverwing offering to keep a sharp ear open for any sounds from the bedroom. But the children must always have been very quiet, as Claire had no recollection of the landlady knocking on their door telling them to get to sleep, as she might have done. Danny and Gerry slept side by side in the corner double bed and Claire was left in her parent's double bed, so that upon their return they could lift her out fast asleep to be laid either at the opposite end of Danny and Gerry's bed, what was referred to as 'topping and tailing', or in the particular year of the incident which is about to be related, to a camp bed under the window.

Claire feigned tiredness until she thought her brothers were asleep and she then quietly slid out of bed by the light of the moon shining through the window. Her mother had the day before bought a new pale blue nylon blouse with a lace collar and Claire wanted to try it on. After putting on one of her mum's bras and padding the cups with some rolled up socks, finding the new blouse hanging up in the wardrobe she put it on. It fitted her perfectly. So emboldened she decided to wear Olivia's new navy blue skirt and jacket. Again, a perfect fit. Wearing the outfit caused Claire to feel so wonderful, and so she decided to go 'the whole hog' and wear her mum's navy blue court shoes. By this time she was in her second heaven, feeling so lovely and so beautiful. She really did not want to take the clothes off straight away so she lay on the bed to let the whole experience sink in. Her thoughts were that this was what being a woman was all about, feeling special and wearing nice clothes. Wearing them was natural for her as a girl growing up and she saw nothing wrong in what she was doing. After a while though, Claire thought she had better undress and put the clothes back where she found them. That done she climbed back into her parent's bed and quickly fell asleep in innocent happiness. She knew nothing more until she woke the next morning in the camp bed under the window. She washed, dressed in the boy's clothes she was expected to wear, and joined her family as they all went downstairs to the breakfast room.

They had finished their cereal, bacon and eggs and fried bread, and were tucking into some toast and marmalade when Danny let rip. Staring at Claire with a cheeky grin across his face he said: "I saw you last night." Claire blushed but kept her head down. Danny went on, "I saw you last night wearing mummy's clothes."

She blushed crimson. "No, you didn't, you must have been dreaming," Claire nervously spluttered, not daring to raise her eyes to look at her mischievous brother.

"Oh no, I wasn't. I saw you," he added, his smile giving way to putting his tongue out at her.

"You were obviously dreaming," Claire said again, without daring to look into his face.

"Wasn't!" He replied. Obviously, this was to be the start of a staccato period of children's banter and so Milton stepped in:

"Shut up you two. That's enough. Eat your breakfast."

Danny wouldn't have this and as his smirk had turned into an accusing laugh, he continued with the accusation. However, in order to show compliance with his dad's command, his words were uttered without a sound, "...*yes I did*" he mouthed, and he put his tongue out again at Claire.

"I said that's enough Daniel." Milton added immediately, suspecting another flare-up. What was going through the minds of her parents Claire had no idea as they all finished their breakfast in silence.

That day they were to go to their day-chalet as usual, overlooking the South Bay sea water bathing pool. Her thoughts were on high alert though, aware and very conscious that her brother Danny had rumbled her. She therefore had to be on guard from this time onward. But strange as it may seem, many years later in adulthood, when Claire mentioned the incident to him, he had no recollection of it. She had developed a fantastic memory, her brothers obviously had not.

Claire was pretty sure by this time that Olivia knew that her "daughter," in the guise of 'her son William', was dressing up in her clothes like all normal girls, but kept the secret to herself. Often while on holiday, Claire would lie in the camp bed and reach out for her mum's shoes, which generally were left on the floor tucked under the end of their bed. The more she thought about things, she was sure that her mum had, on perhaps more than one occasion, found her shoes at the bottom of Claire's camp bed when she and Milton arrived back from a visit to their usual pub.

But the big crunch was yet to come. Home from school sports one Monday afternoon, Claire was creating a design for her art homework while sitting at the dining table. Her mum was sitting on the left of the fireplace in one of the pre-war style armchairs Milton and Olivia had been so proud to buy in 1938. Her mum was embroidering flowers, her constant pastime, on a new tablecloth. Sometimes Claire was thrilled when her mum showed her what she was doing and how she formed the stitches. But on that afternoon, without looking at her directly, Olivia made a startling statement: "You know the new navy high heels I bought?"

"Er…yes," Claire nervously replied, already starting to blush.

"Well, they are too tight for me. Would you wear them in for me, you know around the house to ease them in a little?"

Claire hesitated as she started to reply, "Er…" To say she was shocked by this request is an understatement as she was absolutely devastated. It was pretty obvious that her mum knew that she had been secretly wearing her new shoes and wanted to bring the issue out into the open. Claire's only thought was what her extremely volatile dad would say if he got to know any of this. Milton hated all forms of effeminacy in men and boys, no matter how justified it might have been. Naturally, Claire did not want to be the object of any more ridicule than she already had to endure from his mouth. The thing was, should she open up to her mother and be totally honest with her, hoping that something could be done to help the situation? But if she did, her mother may tell her dad, and she could not risk any more humiliation. Consequently, Claire had to think quickly to avoid a situation that could so easily get out of hand. "No, boys don't do that sort of thing," she eventually blurted out, while her face was obviously as crimson as one of her dad's fat home-grown tomatoes.

Claire cannot remember the reply her mum gave her, if she replied to her negative response at all, but it could have been something like "I just thought I would ask." In actual fact, Olivia had really nothing to lose as obviously 'William' was stunned at her question.

It was about that time that Claire had experienced her father throwing a pointed kitchen knife at her mother and as she moved sideways to avoid it, the knife ended up sticking through a panel in the dining room door, its handle quivering wildly. There was the other time when her dad threw a poker from the fireside at her mother while she was setting knives and forks on the table, and once again she ducked or moved aside as it sped past her and sailed cleanly through the bottom glass pane in the windows at the side of the French door. Was it any wonder then that Claire did not want her dad to be reminded of what she was? His temper was well known.

It was obvious beyond any doubt that her mum knew of her growing gender problem, and maybe Olivia's question was framed to try to bring Claire out of her shell. But she was scared to death of her dad being told so the matter was not pursued right then and there. Keeping her head down on her artwork, trying to avoid the delicate situation, Claire really didn't know what to do or say next. Her mum on the other hand, obviously wanted to raise the issue of 'her son's' gender problem but seemed unsure as to how to approach it. Her next words brought the hot flush back to Claire's cheeks: "You know William, had things gone the way I wanted, you would have been the daughter I craved for. I was going to call you Claire. My grandma was called Claire, that's why I chose it."

Shock of all shocks! This was building up into some sort of confession perhaps? There was a long silence, but it was Olivia who continued. With tears forming in her eyes she tried to remember and relate past events. "Grandma Claire was from County Donegal in Ireland and my other grandma, Grandma Gertrud Levinstein, was from Germany. They both had dark hair but Grandma Gertrud used to wear hers in a chignon." Olivia was musing, sitting in her chair and staring into the fire, "I did so want a daughter. It would have been so lovely," she continued. "We could have done so much together, sharing our clothes and shoes, experimenting with make-up, going out shopping together and you learning to knit and to embroider."

There was another long pause as she bent over her embroidery. "You do know that you were born a hermaphrodite, don't you love? The specialists apparently also call it *intersexed*." She didn't wait for Claire to answer and continued rambling: "You were such a pretty thing and I was so happy gazing at you as my baby girl." By this time Olivia was actually weeping and looked up at 'her daughter' through sad but loving tear-filled eyes, appealing for understanding.

Claire turned around at that point and looked her mother full in the face, and asked in all innocence: "Why mummy, what happened?"

Her mum just stared at her wiping her tears away with a very soggy hankie clutched in her left hand. Claire thought it might be safe to open up a little as to what she was experiencing in her confused thoughts. Olivia stared into the glowing coals in the fireplace as Claire or 'William continued. "I suppose you had guessed I have been trying on your clothes and shoes but I can't help myself. I feel like a girl. I want so desperately to be a normal girl and to do the things other girls do, but when I look at my body I become so sad that it is not developing as it should do for a girl."

Olivia reached out her hand toward 'her daughter' and they held hands at that point, just looking at each other. Claire continued: "The problem is that I know my dad hates me and I know it is because of how I see myself, as a girl. So knowing how I was born is of great interest to me mummy. It helps me fit pieces together into a jigsaw. In some small way what you are telling me explains why I feel like I do, but I am scared to death of daddy. His ridicule of me in front of Danny and Gerry really hurts. If he was aware that I really am a girl I am feared he might kill me as I know he hates all forms of effeminacy in boys."

"No love, he would not kill you as if he did, he would be blamed and go to jail. But he did threaten to walk out on me after you were born, just because you had genitals of both genders. We had been told by two of the specialists at the Infirmary that your condition was all in the mind. We were advised to raise you as a boy and all would come right in the end. We were told that rearing you in a boy's world would solve the gender issue."

"Mummy, that is not true. I know within myself that it isn't true."

"Well, love, that's what we were told, and your daddy is still convinced that you will gradually grow into a normal man. He does want to be proud of you and he wants to see you taking an interest in normal boy's things."

"That's the problem mummy; I am not interested in boy's things. I just want to be a girl, and my interests are those of a girl, not a boy." By this time the comments of the two of them were going around in circles, each of them knowing that Claire's situation was hopeless. She could not change her mind, but only she herself was aware of that. Other people saw her dressed as a boy and when she was in the swimming pool or on the sports field, she looked like a boy. She had therefore, to think very carefully about her future and what she was going to do to try to fit in with society and be in some way, even if miniscule, what her dad wanted. Claire really did worry about her future and how things might turn out.

Olivia and Claire both shrugged their shoulders as they looked into each other's eyes. Just then they heard the driveway gate open and close as Danny and Gerry came running down the path from St Edwin's. Olivia and Claire never did fully finish their discussion. Olivia knew, as Claire did, that they had to appease Milton. On Claire's part, she had to try in some small way, to be what her father wanted, no matter how painful it was for her. On her mum's part, she had to weep to herself and keep quiet. She knew the consequences of the truth coming out, and the future did not look good on that score.

So Olivia had explained to her daughter how she had been born with the parts of both male and female, and that the hospital had said it was normal to allow the female parts to prevail. She had added, "But it was your daddy who refused to accept you as a girl and took things into his own hands." There was a short pause as Olivia reluctantly added: "He reasoned that he would be less than a man if he had a daughter and not a son. I know it is ridiculous but that is your daddy. He has some funny ideas."

The two had comforted each other crying and holding hands, but after Claire had related her side of things Olivia stopped sobbing, straightened up and said: "No matter love. What's done is done. Get back to your homework Claire, I mean William." Just at that moment Danny and Gerry rushed into the dining room full of their antics at school and they took over the conversation. Claire collected her drawings and charcoal and went up to her bedroom. Now that the cat was really out of the bag, she wondered if her mum would say anything to her dad.

The knowledge of her birth and what her mum would have loved to happen were what Claire would have liked too. She desperately wanted to be the daughter her mum wanted. Indeed, in so many ways she was that daughter, but there were other considerations beyond the control of both of them. Had there been the opportunity, Claire felt sure that her mother would have been only too pleased to help her correct her physical gender.

But she had already discovered in a book she had read at the senior library, that change of gender at the age of fourteen was forbidden in the UK. Anyone caught in the gender trap, as she referred to her problem, had to have permission from both parents for a start, and she knew without a shadow of a doubt that her dad would never give his permission. Besides that, no one under the age of twenty-one had been given permission in the UK to change gender. It was a forbidden issue. In fact, the number of cases throughout the world of people changing gender was so small as to be almost negligible. The first experiments had been in Germany in the 1930s, but little was recorded of the results, and especially not available to the medical profession in the UK while the country had been at war with Germany. Later in life, Claire was to learn a lot more of her condition and solutions for her ongoing well-being. But in the mid-1950s, there was little published information other than referring to gender dysphoria as a mental problem.

21

Into Politics

Dressing up at home took two forms. The first when Claire was home from school, especially from 'Monday Sports' due to rain and when her mum had gone out shopping; and the second was when she was alone in her bedroom, supposed to be in bed asleep. In situations where her mum was out during the day, Claire knew where everything was in her mother's bedroom, especially in her section of her parents' joint free-standing clothes closet, which they called a wardrobe.

Olivia didn't have a lot of clothes as she had to ask Milton for the money to buy them, or if she had saved enough from housekeeping that her husband gave her every Friday. Generally, Olivia had very little money of her own when her children were little; merely what she might have saved from money that usually went on 'the bairns'. Olivia hung her few items of clothing at the left-hand-side of their wardrobe and the five pairs of shoes she possessed were placed under them on the floor of the closet. Milton hung his suits, and he always wore a suit for every occasion, on the opposite side to Olivia's clothes. Claire knew that in her mum's dressing table drawers she kept her undies and the little make-up she was allowed to wear. Milton didn't like his wife wearing much make-up, or 'stuff' as he called it. That is unless they were going anywhere special, when she was allowed to apply some foundation and/or powder and a little lipstick, which she spread with her little finger. Occasionally, she would run a lead pencil over her eyebrows, but she did not possess any mascara. Her blusher, if one can call it that, was a tiny round card box of rouge, which she rarely used. Claire had noticed that to achieve the effect of blusher, her mum would smear some lipstick on her little finger and gently spread it along her cheekbone and then blend it in. She knew that her mum had some foundation but she rarely saw her wearing it, although she thought she must have done for special occasions, attending a baptism or a wedding, for example.

Claire's problem was, like all girls growing up, that she needed to practice applying her make-up, and the only real opportunity she had to do this was when the household was sleeping. But, not being able to buy her own make-up, she had to come up with an alternative to actual cosmetics. For this, she could only use watercolor for her lips and eyebrows and sometimes artist's guache, which gave a more vibrant tone. The trouble with the latter was that the color vermillion which she occasionally applied to her lips, did not wipe off very easily. It stained the lips and the next morning quite often she had to try again to wipe it off, which was not always successful, much to her chagrin. Olivia obviously noticed too and tried to hide her amusement as she stared at 'her son' eating 'his' porridge. Claire constantly experimented with different shades of pink on her lips and cheeks and added color to her eyebrows too, after plucking them slightly. She had not gone to the level of applying an eye liner at this stage – that was to come later.

One evening, when it was still daylight due to British Summer Time, Claire had been in her bedroom doing homework when she heard the driveway gate being opened. She stood up to look out of the window. Her eyes must have been like saucers as she stared at two black-clothed monks entering their driveway. As they walked down the driveway toward the scullery door, Claire stood motionless wondering what to do. Silently she opened her bedroom door and crossed to the stair landing so that she could hear any conversation that might prevail. Her heart was in her mouth. Claire had actually forgotten the discussion she had had at the religious vocations exhibition a few weeks earlier and it was plain to see that the Passionist Fathers hadn't. After initially hearing raised voices and then the scullery door banging shut with some force, it was blatantly obvious that the visitors had not been welcomed into the house. A few seconds later she heard the gate open and close again and rushing to the window saw the monks walking away. One of them turned around to look at the house and saw Claire standing at her bedroom window. He gave a shrug of his shoulders, as though to say *well, we tried*. Claire waited. Sure enough the command came: "William! William, get down here this minute. I want a word with you." Her dad had issued another of his dictatorial demands.

Claire knew she was in for a grilling from him and gingerly left the sanctity of her bedroom. With her heart filling her mouth entirely, she descended the stairs, counting each step methodically. Milton was waiting for her outside the dining room door, and ushered her inside with a wave of his hand: "Get in here. I want words with you."

Claire glided past her irate father into the dining room and stood waiting for the usual rebuke. She had become quite accustomed to his tirade when he considered 'his son' had stepped out of line.

The onslaught began immediately by poking her in the chest: "What do you think you are doing telling those black-robed monkeys, those bloody holy Joes that you would like to join them?" Claire hung her head. "Have you completely lost what little brain I thought you might have?" She continued to look at the floor. "C'mon, I'm waiting! What have you say for yourself William?"

"Sorry daddy, but I had forgotten about speaking to them at the religious vocations exhibition last month."

"I knew there would be trouble you going to that thing." He was silent for a few seconds, staring at her and then stood looking out of the dining room window. "Why did you tell them you would like to join whatever they call their monkish community, without asking my permission?"

"Because I am interested in serving God and it seemed a good idea to join them in the monastery. But since then I had forgotten all about it."

He looked out of the window again into the back garden. Turning toward her again, he stared her in the face. "So you have forgotten about it. Is that right?"

"Yes."

"Good! So we shall hear no more of that silly nonsense again, shall we? I am not wasting my time working like a Nigger to get you through High School only to find that you want to throw it all away in a religious nut house. So you can just forget all those stupid ideas?" Claire nodded her head while still staring at the floor. "Well, go back to your homework. I don't want to hear another word on this. Is that clear?"

"Mmm!" She murmured as a weak answer, still hanging her head.

"What did you say?"

"Yes."

"I should bloody well think so." Her dad had won again. She had been destroyed. The matter was simply pushed aside by her dad as another of her scatterbrained and idiotic ideas. However, rather than put the matter out of her mind, she still harbored thoughts of being in a religious order, as a way of containing her gender dysphoria. Claire thought maybe she could hide herself away in a monastery and it would vanish. She prayed to all her favorite saints and hoped that Jesus would either change her into a proper girl one night as she slept or take the thoughts away. It was to become a vain hope however, never straying far from her thoughts. Claire was to discover in later years that clutching at the religious life was a feeble response to her gender dysphoria. She was caught in a cleft stick, and there appeared to be no way out of her enigma.

At Clark's College, Claire was younger than the average class member and consequently was often bypassed in many things. But she did hold her own in Art, and in fourth year she had been chosen as the school artist, especially to produce posters for various events, instead of having one or two produced by a printing firm. These were the days of the *Gestetner* machine and many years before the photocopier. Her posters were sprayed with an art fixative and then pinned to the school notice board by the main entrance on Woodthorpe Lane.

In the senior years also, Claire took over the administration of the school music club and introduced its members to the classics while they interspersed such sophisticated sounds with the whines of Johnny Ray and other popular singers of the period. They had to be careful though, as Mr Hinton, the senior master often stepped down to the basement venue after school hours, to check on 'the little rascals'. Claire wondered if Mr Hinton thought they might be conducting a drunken orgy in the building's depths.

Prepared for such an eventuality as the sudden appearance of their senior master, the students always had a lookout near the steps up to the main floor. When the door burst open with the pronouncement: "Freddy's coming" Claire quickly removed the latest pop single to replace it with a Chopin prelude or some other similar piece she had to hand in readiness. By the time 'Freddy' Hinton entered the classroom, he saw little angels listening to classical music and seemingly enjoying it by the smiles on their faces. Butter would not have melted in their mouths – or would it?

At High School, Claire also founded a philatelic club after classes, at which they would exchange duplicate stamps in their individual collections. These were known as 'swaps'. Often on some Fridays, after classes, the senior students would meet for debates and other worthwhile events to improve their perception and language skills. Although Claire was not 'sporty' or one who followed modern trends, she did fairly quickly become a member of the debating team, especially where politics was concerned. This was encouraged by her dad, who had switched from supporting the British Labour Party in 1950, to supporting the Conservative Party the following year. By this time, his factory, which he still referred to as 'the works' was doing fairly well financially and he apparently thought he should support the right-wing Tories instead of the left-wing Labour Party. His reasoning was that as he was now a businessman, not working for someone else, he should put his allegiance behind the party that supported big business, and not the party of the workers, whom he now started referring to as "the Socialists."

As a result of being brainwashed by her dad in Conservative party politics, Claire was encouraged to join Micklegate Young

Conservatives and with her dad's influence, she was duly admitted. Having become a member of East Aireborough Conservative Association and elected as its chairman, Milton's influence meant that Claire was nominated as vice-chairman of her local Young Conservative branch. However, the activities of the branch seemed to revolve around the distribution of leaflets at election time, apart from having social events to raise party funds. But what the membership did for Claire was to help her focus on national and social concerns, as seen a few years later when she abandoned right-wing politics. She had become sympathetic to the plight of the poor, the needy and the underprivileged and found the Conservative Party unsympathetic to her causes. She was to see the Conservative Party as the party of the wealthy, the aristocracy and big business. In contrast to this, she saw the Labour Party as supporting the poor, the workers, intellectuals, and teachers. At the time she was in rebellion, and saw the Labour Party as the ideal. She knew her paternal ancestors had been hardworking coal miners and her great grandfather had even been a strong supporter of James Keir Hardie, the Scottish Labour leader. Among many, Hardie was regarded as the real founder of the Scottish Labour Party from his roots in Motherwell and Glasgow. Claire wondered if her great grandfather's support for Keir Hardie was one of the links in her paternal Scottish ancestry. She wondered if her family had moved from Glasgow to Yorkshire to work in the coalmining industry.

However, that aside, a few years later Claire was persuaded to join the Young Liberals on becoming friendly again with a boy who was in the class above her at Clark's College. Milton got to hear of her rift with his beloved Conservative Party and threatened to kick her out of the family home. He didn't, but a few years later he was to disown her for another reason.

22

The Red Shoes

Claire was appointed as a prefect at the Regal Cinema in Micklegate and was privileged to be able to watch movies at a cheaper entrance charge. When she was not on duty as a prefect, however, instead of a one-shilling ticket to go through the front entrance, she was charged only three pence to sit in the front stalls at a children's matinée, and six pence to sit elsewhere. As a prefect, it cost her nothing when she was on duty, which entailed keeping the audience in order. The usual children's performances comprised a couple of short movies such as an episode of *The Three Stooges*, *Charlie Chaplin*, *Laurel & Hardy* or *Abbott & Costello* with a main feature movie which could be a Western with Roy Rogers, Hopalong Cassidy, The Lone Ranger, Batman or Superman or other major movie stars of the time suitable for children. One Saturday however, there came a great movie that changed her life – *The Red Shoes* starring Moira Shearer.

Claire didn't know that the Danish author Hans Christian Andersen had written a story of a girl who danced and danced whenever she wore a pair of special red ballet shoes. But she had to admit that she had not been specifically looking for such a story in the children's or adult section of Micklegate Public Library. On the other hand, had she discovered the book and borrowed it, she was sure her father would not have allowed her to read it. Milton, she thought, may be aware of her inclinations toward dance, and especially ballet and may have put his authoritative foot down. Nevertheless, Claire had to watch the movie, which was to become a special feature at a children's Saturday afternoon matinée. She was spellbound all through the movie and in Moira Shearer she saw herself dancing. Claire cried over the ballerina's magnificent performance, she was so beautiful and talented and truly a great star. In Claire's mind, she herself was that star and lived her life for the rest of the day as that particular actress. So Claire became the actress Moira Shearer, or the character Victoria Page in the movie. She must have walked home in a daze that afternoon and on her late arrival at home, Olivia asked: "What's the matter with you, William? You seem to be in a daze."

"Nothing mummy," Claire answered as though her voice was coming from an ethereal cloud hovering in the distance.

"What have you been watching at the Regal, some stupid Western or something?"

"No, I just watched the most beautiful woman in the whole world dance in the ballet *The Red Shoes*." Claire looked into space as though she was still watching the movie.

"You watched what? *The Red Shoes*? What's that all about?"

"It's about a girl who wears a pair of red ballet shoes and she could not stop dancing when she wore them."

"Oh, so it wasn't about the real world then?"

"Hmm?" Claire questioned in a sort of whisper as she was still living the dream.

"I said it was not about the real world or real life, just some sort of nonsense I suppose." By this time her mother was looking at her in a strange sort of way, as though her thoughts were trying to leap out of her face. Olivia stared at 'William' and put down the iron. With hands on her hips she said quite forcefully, almost with malice in her voice: "Well, you can just forget that stupid story and go and fetch some coals for the dining room fire."

Claire dreamily wandered into the dining room for the coal scuttle and ethereally walked out of the scullery door and, opening the coal-house door next to it, began to shovel coals into the scuttle. After a few minutes Olivia opened the scullery door and shouted: "Hurry up with that coal William, the fire's almost out. Are you day-dreaming as usual?"

Claire completed the task forced upon her and was about to climb the stairs to her bedroom when Olivia commented: "Don't tell your daddy what you watched this afternoon or there might be strong words from him, as you well know by now."

In her bedroom, she flung herself onto the bed and fell asleep dreaming that she was dancing, wearing red ballet shoes. After wanting to be a ballerina for so many years she had finally found her idol, Moira Shearer. She loved everything about her, from her beautiful face to her mass of red hair but more so her skill and talent as a ballet dancer.

She was awakened by Danny who was shaking her violently and shouting: "Mummy says you've to come downstairs. Tea's ready." Claire woke with a start and told Danny to get out of her room. He did thankfully, albeit putting out his tongue in the process, and she went across to the dressing table mirror and sitting down in front of it stared and stared at the image before her.

"William, get yourself down here now or you get no tea." Claire had been warned and this temporarily brought her back to the real world that her mother wanted her to live in, not her dream world.

At the dinner table there was the usual banter between all of the children until Milton asked: "So what was the matinée film about today Danny"

"Oh, it was just some stupid girly thing, about a woman who couldn't stop dancing. You wouldn't have liked it daddy as it was all about ballet and it had lots of poofter men in it prancing around with the girls."

"Was it really?" Milton quizzed as he put a piece of one of his home grown tomatoes into his mouth. "Was William there too?" he asked Danny, not asking the 'his son' sitting directly across the table from him.

"Yes, SHE was; all googah and dreamy eyed as usual," Danny shouted while staring Claire in the face, and then putting his tongue out at her. The table went quiet. Danny had used the 'she' word describing Claire and they all knew what that meant.

Claire's face was flushed down to her neck and she dare not look up from her plate of salad. Nevertheless, they finished their tea in silence and waited to be granted permission to leave the table. Surprisingly, nothing else was said after Danny's comment and Claire thought her dad had gotten over the shock that she had watched a whole movie about ballet. That night she took the ballet shoes off her wall, where they had been hanging despite her mum's warning weeks earlier. She hugged them to her cheek as she drifted off to sleep; once again dreaming that she was Moira Shearer in *The Red Shoes*.

Oh, how Claire wanted to dance. It was to her an extension of the music of Tchaikovsky, which she adored. As a girl, it was so natural for her to want to dance and quite often in her dreams she danced, sometimes into the sky and among the clouds. She assumed later in her life that this was what some people saw in her, especially her siblings – 'with a head in the clouds'. But sixty years later, when she was well into her seventies, having had many of her childhood dreams fulfilled, the objections of her father to everything she held dear were to become 'times of great sadness'.

Unknown to her parents she did manage to see *The Red Shoes* three times that week although her parents thought she had been involved with other events she related to them. Claire assumed that they believed her although she did have doubts on this when she was going to sleep, after sitting in front of her mirror, trying to enhance her eyes like those of Moira Shearer in the movie. All through her life she was to re-live those days of ecstasy, believing that she could become like her role model if she were strong enough to challenge her father's bigoted ideas. If it came to the crunch would she be successful? She didn't know. All she did know was that she had to try to become an independent woman who knew her own mind and would at some stage in her life seek to fulfill her dreams.

In her teens, any sign of femininity in her was smashed by her dad with hurtful comments. Even as a member of the boys gymnastics team at high school, the sports master often referred to her as 'girly'. So if he could see through her, she assumed her dad did also. The rift between Claire's father and her was to shape her life for good. In adulthood when she was living with Sharon, the latter once commented that Claire was very observant of her surroundings, and that for some strange reason she never used the word 'pretty'. Claire had to explain that in her younger days she was ridiculed by her dad for using that word. She mentioned his constant ridicule of her, and when she used the word 'pretty' he seemed to go ballistic. Sharon had asked why, and Claire told her that her dad believed that only women used such a word and the use of it reminded him of the way she was born and maybe his own involvement in the mutilation of her genitals.

23

The Tin Tray Affair

But no matter what Claire did or thought, she was constantly considered 'weird' by her family. Her love of classical music and modern jazz was a case in point. While she was at high school, most evenings she would retreat into the front room, referred to as 'the sitting room' although it was rarely used as such by anyone else in the family. There she listened to classical music while she completed her homework. But, on more than one evening a week her mum would open the door and demand: "Your daddy wants you in the other room with us instead of sitting in here by yourself."

"But I am not interested in watching television." Claire would explain with conviction each time.

"I couldn't care less, it isn't natural you sitting in here by yourself."

"But I have to do my homework."

"You can do that at the dining room table."

"But with the television on in the background I wouldn't be able to concentrate."

"That's something you have to get used to William. I want you in the other room now!" Always it was a command, and with that she would walk out, leaving the door open. Claire had no choice as she was constantly in her dad's bad books. So she would put her homework away and sadly slink next door into the family's main room which they referred to as the dining room. There, her parents and her two brothers would be watching some mindless show on the tiny black and white screen, with its pale blue, pink and green colored plastic sheet hanging in front to give some semblance of color television. On the particular evening about to be related, her father told Danny and younger brother Gerry to 'budge up' so that she could sit down on the sofa. The 'two scalawags' as Claire referred to them, did so under great sufferance. She would sit there with arms folded in determined revolt, her face showing her disgust at what they were watching. Danny leaned over and whispered in her ear, "You're weird."

Claire would have loved to slap his face but knew that her parents would take Danny's side of the argument as usual, so she was forced to bide her tongue. It didn't matter what homework she had to do, she still preferred to sit by herself in the front room, either reading, painting, drawing or writing. She liked her own company as she could think what she liked, instead of being molded into the moron that her dad obviously preferred. Her brothers were growing up in her dad's mold but she was sure that in her dad's eyes, she was an 'abnormality'. Well, was it a surprise to her now, knowing how she was born?

At the end of her final school year a ball was to be held at the Capitol Ballroom in Meanwood. For weeks before the event some of the senior students had been taught how to dance and Claire enjoyed this as anything to do with dancing was of great interest to her. She loved movement and especially dancing.

That year Claire's senior class was to put on a play, written by some of the senior boys such as Murdo Fallon and Johnny Burton, head girl Betty Holbrook and deputy head girl Mary Keeton. It was to be a one-act play of a court room in which the teachers, or rather a parody of them, were to be put on trial for various misdemeanors. As usual, being younger than the others, smaller and somewhat insignificant too, Claire was not selected by the organizers for any notable part. Had they but known it, she was a good actor and in later years was to be a member of a three thespian companies, and a playwright too.

In the class play, one of the boys, Gerry Slant, had to dress up as one of the female teachers. The practice for each part took place at lunch time in the gymnasium and one of the girls had taken a pair of high heels for Gerry to wear at the dress rehearsal. Claire was leaning against the back wall of the gym thinking that what she was about to witness would possibly be good for a laugh. She was not wrong. Gerry Slant, blushing bright crimson, was steadied by two of the senior girls as he gingerly stepped into the high heeled shoes, after being told by them to take his 'smelly' socks off first. The girls then encouraged him to walk forward a few steps, bending his knees to compensate for the height of the heels. Of course, Gerry could hardly walk in them as he had never worn women's shoes in his life up until that day. In truth, Claire considered that he was absolutely useless, and as she watched the charade she was smiling inwardly. She knew without a shadow of doubt that if they had chosen her, she would have had no problems at all in walking in the shoes. Her eyes glazed over with sadness, tears starting to form. In a soft breath she muttered, *I should have been chosen for that part as I am a girl and can easily walk in high heels.*

Claire's friend Johnny Hartwith, whom she had befriended because everyone ignored him too, due to him having a hair lip, heard her whispering to herself. "What did you say William?"

"Oh! Nothing Johnno! It's nothing at all."

"Are you okay?" he asked staring Claire in the eyes.

"Yes, I'm alright," she said, turning her eyes to the front.

She was, of course, totally insignificant like Johnny, and anything she said would have been ignored, or so she imagined. When the controlling group selected people for various parts, Claire was not chosen for any of the major or even minor roles, and after everyone was selected, she was the one left standing there with Johnny. *What could they do with us,* she wondered.

What transpired was that she was to be the smallest and last member of 'the Jury', the collective opinions of which was to commit each 'teacher' to a life of penitential servitude. When the decision of each member of the jury was sought, Claire, being the last one to declare a verdict, had to vote against the "guilty" verdict, voiced from the rest of 'the jury'. She had simply to stand up and shout, "Not guilty."

Her friend Johnny was to sit next to her in the jury and when she uttered the opposing words, he had to stand up and bang her on the head with a tin tray, so that the 'clang' echoed around the hall. Claire had told Johnny not to hit her too hard or she would not walk down Woodthorpe Lane with him anymore, after school. But in truth she was the joke as usual, 'useless' as her dad constantly reminded her.

Claire cried every night when she went to bed, as she was so devastated over her gender dysphoria. She was totally convinced, without a shadow of a doubt, that she was a girl and would have passed easily had she been allowed to change gender at that age. But changing gender was not only a forbidden subject in many ways, but in the music hall, and in the media generally, it was regarded as a big joke. The public in general regarded change of gender as 'having the snip'. Medically it was regarded as having a mental disorder. There were such men who flipped their gender for the stage, such as Danny La Rue, the Irish Catholic comedian who dressed as a woman in pantomimes and night clubs and in at least one movie Claire was to see him in, many years later. He was a transvestite, a drag queen, one who dressed up in the opposite gender as entertainment. He seemed to be quite successful at it too.

A few years previously Mr & Mrs Rooney from next door, had taken her to watch a pantomime at Aireborough Grand Theater in which Danny La Rue had been one of the main actors. It was a performance of Cinderella and after thinking she could have easily taken the part of Prince Charming, played by a woman, Claire was impressed with the professional acting of one of the Ugly Sisters. There were two ugly sisters and one of them was decidedly 'ugly', and obviously a man dressed up. The other one was not ugly at all. In actual fact she had been quite attractive. It was during the interval when the Rooney's and Claire had been sitting in their seats in the stalls, spooning ice cream into their mouths with tiny wooden spades, when she was asked by uncle Henry: "Well, William, what do you think of the performance?"

She made very grown up comments apparently as she loved acting, but then said: "I thought one of the ugly sisters was quite beautiful and not ugly at all."

Henry laughed. "Which one do you mean William?"

Claire explained what Danny La Rue had been wearing and Henry laughed loudly, "That ugly sister is a man dressed up William."

She was stunned for a minute, thinking that Uncle Henry had misunderstood her. So she repeated her comment and he in turn repeated his back to her. Apparently Claire went very quiet with her eyes open like saucers. "Are you alright lad, you've gone all queer?"

"Yes I'm alright; it's just that I feel I have been tricked. I thought one of the ugly sisters was actually a woman. I didn't realize it was a man dressed up." Claire didn't say any more, as she was so dumfounded at the revelation.

Claire mused to herself that if a man like Danny La Rue could look very convincing in public, except that he had a deep voice for a lady, then maybe she would be able to pass as easily as a girl. *Very interesting!* Claire thought to herself. *Very interesting indeed! Uncle Henry.*

24

Religion Again

As Claire entered her final year at Clark's College, she was placed in class 5/12, which was the upper of the two final years. She had taken over Catholic assembly from Tony Ackerman, a 'teddy boy' in her view. Tony's idea of being in charge of Catholic Assembly was to have everyone sitting down folding their arms and keeping quiet. He had not led the assembly in any prayers as to him being Roman Catholic meant that they just had to desist from attending the 'Protestant Assembly', which began each school day. So when he left Clark's College to help his dad in their retail electrical shop, Claire simply took over and there was no objection from the few Roman Catholics in her year.

Each morning she would start Catholic Assembly with the *Our Father* the *Hail Mary* and *Glory Be* and sometimes they would say 'the Apostles Creed', which at the time Claire was not aware of the fact that the so-called 'apostles' had not written it. It had been composed in the fourth century. After prayers she would read her fellow Catholics excerpts from the lives of the saints, using booklets which she had in her own collection, published by the *Catholic Truth Society*.

The strange thing about this period was that Claire was apparently seen by some of the Protestant students as a cross between Jewish and Catholic. She thought this may have been because of her almost black hair, or the fact that the Protestants were confused by the fact that the classrooms used by Jews and Catholics for their religious assemblies were next to each other on the ground floor. Whatever the Protestants might have thought, Claire had no influence on the matter. It was many years later she learned that her distant ancestry was indeed German Jewish, but her forebears had been converted to Christianity to escape persecution.

The confusion in this came as somewhat of a surprise to Claire, happening one day when the senior students had been on a coach trip to Fountains Abbey. It was customary on the return journey in the coach to sing songs to while away the darkness outside. On that occasion, Claire recalled, some of the boys started singing a song called *The Quarter-Master's Store*. They would pick someone in the coach and add their name to the song so that it rhymed:

There was Mitch, Mitch, climbing out of a ditch,
In the store, in the store.
There was Mitch, Mitch, climbing out of a ditch,
In the quarter-master's store.
The chorus line was always the same:
My eyes are dim I cannot see,
I have not brought my specs with me,
I have no-ot brought my specs with me.
When Claire's name was mentioned it became:
There was Wilson, Wilson, coming out of Bilsen,
In the store, in the store.
There was Wilson, Wilson, coming out of Bilsen,
In the quarter-master's store.

What they had done was to change the pronunciation of the name Belsen, into Bilsen to cause it to rhyme. Whether they knew that Belsen was a Nazi concentration camp for Jews is unclear, but they obviously remembered from news bulletins that Jews had been housed in an extermination camp known as Bergen-Belsen. Obviously, the words fitted for the song, but Claire was not familiar with the particular concentration camp. All news on BBC Radio about Germany was usually turned off by her father, who regarded all Germans as filthy people, and that Jews were no better. Throughout World War II, Claire's dad had shown extreme hatred for all foreigners, no matter where they came from, especially Germans and Irish. Had he known that his wife's Levine ancestry was German and Irish, and many years earlier Jewish, maybe he might not have married Olivia after all.

Claire was fascinated by Judaism and wanted to know as much as she could about it, not that opportunities ever came up. To confuse the issue, Milton, having been raised as a Baptist, had converted to Roman Catholicism in order to marry Olivia. But to him the conversion experience hovered around her parish priest in Harehills allowing her future husband to play the church organ, or so his story went. Claire never knew that her dad could play the organ, or any keyboard instrument for that matter. It was later that he bought her a plastic banjo-ukulele and taught her the chords for George Formby songs such as *I'm leaning on a lamp-post at the corner of the street*, *Song bird come share a tree*, *Show me the way to go home*, *I'm tired and I want to go to bed*..., and such like. She really wanted to learn to play the piano but her dad was too stingy to buy one. Maybe if they had a piano it might prove that he could not play a keyboard after all. However at the time, Claire didn't think this far ahead, only that she would have loved to play the piano and her dad would not buy one.

But back to the religious issue! Claire could not remember her parents ever attending Mass at St Brigid's. They may have done for her First Communion or her Confirmation, but she had no memories of them being there. She did remember walking to school wearing a clean white shirt, blue tie and short gray pants for those particular events and being so jealous of the girls wearing their lovely white dresses, veils and tiaras. After their First Communion, the children went into their classroom for the customary 'communion breakfast' which was not plates of bacon and eggs, that the Wilsons might have had at home, but some sandwiches, buns and cups of lemonade. Claire didn't regard this as a real breakfast.

She must have been perhaps about the age of thirteen when her parents allowed her to choose a budgie to share with her brothers, buying it from the man who lived in the corner house as he had an aviary full of them. However, Claire was the one who was asked what name the bird should be called, and choosing the name *Tuppy* as she pretended it only cost twopence. It was a girl budgie as it developed a brown thickening over its nostrils, as Claire knew that the male's nostrils were blue. Over the early months of the family having *Tuppy* living with them, she appeared to prefer to land on Claire's shoulder rather than those of other members of her family. She could only assume that the budgie and she were kindred spirits, both females, but in reality perhaps it was because she was the one who spoke to the bird more than the other members of the family. Plus Claire was the one who changed the bird's water tube, filled up her seed tray and replaced the sandpaper sheet at the bottom of her cage. After a few weeks of her getting used to the family, Olivia suggested they let *Tuppy* out of her cage for a fly around the dining room. This was fine but comical as she tried to land on Milton's open copy of the *Yorkshire Evening Post* while he was trying to read it. He had had enough when she started to land on his sleeve and nibble the edges of the paper. Her favorite position after a while was to sit on Claire's shoulder and chirp into her ear. In reply Claire started copying her whistles and in return she copied her mistress back.

But poor little *Tuppy* didn't last out the year though, and Claire pleaded with her mum and dad for them to get another one immediately. That was when *Tippy* came to join the family. Once again Claire approached Mr Smythe, in the corner bungalow and asked if he had one available. He bred mainly canaries and finches but he also had an aviary of budgerigars. So he agreed to sell Claire one of his blue and white ones. The same routine the Wilson family went through with *Tippy* as they had done previously with *Tuppy*, another female too. But calamity struck again and this new darling died within six months for no apparent reason. Milton made the comment that perhaps it was because she was already an old bird when they bought her.

The last of their three budgies was named *Chippy* and she lasted much longer than her predecessors. In fact, she was still alive when Claire left to go to London a few years later. But *Chippy* was really her pet. As soon as Claire arrived home from school, Olivia told her that her new pet would sit on her perch and "go all google-eyed", until Claire took her out of her cage and placed the bird onto her shoulder. Claire's mum said as soon as she opened the metal gate to their driveway, *Chippy* knew it was her and stared into space until Claire approached her cage to let her out.

Then of course there was the story of the pet mice that Danny and Claire had. She had a white mouse and Danny had bought two brown mice. What he didn't know was that they were of different sexes and started breeding. The children kept their mice in the garage, as Milton preferred to leave his car in the driveway outside the scullery door. But after a while Danny's mice started to smell something terrible. The real reason was that he didn't bother to clean them out and eventually they died. But then Danny, mischievous Danny, sneakily murdered Claire's white mouse after his own had died. She knew it was Danny as he dropped enough hints about his wicked action, but when she appealed to her mum for some form of retribution against her brother, Olivia refused to take sides. "It's your problem William. You are supposed to be a big boy now and should accept that maybe your mouse has died instead of accusing your brother."

Was there no justice in this world? Claire thought. She wanted to slap Danny across the face but knew full well that he would scream blue murder and she would be the one to be blamed. So she had to simply accept the fact that in no way could she trust her bother Danny ever again. However, Claire was left with *Beauty*, her English-Butterfly pet rabbit, and of course *Chippy*. Quite enough of a handful for her at the time, as her gender dysphoria was getting bad again.

The pure frustration Claire experienced at not developing like other girls at school caused her to constantly cry her eyes out each night when she climbed into bed. It was so unfair. Why did God leave her like this, hanging off the edge of a cliff? She constantly prayed for him to change her overnight into a proper girl, only to find the next morning that her prayers had not been answered. Was she to spend the rest of her life in frustration? Would God ever listen to her? Was there a God at all? But yet the priests were convinced that there was a loving God and surely their prayers were answered weren't they? Or was it all in the mind? Maybe she was going mad and needed some medical help, but who could help her? Didn't the few stories she had read, say that all those who thought they were in the wrong body were mad? Maybe her parents thought she was going mad? Why was she here after all? So many questions Claire asked herself in her midnight stupor, for which she had no answers.

There was another matter which was upsetting her around this time too, that of her dad's bigotry. Milton's attitude to her reading what she wanted was becoming a sore point to him. He always wanted to know what books she had borrowed from the public library, all of which he disapproved of, even if they were mainly novels. She often borrowed adventure stories but her dad considered these as 'flights of fancy'. "No use at all!" he would declare. All they would do would be to give her ideas about other lands and people, all inferior to England.

Claire's dad also disapproved of the music she listened to. While Claire liked the sound of dance band music, her dad constantly stressed that there were plenty of British bands to listen to instead of the American ones she preferred. Yes she did like to listen to the strains of Victor Sylvester and his Orchestra, but her dad frowned upon her selection of Count Basie and his Orchestra, Lionel Hampton, and such as Duke Ellington and his Orchestra too. The reason for Milton's dislike was that those artists did not have white faces. Her father was gradually coming to the opinion that she liked the music of what he referred to as *Black Men*. This attitude drove Claire wild. It was just the same as whenever a Jewish artist appeared on television. Milton would remind her time and time again that they were Jewish. So, in order to avoid friction with her dad, she had to downplay her choices in music. When she said she liked to listen to Beethoven, or Schubert, Delibes, Tchaikovsky or Mozart, he frowned in disgust as they were not British. In the case of many of her favorite composers, who happened to have been born in Germany, Claire was berated for choosing those who were from an enemy of Great Britain. It appeared to Claire that the hatred her father had engendered during the Second World War against the Germans. His hatred of the Irish over many years, was still in evidence too. However, in order not to anger him, she decided that she should assume that his attitude might change at some point in the future. But again, she wondered if it ever would.

25

Choosing a Career

Claire was so very scared that if her dad so decided, there was a strong possibility he could have her committed to *Menston Lunatic Asylum*. This was a strong fear she had when she was at home with her parents. She had made so many unintentional mistakes in her short life so far that she felt it only needed one major gaff regarding her gender and she would be in what was known as 'the dark green van' to the 'funny farm'. So much was this thought uppermost in Claire's mind that every time she heard a vehicle stop outside the house, she would rush to the window expecting to see two men coming through the gate carrying a straight-jacket. As it was, the only green van that ever drove into her end of the street, and called at their house was the *Rington's Tea* van. The Wilsons always drank *Rington's Tea* of course.

The expectation of the men from *Menston Lunatic Asylum* coming for her was becoming somewhat of a recurrent nightmare, however, and she prayed to all the saints she knew to intercede on her behalf to Almighty God. She wanted them to plead for her to wake up one morning to discover that she had become a proper girl like all the others in her class. All this was despite the fact that in her miniscule bedroom opposite her bed, high up on the wall, she had pictures of the Sacred Heart of Jesus and the Sacred Heart of Mary. Claire never gave a thought at the time to the fact that they looked like Italians. At that age she was not aware of the real historical fact that if they existed at all, they would have been Jewish. Everything in the Church was geared to Jesus Christ being the founder of their Holy Roman Catholic faith. He had appointed Saint Peter as the first pope, and that was that. End of story as far as the Church was concerned. It wasn't until many years later in her retirement that research for her PhD showed that none of this was historically true. But then, that is another story altogether.

As Claire entered her bedroom she had a cream-colored plastic holy water stoop with a fluorescent crucifix over it, near the door and she would bless herself going in and out of the room. She had obtained permission from one of the priests at St Brigid's to fill a small bottle with holy water from the large earthenware jar in the church porch. On the wall of her bedroom she had holy cards pinned to the wall at the side of her black-painted plywood dressing table. These holy pictures were of some of her favorite saints; Gemma Galgani and Maria Goretti in particular, but also at this stage she was adding holy cards of Passionist saints, St Paul of the Cross, St Vincent Strambi, Blessed Dominic Barberi and Blessed Gabriel Posenti. Claire could not understand why there were no women saints among the Passionists, only men. At that time Gemma Galgani and Maria Goretti had not been claimed as Passionist postulants, only many years later were these young girls added to the list of Passionist saints. Over her bed Claire had always had a crucifix about 20 cm high, but she had added behind it a large cross, cut from some Masonite and had painted it black. Claire thought it looked impressive.

When her mum had persuaded Milton that it would break some of the ice between himself and 'his eldest son' if he was to redecorate the bedroom for 'him', Claire had been allowed to choose the wallpaper herself and had helped her dad to apply it by pasting the sheets before he hung them. The window wall and the wall behind her bed were to be in maroon with a crisscross pattern of vine leaves in silver, and the side walls were to be papered with a design in pale yellow, with silver stripes from top to bottom. Today Claire cringes in horror at her former choice, but then, the world looked different in those days before she became a student at Aireborough College of Art.

As a result of the constant thoughts of her enigma, her gender dysphoria, her school results at the end of term were tumbling further and further downhill. In fact, by the time she completed the mock GCE exams she was placed second equal at the bottom of the class. Considering she had been a model pupil when she started at Clark's College and had been top in her class only three years earlier, she was ashamed of herself but found it very difficult to rise to the occasion. Claire was constantly thinking of her future as a girl forced to dress as a boy. How was she going to cope? She almost became a nervous wreck with lack of sleep frustrated over her gender. While she looked forward to going to bed each evening, it was mainly because she could be herself behind a closed door. Having been described as a 'day-dreamer' at both primary and high schools, she certainly lived up to her name inside her private cell of a room.

Looking back on those months and years, Claire fully believes that if any child feels that they are living their lives in the opposite gender to that which they believe they should be, then they ought to be allowed the freedom to seek medical and psychological advice. In later years, as she studied her condition, especially as the world entered the 21st century, she was aware of many cases worldwide which had been brought to the attention of the media. But the backlash, especially of fundamentalist Christians and Muslims has been such that murder has been threatened, and in one or two cases carried out without the perpetrators being brought to justice. She recalled one instance in the USA where a mother allowed her 11-year-old 'son' to wear girls' clothes because he was convinced in his own mind that he was a girl, and the school even accepted the situation. But once the matter had been covered by a local newspaper, all Hell had broken loose, and the parents were threatened by some local Pentecostal Christians, Roman Catholics, Episcopalians and Baptists. As a result, the family had to sell up and move to another district in fear of their lives. Some of the comments made by the fundamentalists were that God had created the child a boy and the parents had no right to overrule God's decision in allowing their son to dress as a girl. The parents in this case were likened to Satan by the Christians. Religious fundamentalism was fast becoming a poison in Claire's view, all caused by a misunderstanding of 'The Bible'.

In the GCE exams, which Claire took in 1956, she passed the subjects of Art, French, English Language, Mathematics and Geography. In her conversational French examination she sat opposite the examiner and chatted to her quite easily. She was later told that she had been awarded the highest mark in the school in French and was highly commended for her colloquial conversation. Achieving these results meant that an entry to the College of Art was assured as they required all entrants to have five subjects at 'O' level, which included Art of course, and that was her favorite subject.

But prior to achieving this result, Claire had had to endure a terrible period with her father over her future career. It came about when her father asked 'his son' what 'he' wanted to do after leaving school. Claire told him that she wanted to be a ballet dancer as she just loved ballet. "You want to do what?" he asked her, his red nose shining like a beacon and saliva from his mouth spitting in all directions.

"I want to be a ballet dancer."

"You have to be out of your tiny twisted mind. If I let you join all those pansies prance around the stage, we would be the laughing stock of all the neighbors, not to mention our family. No William, there is no way I am going to let you insult me by becoming a bloody pansy dancer. So you can put that idea right out of your stupid twisted mind."

"But why daddy, I don't see why? I love ballet. Kirsty goes to ballet school why can't I? It just isn't fair."

"Because I'm telling you! You are not going to do ballet, and that's final. Kirsty's a girl and girls do ballet, boys don't. No son of mine is going to be a poofter ballet dancer. That's the end of it." Claire was told to think again.

She was devastated, and was about to remind her father that she was a girl and not a boy. But then she remembered that if he was at home when ballet came on TV, he would switch the channel over for another, or switch the set off entirely. Often he repeated his time-honored phrase; "I don't want to watch those pansies frolicking around the bloody stage." Adding that in his view they were not real men but poofters.

Two weeks later she told her father that her next choice of career was to be a fashion designer and, although quaking in her shoes at having to mention it, she plucked up enough courage and did so. "Designing what?" he asked her point blank, staring at her.

"Well, women's and children's clothes of course," as though it was quite natural to make such a choice. Claire was encouraged by the fact that she had been designing clothes most Sunday afternoons, as she leaned over a board on her bed. She used photographs of fashion models in her mum's magazines as guides and loved the idea of being able to create new styles on tracing-paper overlays. But following the previous occasion when she had discussed a career with her dad, she was nervous and expected some adverse reaction from him. When she outlined in greater detail what she would like to do, her father went red in the face and he spluttered angrily: "What did you bloody say – you want to design what?" He blurted at her, saliva dripping from his mouth as he spoke.

"Women's and children's clothes." Claire meekly repeated.

"Are you going stark raving mad?" He asked her, his eyes almost popping out of his head. "That's women's work. Designing women's clothes is for women unless you include the likes of Christian Dior and his pansy boys. No, most certainly not. It is out of the question. I will not have a son of mine working with poofters. We'd be the ridicule of the neighborhood."

Claire was once again about to point out to her dad that she was a girl but thought better of it as his temper was already steaming on boiling point. She did not want him to take out his belt as he had done many times in the past, and 'lather' her backside, as he termed it. Claire was told to think again as he walked away and out through the scullery into the garden slamming the door behind him. Olivia had heard the conversation: "Why do you have to make your daddy so angry, William? He's only trying to help you."

"I'm not trying to make him angry, but he will not let me do what I want to do for a career."

"Your daddy knows what's best for you William. You don't have to go against him all the time."

"I don't. It's just that whatever I want to be, he says it is out of the question."

"The trouble, William, is that you are choosing jobs that are for girls and not the sort of boy that your daddy wants you to be. I think I know how your mind thinks but he has completely wiped out of his mind the way you were born."

"So why don't you remind him mummy?"

"Simply because if I do he is likely to blow his top and create mayhem. Your daddy has a violent temper, as if you didn't know. There is no saying what he might do if I remind him of how you were born. He is of the fixed idea that if you do a man's job, you will turn out to be a normal man. That is what the specialists told us when you were a baby."

That's a load of bull-shit! Claire muttered under her breath as she walked away. Although she was sure that her mum heard her, she didn't carry on the conversation.

So, Claire had to really think hard about her third choice of career. It was obvious that her previous selections were chosen from a girl's point of view. To her this was natural, but as her father had insisted from birth that she was to be reared as a boy, her choices of career did not fit his idea of what he wanted 'his son' to be in life. So Claire's third choice of career was carefully selected as it could be carried out by both men and women equally, albeit that at that time in the British workforce most positions were held by men.

So Claire told her father that her next choice was to be a graphic designer. With growing fear in her heart she wondered how he could possibly object this time. But true to form, her choice of career did not meet with his approval. Her dad's objection this time revolved around the life of someone he knew, who was classed as a 'commercial artist', but who her dad regarded as a complete failure because he and his wife still lived in a terrace house off Woodthorpe Moor and didn't drive a car. He was referring to the artist, Bertram Wade, who designed his 'works' letterheads and brochures. In Milton's opinion Bertie Wade did not earn much money, and *ipso facto*, was a pauper. Bertie was always penniless, and at the beckon call of people like Milton who saw himself as a benevolent philanthropist. Claire's dad's objection to her becoming a commercial artist like Bertie was that she would always be 'on the scrounge', and would not make much money. He had fixed ideas, like so many people, as to who made the most money and earned the most respect. It wasn't those who had university degrees or qualifications but the hard-core of business people who could make money.

It had become blatantly obvious by this time that her dad objected to every potential career that Claire chose. She knew that she was good at art and that her art mistress Miss Carstairs had reported that she had a great imagination and design sense and would do well in one of the artistic professions. She was encouraging Claire to enroll at Aireborough College of Art, but Milton's knowledge of suitable professions was very limited. His mind was clouded by the fact that most of the people working in the art field belonged to the category he described as 'arty-farty', and most of those were his dreaded 'poofters'. Claire was far more intelligent and skilled than her dad would admit to, because her school certificate results were far in excess of those that he had ever achieved. In fact, she knew that her dad had never been to a high school. That had been the privilege of his older brother Clive. If truth be known, she had the feeling that her dad was jealous of her academic achievements and artistic skills and he could not see 'his son' in any position higher than he would have for himself. Consequently, he had suggested Claire could be a draftsman as he had been, or become a surveyor designing buildings. Of course, she knew that being a draftsman was way below her capabilities and as far as being a surveyor, she knew that surveyors did not design buildings, they measured them or measured land. Her dad really did not know the difference, but she did, and she didn't see her doing anything like that. What really bothered Claire was that although her mum had been to high school and secretarial college, albeit in the commercial section of Clark's College, she did not give 'her son' any support whatsoever to go on to study for a degree. Milton would not have agreed to this anyway as he believed all academic graduates to be losers.

26

The Office

About three weeks later, Milton arrived home from work late one afternoon and before Olivia had put the dinner on the table, he instructed Claire to find a piece of unlined paper and a pen as he was going to dictate a letter to her. Naturally she was puzzled as he had not said to whom it was to be addressed at that point or, more importantly, what the letter was about. Speaking to his wife quietly he told her he had seen an advertisement in the *Yorkshire Post* that morning for an *architect's assistant* and he decided that as architects were a class apart and obviously earned lots of money, 'William' should start at the bottom as an articled clerk and work 'his' way up. Milton had fixed ideas on everything, a fact that has previously been outlined. So Claire's dad knew what was best for her. She, 'his son', was absolutely useless, so how could she know what her future held. In his own words he had sweated and toiled to put her through a private high school and he was damned if she was going to spoil his plans for her future. He had decided that he didn't want 'his poofter son working in his own business as that was for real men, and it transpired a few years later that Danny and Gerry had been chosen by him to eventually take over his business. That's why he chose their first jobs for them too – Danny working on the factory floor in *Yorkshire Copper Works* like Milton had done in his youth, and Gerry in another engineering workshop, *Hudson Verity*, where Milton had also worked for a time. He had contacts and that was the way to carry out good business, especially when it came to finding jobs for his heirs.

But that particular afternoon Claire had to write exactly what her dad told her to write. There was to be no variations allowed as he knew how to write letters – she didn't. He dismissed the fact that at Clark's College, the senior students had been practicing writing letters for potential jobs for the last month, during their English classes. But Milton's attitude was that teachers knew nothing about the 'real' world and were not capable of teaching their students how to write effective letters for jobs. He regarded the guide letters in the books in high schools as equally useless, as they too had been written by academics. So Claire had to write word for word what her dad dictated to her, as though it was written by her, and in it she was to ask for an interview. Fifteen years later, Claire was to find the letter she had written and she had to laugh at its archaic language. The letter Milton dictated in essence was more like those composed in the nineteen-twenties rather than the nineteen-fifties. So different to those Claire and her fellow students had been learning to write at school. But she duly complied with her father's wishes, as to do otherwise would raise his temper enormously. She had encountered this so often, growing up into adulthood. "Now sign it. I presume you are capable of signing your own bloody name."

"Of course I can, and please don't swear at me daddy."

"Don't you be cheeky to your daddy, he's only trying to help you," said Olivia as she walked into the room with some knives and forks and laid the pile of bone-handled metal at Claire's side. "You've some room to talk, writing dirty filthy words on lamp posts." Would her parents ever forget that unfortunate incident many years previously?

"But supposing I don't like the job. I wanted to go to the College of Art and Miss Carstairs says I could be very successful in one of the artistic professions."

"Look know-all, she doesn't know you like I do. I will not have you mixing with poofters at that arty-farty place. I have just about had it with you and your idiotic ideas. Do I make myself clear?"

"But dad…"

"There's no 'but dad' about it my lad, you will do as I say or you're out that door. You are not too old for me to take my belt to you again and I mean what I say. You will do exactly what I want you to do as I know better than anyone else. Is that understood for the last time?"

Claire nodded, holding back tears. But yet if she was successful in getting the job her dad had seen in the paper, then it might give her some sort of independence. Perhaps she might be able to earn enough money to do what she really wanted eventually. New possibilities opened up in her mind at that point and she became compliant.

The problem in Claire's psychological development, however, was that she knew for definite that she was female, and not the male that everyone assumed, because of what her dad had told the registrar at her birth. So when it came to what she was to wear for her first job interview her mum had her dressed in a shirt with a separate collar which Olivia had bought for her from Raefe Bullimer's gentleman's outfitters next to the National Bank in Station Road. The collar had to be attached to the shirt with collar-studs and Claire hated this. She had never worn anything so uncomfortable in her life. Olivia had bought 'William' a pair of beige trousers and a tweed jacket as 'his' advance Christmas present and a gaudy red, white, gray and yellow tie. The top coat Claire was to wear, as the weather was still very chilly, was to be a navy blue serge hand-me-down from 'Uncle Edwin' next door. The top coat dwarfed her. It is a wonder they didn't insist she wear a bowler hat like Edwin did too.

After traveling on the tram down to the city center, Claire walked up from City Square carrying her art portfolio to the interview with Mr Henry Worthing, ARIBA, chartered architect. His office was a rather dingy affair in a dirty red brick building in the same street as the College of Art. Mr Worthing looked at all her paintings with interest. "With paintings such as these, William you could be anything you want, a top commercial artist or even a fashion designer, why have you chosen architecture?"

"Well sir, it was my father's suggestion."

"Oh I see, and do you know much about architecture?"

"Not much sir, only what I have learned from school, and my dad says architects do drawings of buildings like surveyors and draftsmen."

"Well, I am afraid your dear father doesn't understand very much about the professions. Draftsmen produce drawing of technical items, machinery and the like. Surveyors do just that – survey. In the building industry there are building surveyors who measure buildings and produce drawings of them, but we do that for ourselves here. Quantity surveyors measure buildings and calculate their costs. So there's a lot more to it than you might have understood, or that your father has led you to believe. However, let's have a look through a few more of your drawings, shall we?"

From her art work, Mr Worthing selected a couple of paintings which had buildings in them and said he saw her potential. Especially that she could illustrate buildings very well in perspective. He asked if she had ever done any technical drawing and Claire explained that at Clark's College there were limited opportunities for this.

"No matter," he said, "We architects don't do much in the way of technical drawings, so it would not have been much of an advantage to you I suppose, except to learn how to work at a drawing board and produce details."

Claire was pleased to learn this as it deflated her dad's ideas as to the work of an architect. At the end of the interview, which she didn't really like, as Mr Worthing was a smoker and puffed cigarette smoke around constantly, Claire looked forward to getting out into some fresh air. Mr Worthing said he would let her know within a few days as he had some other people to interview.

Four days later, a letter in a pale blue envelope arrived addressed to Mr W. Wilson. By the time Claire had arrived home from school, the letter had been opened by Milton at lunchtime and then placed back in its envelope. On being summoned into the dining room, she was presented with the letter, which her dad had removed from the envelope and unfolded for her to read.

Milton was delighted that his letter had won 'his son' the job but Olivia reminded him that it might have been 'William's' art work and presentation that had perhaps been the deciding factor.

"Nonsense," Milton said, "If he hadn't written down what I told him, then he would not have got the job. He's only a boy. He has to learn what's right as I keep on telling him."

Olivia bit her lip and went very quiet. Her husband was always right – of course.

Mr Worthing's letterhead was very official-looking, the lettering being in a scrolled font. It thanked Claire for attending the interview and Mr Worthing said he could offer her the position of architect's assistant for a probationary period of six months at £2 a week. At the interview Mr Worthing had told her that the title 'articled clerk' no longer existed and she was to be paid a wage instead. She had to write back and accept the position by return and state when she could start in his office. Milton once again told her to get pen and paper and he would dictate a suitable letter in reply. Claire saw this as total interference in her capabilities, but she knew the consequences of objecting and complied obediently. "You know you are very lucky that he is going to pay you to work for him?" commented her father, obviously still believing that many architects still took on articled clerks. She wondered how many years it would take for her father to change his opinion, if ever.

"Mr Worthing told me that articled clerks no longer existed in architecture, that that practice was outdated."

"William, will you stop giving me your views. You know absolutely nothing about the business world and must be guided by me in everything as you are completely useless. If I tell you that you are lucky to be paid a minimum wage, then you must accept the fact. No 'ifs or buts'. Most architects have articled clerks. Mr Worthing obviously doesn't know this as he is only a relatively young man." Claire had been told. Her dad was always right – and that was a fact.

Claire allowed herself a two-week break to go with her family for their annual summer holidays to Scarborough and gave Mr Worthing a particular day on which she would present herself at his office at 9 O'clock on the Monday morning mentioned in her reply.

Mr Worthing had quite a reputation as the 'Renaissance Architect of the North' she was later told, but doubted it as his buildings seemed to be modeled on houses from the Cotswolds in the south of England, not exactly the same as traditional houses in Yorkshire. Nevertheless, he was successful in his own right, and was later to become a Fellow of the Royal Institute of British Architects. Claire was to join his office which was then situated on the top floor of a former terrace house in Vernon Street, right opposite the side door of the School of Architecture and obliquely up from the main entrance to the College of Art. The ground floor was taken up by some men selling second-hand gas stoves, and on the first floor were the offices of a local firm selling fire extinguishers. The staff of Henry Worthing's architectural practice had to climb four flights of steps to get to the rather pokey landing which had a door to the right into the ladies toilet, and opposite to the secretary's room with a reception bench covered in gray linoleum. *Not exactly salubrious*, Claire thought. But it was a job.

On her first day in the office she was fitted out with a very starched white smock to wear over her clothes. This was meant to protect the fabric from pencil dust and the dirt that seemed to be everywhere. Mr Worthing didn't wear a smock as he was the boss. He wore a tailored Saville Row suit with a flared waist to the jacket, and rather effeminately held a cigarette between his fingers just about all of the time. Through the fog of cigarette smoke constantly around his face, one could make out a pair of spectacles with round frames to the lenses. As already hinted, Mr Worthing reeked of tobacco and Claire had to get used to holding her breath when he was near. Fortunately, he seemed to spend most of his time in his own office at the end of the corridor, it being his private domain. At his huge leather-inlaid desk, which he occupied infrequently, he sat in a leather chair, smoking. When he needed to sketch anything, he sat on a high stool at a bench on which his drawing board was placed, in front of the window. His walls were covered in the photographs of some of the houses he had designed, and on the wall opposite the window he had a series of William Russell prints of female nudes in Italian settings. Claire was later to be told that her boss was also a 'gentleman farmer' from Collingsby. His architectural practice was often supported by the insertion of funds from his two farms, especially the milk from his pedigree Friesian dairy herd.

Next to Mr Worthing's room was a tiny room with a desk and a drawing board, the domain of Mr Harvey Peterson, LRIBA of Linton He was Mr Worthing's first partner, and was also a smoker. He too seemed to have a fog permanently surrounding his head.

In the drawing office, which took up most of the upper floor, a long bench stretched the length of the wall facing the street. Next to the small window between Mr Peterson's office and this room was the drawing board and adjacent green-painted metal table of the newest partner, Mr Gerald Robinson. The drawing board at the opposite end of the long bench to Mr Robinson's drawing board, was that of the first assistant Vernon Clarkson, a young man who seemed to spend most of his time telling jokes, most of which were in Claire's view quite rude. This drawing office was to be her work place, using the drawing board next to Mr Robinson.

Claire's job as junior assistant was to collect the morning papers, the *Daily Mirror* for Mr Worthing, the *Daily Telegraph* for Mr Peterson and the *Daily Express* for Mr Robinson. Mid-morning she was to make milky coffee and take it to every person in the office, and in the afternoon she had to make tea. To heat up the milk in a pan she had to use a gas ring on the floor in reception, where the secretary sat typing. The latter didn't seem to do anything apart from typing, and doing her make-up. That was Betty.

At lunch time Claire was generally called upon to go to the shops to buy any food that the staff required for their mid-day meal. Mr Worthing was in the habit of taking a packed lunch, made up for him by his neighbor Mrs Coles who, Claire discovered many years later, shared an adjoining door to Mr Worthing's living room. It appeared that the two of them were very friendly.

Mr Peterson also took a packed lunch prepared for him by his dear wife, and only occasionally asked Claire to buy him a tomato or an apple, when his wife had forgotten to buy some. In complete contrast, Mr Robinson wanted her to buy everything he ate at lunchtime. This generally comprised either a pork pie, which he often jokingly referred to as a 'porco piario', or a mold of brawn, a tomato, a buttered bread cake and an apple or a custard tart. Vern took his own packed lunch too, made up by his mam. Claire took a packed lunch most of the time as she could not afford to buy anything on her small wage. She had to give her mum her £2 every Friday and she would give her back ten shillings, from which Claire had to pay her own tram fares and anything else she needed during the week. This was the period when a tram fare into the city center was only twopence. A far cry from today's prices of course, although the trams were discontinued eventually to be replaced by buses belching diesel fumes from their exhausts.

Claire's first 'architectural' duties were to learn how to use the printing machine in a rear store room, and with this to print drawings on tracing paper or tracing cloth. The printing machine was a rather antiquated contraption and it stunk of ammonia. She had to lay the tracing paper over a sheet of yellow-colored paper and lay the two sheets around a glass drum, hold them in with a thick piece of material, switch on the machine and wait an appropriate development time. Then she had to place the rolled up piece of paper into a long wooden box in which there was a tray of ammonia. It didn't take long for her to feel ill and, at the suggestion of his staff, Mr Worthing decided to update and bought a more modern machine. This new machine functioned on what was called a semi-dryline process and Claire had to feed the tracing paper and lemon-colored paper together into the base of a revolving drum after switching the machine on and turning a dial for the length of development time. When it came out, the lemon-colored paper had turned to white and she then had to feed it through some rollers at the top which picked up liquid from a tray. As she peeled the paper from the rollers it was very damp and she had to peg the print up on some wires strung across the room, to allow it to dry. This generally took about half an hour, ready to be sent in the post or taken somewhere by a member of staff. After the first week getting used to her mundane tasks, which seemed like forever, she was given the chance to do some drawing at a drawing board. At long last, some real work.

One morning Mr Worthing called Claire over to the drawing board closest to the one Mr Robinson used. He pinned a print of an old building in Park Row onto the board and then a piece of plain tracing paper over it. He then showed her by example what he wanted her to trace through from the drawing below. The problem was that she could not reach the upper section of the drawing board as she was not tall enough. To remedy the problem Vernon took out a wooden platform from under the bench for her to stand on. Ahah! Now she could reach the whole of the drawing and started work immediately much to her immense satisfaction. The traced drawing took two days to finish and Mr Worthing then took over again and added some straight lines to the classical building. The drawing was of the front elevation of a department store known as Marshall & Snelgrove and Mr Worthing, as their architect, had been commissioned to add another three stories using a façade treatment known as curtain walling. It was a system of construction that did not respect tradition but was the latest trend and was cheap. Many years later when Claire lived again in Aireborough for a short time, the building which she had previously traced had been demolished and a new modern building clad in granite erected in its place. Such was the price of progress.

27

The Religious Life

During Claire's first year in Mr Worthing's office, she once again felt a call to the religious life. The atmosphere at home in Micklegate had been so volatile with her father that she could not stand living under the same roof as him. Every meal time there were arguments and criticism of her by him. Her mother had seen some *Catholic Truth Society* booklets about the lives of the saints on the chair at the side of Claire's bed, and had told Milton. As a result he had instructed his wife to confiscate all 'William's'religious books and burn them. Claire was distraught and devastated at this attack on her liberty and freedom to read whatever she liked, especially the lives of the saints. She was seventeen years old for goodness sakes, why couldn't she read what she liked? Claire had had enough and decided to leave home. In this she felt she had no choice. She had to make a stand against her father's discrimination, bigotry and mental cruelty.

Claire had been planning the move for a few days and had secreted clothes and essentials out of her room in a briefcase her parents had bought her. Her dad having told her that as she was now working in business, she should have a briefcase. That had been their first Christmas present that year, and it had been useful to transfer some of her clothes to the office. There she had hidden the clothes in the store room, and on the following Friday she planned to leave. Instead of going home after work, she visited St Brigid's presbytery and spoke to Fr Killen. He was very understanding and after a while consulted with the parish priest Canon Cordingley. They did not call Milton or Olivia, which with hindsight they should have done, but decided to ring the Passionist monastery in Ilkley. It was about 6 pm when it was suggested that she catch a tram into town and then take the Ilkley bus from the Wellington Street bus station used by the *West Yorkshire Road Car Company*. From the bus stop in Ilkley town center Claire then had to walk down over the bridge and up the hill on the other side, to the Monastery of St Paul. By the time she arrived, it was about 9.30 pm and everything was being bathed in the enveloping darkness. Nervously Claire rang the bell adjacent to the main entrance door, with its iron straps and heavy bolts. A monk, wearing a black habit, cloak and skull cap opened the great door for her to enter, and then greeted her with much warmth. He took her bag from her and ushered her into a huge refectory where she was given a hot meal, saved for her by Brother Jerome, the cook.

By the time she was finishing the apricot crumble, smothered in custard, a more senior monk arrived and sat opposite her. This was Fr Peter, the one who supervised the ones in training, the *confratii*. He listened to Claire's story and she was offered a room in which to stay while things were sorted out at home. It should be remembered here that although Claire knew herself to be a girl, she was dressed as a boy and had trained herself in the speech and mannerisms of young men. She had had to do this to survive in what she was slowly coming to accept was a hostile world. She had to play by their rules. At this stage in her young life she felt she had no choice.

So Claire stayed at St Paul's Monastery for about two weeks, traveling on the bus into Aireborough every day to go to work, and then back again at night to the monastery. While she was there she became friendly with one of the young monastics in training, Confrater Ricardo, known by his brother monks as "Ricky." As it was summer, Ricky and 'William' often went for a walk after the evening meal to sit under a tree or on a convenient bench, either on one of the moorland tracks or in the open-air chapel. The 'chapel' was very quiet and had carved stone *Stations of the Cross* at the perimeter of a graveled 'nave'. On the second Saturday that she was staying at the monastery Ricky and "William" went for a walk through some of the surrounding paddocks when the skies opened and a thunderstorm forced them to shelter under a huge Sycamore tree. Sitting there under the spread of multi-fingered leaves they chatted about so many things, especially about the Passionists and what was expected of the students. That evening she was invited into the Confrater's common room and was totally amazed to see them jiving to the latest pop tunes. This was indeed an eye opener. She had thought that people in religious orders were different from those in the outside world, only to discover that this was not the case at all. Some of them smoked cigarettes and swore frequently, not the sort of persons she chose to associate with, given a choice in the matter.

Unknown to Claire, her mother had been ringing Mr Robinson in the office every few days to ask him to persuade her to go back home. On Claire's part there was one stipulation which she outlined most clearly, that if she was to return home to Micklegate, her dad should stop poking fun at her with a mouth full of criticism. With these demands eventually met, Claire agreed to return home to her mother's hugs and the cool distance of her dad. Danny and Gerry did not know what to make of it all, so remained quiet. Olivia had advised Claire to try to make life a little easier for her dad and to involve herself with the normal activities of other teenagers in Micklegate.

Having been invited to join members of Micklegate Young Conservatives to attend a dance in Bramhope, an outer suburb of Aireborough, Claire accepted knowing that her father would be pleased. But, traveling in the back of a small van without windows, they had to collect a young man reeking of cigarettes from the village of Scarcroft and, by the time they picked him up and had him join them, they all felt like sardines in a tin can. Claire was beginning to feel nauseous and claustrophobic, especially breathing in the stale cigarette smoke still clinging to the clothes of her companions. So much so that by the time the van arrived outside the village hall in Bramhope, where the dance was being held, she felt decidedly ill. At this time also, Claire was going through yet another of her occasional periods of intense religious conviction. While she experienced and really enjoyed seeing and being with so many other young women, dressed as she would loved to have been herself, had her father not have registered her as a boy at birth, she allowed her religiosity to overrule her head and sought quietness, instead of public dancing and loud music.

After standing by the back wall in the dance hall for a short time she quietly left. Having been given the keys to the van, she sought solace sitting in the back of the van ready to go home. Apart from concentrating on her religious aspirations, she was turned off by all the cigarette smoke, which made her feel so nauseous, in mind and in body. Also Claire was hung up on her gender problem too. She thought if she turned her attention to her Catholic faith, the constant thoughts of being a woman might vanish. Surely these would not be with her all her life? At this stage in her understanding of gender dysphoria, some of the medical books she sought in the central library in Aireborough City center talked of it as being a psychological illness. That being so, Claire was convinced that she was ill and needed the peace and quiet of the cloister to restore her to some semblance of equilibrium.

By mid-year, she had decided to tell her mum that her love of the religious life had not waned, contrary to the assumptions of both parents. Consequently, with the help from Fr Killen, one of the curates at St Brigid's, and a visit to the Father Provincial at the Minsterfield Monastery in Northumberland, she was able to get a placement at a College for 'Late Vocations' at East Leigh, near London, in the south of England.

Claire's parents, upon being told 'their son' had been accepted at a college to become a priest, realized that they had lost the argument. As a result they no longer fought the issue, simply ignoring it as though it was invisible.

But the morning soon arrived for Claire to leave home in Micklegate to travel to the south of England. Her dad ignored her by going to work at his usual time without even saying goodbye and her mum, having made 'her son' some breakfast, had obviously been told not to offer 'him' any consolation. Olivia didn't even have enough love or decency to go to the scullery door to see Claire off. Such was the gnarled relationship and lack of love

Claire thought her mother had for her offspring. Olivia had been ordered by her husband to remain seated in her lounge chair by the fireside. This was to be their defiance against the Church for stealing 'their son'.

Claire went over to her mum to give her a kiss but Olivia turned the opposite way, offering a cold shoulder instead. "Bye mum." Claire muttered in sadness as she stared at her mother. "I'll write to you."

There was no answer. So Claire dragged her huge suitcase down the back steps to the drive way and struggled with it along to the corner of the street where Sandy Peth met Hawkhill Drive and across the road to the tram stop. She was convinced that neither of her parents had any inkling of what she was going through, or even any compassion for the enigma that she struggled with.

Alighting in City Square, Claire trudged across to Central Station where the Hendersons were seeing their son Martin off to the same college. Mr and Mrs Henderson had heard from their son about the objections of Claire's parents. So they gave her, in the guise of 'William' the assuring hugs that had been missing. The two boys, Martin and 'William', sat opposite each other in the railway carriage as they traveled down to Kings Cross in London.

Although Claire did well academically at Fisher House in East Leigh, the acute problems she constantly experienced with her gender were making her very restless and insecure. One particular evening, it was a saint's feast day; Claire had been at a party in one of the adjacent dormitory houses, when she could stand it no longer. She left the gathering which was in full swing in one of the common rooms, and where just about everyone was on the brink of inebriation. Stepping into the wind and drenching rain she knelt beneath a statue of *Our Lady* set on a small plinth. Kneeling there, crying her eyes out and speaking aloud her heart-bleeding questions, she earnestly pleaded for help and guidance on what she was supposed to do with her life. The wind and the penetrating rain dulled her surroundings, but as usual there was no answer from the sky above the statue. There were no words of support or encouragement. There was no huge hand reaching down to cover her drooped shoulders with tenderness. Claire was utterly alone with her dysphoria. There was no one in the whole wide world that could help her, just the rain running down her neck and the cold breeze chilling her to the bone. That night she sobbed herself to sleep again, as usual.

She could not see her becoming a priest in the Passionist Order, even if she could disguise her true gender. So she decided she ought to step down to a lower level and become a lowly brother, working on her humility. Maybe she could smother her gender problem in work and prayer. With this in mind she approached the rector of the college, Fr Leon, SJ explaining to him that she didn't think she was cut out for the high life as a priest in the Passionist Order. Claire watched the look of surprise spread across Fr Leon's face, trying to discern his facial features through the permanent fog of cigarette smoke which surrounded his features. The rector said he would make a recommendation to the Father Provincial of the Passionists for her and suggested she be admitted to their noviciate as a potential lay-brother. Knowing that Claire was a worthy student, especially in advanced English, French and Latin, in which classes she was in the top five, Fr Leon said he was somewhat perplexed that she was quitting. Not because things were too difficult for her but for some other reason, which he could not fathom.

He stared hard at her through the smoke drifting from his mouth and nostrils, obviously trying to get her to disclose her real problem. Of course, she could not tell him of her gender dysphoria, that was a matter between God and her. Claire had read the story of one Italian girl who had approached her local parish priest and told him in private that she felt she was a boy. The young girl's pastor told her to stop such wicked thoughts immediately, and warned her that if she went ahead with any medical treatment she would be damned to Hell. She was found a few days later having hanged herself from the light cord in her bedroom. Claire vowed that this was not going to happen to her. But yet she still had to come to grips with her enigma and somehow find an answer, no matter how long it would take.

Shortly after the interview with Fr Leon, Claire went on a week's retreat to the Monastery of St Gabriel at the London suburb of Highfield. This was a really huge building and its corridors were tiled in what looked to her like marble, the noise of her shoes echoing off the walls and ceiling. The guest master allocated her a nice room on an upper floor overlooking the cemetery, with the parish hall at its far end. Claire went through intense brain-storming at St Gabriel's, but could see no future other than the architectural career that her dad had gotten her into. She knew nothing else as she had tried to work in a bank, the insurance industry, the teaching profession and now the religious life. She was thoroughly fed up and confused as to her future. Thankfully, suicide did not enter her thoughts, as if it had of done, the choice would have been easy for her in her state of mind.

So it was on the following Friday evening Claire leaned on the window sill of her cell looking down Highfield Hill toward the parish hall. She watched young couples stepping along the footpath to the hall where a dance was in progress. Instantly she became jealous of the girls who were wearing pretty dresses and she would really have loved to go dancing herself. This was a complete about-change from her feelings a few months previous, when she couldn't get away from a dance hall quick enough to enter the religious life.

What was she to do? How could her mind change so much? Was this part of the sickness she had read about? Shouldn't she beg to be seen by a specialist psychiatrist? Instead, she continued to lean against the window sill crying her heart out again, a common pastime of hers. Her prayers for guidance mingled with her tears, but instead of flying up to an imaginary 'Heaven', they dripped onto the stone window sill. In a trance, as usual seeing herself as a beautiful young woman tied up ready to be fed into the fires of the Inquisition, slowly the mist in her mind began to clear. It became obvious that all she could do was to go back home to her parents. In this frame of mind, she decided to write her mum a letter. Claire was aware that there was a new part-time course starting at the School of Architecture the following January, so maybe she could be accepted on that.

While she had a writing pad in her case, she realized that she had no envelopes. But rarely getting stuck with any such problem, she fashioned one out of the writing paper and glued it together. Without a postage stamp she mailed it home on the Sunday morning after Mass. Then, one morning mid-week, allowing time for her mother to get her letter, and when the community was in the quire, she silently slipped the latch on the front door of the Monastery and let herself out onto the street. Struggling with her huge suitcase, Claire walked down the hill to the underground rail station. This would take her to Kings Cross and the long train ride back to Aireborough.

Knowing that her parents had moved to a different house in one of the outer villages of Aireborough while she had been at the college, she caught a *West Yorkshire* bus in the Vicar Lane bus station and traveled out to what was to be her new home in Rigton, a village between Aireborough and Wetherton. After stepping off the bus at Rigton Bank Top she trudged up the hill in the pouring rain to her parents' new home, dragging her huge suitcase behind her. With her heart in her mouth she climbed the steep driveway to the back door, put down her suitcase beside her and knocked. After a minute or so, the door was opened by her mother. Claire stood there in the rain waiting for some response from her. "What are you doing here?" Her mum asked, rather abruptly, not making any attempt to step aside to let her inside out of the rain, "you're supposed to be at College." She added.

"Didn't you get my letter?"

"What letter, we haven't had any letter from you saying you were coming back home." Well this wasn't surprising as neither her dad nor her mum had said goodbye to her a few months earlier from where they had lived in Micklegate. While Claire had been in college her mum's spasmodic letters could have been said to be almost non-existent. Her 'eldest son' was not the flavor of the month in her husband's eyes. Claire having disobeyed the decisions he had made for her life. "You'd better come in and see what your daddy says when he gets home from work." It seems this was all the welcome Claire was going to get.

She stepped inside and left her suitcase in the hallway near the staircase. Olivia made a pot of tea. "I suppose you want a cup of tea, do you?" Olivia asked, followed by a nod of Claire's head. Olivia's 'daughter' explained to her why she had left East Leigh and that she was going to go back to the School of Architecture. "If they'll have you; you have left them twice already, maybe they won't have you back?" was the negativity she offered her as conversation. She did not ask Claire anything about her time at East Leigh or of any other matter. "If your daddy says you can come back home, then you can have the room at the side as it will be big enough to have a drawing board in there if you wish, provided they will accept you back at College."

The room needed some re-organizing as it had been used as a store room. Danny and Gerry had chosen to use the smaller bedrooms, Danny in the back room with its ship's bunk, and Gerald in a single bedroom to the front. But the large room was not a problem for Claire's imagination. She went into the sitting room and sat down to await her dad coming home from 'the works'. At about 5.30 pm Milton came through the kitchen door and Olivia told him that 'William' was back from College and sitting in the other room.

Contrary to what she had fully anticipated, her dad appeared pleased that she had returned home, assuming that she had turned her back on the religious life for good and might, at long last, settle down to a normal life as a young businessman. A life based on what he had planned for her future. Now, however, he seemed more concerned as to how she could have afforded to pay for the train fare up to Aireborough. Claire explained that the Father Provincial of the Passionists had sent her a £5 note with which to buy a train ticket to the Noviciate. Since she had decided to take a train up to the north of England instead, she used the money to buy her train and bus tickets. Milton took his wallet out of the inside pocket of his suit jacket, he always wore a suit even for gardening, and gave Claire a £5 note to reimburse the Father Provincial. "Now make sure he gets it, and let that be the end of the matter."

She assumed that that was her dad's way of brushing her religious ideas out of the window and that finally she might be seeing some sense after all. The following Monday Claire visited the School of Architecture and registered for the new full/part time course. Contrary to her mum's warnings, she was welcomed back to study there. The principal, Frank Wedgewood, was aware of her previous design work and was very understanding. It was not uncommon for students to leave their courses temporarily for work experience, or to follow another avenue toward their future. Mr Wedgewood was a wise older man and understood Claire's actions to some extent, even if he was lacking knowledge of her real dilemma, her gender dysphoria.

One day, the following week, her dad arrived home from work with a tubular steel drawing board frame and a contraption which engineers used instead of a tee-square. Claire was not used to this as it would not let her draw continuous long lines, only short ones. Milton thought that architects were behind the times, still using old-fashioned tee-squares. But she did not want to start an argument with her dad as he was bound to be critical of her views. Instead she worked out that, as her dad never entered her room, she would use a tee-square with a counter balance. So the device her dad had brought home for her was relegated to the top of the clothes closet.

28

A Robbery

After re-registering at the College of Art School of Architecture, Claire walked up Woodthorpe Lane and visited Mr Worthing's new office in Blenheim Terrace. He was glad to see her and offered to reinstate her in her former position. In this new building she was to be in charge of the drawing office at the rear of the top floor, overlooking the terraced streets of the Blenheim's. The two part-time courses on which she had previously been registered, had entailed her attending at the School of Architecture for two days a week and working in the office for three days. In contrast, the new course entailed six months full time at college and six months working in the office. This suited Claire better as it allowed her to focus on projects and not have her mind distracted as much as it had previously.

Attending the previous two courses, she had been the butt of jokes by other students as she was the youngest among them. This time Claire really hoped it would be different. Their 'studio' was the top balcony of a former Methodist church in which the School of Architecture was housed, although some of their art courses and almost all lectures were held in the main College of Art building. From their high-level studio, the sounds of the student's sonorous, although often discordant, chants echoed throughout the whole of the former church nave and they were constantly being told to be quiet by members of the staff walking down below. Often, when some of the students started singing, Claire would sing descant, and she thought the combined result was rather nice. But her days were ruined often by two other students: Raymond Burnley and Marvin Burneston. Ray used to antagonize her so often that she would lose her cool with him and of course, typical crazy man, he loved to get her riled. He was a bully, in fact, so was Marvin.

One morning Ray was chatting to Claire at the side of her drawing board when he began playing with her assortment of drawing pins which she kept in an empty *Megazone* throat-lozenge tin discarded by her mum. Ray opened the box and within a split second had dropped one of the pins on the floor. Claire said to him with new strength in her voice: "You drop all those and you will pick them up."

"Oh Yeah, and with whose Army?"

"You'll find out," she blurted menacingly. But, as if programmed, Ray did actually drop the tin and Claire really flew into an unholy rage. "Pick those up," she shouted at him, pointing at the scattered drawing pins on the floor. She stared at him with intent, her hands on her hips waiting for some response from his startled but somewhat cock-sure demeanor.

Ray had not expected her threat to be exercised so explosively, not having realized that Claire could be so forceful. But, against his normal bravado and inclination to be mischievous he bent down as meek as a lamb, and picked up every single one of the drawing pins, placed them back into the *Megazone* tin, closed the lid and placed it gently at the side of her drawing board. He didn't offer any apology, merely slinked off to his own drawing board in the far corner. Purposefully Claire said nothing either, merely continued with her drawing, head down. Some of the other students sensed the friction and jeeringly uttered "Whehhey!" She had won.

As for Marvin Burneston, he was a real nasty bully. After classes one evening Claire was in the public phone box in Vernon Street speaking to her friend Diane Fernley, who lived in Baildon, near Shipley. Claire noticed Marvin standing outside the cast-iron phone box painted in its customary post-office red. He was tapping his foot in an agitated manner, impatience personified, glowering at her through the small horizontal glass panes in the door. After a few seconds he opened it and demanded that Claire end her call. She dismissed him with a wave of her hand but he, being much taller and heavily built, reached over and, putting his finger on the button in the telephone cradle, wrenched the phone out of her grip. Claire's call to Diane ended abruptly of course and she was livid at Marvin's bold-faced cheek. "How dare you? You pig!" She shouted at him.

"I have an emergency," he said in a rather surly manner and pushing her further out of the door closed it behind her. Marvin started tapping the button on the cradle like fury. Claire stood there not knowing how to tackle this bully and fumed with hatred of him standing in the box, with his red hair and bushy beard. She hadn't realized until later that he was tapping out a number because he didn't have any money to pay for his call. "Don't worry I will get your number back for you," he shouted through the thick glass panes, with a dirty grin across his face. "Hello, Dermot, it's me. Tell mum I am still in Aireborough and will be home in about an hour. Bye" Then turning toward Claire he asked: "Now what was the number you were speaking to?"

She told him and he proceeded to tap out the number, handing her the phone before it had connected. He swung open the door and vanished up the street.

"Hello?" It was Diane's voice. Marvin's tapping had worked and fortunately Diane was still standing in the phone booth in Shipley. When Claire told her what had happened, Diane accused her friend of being weak, and not standing up for herself. Claire explained in greater detail that she had no choice as he was a big man, not just very powerful but very forceful too. Not one to be messed with. Thankfully, Diane realized the situation and joined Claire in her anger against Marvin the bully.

At this period in her life, Claire decided that if being involved with extra-curricular activities was a way of getting through her gender dysphoria, then she would become active in village life by becoming Youth Club Secretary. As 'Hon. Sec.' of Rigton Youth Club, her work was simply organizing special events in addition to being on hand for the Tuesday evening meetings, for indoor sports and dancing, and looking after week to week correspondence. In this period, Claire asked her friend Glenys Stevenson, who at the time was working as a nanny with a family in Ling Lane, Scarcroft, to help her teach the Youth Club members ballroom dancing. Glenys and Claire had met previously at the ballroom dancing sessions held in the Constitutional Club in Overton Road. Their teacher was Anna Katlovski and with her husband Sam ran the Katlovski Dancing Academy. Glenys and Claire had been working toward ballroom dancing medals so prized by everyone in the academy, but forced to retire due to lack of time to spend on their pastime, plus the cost of traveling by bus from their respective suburbs. Fortunately, in her present job Glenys was able to take time out one evening a week to visit Rigton Youth Club to join Claire in teaching the members to dance.

By this time Claire considered that she was beyond her 'youth', and sought other ways to occupy her time and thoughts. Having been a scout in St Brigid's troop a few years earlier, and having been a member of the scout group at the seminary she had attended in East Leigh, she decided she would lend a hand with the local troop. The group leader gave her a free hand when he could see that she certainly knew her scouting. But over the following year she set out to revolutionize them.

One of her major objectives was to get the scouts away from the 'Army' image, especially in wearing the color khaki. Consequently, she suggested to the *Troop in Council* that they change to wearing green shirts and the patrol leaders agreed. Their neckerchief had been a dull gray with maroon edgings for a number of years, and Claire considered this so drab and dull. So she managed to persuade them to change the colors to vermillion with a thin white edging.

All was going well until Blodwen Edwards, the cub leader, and Claire decided to repaint the cub room in lime green because they had obtained the paint without cost. They thought that the parent's committee would easily approve. However, the chair of the parent committee, Henry Brownridge, went ballistic and ordered the room to be repainted in a 'normal' color. The two girls were in disgrace. So much for making changes!

After Claire's twentieth birthday, she answered a call from the *Yorkshire Evening Post* for young people to serve on their newly created *Teenage Page Panel*. As a direct result of her previous activity of sending countless letters to the editor on various topics, she was invited to sit on the panel. This was despite the fact that she was legally outside her 'teens'. The panel was to meet every couple of weeks in a conference room at the *Yorkshire Conservative Newspaper Company* to discuss various issues of importance to contemporary youth. Their discussions and findings were to be printed in the *Evening Post* three days after their sessions.

Two of the panel members, Leo Mendel and Cheryl Bazin, were in tears over the Arab invasions of Israel. They had explained to the other panel members at one of their discussion sessions why they had decided to leave the UK and migrate to Israel, termed an *Aliyah*. Claire, in the guise of 'William Wilson' was still classed as a Roman Catholic and the Catholic doctrines against the Jews bothered her. In the Roman Catholic Easter services the Jews were described as 'perfidious', a word which her dictionary defined as 'treacherous'. Claire could not for the life of her see why, and she would have loved to have been able to join Leo and Cheryl in migrating to Israel. It was many years later Claire discovered why the Roman Church had used such derogatory term against Jews.

Sha'ul of Tarsus, known to Christians as Saint Paul, was a Roman citizen who, according to one book Claire had read, had converted to Judaism in order to marry a woman with whom he had fallen in love. Subsequently, he had turned his back on his original religion of Mithraism to embrace Judaism in order to marry the girl. Later, Sha'ul claimed that it was the Jews that had murdered the person whom he referred to as *Iessou Christou* ("Jesus Christ" in English). The fact was, according to the historical record, it had been the Romans themselves who saw *Yeshua ben Yosef*, known as 'Jesus' by English-speaking Christians, as a potential trouble maker. Henceforth, the Roman Church began a systemic victimization of Jews. As a result of Claire's feelings, and the explanations of Leo and Cheryl, she once again started taking an interest in Judaism.

The following year, the arguments with her dad were still very much in evidence and once again Claire felt she had to leave home to gain some semblance of peace. Finding a bed-sitter to rent in Chandos Park, without much performance she left home again to live her own life. One of the problems, however, was that as she was still scout leader in Rigton and she had to travel to the meetings every Friday evening. That meant that she had to pass her parents house after alighting the bus and walk up the hill to the scout hall. Purposefully she did not call in to see her mum and dad as she passed their property. She knew if she did, it would inevitably lead to yet more arguments with her dad.

Claire's 'rebellion' did not last long, however, as her top-floor bed-sitter was burgled by a neighbor. A few items of value were stolen, including the scout subscription monies from the meeting at the end of the previous week, plus her camera. A week later, Vernon in Mr Worthing's office, came back from his lunchtime stroll one day and said that Claire's camera was in a second-hand dealer's shop down Lower Briggate. Vern had recognized the camera as she had purchased it from him the previous year. Claire asked her boss's permission to walk down to the second-hand dealer and confront him. Thankfully Mr Worthing saw her dilemma and gave his permission.

It was indeed her camera in the shop window for all to see, on display in the middle of a number of other items. Claire went inside. "You have a stolen camera in the window."

"No I haven't young feller, I don't sell stolen goods."

"Well the camera was recently stolen from my bedsit and it is now in your window. I can recognize it easily. Would you take it out of the window for me please?"

"No, I won't. How dare you come into my shop and make wild accusations at me about a stolen camera?"

"Okay mister, if that's your attitude we'll see what the police have to say about it." With that she stormed out of the door and strode across town to the crime detectives near the town hall. Claire explained the situation to them as they already had the case listed as a burglary. Two of the detectives accompanied Claire back to the second-hand dealer. They looked in the window and there was no sign of her camera. Claire went hot and cold in rapid succession, imagining the shop owner denying that he had had a camera in the window. Claire quickly put two and two together and guessed the police might have been wise to this tactic. She went inside with them and one of them walked up to the counter and gestured with his hand for the owner to hand over the camera. The man, recognizing Claire from her previous accusation, reached below and placed her camera on the counter top. Detective Sergeant Wetherill asked her "Is this your camera William?" Claire nodded her head. "Okay Jim, we've warned you before. Show me your purchase book." Making a note of who sold the camera to the dealer, the detective sergeant handed a receipt to the guy.

As they went out of the shop Claire stopped and made the comment, "Oh I forgot, there was a light meter with it too. It was in a leather pouch attached to the camera strap. It must have been removed." So the detectives went back into the shop and the owner knew exactly what they wanted and produced the light meter from under the counter.

"Is this it?" Detective Sergeant Wetherill asked her.

"Yes, that's it."

"Okay, add it to the charge sheet and receipt," he told his colleague.

So the detectives now had the name of the person who took the camera to the dealer and called on Claire's neighbor later that afternoon. The culprit was the guy who rented the bedsit across the landing from her in the apartment house where she was living in Chandos Park. The police charged him with breaking and entry and the next morning she had to attend at court to identify him and her belongings. The young man was sent to jail for six months and Claire was so scared that she decided to move back with her parents, and to put up with her father's criticisms for a while – until the next time. Olivia was pleased. Danny, Gerry and Milton were not as pleased as it meant more friction at the meal table. But Claire was determined to keep her cool.

29

Pictures at an Exhibition

The next summer Claire's parents invited her to join them and her brothers Danny and Gerry on a two-week vacation at a holiday camp in Prestatyn in North Wales. This was a great opportunity to show them that she did not get up to embarrassing tricks all the time. Milton had his reservations though, as according to his reckoning, 'William' was absolutely useless.

It was at this holiday camp that Claire's love of classical music really began to shine, but in and through unusual circumstances. It was announced over the camp's speaker system that there was to be a fancy dress competition at the resort's weekly ball. As it happened that year, Milton's business partner Gordon Hogben, a man the children were in the habit of calling 'Uncle Gordon', had decided to vacation at the same holiday camp with his wife and family. His wife Gwyneth was referred to by the Wilson children as 'Aunty Gwyn' and the Hogben children comprised their eldest daughter Catherine, son Matthew, and their younger daughter Janice. Their youngest son Paul was not there that year as he was in hospital with a rare muscle-wasting disease. It transpired that the two business partners had decided to take their families to the same holiday camp that year. Other years both families had leased holiday chalets adjacent to each other, overlooking the South Bay Pool in Scarborough. So this particular year was indeed a change of habit for both families.

The event which is the subject of this tale was to become the highlight of the entire holiday. It certainly was for Claire at least, even if her brother Gerry was to get his facts wrong in his dotage.

Both families had planned to attend the camp ball and to enter the fancy dress competition. The two mothers had decided that Gerald, the youngest of the Wilson boys, should dress up as a girl and Janice, the youngest daughter of the Hogbens, should dress up as a boy. Claire thought this was going to be interesting, being that she knew herself to be a young woman, compounded by her continuous enigma – her gender dysphoria. Olivia was watching 'William' like a hawk to see how her hermaphrodite-born son would react. Of course, by this time in Claire's life, although dressed like a young man, she was certainly a girl screaming to extract herself from her socially perceived role, and her mum knew it. But Claire did not want to be a part of the charade, not even to watch the spectacle of Gerry dressed up in one of Aunty Gwyn's frocks, wearing a borrowed tiara on his head, and wearing a pair of Aunty Gwyn's open toed sandals on his feet trying to walk like a girl. Janice, on the other hand, was to dress in Gerry's high school uniform, cap and short pants included. But Claire was made to see them both dressed, her mother eying her with interest. She then left with the Hogben's eldest daughter Cathy, to attend a classical music evening in a nearby house. Claire felt sick seeing Gerry dressed in an evening frock as it should have been her. But she could say nothing.

Claire and Cathy walked around the corner to the house where the classical music evening was to be held, to join a number of other devotees as they listened to long-playing records. Cathy sat opposite Claire in an armchair and the latter sat in an upholstered dining chair. The gathering was to listen to *Pictures at an Exhibition* by Russian composer Modest Petrovich Mussorgsky. The organizer of the event advised that he had a copy of the score available if anyone would l.ike to take a look at it. Claire put up her hand and was presented with the booklet containing the score of the piece they were about to hear, plus the score also of *Night on Bald Mountain* by the same composer. Claire was thrilled, as following the music score would take her mind off a particular event underway in the camp's ballroom.

As the evening progressed, Gerry and Janice won first prize in the fancy dress competition and when the two families got together the next day, it was all they could talk about. The parents, had no interest whatsoever in listening to Claire and Cathy's classical music experience; they simply did not want to hear about the event. Needless to say, Claire always remembered that evening and *Pictures at an Exhibition* became one of her favorite works, alongside Bach's *Brandenburg Concerto No.3 in C Major*. Strangely enough, many years later she reminded Gerry of that evening and his memory of it was that Cathy was his partner in the fancy dress competition. He was wrong of course as Claire always retained a very vivid memory of that particular evening.

Back home in Rigton Claire had been invited by a couple of others to drive over to Thornley one Saturday evening to attend a dance at the local hospital for sick children. It was there that she met Jane Stewart, one of the nurses. They supposed they might have been drawn to each other as they were both fairly quiet souls and didn't stand out in a crowd. So Jane and Claire, as "William," started meeting when Jane was not on duty at the hospital. About the same time, it so happened that the youngest son of the Hogben family, Paul, whom Claire knew, but who had not been at the previous holiday camp due to his long-standing illness, was in one of the wards.

One evening, Claire decided to visit Paul, and Jane had broken all the rules and allowed her friend to sneak into his ward unannounced. As it was a warm summer evening Claire arrived after the children's evening meal and Jane let her in through one of the French doors to the ward. Claire had taken Paul a couple of books and a *Dinky Toy*, a miniature model of his dad's car. Naturally, it transpired that she could see Jane when she came of duty an hour later. Claire had traveled to Thornley on her bicycle and the ride back to Rigton was pleasant under a clear summer sky full of stars.

One evening Jane and "William" met in Wetherton and walked down by the River. It was a balmy evening and after a short walk the two of them laid down under a tree, looking up at a clear starry sky. "Jane, may I ask you something?"

"Yes William, what is it?"

"Well, I wonder if you could help me."

"Go on then, ask me." Claire thought later that Jane was expecting a question to do with their relationship.

"Well, with you being a nurse, have you ever had to deal with children who were born with two genders? I think the term is hermaphrodite."

"Not really. I have never heard of the term."

"Well, my mum told me a few years ago that I was born a hermaphrodite as I had the genitals of both male and female."

"Oh, now that you put it like that, I have heard of it but we don't have any cases in Thornley hospital. So you were born with both genders William? How very interesting"

"Yes, according to my mum I was. But dad organized for me to have my female parts sewn up as he didn't want a girl in the family."

"How strange! Why not? Does your dad have a problem in accepting girls?"

"Well, according to my mum, dad has the idea that only real men can sire boys and the wives of men who he regards as poofters, only give birth to girls."

"Oh William, you don't believe that nonsense, do you?

"No Jane, I don't but to be quite honest, I know that I really am a girl but have had to live my life and dress like a boy."

At this Jane put her arm around Claire and snuggled closer. "William, I love you for opening up your secret to me. It makes me feel special in your life."

"Well, you are special Jane as I love you too, but from what I hear other youths telling me of their escapades, I don't feel the same as they do about girls as I am one myself."

"There's nothing wrong with that William. You are just you and it makes you special. Why were you called William, if you are really a girl?"

"Well, my grandfather was called James William Wilson and my dad wanted to name his first born son after his father, who died when dad was only fourteen."

"I gather that your mum had no say in the matter. So had she a preferred name for you if you were born a normal girl?"

"Yes, she told me that my name would have been Claire."

"What a lovely name. Would you like me to call you that name?"

"Oh, I guess it is too late for that now Jane. Far too late!"

"Don't say that Claire, at some time in the future you may get to be called the name your mum wanted to call you."

"I wish!" Claire commented.

Jane and her friend laid there with their arms around each other appreciating what secret the latter had laid bare. Jane felt special that her friend had confided in her and Claire was pleased to share her burden. But it would not help her immediate future, only that she had a kindred spirit to speak to confidentially.

Claire's secret was out in the open, but with restricted access. Slowly Jane and Claire drifted apart as 'William' continued 'his' studies in architecture and Jane to travel to Canada with her father, after the sudden death of her mother. The only time Claire was to see her again was in Wetherton market place many years into adulthood. But then she wondered if it really was her. Was she still pining after the other woman in her life, who knew of her secret?

About this time also, Claire's twenty-first birthday came around. She didn't think her mum and dad would let her have a party, let alone a big one, as parties had been banned since childhood. But as Claire had been using Rigton Village Hall for various functions, including events for the Youth Club, Rigton Players (an amateur thespian group) and the Young Conservatives, Olivia suggested she book the hall for a twenty-first party. Claire was over the moon at this news and as Jane had not at that point gone to Canada, Claire asked her if she would help her organize it when she wasn't on duty at the children's hospital. She agreed and so the two of them set to and arranged a gathering for about fifty people. Olivia was amazed that 'her son' had so many friends, but all Milton was concerned about was how much it was all going to cost him. However, the day and the evening approached and 'William' was guest of honor with Jane by 'his' side. Now that she knew Claire's secret it was so much more special.

But one of the old problems raised its head again, that of Milton's bigotry against anything German, American or Irish, or anything that was not British. Milton hated everything German because of World War II, and Claire later wondered if he had known that Olivia's ancestry was German; he despised Americans because his beloved sister had married a GI and after migrating to the USA sent for her mother and stepfather who joined them there; and the Irish were always in his criticisms because Ireland was neutral during the war and did not support the British cause.

Added to this was the fact that with the money Claire had been given as gifts for her twenty-first birthday, she had bought lots of 33-rpm long-playing records of artists who were in her dad's perception 'Black Men'. Apart from one or two classics by Beethoven, Mozart and Schubert, she had purchased records by Erroll Garner, Dizzy Gillespie, Lionel Hampton, Miles Davis, Charlie Parker, Thelonius Monk and John Coltrane – all Afro-American. It never occurred to Milton that 'William' preferred their music to the strains of Henry Hall and Billy Cotton and other British musicians. So, even Claire's choice of music caused her father to become angry.

30

Diane

Hiking across Ilkley moor with her brother Danny one Saturday, Claire met Diane Fernley. The two of them subsequently became good friends and often Claire would go to Diane's home in Baildon, where she lived with her parents in a ground floor council flat. Her dad was confined to a wheelchair as he had multiple sclerosis and couldn't walk. Her mum, on the other hand, was hale and hearty and was in the habit of going out dancing and to Bingo sessions almost every evening. Claire thought this was unfair on Diane's dad so sometimes Diane and Claire would stay in to keep him company. Otherwise they would go out for a walk or to see a movie. One Sunday evening Diane took Claire to her local Primitive Methodist chapel for an evening service. Claire had never before been to a religious service in a Methodist chapel and was really interested to see how they might be different from those in her local Roman Catholic church. Claire as 'William' was obviously seen as 'a good catch' by Diane's dad as he never seemed to stop making suggestions about marriage.

But Mr Fernley appeared to have gotten somewhat suspicious when the two friends spent a weekend together in Blackpool. There had been nothing to worry about it as far as Claire was concerned as she was still naïve about sex. She supposed it might have been assumed by Mr Fernley that his daughter would soon become pregnant, in common with what he had heard happened among young people. But such an idea was far from Claire's thoughts as she really didn't know what to do about such matters. In reality she didn't know what went where, and Diane was simply a good friend and nothing more. One might presume one step up from a normal platonic relationship.

On evenings when it was foggy and the buses stopped running, Claire often phoned home to explain to her mother that she was sleeping over at Diane's place for a night. It was later to amuse Claire that all her mum seemed to be concerned about was what she should do with the dinner she had cooked for her. That was all she seemed to care about, no concern that 'her son' was stranded in the fog somewhere. In emergencies such as this, Mr and Mrs Fernley allowed 'William' to sleep on the sofa in their living room. Olivia wasn't concerned about this – only the matter of who was going to consume the meal she had cooked. No doubt at all that Gerry would consume it in five minutes flat.

Diane worked in a government department in Warkfield and sometimes took the train over to Aireborough, so that she and 'William' could go for a coffee or see a movie. One evening Diane went directly to Mr Worthing's office as Claire was working late. On that particular evening, Claire remembered asking Diane to wait for her and to sit on a chair by a table in the middle of the room. Claire had no sooner finished what she needed to do on the drawing, listening to the cleaner vacuuming Mr Worthing's carpet in his office downstairs, and emptying the waste bins, when Diane asked her a strange question. "Would you do my make up for me William?" she asked.

"What?"

"I asked if you would do my make up for me."

"Why should I do that?"

"Well, you are an artist and who better to do my make up?" Diane looked at Claire sideways, with a smile on her lips and added, "Plus I have the feeling that you would like to do it." What could Claire say to that?

So she agreed and wondered if Diane realized that by this time in Claire's life, albeit in her own bedroom, she was practiced at applying make-up. But as Claire applied Diane's foundation the cleaner looked through the glass upper half of the drawing office door in complete amazement. By the time she was applying Diane's lipstick, her friend appeared to be in a dream. Claire stood back to admire her handiwork, and Diane reached for her powder compact to look at herself. "Oh, that is so nice William. How can you do it so well? It is better than I do it myself. Have you done this before?"

Claire gulped – "Well, I have done stage make-up, so it is easy for me," was all she could offer Diane in reply.

By doing Diane's make-up of course it had drawn attention in Claire's own mind to her gender dysphoria once again, which lurked under the surface most of the time. What Diane didn't know of course was that Claire was already quite experienced at applying make-up, practicing a number of times a week in her room. Those private periods were cherished by Claire as she could dream of being the beautiful woman she knew she was. Quite often she tried to dream herself to sleep by imagining that she was placed in a mold, and when she came out of it the next morning she had the body of a normal woman, instead of having the weird body of a male and the mind of a female.

One Saturday Claire invited Diane home to meet her parents. After introducing her friend to her mother, she could not stop Diane from wandering through to the living room to meet her dad. Olivia held Claire back by putting her arm out as restraint: "Do you want me to tell her what you are?"

Claire blushed crimson at this question and realized in a flash that her mum was going to tell Diane that she was born intersex and despite her female genitalia having been suppressed at birth 'William' was constantly cross-dressing. In other words, 'William' was in reality a girl. "No, don't say anything to her please, that is my job."

"Well, make sure you do, as it wouldn't be fair on her if you didn't." Olivia then wandered through to the living room herself. This was very weird. Just who had guessed her secret and who hadn't.

But Claire's friendship with Diane had to stop as it was affecting her architectural studies at the College of Art. All this about the same time as her flat had been broken into in Chandos Park. Claire had already broken off the relationship with Diane, but by this time the latter had fallen hopelessly in love and would not accept the break-up.

One morning, having taken a day off work on the grounds that she was sick, Diane turned up at College crying her eyes out. Margaret, the School of Architecture secretary, arrived in Claire's studio.

"William, I have a rather distraught young lady in the interview room asking for you."

Claire moved toward the steps that took her to the lower floors, and her fellow students, having overheard Margaret, let out their usual: "Weh-hey!" to Claire's.

"Now cut that out, you're only jealous."

Subsequently, Claire decided to take Diane to her bed-sit in Chandos Park in order to try to console her, but the truth had to be told. The secret had to come out.

After she had told Diane the truth about her birth, Diane said it didn't matter as she still loved her no matter what she was. But Claire knew that deep down Diane didn't really understand the implications of gender dysphoria. Claire persisted and it took her another week to gently let Diane down. In the end it came to an ultimatum; Diane demanded an answer – either Claire/William, was to continue her/his studies in architecture, or commit her future with Diane. As a result, Claire decided to tell Diane that she had chosen architecture as her career over her. In a huff, Diane stormed up onto her feet and left the room in a cloud of nonchalance.

Claire never saw her again, but never stopped thinking about her and what she might be doing. Many years later, having designed a number of buildings in downtown Bradford, Claire wondered where Diane might have been at that moment in time. Personal friendships were to become very important to Claire.

The following months saw Claire struggle with her enigma, while she tried desperately to concentrate on her studies. In many ways it was a case of *who am I? Am I here for a specific purpose?* or *Why does God let me suffer like this?* Questions that lots of people ask themselves but only one person at a time can address their own case. In Claire's instance, she felt that her Catholic faith was becoming a stumbling block in many ways as individuals were not encouraged to think for themselves. The Church had all the answers, through the priests. But Claire could not discuss her concerns with any priest as she was convinced she would have been damned to Hell.

31

Sharon

One of Claire's continuous problems had always been that she needed to be part of society and able to serve it. In Rigton, when her time with the Scouts was waning, she founded a branch of the Young Conservatives. Having been active in Micklegate YCs a few years earlier, she seemed to know all the ropes and approached Mr Bartlet, the chairman of the Rigton Conservative Association, to see if they would support the founding of a branch of Young Conservatives in the village. He agreed and as a result a fledgling committee invited the local MP Martin Foxglove to formally open the branch. The committee Claire had put together comprised local youth whose names had been suggested by the senior Conservatives. At first Claire put herself in the position of coordinator as by this time in her life she had become a skilled organizer, somewhat of a political animal too.

The biggest trouble in Rigton, however, was that Claire was seen by the locals as an outsider trying to put them in some sort of order, which most certainly was not the intention Claire had in mind. Some of the members of the new committee had been together at Tullminster Grammar School, and if she needed support for a particular motion she had to rely on the son of the chairman, who had attended Aireborough Grammar School, and another woman, slightly older than herself, called Petula.

One evening Claire had obtained permission from her parents to hold a committee meeting in the dining room of their home, which had been renamed *Maison Milton* by her dad. It appeared to Claire that he had always been secretly still in love with the period in his twenties when he lived and worked in the South of France. Claire had moved the dining table into the bow-window area, and the chairs, comprising lounge and dining chairs, arranged around the edges of the room. She was sitting with her legs closed, which she always did, until one of young men asked, "Do you always sit like that?"

"What do you mean," Claire asked, looking somewhat mystified.

"You know, with your legs together, like this." With that he brought his legs together from the open position normal for men. It was then that Claire realized what she had done and blushed. She had to be constantly on her guard to copy what men did.

"Oh, that. What does it matter?" …and promptly changed the subject to the business of the meeting.

It was not until she was in bed later, that she felt herself blushing deep crimson in the dark, because someone had noticed her natural female way of sitting. This was disturbing as she did not want rumors getting back to her dad, starting yet another round of sarcasm and discrimination. Claire just had to be more careful until she could stand on her own two feet, and perhaps leave home for good.

However, events went fairly smoothly during the first year in Rigton Young Conservatives, but Claire did notice that meetings which were not marked as 'social events' were attended by only a handful of members. Nevertheless, dances were well attended and the committee relied on the availability of Rigton Village Hall for local events. If they wanted to widen their appeal, they would book the Village Hall in Linton, between Collingsby and Wetherton.

But after a year in the post as Chair, disillusionment set in for her. First, she was upset because the Conservative Party in her mind represented the landed gentry, royalty, the aristocracy, the moneyed class and big business. Claire was interested in ordinary people, the people who were trying to make something of their lives and who were struggling to climb to a higher socioeconomic level. In her observation, she saw their efforts often stymied by high taxation and the 'old school' system. Assuming that the Conservative Party was not supported much by the so-called lower classes, Claire decided that right-wing politics was not for her. She had continued a friendship with another student from Clark's College and it was he, Donal Urquhart, who ultimately persuaded her to join the Young Liberals. Claire was convinced that the political world was totally corrupt, and she wanted to change it. But then that is another story which is bound to come up at a later stage.

Dressed as a young male and having to play the part of one, constantly badgered by three of her uncles and her dad, Claire found herself having to pretend to be dating suitable young ladies. She had tried to become friendly with a couple of other girls in Rigton but suspected that they could see through her. Of the three, she was convinced that one of them, Barbara Stead, knew that she was far more female than male. It seemed that Claire didn't really know how to act the part of a young man when she was dating another young woman. It was very difficult. But ultimately, in 1965, to all intent and purposes living as a male, she was to be married to Sharon Bentley of Overton. While Claire liked Sharon however, she had never really given a lot of thought to marriage due to her gender problem. That being so, she clutched at whatever straws blew her way.

Sharon was the only daughter of a commercial salesman who called on Milton at 'the works' and Claire saw her when her parents occasionally visited *Maison Milton*, on Sunday afternoons, nicely timed for tea and scones. Claire was always embarrassed as she loved to see what Sharon was wearing, most of the time dressed in clothes that she herself might have chosen. If truth be known, Sharon was an inspiration. One particular Sunday afternoon Sharon visited with her parents, and she was wearing a gorgeous pair of metallic-silver colored high heels. Claire thought the shoes so elegant and she wished she had a pair like them. But guessing that she might be blushing due to her jealous thoughts, Claire decided to leave the visitors and retire to her bedroom to work on one of her college projects.

After a few minutes in her room she heard the toilet door open and close. The toilet bowl flushed and the door opened and closed again. Thinking nothing of this she concentrated on her design when there was a gentle knock on the door, only for it to open slightly to reveal the face of Sharon. "What are you working on William? May I see?"

"Er, yes, if you like."

Sharon walked over to the drawing board to look at whatever Claire was designing. She looked but, if truth be known, her face indicated that she did not really understand what she was looking at. Her head turned to look out of the window at the view. It looked across the fields to another village in the distance. "You have a lovely view up here, William."

"I suppose I do, but I am mostly too busy working to take much notice."

Just then Sharon's dad called up the stairs to say that they were about to depart. Claire walked Sharon over to the door and opened it for her.

"Bye! Sharon"

"Bye!" was the soft reply as Sharon walked down the stairs to join her parents.

A few weeks later, Claire was sitting at a table in the Central Colleges Refectory with some of the other students from her year in the School of Architecture. On the other side of the hall Sharon walked in with some of her co-students from the Secretarial College next door. Claire saw her and waved. Sharon saw her and waved back. At this, Claire's fellow students looked around and saw Sharon waving to their colleague and turning to her again, jeered in her face: "Oy, oy, what's this then. Keeping a secret from us, are you?"

"No, she is a friend of the family."

"Oh, yes, a likely story," joked Ralph Duncan, "a secret love affair, is it?"

"Give over Ralph, I told you. Her dad knows my dad and quite often they visit us Sunday afternoons, when my dad and her dad can have a chat. That's all it is. Okay?"

Ralph allowed a smirk to spread across his face but Claire's explanation had been accepted by the other students and the subject changed. The die, however, appeared to have been cast.

It was during the following six-month period when Claire had to work full time in Mr Worthing's office and in the evenings attend lectures at the School of Architecture, that the ice was broken. In the drawing office of Henry Worthing's practice in Blenheim Terrace, was a young assistant called Eric. Claire and her office colleague were occasionally in the habit of walking down to a cost-effective restaurant in the basement of Aireborough Town Hall for their lunch. Eric had been asking Claire for some time how to date girls, and as she was about twenty-three years of age at the time and full of the blarney, she decided to look for an opportunity to climb up in Eric's good books.

The opportunity arose as the pair walked out of their office forecourt one day. As the pair walked out of the parking area at the front of their building to walk down Woodthorpe Lane, Sharon was walking up the lane by herself. Here was the ideal opportunity Claire had been waiting for:

"Look Eric, let me show how to date girls, like I explained the other day. Okay?" Claire had gained his undivided attention. "You walk past me when I stop to speak to this girl walking up in front of us." Eric obeyed in wonderment, and at the same time with some considerable amusement. Claire stopped in front of Sharon and Eric continued walking before stopping to look back at the action about to be played out. "Hi Sharon, how are you?"

"Very well, thank you William."

"How are your mum and dad?"

"Fine, thanks, and yours?"

"Oh fine, thanks. Listen I meant to call you. I wondered if you would like to go out one evening, you know, to see a movie or go for a walk perhaps."

"That would be nice, thank you William. When did you have in mind?"

"Oh it is up to you really, what evening would you be free? I could catch the bus and get to your house by seven o'clock maybe."

"Well, Wednesday is good for me if that's alright for you too."

"Great. Look I'll pick you up at seven on Wednesday, is that okay? Sorry but I have to dash as my friend is waiting for me. Bye." Claire caught up with Eric.

"How did you get on," he asked, anticipating the worst scenario.

"I am taking her to the pictures on Wednesday evening"

"No joking William! Is that for real?" Eric's eyes were like huge saucers as he stared at Claire. "That's so cool. Is it as easy as that?"

"Yes, I asked her out on a date – just like that. That's how it is done Eric. It really is so easy." Later in the week Eric asked how the date had gone. It was then that Claire had to admit that she already knew Sharon. She felt she just had to tell him the truth, as by that time he had withdrawn into his shell once more, scared of asking anyone out.

So Sharon and Claire, with the latter dressed as a young man and having practiced men's mannerisms and actions, saw each other regularly over the next couple of years. They mainly went walking in the local woods, or to see a movie. But one weekend they decided to go for a three-day trek into the Yorkshire Dales National Park. As they planned to stay in youth hostels they packed a sleeping bag each and Claire added a small tent to her rucksack too, along with something to cook on and to eat and drink from. Taking a *West Yorkshire* bus to Hawes in the Yorkshire Dales National Park, they then followed their Ordinance Survey map through Langstroth Dale. The first night they called at a farmhouse and asked if they could pitch a tent down by the beck. Permission was granted and the pair pitched their tent, cooked a meal of sausage and mashed potatoes, which they drank with a mug of tea each. But then the rain started to pour down outside, running down the canvas above their heads. But undaunted, they snuggled down to sleep, after first trying to both sleep in one sleeping bag. Quite an ordeal until they realized the impossibility of the task.

The following morning they called at the farm to pay for their stay and the farmer's wife invited them inside her kitchen. Not only were Sharon and Claire then offered a mug of steaming tea each but a plate of fried bacon and egg, with lashings of toast.

What wonderful people these farmers were. This set the pair of them up for the day which turned out to be quite wet, not only above their heads but more assuredly under their feet, often trekking through peat bogs. After a really long day's walk they finally arrived at the youth hostel in Kettlewell, where they could sleep the night and partake of a meal that the hostel manager and his wife provided for them for a reasonable price.

After a good night's rest, they had breakfast, performed their work and then as their boots and clothes were still soaked through from the previous day, Claire found a telephone box in the village and rang her dad to ask if someone from home was available to collect them from Kettlewell Youth Hostel. Milton seemed annoyed but said her brother Gerry would drive out to pick them up and for them to stay at the hostel so that he knew where they would be. Her brother hardly spoke to them on the return journey, seeming as though he was jealous that they had enjoyed themselves despite the rain. But then, Gerry always seemed to be jealous of anything Claire did.

It was during her final year at College that Claire decided to buy a motorbike. She described it as a motorbike but her Uncle Clive laughed: "You call that a motorbike?" He showed them a photograph of himself on a 'real' motorbike and laughingly called theirs 'a powered bicycle'. Nevertheless, it did get them to places they might not have gotten to on a bus. The only problem was that Claire had nightmares of people stealing her bike while she was in college. This never happened however, but the nightmares carried on for many years.

Her brother Danny had left home by this time to live with a girl from Heckmondwike. One particular day he rang Claire to ask if he could meet up with her to discuss a problem he had. She wondered what sort of problem she could sort out for him, considering that he had always been a constant trouble to her from early childhood. Danny suggested they meet at a particular café in Aireborough. His problem was more severe than Claire had realized – he had gotten his girlfriend pregnant. Daniel Lester Wilson was to become a dad, and he was only in his early twenties.

"Would you break the news to mummy and daddy for me William? Please?" Here was her mischievous little brother, one who had been in the act of trying to kill her three times, asking her to help him. He had tears in his eyes and Claire felt sorry for him. She knew the phrase "blood is thicker than water" and wondered if it was meant for occasions like this. Would she be able to help her brother?

"Yes, I will Danny, no problems. Leave it to me and I will try to smooth things out for you." What else could she have done? What else could she have said? Yes, she was always the optimistic organizer, set to become the smoother of troubled waters throughout her life. This exercise was to be the first of a number of times when she was called upon to sort out a problem in a crisis. In Danny's case, it certainly was a crisis.

"Thanks William. I knew I could rely on you. When will you tell them?"

"I think I might have to wait until Gerry has gone to bed one evening, when mum and dad are by themselves. Maybe tonight I might get the opportunity. I'll call you when I have told them."

So, that evening, after Gerry had gone to bed Claire opened Pandora's Box. "I saw Danny today in Aireborough."

"Oh!" Olivia nonchalantly remarked. "How was he? Was he well?"

"No, he wasn't actually." Her parents looked at her at this comment. She had their attention.

"He had some rather bad news he wanted me to tell you." Olivia and Milton's ears were now fully open. "He has gotten his girlfriend Elspeth in a spot of bother."

Olivia immediately knew the full story. "He has made her pregnant hasn't he, the little Devil? I knew it would happen sooner or later with Daniel." Olivia started crying while Claire's dad went red in the face as though he was about to explode. Claire knew the signs from past experience.

"Yes, that just about sums up his dilemma. He wanted me to tell you as he is too ashamed to tell you himself."

"The rotten bugger! I'll kill him! After all I have done for him, getting him his job. We must keep this news from the neighborhood or we will be the laughing stock of the street." Trust Milton to turn the problem back on himself. "Tell him I want to see him, will you William, and I will sort things out." That was how Claire's dad approached everything. He would sort things out.

So the next day Claire rang Danny and gave him the news that she had been told to impart. Subsequently, Milton was to 'sort things out' by making sure that a wedding was on the cards as quickly as possible in the nearest Catholic parish to where Elspeth Partridge lived. 'William' was to be "best man" and Gerry an usher. Milton gave Danny and Elspeth a deposit to lease a semi-detached house in Micklegate and took Danny into his business to learn the trade, so to speak. The problem had been sorted. Milton had triumphed again. His face had been saved.

But the time came when Claire felt that her parents and those of Sharon expected the two of them to announce their engagement. In many ways Claire felt trapped in the formalities of the social correctness of the day. Yes, she had come to love Sharon as much as she believed she could love anyone. Yes, Sharon was special, but Claire had previously never given much thought of being actually "married." But on the other hand, she secretly wondered if her gender dysphoria might vanish if she were married. Maybe being married to Sharon would free her of the turmoil she constantly experienced in her mind. She did however wonder if it was possible for two women to be married to each other, as Claire still felt herself to be female. The only difference was that she had to dress as a man, having been registered as a boy at birth by her very bigoted father.

Sharon's parents lived in Overton and Claire often spent an evening with them, watching television after first listening to *The Archers*, a popular BBC Radio soap. The main problem Claire had, sitting there among them, was that Sharon's father smoked and by the time the radio was switched off, the room was full of second-hand cigarette smoke. Yuk! In summer she just had to get outside into the fresh air as soon as possible and often suggested that Sharon and her go for a walk.

Milton had bought his family a large tent a few years previous to this time. It was so large that it had two separate bedrooms, a rear kitchen, a dining area and a front entertaining section under a canopy. This dropped down at night or when the weather was bad. Milton decided to launch his tent publicly soon after its purchase and drove the family to Windermere, in the Lake District National Park. There they pitched their new acquisition at the side of a large field alongside the somewhat smaller tents of other campers. What Milton had not allowed for was the weather forecast, which didn't look promising. So much so that the first morning they all awoke to find the roof of the tent sagging and on a peek through the windows they discovered that it had snowed overnight. Yes, it had snowed in May, when they were well into spring and only a month before summer was to arrive. The snow had even settled in the field to a depth of about fifteen centimeters. That was the British weather for you, at Whitsuntide even.

The next use of the tent was to be on a holiday in Europe. Instead of visiting France, as was Milton's usual destination, he had decided to take the family to a village on the Italian Riviera. As Danny had left home by this time, the spare place in the car had been offered to Sharon. The only problem with this was that 'William' and Gerald had to sleep in the dining area, allowing Sharon the full use of the second bedroom. Gerry was miffed over this as usual, but Claire obviously didn't mind.

The campsite had been built on a hillside which gave magnificent views from just about every camping place, each site overlooking the Mediterranean. While the access driveway to each camping site was rather steep and winding, a car parking area was sited next to each tent space. Some holidaymakers arrived by bus, which stopped at the bottom of the hill at the entrance to the camping site. To accommodate these campers, the administration had one of their operatives, Bruno, ride his motor-bike and sidecar down to greet the new arrivals and to transport their luggage and camping gear to their allotted campsite. This fascinated Claire, always one to listen intently to how others conversed with each other. It seemed that if Bruno was not at the camp office when needed, they announced over the *Tanoy* system: "*Bruno, venire in ufficio per favore*" meaning "Bruno, please come to the office." This sentence was to stick in Claire's mind for the rest of her life. It seemed that her brain tuned in to unusual non-English words or phrases.

On returning to England after their vacation, Claire decided to buy herself the motorbike already mentioned. Of course, Uncle Clive just had to keep reminding Claire that in reality the motorbike was 'a ladies motorized cycle', its engine merely 49 cc compared to the powerful Enfield he had ridden as a young man. Milton had equated with this as he also had ridden a powerful 'man's machine' in his prime. But for Claire, this was just what she wanted, a machine which didn't cost much to run, which would transport her to college and back safely. She bought a safety helmet and plastic over coat to protect her as the winter rain and wind really bit into her skin. The connection with their Italian camping experience soon came into line with Claire's purchase. Having been paid £60 by Milton in payment for producing a set of drawings for an extension to his factory, she had managed to save the balance toward the total of £85 for the machine, bought from a bike store in Lower Briggate in Aireborough. It had to have a name, the bike that is – didn't it? 'Bruno' that was it – *Bruno, venire in ufficio per favore*, she recalled, and quickly stenciled the name on the back of one of the leg guards, which were a feature of the bike.

Bruno was to become a savior in many ways as it was now easier to get to many places, previously only accessible by bus or train. One particular avenue was that she could now apply for jobs in places other than Aireborough. Although Aireborough was her base, and would be for some time yet, it meant that she could travel to York for jobs during her college holidays. She therefore applied to work in a practice in the suburb of Acomb. The base practice was in Liverpool, but the partners had opened an office in an outer suburb of York in order to carry out design work on a number of Yorkshire projects on which they had received commissions. To get there, Claire could use her new-found mode of transport. *Bruno* was constantly in great demand by her.

The architectural practice was housed in an old 'Thomas Fairfax' Manor House which had been restored to a semblance of its medieval glory. On being told some history of the house, she wondered if it were true that the great and powerful Sir Thomas Fairfax had lived there. It was not until she was to be engaged in work to another 'Thomas Fairfax' manor house in Bilbrough a few years later that she discovered it doubtful that the famous man had lived in Acomb. It was true that he was buried in Bilbrough, just outside the York boundary but as he had retired to Nunappleton, north of York, it seemed very unlikely that he would build himself two manor houses. On this assumption, Claire considered that maybe it was one of his relatives who had built the house and public misconception had blossomed.

The office itself comprised the lower rooms of a two-story mansion situated in the main street. Claire was allotted a drawing board alongside the local partner's wife, opposite two men at their own respected drawing boards. The room was uncarpeted, the boards stained and highly polished, looking over a quiet garden with a high hedge to the rear. Next door was another drawing office which was the domain of three rather uncouth, rude and disgusting men. These individuals were allowed to smoke and their walls were covered with what Claire considered 'dirty pictures'. Thankfully, she only had to visit that particular room once during her period working in the practice, and that was more than enough.

The following year Claire obtained a working holiday period with an architectural practice near City Square in Aireborough. Her interview was with the younger of the two partners, who, she considered, devoured her portfolio of work. She got the job and was told later by one of the assistants that her new boss probably was looking for inspiration in her work. By this time Claire had a reputation for designing projects which were out of the ordinary, so perhaps she was the victim of plagiarism.

Just as she had been a tiny cog in the wheels of the previous practice where she spent her whole time drawing a perspective for publication, in the new practice she was to spend most of her time working up details on her boss's project ideas. What disturbed her was his attitude toward women. Her boss was to show himself as a lecherous beast as he tried to take advantage of his secretary following his downing of many pints of beer one Christmas. The crunch came when her mother arrived to confront him, to be attacked by her excellent use of the English language. In response he kicked them both out of the door with the shout "Bloody Jewish bitches." Claire felt that this just about summed up her boss, a typical man who thought he was God's gift to women. In this he fell down in her previous high estimation of him. He had been removed from his pedestal and was no more than a common lecherous devil. Claire was opening up to the world, proving that she certainly was not the 'young man' that her father wanted her to be. She had none of the characteristics necessary to confirm that she was a man, even if she had something between her legs that society used as their confirmation. She still felt that she was a young woman and her thoughts told her that this was very much true.

32

Disowned

Prior to getting married, Claire had seen a derelict house on Blackman Lane, up the hill beyond the Bentley Arms, supposedly England's oldest public house. Heath Lodge had, according to a local source, been a shooting lodge of Viscount Bentley and it dated back to 1729. Its walls were about 60cm thick, but if she bought it she would need to replace all the rotting windows, lay a concrete floor to replace the stone flag floors, and add a kitchen as an extension. Milton was by this stage pleased that his strategy of nurturing her out of her gender dysphoria, was working. This was reinforced by his constant reference to her as a young man, so that her transformation from being a hermaphrodite would be complete.

Her dad had told her that he had decided to set each of his sons up with a gift of money with which they would be able to obtain a mortgage. So saying, he advised them that he would give the two of them the ten percent deposit on the £8,000 loan from Wetherton Rural District Council in order to buy the property. Consequently, Claire set about preparing the drawings and engaged some men to start work on demolition of parts of the house, and the repair of its outer walls.

The men whom Claire contracted to start the work seemed somewhat lacking in enthusiasm. Nevertheless, it came as a shock to discover that, having been offered a more lucrative offer from another customer, the builders decided to drop the work on Heath House home in favor of working for a wealthy family in a nearby village. This was where Claire's Uncle Leopold came in, as his wife Katarina had told her that he had always wanted to 'do up' a cottage. But while Claire was in the process of discussing the project with Uncle Leo, Milton interrupted and said he would arrange things with his brother-in-law. That being to Milton's satisfaction Claire's uncle took on the work with gusto. The big problem was that she had not bargained for her dad's bigotry, and something blew up between Leo and Milton. Later, she was to discover that her dad had argued with her Uncle Leo and the latter had walked off her project saying that he would never do anything for her dad again. This was yet another family squabble. Considering that both families had been reasonably friendly before this incident, her Uncle Leo and Aunt Kate would never speak to her parents again. The overriding problem appeared to be that Milton considered himself superior to most people and especially to those in Olivia's family. This was not surprising as Claire's dad was very critical of other people in general.

But, perhaps feeling guilty over the impasse, her dad and her brother Gerald had decided that they would finish off the work yet to be completed on Heath Lodge themselves. Gerry, true to form, constantly reminded Claire to keep away from the house as she was useless at anything. Unknown to him and other members of the Wilson family, they were totally wrong in this assumption. Claire was later to prove that she was more than capable of rising to any task she set her mind to, as the future was to illustrate.

Wanting to impress her family that she had style, Claire had previously decided that Sharon and she would get married in a beautiful Roman Catholic convent chapel in the nearby village of Pinkerton. While the building looked old, it had been built in 1827 yet modeled on an old Anglo-Saxon church, with a beautiful entry porch, and each interior column carved in a different design to the next one. Claire had selected music for the traditional wedding ceremony by her favorite composer Johann Sebastian Bach and the parish organist was actually very good indeed.

When Sharon arrived with her father she took Claire's breath away as she looked a perfect picture. Claire's biggest problem however, was that she had to dress as a man, like the two fathers and her brother Danny as best man. But what on earth could she do about it? Simply nothing! Her brother Gerald, Cousin Robin, and a friend called Sean were groomsmen, all wearing formal black tails, gray vests, striped pants, gloves, and gray top hats. Claire's extremely painful dilemma was that she wished she was Sharon, looking so radiant and beautiful in her dress. The Latin nuptial mass was performed without a hitch and the two of them were then driven to the Bentley Arms in Rigton, just down the road from their restored cottage.

After the wedding reception Claire had arranged for Sharon and herself to be driven to a private bus station in Aireborough, which was to take them to Manchester airport from where they would fly to the Canary Islands for their honeymoon. The honeymoon was a package-deal holiday from a brochure that Claire had obtained from a travel agent in Aireborough. On her wage as an architect, she could not afford anything lavish and so to keep costs down, she had to choose from the choice of destinations in the brochure. By this time, Claire was working with a small practice in Aireborough city center and her wage was extremely low. Throughout her architectural career so far she had been telling her father, who had chosen her future for her while she had been at high school that architects earned very little money. In response, every time she broached the subject, he would tell her that she didn't know what she was talking about. She simply had to start at the bottom of the ladder and work her way up like every young man had to do. He totally ignored the fact that, while he had also chosen the careers for her brothers, he had taken them both under his wing in his own business. Consequently they had an assured financial future, Claire, as 'William' didn't. Consequently, it was to become a constant struggle to make ends meet.

From the airplane, Claire (as 'William') and Sharon, together with other passengers, were collected by an agent from the packaged holiday company and driven through the rough roads from the airport into the town where their hotel was located. It was therefore quite late when the coach finally arrived at Hotel Santander and the two of them were shown to a room overlooking the swimming pool.

It was while Sharon was taking a shower that Claire began to have doubts about the success of the relationship. Prior to talking about marriage, struggling constantly with her gender dysphoria, she had thought that maybe if they were married, the struggle with her enigma would vanish once she was in a normal stable relationship. Now, staring down at Sharon's clothes on the double bed in front of her, niggling doubts pierced her brain. Looking at the beautiful traveling clothes, Claire felt that her enigma was going to boil up and spoil everything. She had hoped that it would vanish if she made every effort to live like a man and get married. So far, albeit after only a few hours, all the marriage appeared to have done was to make her symptoms worse, not better. Claire may have made a really big mistake. Nevertheless, the deed was done and there was no going back. How on earth was she going to cope with the ongoing dilemma?

The honeymoon was not a complete failure however, as the couple traveled throughout the islands visiting churches, pottery, glass and leather works, simply enjoying each other's company; and relaxing or laying on one of the many beaches. What Claire had really not thought through properly was the future. She could not tell Sharon about her gender dysphoria, and this was to become a huge issue over the next few years. Many years later Sharon admitted that throughout their life together, she had noticed that Claire exhibited a lot of feminine traits. But at such times Sharon had dismissed these thoughts as fantasy.

The other problem was that on their return to the UK, they had to stay at Claire's parents' house in Rigton for a couple of months, sleeping in her old bedroom. This was while their future home was being finished in her dad's spare time, with some help from her brother Gerry. The period living with her parents commenced peaceful enough with everyone in high spirits. If anything could mar it, it would be Gerry's jealousy of 'William'. This was becoming annoying. Toward the end of the first couple of months the strain of staying with Claire's family began to make itself felt in a big way. Her mum especially seemed to go out of her way to criticize Sharon. Consequently, the day when they could leave *Maison Milton* could not come soon enough.

It was a very cold and bleak day when the pair decided to move into Heath Lodge. The only heating they could afford, even on their combined wages, was an electric convection heater in the open dining area and a modern open coal fireplace in the living room, both forms of heating being totally inadequate for the size of the rooms. They had not been in the house long when Claire's foot went through a floorboard in the living room due to a previously unknown infestation of dry rot. They could not afford to have it repaired as Claire's wage, working in her new job as an architect at the city architect's department, was extremely low at £24 a week. She had bought a second-hand pale green Morris Oxford because they were living so far away from a bus route, but it soon had to be sold back to the dealer, as she could not afford the cost of petrol on her low wage. But in order to get to the nearest bus stop, they had to walk along the side of a couple of plowed paddocks to the main Wetherton Road in the village of Scarcroft. The alternative route was to walk down the very steep hill to Church Lane, which might have seemed fine, except that the walk back at night, in the dark, up a very steep hill, was so tiresome. It was much more treacherous in winter too when there was ice and snow. Sliding back down the hill was no fun and it was occasions such as this that the walk through the fields was far more amenable.

Both families expected Sharon to fall pregnant almost immediately but this was not to happen, as she was too hyped up. Having to work in an office near the city bus station she decided to quit her job as a secretary to a biscuit manufacturer. In order to fall pregnant she was advised by her mother that she had to concentrate on being 'at home'. This was all very admirable to Claire, but as 'William' she really was not sure exactly what to do to get Sharon pregnant. However, by process of elimination the two of them worked it out between them and, a few weeks later Sharon's doctor confirmed that she was pregnant. So although being born a hermaphrodite, contrary to popular medical understanding, Claire, as 'William', was eventually able to produce semen to fertilize one of Sharon's eggs. This might seem quite basic to the reader, but one must realize that Claire was not sure whether what she possessed 'in the basement' so to speak, was what real men had between their legs. Many years later, in fact in her retirement, Claire had to have some tests carried out and she was told by a specialist that she did not have a prostate gland. This confirmed to her medical team that she had not been born normally. Also discovered in later life, was the fact that her body produced a far greater amount of the female hormone estrogen, than the male testosterone. It was not until 2015 that a man in the USA was found to have both male genital parts and a womb in addition, with active eggs awaiting fertilization. Previously this was thought to be impossible, so the scientific and medical journals had to be re-written.

The problem for Claire was the way she was able to produce the semen. To create an orgasm she found that she had to imagine that she was the woman in the relationship, exactly as Claire had done many years earlier in her teens. What she discovered was that 'marriage' did not change the cross-dressing habit she had gotten into in her previous life, so she continued to dress as a woman when the opportunity arose. If Sharon was out Claire was in the habit of trying on her clothes in order to satisfy her natural feeling that she was still the woman that she knew she was. Even, on one occasion having bought Sharon a gift of some false eyelashes, Claire felt she had to try them on herself first.

Her gender dysphoria was certainly still alive and more active than ever, but she could tell no one. This resulted in the mental anguish becoming almost unbearable. She was scared of mentioning it to her doctor as this might get back to her dad and she was sure he would have murdered her, if nothing else but to save his own face. But whether he would have done so or not is neither here nor there.

Financially Claire was having problems making ends meet on her architect's salary. Sharon insisted that Claire hand over her weekly wage every Friday, in those days given to each employee in a brown envelope. Sharon's father had done the same and handed over his wage to her mother, and Sharon was not happy unless she was controlling the purse strings. Nevertheless, it was a real struggle and the two of them looked for an alternative.

While recalling events concerning Heath Lodge, perhaps the ghost should have a mention. One evening, Sharon and Claire had been to see a movie at the Clock Cinema, at the bottom of Easterly Road in Harehills. After buying some fish and chips for their supper, they sat in front of a roaring fire and scoffed their scrumptious feast. It had been raining earlier but the rain had stopped to leave the moor calm for the night. So later, in a comfy bed the pair of them sauntered into the *Land of Nod* without a care in the world.

It was just after midnight when Claire was awakened by a loud tapping noise, and climbed out of bed to see what was causing it. She realized that the noise was coming from the hallway between the kitchen and the dining room. After donning her thick dressing robe in the darkness, she wandered out of the bedroom onto the open landing which looked down onto the stairwell. The noise was just as loud and sounded like the handle of their large golfing umbrella tapping on the linoleum floor tiles. This was very mysterious.

Stepping back to the head of the stairs she flicked the light switch on and dashed down the stairs like fury to catch the unsuspecting 'thing' that was causing the noise. But when she arrived at the foot of the stairs and looked, there was nothing to see apart from the umbrella. Simply nothing! By this time Sharon had come out of the bedroom and asked, "What was it William?"

"I don't know. I thought that there might be a logical explanation for the noise I heard. It was as though a draught was coming under the front door to move the umbrella up and down, but there is no draught as we have the fabric sausage along the door's base. There is simply no way that any tiny creature such as a mouse could lift this umbrella either. It is a complete mystery."

The next day Claire mentioned the incident to someone at the shop, just up the road and the answer was as plain as day to them: "It was the ghost come back to haunt you." They said, with all conviction. Others in the shop agreed. It had to be the ghost of Heath Lodge.

Before they had married Claire had wanted to migrate to Canada. She had tried to migrate to the USA when she was a student at college, and even been promised a job with an architect in central Ontario. Prior to that even, she had been offered a place at Rhode Island School of Design but cancelled all thought of it on meeting Sharon. Now she contemplated Canada again but the thought vanished due to arguments with her dad. He had received a letter from his mother, Claire's Nanna Mariner, saying that America was a terrible country and Canada was even worse. She had told her son that there were people sleeping rough on the streets in Canada and people were very poor. It appeared that Claire's American relatives were in the habit of crossing over the border between Detroit, MI and Windsor, ON, where they could buy cheaper food than in the USA. In the act of shopping, Claire's Nanna had seen some poor people sleeping on the streets. What she had not seen was the far greater number of people sleeping rough on American streets. Nevertheless, the seed was sewn in Milton's mind that migration to Canada was lunacy. As a result Sharon and Claire went to see a promotional movie about Australia, without telling either of their parents.

Claire's Uncle Jeremy and Aunty Deborah had migrated to Sydney many years earlier, with her cousins June, Jimmy and Deborah, only to be followed by her godmother Aunty Irma, Uncle Duncan and Cousins Olivia and Ivan. But when Claire eventually felt that it was time to tell her parents that she and Sharon were thinking of migrating to Australia instead of Canada, Milton told the two of them to sit down while he gave them some 'home truths' about Australia.

Claire's dad stared at her and in all seriousness told the two of them that her Uncle Jeremy would have been sent to jail in Aireborough had he not emigrated, as he was a crook. He said that Australia had been founded almost as an open prison, a convict colony, and it was still a land full of criminals. He made the comment that it was only fitting that the land of convicts had welcomed Jeremy and his family as one of their own. A few years later in Australia, Claire was to confront her godmother and asked her if she knew anything about Milton's accusations. Irma was annoyed and boldly stated that none of it was true. It appeared that Milton had disowned Jeremy, at one time his best friend, because he had decided to leave the UK.

Milton didn't have a good word to say about any member of the Levine family at all. Whether it was because he had discovered they were originally German or not, Claire could not be sure. Considering that her Uncle Jeremy and her dad had been friends before her parents were married, the relationship between the two men appeared strained. It had been Jerry Levine who had introduced his sister Olivia to Milton Wilson when they went dancing on Saturday evenings. Claire had wondered if her father had in fact been acutely jealous of her uncle and his family, but yet on the other hand she had to consider the other factor. That was whether or not there was any truth in her dad's claim that Jeremy was guilty of some misdemeanor.

It was a number of years later that Uncle Jeremy opened up and told her the truth about his reasons to migrate. Jeremy had been trying to build up a small business while he was working for another company in Aireborough, but his employer had discovered his intentions and sacked him. Claire then compared this explanation to that of her dad's actions when he set up his own business. There appeared to be a glaring similarity. Milton had been working for Burnley Aircraft during World War II and had started his own business initially repairing cars, and taken two other members of staff from the aircraft company with him in his venture. So in effect what her dad had been doing was no different to what her Uncle Jeremy had done. But Milton, always the romanticist to put himself in a better light, made it seem that his actions were clean and those of Jerry Levine, his former friend, were dirty. This was the way her dad did business.

Claire had learned this the hard way many years earlier when she was at high school. Her dad had told her of the times he bought cheap products and then sold them for a higher price. He said he once put an advertisement in the *Yorkshire Post,* which said: *How to get rich quick. Send half-a-crown and a self-addressed envelope,* and he gave a box number for replies. He then began to laugh and told Claire that he had some cards printed with the words: *Do as I do* and put them into the self-addressed envelopes after pocketing the half-crown postal orders, and sent them back to the enquirers. To Claire this was fraud, but her dad considered it legitimate business. To Claire's mind, this was capitalist crime, and in time she came to despise capitalism as greed.

But trying to show her dad that she had initiative and was not exactly 'useless', at high school she had copied his example and found that she could buy bankrupt stock from a shop in the Grand Arcade and sell it for a higher price. She bought some writing pads for three pence and sold them for sixpence. Then she bought some exercise books for sixpence and after removing two center pages, still with more pages than the official school exercise books, she covered them with brown paper and sold them for a shilling compared to the school exercise books which were one and sixpence. With the spare center pages Claire produced a class magazine of four pages called the *Ping Ling*. She drew a picture on the front of every copy, and her friend Jake Ricall wrote a story about airplanes on the inside. Claire added a crossword and some jokes, and copied some short quips from the *Readers Digest*, and then sold the 'magazines' for a penny each. Eventually, someone discovered the same store, and that stopped Claire's little 'business venture'. Added to that, the other students in her class worked out that they could buy one copy of the *Ping Ling* for a penny and then sell it on to other students for a halfpenny. That was the end of Claire trying to copy her dad's capitalist business ideas.

The evening before Sharon and Claire were to fly out of England for Australia, there was an evening gathering at the home of Sharon's parents, Norbert and Lucy Bentley. Half way through the evening, Milton took Claire (whom he still saw as his eldest son 'William') into the Bentley's dining room and reminding her that she was going to a land of convicts. He told her that he disowned her for deserting the best country in the world and that she was a big disappointment to him. He stressed that she had turned out rotten after going against his wishes for her future, reminding her that he had known what was best for her, and what she had effectively done was to squander the money he had paid out for her education. He added that it all started when she was a 'little boy' and joined Micklegate Children's Library. It was not natural for little children to read fancy books about other countries as it gave them ideas that other countries were better than Britain and that was all wrong. Britain was not only the best country in the whole world but it was the richest and mightiest. Truly, her dad's attitude of Britain was equivalent to Adolf Hitler's view of Germany.

Claire was devastated and could not understand how a father could say such nasty things to his flesh and blood. Milton said: "Your brothers are like gold compared to you William. They don't disappoint me time and time again like you have done over the years. Book learning and college study appear to have turned you against your family, but Daniel and Gerald have remained loyal to your mummy and I, and have a great future in the works. You, on the other hand, have got too big for your boots and are now flying off to a land of criminals. To me you are no better than the convicts who live there. You are a disgrace to England and to our family, a complete disgrace. So you go to Australia without my blessing and as far as I am concerned you are no longer a member of the proud Wilson family."

With tears welling up in her eyes, Claire tried to answer her father but he put up his hand to stop her. The one-way conversation was at an end and Milton walked out of the door and back into the Bentley's living room to join the others. Claire stood there transfixed to the spot. She heard her father say to her mother that it was time for them to go home and that she had to get her coat on. Still standing there in a state of shock, Sharon joined her and asked what 'his dad' had said. Claire told her that she would tell her later as she was in no mood to speak at that moment. Internally, Claire vowed that from that evening onward, she had no father. He had cut himself off from her, not the other way around. He was so pumped up with his own self-importance and opinions that nothing would ever change him.

Sharon gave birth to Tanya in March 1967 and the family was waved off at Yeadon Airport by the Bentleys as Claire and Sharon's boarded the flight down to Heathrow for their Qantas flight to Australia. The Wilson family totally ignored the threesome and did not say goodbye to them. On arrival at Kingsford Smith Airport in Sydney, Claire, Sharon and Tanya were met by most of Claire's Australian family. Cousin Deborah's husband Donald Mackenzie drove them to their home in Abbotsford where Uncle Jeremy and Aunty Debby were waiting for them on the front verandah. Uncle Jeremy was wearing a light short-sleeved shirt and shorts and Aunty Debbie a light summer dress. Quite a change from the cold weather Claire and Sharon had left behind in England. Sharon, Claire and Tanya were to stay with Cousin Debbie for a week or so until they found somewhere to live. Their first weekend, however, was a round of parties and they were overwhelmed by the friendship of Claire's Australian family in Sydney, in stark contrast to family members in England who had turned their backs on them.

33

Australia

Claire found a house to rent in the suburb of Dundas, and the family moved in with the basics until their crate of furniture and household effects arrived a few weeks later. Claire had been promised a job with an architect in Philip Street, Parramatta prior to landing in Australia, but when she called at his office, his wife Myra told her that James had passed away since their initial contact. Consequently, the job she had been promised melted into nothing. Not daunted, Claire looked in Positions Vacant columns of the *Parramatta Advertiser* and seeing a job opportunity, arranged to attend an interview with a small builder in a three-story office block in George Street.

Donald O'Brien had started his apprenticeship as a joiner in the outer suburb of Riverdene and had done well for himself. He was now the boss of a small-time building contracting business. Having only the previous week sacked his draftsman he was looking for an architect or draftsman to take charge of his drawing office. At her interview Claire was scrutinized by three men: the boss Don O'Brien himself; the Accountant, an Englishman by the name of Humphrey Haddlington and the chief estimator Brad Turner. After her interview she was told to wait in the drawing office while they discussed her application. It did not take long before Brad Turner, the estimator, came in followed by Mr O'Brien to advise her that they had decided to give her a chance. The wage was a lot better by far than she had earned in England, and surprise of all surprises, she was to get a company car too. Brad was to get a new Ford Fairmont and Claire, as 'William', was to have Brad's Ford Falcon.

But things were not happy for her as Mr O'Brien had never employed an architect before, the previous draftsman having been more open and malleable to Mr O'Brien's ideas. So 'William' was thrust into the nitty-gritty life of a builder's office from day one, and within the first few days Mr O'Brien came up with a real challenge.

The guy they had previously employed had designed a private nursing home in Gladesville, part of which he had placed in front of the legislated building alignment line. Consequently, after the building inspector had noticed this error, the local council had told the building contractor to move the front wall behind the enforcement line which ran parallel to the street frontage. This they had complied with early on in the contract, but when the building reached roof level, nothing fitted. The roof joiners reported that the gutter would not be level.

Claire studied the situation carefully and asked her boss if he had ever constructed a roof with what was known as a 'bastard angle'. No, he had never heard of such a thing but listened. So Claire explained that they should build the roof on both sides so that the gutters and ridges were level and then let the slope of the roof take up the variation. In other words, while the gutter lines and the roof ridge remained horizontal, the roof pitch varied. The roof carpenter was informed and by the end of the following week the building was roofed successfully with *Wunderlich's* Marseilles-pattern terracotta roof tiles.

There were many interesting schemes that Claire was to tackle over her first few weeks – from producing drawings for factories, blocks of apartments, referred to as units in Australia, and yet more problems that were thrown at her by her boss. One day Claire heard a commotion in the next office, and naturally she enquired what was going on. She was told that one of the firm's employees had been killed at a car dealership they were building in Lindfield, one of the suburbs north of Sydney. Apparently no one had thought to put a protection rail around the square hole in the first floor concrete slab which was to house a parts lift. Claire was in total shock because of their negligence. The company was sued over this incident, which she thought was the right thing to do, and it forced them to add protection rails where previously they had not bothered.

It transpired that Mr O'Brien, Claire's boss, didn't like trade unions and refused to let any of his workforce join one. For Claire, this rang loud bells as her father had been of the same opinion. Now her boss had to sit up and realize that he could not carry on in business without allowing his men to join a trade union for construction workers. She was beginning to wonder if she could continue to work with such a bigoted employer.

On another matter, Claire had been looking at development sites with a realtor from Auburn, and she had designed some lovely villa homes for the sites, not aware that her boss didn't like them. To his mind, they were too modern. Nevertheless, Claire defended her designs as she had already visited many of the show homes in the northern and western suburbs, and seen what other builders and developers were building and selling quite successfully. Mr O'Brien said that he disagreed with Claire's ideas. "What kids want nowadays are the same red brick double-fronted houses as their parents. Not some newfangled English designs." That was to put Claire in her place.

She stood her ground explaining that her designs were definitely not English and that times were changing. She reminded Mr O'Brien that other house builders had show villages with houses of modern designs. It appeared that Mr O'Brien was not going to be told by this young Englishman that he didn't know what he was talking about. Now where had Claire heard those words before?

Fifteen minutes later, Mr O'Brien asked his secretary to call 'William' into his office. Claire stood before her boss, not being asked to take a seat as he once again damned her professional opinion. "You have a lot to learn about Australia William. You can't impose your English ideas on us here."

"But my designs are in fact Australian, not English Don." But her boss was not listening.

"You can't come over here young man and try to tell us what to do. We have our own ways of doing things and I know what sells." With that he dismissed her explanation with a wave of his hand. "You are obviously not suited to our ways here and I am terminating your employment with me at the end of the week. You may go now."

Claire walked back to her desk and after looking through the jobs vacant column of the *Sydney Morning Herald*, found a position with an architect in Chatswood. She rang the boss of that practice and arranged to attend an after-hours interview a few days later. However, shortly after her contretemps with Mr O'Brien, she was called back to his office again. He threw her insurance cards and a pay check on the desk in front of her and suggested that rather than leave at the end of the week, she should leave immediately. Claire was mortified. How could she be dismissed like that, wasn't it illegal? Apparently not! She realized that Mr O'Brien appeared to be what some referred to as 'a hire and fire merchant'. If a member of his staff disagreed with him over a matter, 'out the door' they went. To Claire, he was a petty dictator and surely he would not last long in business if he carried on acting in that way?

Donald O'Brien's meteoric rise as a builder from being a carpenter in a remote suburb, told Claire that he was a hard taskmaster and that there was no way she could work for such a man. But, many years later, walking through the streets of Parramatta, she noticed a tall building built by Donald O'Brien's company. To her, this showed the ruthlessness of the man, not his success. However, his hardness for business, and his methods led him to become one of Australia's leading developers. To Claire's understanding he was a typical capitalist, out to make as much money as he could and to hell with everyone else. Her early years in Australia were shaping up to show her that Australia survived on ruthless capitalist employers, supported by corrupt politicians. But then, she was to discover that that was typical of the world, not just Australia.

A few days later Claire began work in an architectural practice in Chatswood. In those days nothing like the skyscraper subcity it is today. Her main work was initially to write and illustrate a brochure for the Mobil Oil Company. The theme of the document was to market a new design of petrol stations, and to trial a new logo for the company. Unfortunately for her however, while she was in the middle of this work she took ill with a very bad cold and her boss threatened her with the sack – sickness or no sickness.

Although Sharon had rung the architects' office to explain that 'William' was ill, the senior partner sent a telegram demanding that Claire ring him personally. Consequently, she got out of bed and dressed as warmly as she could to walk to the public phone booth that Sharon had previously used. Claire's boss warned her that she was paid to perform, not to lay in bed feigning illness. With that ultimatum she saw the writing on the wall that here was another strict taskmaster for a boss, and she had to look for yet another position, hopefully closer to home. In the meantime, in her dressing robe, she set to work to produce some perspectives of the service stations the practice was working on for their client. The following day, feeling somewhat better than she had done previously, albeit still sniffling, she took her artwork into the office in Chatswood. Her boss and his partners looked at them with interest.

"If that's what you can produce when you are ill William, then you can be ill more often if you wish. These are good and just what we wanted. Congratulations."

In the meantime, unknown to Claire but mentioned by Sharon a few years later when they were having relationship problems, 'William' had been the subject of a conversation with Father Mark, the curate at St Peter's, the nearby Roman Catholic church. What Claire gathered was that Sharon had taken a fancy to Father Mark and looked forward to his pastoral visits. It was obvious that Sharon had been opening up her thoughts about her husband. But without knowing Sharon's partner personally, Father Mark had suggested that 'William' might be sick and in need of psychiatric help. What Sharon had been telling Father Mark was never disclosed and Claire, not being able to form any idea, could not even fathom a guess. But as she discovered in later years, that Sharon tended to be somewhat of a flirt with the right man and one's imagination might provide a scenario.

All Claire could think was that Sharon saw the priest as a lovely man and gradually opened up her innermost feelings. Sharon told Claire many years later, that she saw the feminine side of her husband quite often and it confused her. Sharon's dad had been a tall, broad-shouldered man, and Claire gathered that she compared all men to him. Obviously as 'William' was much smaller and in her words showed feminine tendencies, "he" was somewhat of an enigma even to her.

Having had to travel some distance from Dundas to Chatswood, Claire decided to look for a position closer to home. Consequently, she applied for a position as architect to a medium-sized architectural practice in Marsden Street, Parramatta. She was interviewed by Mr Lindsey Blackman and started work with his practice as soon as she was able.

Not too long after Claire, as 'William', had joined Mr Blackman's practice, her new boss realized that she knew her job really well and he thrust his new architect into the Australian design scene with a vengeance. Fortunately, Claire had applied for membership of what was then known as the *Royal Australian Institute of Architects* (RAIA) almost as soon as she had arrived in Sydney. She was helped in this by a sales representative called Dirk Engelveen, who introduced her to a few top architects over a beer after work one evening. As a result of these introductions, Claire had her sponsors sewn up for membership of, and was duly admitted as, an Associate of the RAIA. Her architectural degree from Aireborough College of Art School of Architecture was accepted by the Institute and finally life began to turn around for her.

After a few months 'William' was invited to join Mr Blackman and his partners, Clem Drucker, Wilf Bainbridge and Gerald Harvey, and their associate Jack Jackson, to attend the RAIA Christmas Cocktail Party in the half finished Sydney Opera House. They drank their *cocktails* with other members of the institute under the sweeping shapes created by Danish architect Jörn Utzen. A few years later, Claire was pleased to learn that the Institute had held a referendum to decide whether or not to drop the 'Royal' tag. Consequently, the vote was unanimous and the

Institute returned its 'Royal' charter and became the *Australian Institute of Architects*. As far as the Sydney Opera House was concerned, the RAIA was the first organization to be allowed into the unfinished structure. Claire's memory of this occasion was to stay with her for the rest of her life.

Sharon had attended the cocktail party with Claire and the latter thought her marriage partner looked so lovely wearing a pretty pale blue taffeta dress. If truth be known, Claire was jealous, as she wished she had been able to wear such a beautiful frock on such a festive occasion. Unfortunately, Claire had to continually remind herself, due to her father's bullishness at her birth, that she was still stuck in the gender trap. Claire was a woman who had to live the life of a man and it hurt all the time. It really hurt, oftentimes driving her to despair and depression. But who would have guessed and who would know how she felt as she could tell no one. This was part of her enigma, albeit a small part.

When it was time to leave the RAIA function 'Uncle' Gerald and his wife, the latter of whom seemed to treat Sharon and 'William' as her offspring, asked if Claire could drive them to their car which they had left in a car park in Camperdown, near the University of Sydney. Gerald's problem was that both he and his wife had drunk too much, as it happened Claire had too, and although she knew her way up Broadway toward the Parramatta Road and Camperdown, she was told later by Sharon that she drove through just about all the red lights on the way to Gerald's car. How Claire then drove back to their new home in Seven Hills, she had not the faintest idea the next morning. Fortunately they had not met with one police car. Today, it certainly would be a different story.

Sharon and Claire were managing fairly well together as the latter's wage allowed them to live a good life. It was while they were living in Eighth Avenue, Seven Hills, that James Marcus was born. He was christened in the tiny Roman Catholic chapel over on the Windsor Road, served by the parish priest of St Bernard's in Castle Hill. By this time Claire, alias "William," had joined the Jaycees, the Junior Chamber of Commerce, and attended evening meetings regularly. In the meantime, Sharon became restless and wanted to return home to England. If truth be known, Sharon had not exactly settled into Australian life as well as Claire had and she yearned to see her parents again, especially her father, on whom she doted.

The Wilsons agreed to sell their new house in Seven Hills and Sharon was to fly back to Aireborough leaving Claire to oversee the sale of the property. Living on her own in the house after Sharon, Tanya and Marcus' departure, was an opportunity for Claire to indulge her fantasies. Each evening, when she was not attending a meeting of the Jaycees, she would dress up in clothes she had bought in Parramatta. This was bliss, having no interruptions. So much so that she sat in front of the dressing table and practiced applying make-up to her heart's content.

But it did not take long for the property to sell and she soon found herself flying across to Edmonton, Alberta, where she hoped to find a job. They had obtained immigrant status for Canada and upon arrival Claire took a connecting flight across the Rockies to Edmonton. She was met off the flight by Alphonse (Alf) Martel, the President of the Junior Chamber of Edmonton and Patrick O'Donohue, an Irish member. After driving her to the local hostel of the *Young Men's Christian Association* (YMCA), where she was offered a room at the front of the building, Claire registered as 'William Wilson' for at least a week or so. After dropping her bags in the room she went out again with her new friends.

The 'gang' took her to a large bar to meet up with some more members of the Junior Chamber, and it was here that she rapidly learned the ropes about ordering beer in a bar in Alberta. It seemed that patrons could not go up to the bar counter to order drinks as was the practice in Australia. Instead, one had to wait at a table while a drinks waiter arrived to take their order, it being the law that only a waiter was allowed to carry drinks from the bar counter to a table. Rule number two was that everyone drinking had to put an equal amount of money in the center of the table to form a 'float'. Each time there was a fill-up of glasses, the money was taken from the float. It all made sense to Claire in many ways, but was so different to what she had been used to back home in Australia.

As she had not all that long ago arrived off a flight from San Francisco, having only eaten some peanuts and pretzels on the airplane from *San Fran* to Edmonton, her stomach was somewhat sensitive to the tiniest amount of alcohol. Alf suggested they all eat and ordered hamburgers all round with a large bowl of French fries to share. Claire was so hungry that she tucked unto her portion with relish, albeit her first Canadian hamburger. Unfortunately, it did not compare well with the gigantic juicy Australian beef burgers she had been used to in Sydney. But that was her opinion, and these were the days before *McDonalds Restaurants* appeared in almost every town and city in the Western world. Nevertheless, Claire was fed too much liquor that first evening and on returning to her room at the YMCA, she threw up in the toilet bowl before getting into bed. Her first night in Canada had not been a good one, she thought. But things could only improve couldn't they?

The following day Claire saw an advertisement in the *Edmonton Gazette* for an architect to join the practice of a Russian, Antonin (Tony) Matsov. Her interview was surprisingly arranged for 5 pm, but she was prompt as usual. She was kept waiting in reception for half an hour until Mr Matsov could see her and eventually he came through from his office. They sat down next to each other at a large coffee table in reception. The two of them chatted for a while and then Claire handed over her résumé which Tony simply skipped through without appearing to take a lot of interest. *Maybe he wasn't really interested,* she thought. Maybe she had come on a wild goose chase as she thought this was a strange way to interview someone. Then Tony Matsov asked to look through her portfolio of work. Here again he didn't appear to take much interest as he casually turned each drawing or sketch over. He had almost come to the last examples of her work when he picked up some small sketches she had produced for an Anglican church she had designed in Aireborough a few years beforehand.

"How long did it take you to produce these?" Tony asked.

"Oh, I guess at the time I did about four sketches a day," she told him truthfully. Tony was impressed. "I have to admit William that I am not too impressed with your work generally," he said as he once again flicked through the previous drawings, "but these I like."

"Thank you."

"Okay, so when can you start?"

"Oh, er, like tomorrow if you wish, or the day after." she blurted out in concealed excitement.

"Okay, you can start Monday morning at 8.30 am, is that okay?"

"Thank you, I will be here ready to start work on the dot."

"Good! Now what are you doing?"

"You mean like – right now? Like – this evening?"

"Yes, that's exactly what I meant. I have to attend a book launch at a hotel downtown at 6 pm, would you like to come with me?"

"Oh well, yes, but what about my portfolio of work, will I leave that here?"

"No, bring it with you. You can leave it in the trunk of my car while we are at the function."

So Claire waited in reception while Tony gave instructions to his wife Viola, who was the practice secretary. Then Tony led 'William' to the elevator and down to the street below. Her new boss walked across to a beautiful gray-colored Rolls Royce Silver Cloud and opened the trunk. *Wow! Is this his car?* Claire thought to herself.

"You can put your portfolio in here, together with your coat if you wish as we are not going to need outer garments where we are going." Obeying his command Claire laid her portfolio down on the pristine floor of the car's trunk and laid her raincoat over it.

That done, they drove off, the engine simply making a soft hiss. Tony Matsov told her that after the book launch they would probably dine with some of his political colleagues. She was shaking in her boots at this announcement as she was totally unprepared for such an occasion. Nevertheless, all she had to do was to stand behind her new boss and let him do the introductions. Claire was his guest that evening, after all was said and done.

The hotel conference room was packed with many people and Claire didn't know how she would survive the whole evening. She was in so much awe of the book launch that she would have preferred to return to the YMCA, pick up a hamburger and then gone to bed. The speeches and clapping out of the way, people started to leave the function. It was then that Claire noticed Tony chatting to two large-framed men, her boss in contrast being quite small in stature. Tony waved for her to join them and introducing her to the men he outlined his plans for her: "William is going to be working with me from now on; he is an architect from Australia." Then Tony led his newest employee to an alcove where he ordered drinks. So Claire had only been in Canada a couple of days and here she was dining with some famous people. To an outsider she appeared to have well and truly landed on her feet.

The reception itself was quite boring in reality, as it was simply an event to launch a new book written by a French-Canadian writer: Rénard Michelson. Claire felt as though she was in Tony's shadow all the time, and even at the table she felt like sliding under it. But she had nothing to lose as all she had to do later was go to sleep in her YMCA room. That being so, she had already gotten into the habit of picking up a hot dog at a street kiosk nearby for her 'supper'.

The men that Tony Matsov was entertaining over a meal certainly had the stature and talk of politicians, and Tony certainly knew how to get around them for business. But as she was to learn later, from no less than the secretary of the Alberta branch of the *Royal Architectural Institute of Canada* (RAIC) that her boss was under surveillance for fraudulent dealings. Had she been aware of this at the time of her employment, maybe she would have thought twice about working for Antonin Matsov.

As the meal progressed Claire was to discover that one of the men was a member of the provincial legislative of Alberta and the other an Edmonton city councilor. They talked above her head as she was totally unfamiliar with either Canadian provincial or city politics. She did however gather that they seemed to be in each other's pockets and those of her boss too.

They had consumed their main course, and drunk copious amounts of wine while waiting for the desert to arrive, when Tony turned to Claire. With the eyes of his political colleagues watching her face, Claire paled in shear fright, as she was asked: "What do you think William?"

"Er, I have no opinion at the moment Mr Matsov as I have only just arrived." He had raised a question which Claire thought was too obnoxious for words, but wanting to give a good impression straight after her interview, she added: "But I guess I agree with you."

"Why do you agree with me?" *Help!* She was stuck, but decided to repeat some of the things he had said to show her agreement. That response, unknown to her at the time, was her undoing. Tony told her on the drive to the YMCA later, that he thought she might have had some gumption and not simply agreed with everything he said. He reminded her that she had to stand on her own two feet and develop her own opinions, however right or wrong they might appear. Claire blushed crimson in the light of the oncoming headlights, but breathed a sigh of relief as she climbed out of the Rolls Royce to walk into the YMCA reception, her portfolio under one arm and her raincoat over the other.

The night porter remembered her from the time she had booked in and recalled that she had been for interviews. He handed the key to her room with: "How'd yer get on with yer innerviews young feller?"

"Great, thanks." Claire nervously replied, "I've gotten a job and start Monday morning."

"Good fer you. Is their office far from here?"

"Well, it's a bus ride and a short walk I guess. It's near the city airport."

The porter nodded and offered the customary "Goodnight, sleep tight," as she wearily walked around the corner to the elevator to proceed to her floor. That night she should have slept well, with happiness, but was kept awake for a while by other residents spewing up their guts after an evening imbibing too much alcohol. Claire vowed that she would not get herself into the same condition, but was later to find that she could not comply with her own intentions.

34

Canada

Over the next few weeks as Claire became friendly with members of the *Junior Chamber of Commerce* (JC), she was invited out to more drinking bouts but could not compete with the guys with whom she shared a table. It was not surprising really, as she had a smaller woman's stomach, she could not drink too much before becoming infected with what she wisely thought of as stupidity.

Being invited to quite a few JC events, on one Social occasion she decided to have some fun and introduced them to a dance that she had invented called the *kangaroo hop*. In this her arms became the kangaroo's front shortened arms or legs and she simply hopped around. It was so funny apparently, they believing it was an Australian dance. Whether they thought Australians were *A Weird Mob* or not Claire was never able to make out.

She opened a current account with the Royal Bank of Canada in Jasper Avenue one lunch time and deposited her travelers' checks. A week later the rest of her money arrived from the Bank of New South Wales and at the earliest opportunity she knew she had to get herself some wheels, plus somewhere permanent to live. As luck had it, one of the other members of the Junior Chamber was an insurance salesman called Rolf Ardmont and he had a car to sell. The problem with the dark green but sleek Chevelle Malibu was that it had a large dint in the passenger door. Nevertheless, the car was relatively cheap. Claire intended having the dent repaired as soon as she could afford it, but her major priority was to find somewhere to live as Sharon and the children were to arrive in another few weeks.

There was a new development in North Edmonton called *Skylark Village*, which comprised some high-rise apartments, double-decker terrace properties and quite a number of three-story town houses. Claire was shown inside one of these and was so impressed she decided to pay a deposit and moved in two days later. She bought a picnic table instead of a normal dining table as their own furniture would arrive before long, and they already had a table and four chairs. She ordered some beds as their own had been sold, and they would have to manage with basic pots and pans which were purchased from a store in one of the eastern suburbs which sold recycled goods. But Sharon, Tanya and Marcus were to arrive before Claire knew what had hit her and she had not bought everything they needed to make them completely comfy. Nevertheless, she reckoned that they would manage until their household goods arrived from Australia.

The day came for Sharon, Tanya and Marcus's arrival. Claire waited in the arrivals lounge at Edmonton Airport as the airplane landed and unloaded its passengers. Panic struck though, as there was no sign of her family. Then just as she was ready to walk back to the arrivals desk, there they were walking down the corridor, the last ones off the flight. Tanya ran up to Claire as soon as she saw her, but Marcus held back as though she was a stranger. Claire was told that her accent had already changed to Canadian, but she was not aware of it. It can't have been by much anyway.

Claire drove them all to their new home in Skylark Village and after they had inspected each room, everyone was pleased with the town house she had selected. The children were soon tucked up in bed and fell asleep in no time.

The job Claire had as architect in the office of Tony Matsov was quite onerous. He kept her working all hours as he always seemed to come to see how she was progressing when it was time to go home. Consequently, by the time Claire arrived home most days, and let's not forget that these were the days before mobile cell phones were invented, Sharon was beside herself with worry. Quite often too, by the time Claire did arrive home, Tanya and Marc were already in bed, and of course, they wanted her to read them a story.

One of the problems Claire encountered was that she was expected to work through weekends too, as the practice had strict deadlines to keep on the main project. Nevertheless, as a family the Wilsons managed to get out occasionally, and Claire remembered quite clearly driving them to Devon Lake for a picnic one Sunday lunch time. Thinking they had left the mosquito menace back in Australia, they had to change their minds. They didn't stay long as the huge number of mosquitoes constantly invaded and bit every member of the family. Instead of being able to enjoy their surroundings, they had to pack up their picnic things into their Chevelle Malibu and drive back into the city.

But there was a surprise in store for the family. Claire's boss Tony Matsov decided that as she had worked through two weekends, she needed some compensation. Sharon had been complaining about Tony working Claire through weekends without extra pay, so he awarded the family a long weekend to drive up to the Rockies. They stayed a night in Jasper and the following day walked on a glacier below Mount Edith Cavell. Claire and Tanya were really interested in the variety of mosses which were growing in the valley bottom as they were of such a bright green, adjacent to the creek which was bitterly cold. Having spent a night in the *Post House Annex* at the side of Lake Louise, the next day they drove down toward Calgary. It being such a lovely day they all agreed that it would be just great to ride up Sulfur Mountain on one of the cable cars. At the top they found a vacant picnic table and began to eat their packed lunches. What none of them had expected was the number of cheeky chipmunks on the mountain, so friendly and cute. They jumped right onto the Wilson's table for handouts. It turned out that no food could be left uncovered as the little critters would grab it and scarper off.

The snow started falling early in Edmonton and it did not take long to find that Claire had to have chains on her Chevelle Malibu. The temperature dropped to below zero too and she learned to plug the engine into the power post near the parking bay at the rear of their town house. But one particular day she couldn't get the car to climb out of the gutter and stepped out to see what the problem was. A passing neighbor had a look with her and declared that she had a tire which was slowly becoming soft. Due to the low temperatures, the air in the tire had frozen and the wheel would not turn. All she could do was to ring the office and explain her problem to them. Ted, one of the older assistants was ordered to collect her as her boss could not afford Claire to slip behind in her time keeping, taskmaster that he was. But at lunchtime, when the air temperature had risen slightly Ted drove her home and together they inflated the car tire. It was only a slow leak and so Claire decided to keep it topped up until she had the time to take it into a garage for repair.

One problem with the early snow was that it was powdery and it caught in the gaps in the tarmac on the road surface and was quite slippery. Claire was traveling to work after lunch one afternoon when, driving on the icy surface through an intersection in Edmonton, a car coming at ninety degrees to her slammed into the offside door. It was a pity it wasn't the passenger door as there was already a dent in that door from the previous owner. Fortunately, the guy in the offending car admitted it was his fault and so Claire was able to have the damaged door fixed on the other driver's insurance.

One Sunday Claire drove the family through a national park but wondered why there was a traffic snarl up ahead. Claire opened her driver door to take a look but soon got back inside again. What she had seen was a huge grizzly bear prowling along the row of cars, maybe seeking a handout. She warned the kids to keep their windows closed, despite their temptation to pat the cuddly-looking bear. As it approached however, Tanya and Marcus soon realized that grizzly bears were huge and dangerous-looking, and cowered down into their seats.

But just as Sharon had shown in Australia, she was not happy in Canada either. It was extremely cold and she was bored during the day, not being able to get a job due to having to look after the children. She and Claire had been looking at houses to buy but the prices were far beyond their reach on the latter's meager wage. As a result, after much deliberation, they decided to move back to the UK. To Claire, it was a blessing in disguise as she could not see her working for Tony Matsov for ever and a day as he was a slave driver. To add to her consternation, the secretary at the Provincial office of the Royal Architectural Institute of Canada told her that her boss was under investigation for fraud. Antonin Matsov had apparently been reported to the RAIC for insider dealing among Provincial Legislative members. They appeared to be in each other's pockets and this, quite naturally, was illegal. Claire was asked if she was able and willing to provide them with any evidence which might confirm the rumors. With this knowledge, the writing was on the wall and the Wilsons decided to leave Canada as soon as they were able.

Previous arguments with her dad that she had encountered prior to migrating to Australia vanished into the ionosphere when she and her family returned to 'the best country in the world'. Her dad was elated as it proved his point. Arriving at Manchester Airport, Claire and Sharon were met by Milton and Gerry and driven across the Pennines to the family home in Rigton, where they were to spend a few days recuperating.

Claire's first priority was to find a job and as luck would have it, a large firm of architects in the center of Aireborough was in great need of experienced architects. Jumping in with both feet in her excitement she was interviewed on a Saturday morning by the senior partner Bernard Kaplan. She was amazed that Bernard was working on Shabbat, but he turned out not to be a stickler for strict Jewish observance. Bernard sat sideways to his desk devouring Claire's references and examples of her design work. He explained the flavor of the work on which the practice of Kaplan, Benson & Partners was currently engaged and then said he would like to offer her a position. "What salary were you thinking of?" he asked her casually.

"Oh well, I had not given it a lot of thought since I have only just arrived back in Britain, and I realize that wages may be different to those overseas."

Bernard looked down a list of personnel which indicated their salaries. He told her he could slot her in between a couple of other senior architects and quoted a salary. "Is that per month?" Claire asked him.

"No William, that's per year."

Claire was dumbfounded. "Oh sorry, but in Australia and Canada I was getting that sort of figure per month."

"Well, the wages are much lower over here and I have slotted you in between two others of similar experience, and that is all I can offer you."

Claire asked if she could think about it and would let him know first thing Monday morning. Back at *Maison Milton*, her parents' home in Rigton, she related the interview to her dad. He didn't bat an eyelid, concealing his surprise that the wages of architects were so low. Claire explained that she had been earning the sum offered per month overseas, not per year. "Well, William you are back in Great Britain now, you have to make allowances." It was no wonder that she had gone overseas in the first place as she was to find it difficult existing on an architect's salary in England. But she had had no choice.

She rang Mr Kaplan on Monday morning as promised and accepted his offer. It meant however, that 'William' and Sharon would have to find a cheaper house to buy than the one's they had been looking at. Milton suggested they may like to try to find a house in Wetherton as Claire's youngest brother Gerald and his wife Veronica were living there. Consequently, the pair of them visited the office of a Chartered Surveyor in the small town, and the couple was shown a detached house on a private housing estate on the East Side. There was not much of a selection on the market in their price range, and as they didn't have much choice they decided to accept it. Claire could not afford a decent car like the ones she had owned overseas and had to manage with an old Morris Cowley. It was a real set down from what they had been used to overseas but, as with the job, Claire had no choice back in England, as her father continued to tell her.

Slowly Claire and Sharon began to make a few friends, albeit mainly among their neighbors. One evening they attended a disco in Wetherton Town Hall together with their neighbors Tracey and Jack, and Marney and Eric from the house on the corner. They all parked their cars near each other adjacent to the old cattle market and walked toward the town hall. Claire held Sharon's hand and then noticed that she was holding the hand of Eric, the guy who lived in the corner house. Claire was puzzled. Why would Sharon hold Eric's hand? Indeed, why would he hold Sharon's hand instead of that of his wife?

In the hall later, as they were dancing, Claire recognized a tune they were playing and guessed that it might have been from 1957 as she always associated music with her surroundings and events. She approached the Master of Ceremonies (MC) and mentioned it to him. He nodded to her and Sharon and Claire continued dancing. A few minutes later, as the music finished, the MC announced that someone had correctly identified the year when the last number was composed. Surprise, surprise – it was Claire. Wow! Was she amazed? You bet she was. Her prize was two free tickets to attend an evening at Batley Variety Club the following week.

So on the appropriate evening Claire and Sharon drove down to Batley and were directed to a table near the stage. Their free tickets included a free meal too and she bought a bottle of wine to accompany the meal. The guest artist for the evening was the Buddy Rich Big Band and of course as Claire loved all forms of percussion, Buddy's drum playing was outstanding and the evening became the real highlight of her year.

Trying to economize, Claire decided to start making items of furniture for the house. Her pride and joy was a tester canopy to hang over their bed head, the latter of which was Australian, made from black bean. Claire copied the shapes of the vertical bars in the bed head but reversed them so that they were facing down on the canopy. It looked great on paper and she was sure that her skill at woodwork could make it look great as a piece of furniture.

After the evening meal one day, when Claire was busy in the garage making the bed canopy, Sharon came in, all dressed up, to say that she was going out to a mother's meeting at the school. Although Sharon had not given any inkling that there was such a meeting, Claire never gave any thought to the issue at the time.

A couple of weeks later however, still working on the tester canopy there was a skirmish. Her neighbor Jack was a retired policeman and was outside his gate threatening Eric Ackroyd from the corner house. Claire didn't know what the argument was about but Jack's wife Tracey came into the garage to speak to her alone.

"William, I hate to be the bearer of disturbing news, but I think you should be told the truth about a certain person." Claire was all ears at this revelation. "I don't think you are aware that Sharon has been dating Eric. He has befriended most of the young women in the street previously and Sharon is his latest victim."

Claire was dumbfounded and stood there with mouth agape.

"I didn't really want to be the bearer of bad news William but I thought someone should tell you." After a short pause to let the information sink into Claire's brain Tracey added: "I think it is better if you confront Sharon with this and get it out into the open air. She ought to admit she is having an affair in my opinion." Claire was open mouthed and stared at Tracey. "Sorry William, but I just thought you should do something about it as this is not the first time Eric has ruined people's lives."

Claire went back into the living room and told Sharon that there had been a skirmish outside involving Eric Ackroyd. Sharon went as white as a sheet. "What was that all about," she asked.

"I thought you might be able to tell me." Claire waited for her reply as Sharon stared at her directly for a few moments before looking at the floor. After a few minutes of silence waiting for her to explain, she opened up and admitted that she had been having an affair with Eric. Claire was flabbergasted. Sharon explained that the times she had told 'William' that she was going to a meeting at the school, she had been dating Eric, and they had traveled into Wetherton to have a coffee and chat on most occasions. Claire was absolutely amazed at all this. How could Sharon do this? Claire was frantic with worry and her life started falling apart right at that very moment. Sharon had been deliberately lying about the times she had gone out, or telling Claire what she had done when she picked the children up from school.

Sharon admitted that she had fallen madly in love with Eric Ackroyd, but that she still loved 'William'. Claire suggested that they go see a marriage counselor but Sharon refused. She had made up her mind to leave and live with Eric, and nothing Claire could do or say would make any difference.

After work one Friday evening Claire arrived home with a huge bunch of flowers for Sharon and presented them to her as she was cooking a meal in the kitchen. Sharon took the bunch of flowers, laughed, and then threw them onto the kitchen floor. "You think that's going to make any difference, do you William? You must be mad. I am leaving and that's that."

Sharon had planned to walk out one morning the following week and told Claire at breakfast that particular morning. As a result of Sharon's proclamation, before Claire went to work, she managed to get Tanya and Marc together in the bedroom to tell them that mummy was leaving and going to live with another man. "Oh, you mean with Uncle Eric?" Tanya asked. So her little daughter already knew what was going on, which was more than Claire did, it seemed.

"Yes. Now you have a choice, do you want to live with mummy and that man or would you prefer to live with me and maybe stay at nanna and granddad Wilson's for a while?" Tanya chose to live with 'her daddy' but Marc chose to cling to his mummy's skirt. He was only three after all.

After breakfast Claire told Sharon that she was going to take Tanya to school and vanished pretty quickly out the door and into the car before Sharon could object too much. She drove hell-for-leather over to her mum and dad's house in Rigton and told them the sorry tale. Olivia fussed over Tanya and things were settled. Claire drove back to Wetherton and told Sharon that Tanya was safe with her nanna and that when she had left with 'her fancy man' the door locks would be changed, so she had better take everything she needed.

Eric was waiting around the corner to collect her and her belongings. Claire drove into Wetherton to buy new locks for the front and back doors and when she returned, Sharon and Eric had cleaned out the house and gone. The house was left in a real mess in their rush to be out. Claire changed the locks and the house was then secure. She then drove to Rigton and then into Aireborough to tell her design department section leader Clive Rushworth what had happened. He was very sympathetic and told her to take the rest of the day off.

The following day Olivia took Tanya to Rigton Primary School where she was enrolled as a new pupil. Claire didn't want to mess up Tanya's education, just because her mum had walked out of their lives.

Sharon was so smitten with her new beau that she didn't seem to see reason. This was perhaps typical of many in her position, and could be said to have been typical of so many throughout history. After a week or so Sharon rang Claire at work to arrange a weekly meeting, so that the children could play with each other. The first meeting was arranged for the following Saturday morning in the village of Tullminster, where Tanya and Marc could play in the children's playground off the main street.

Sharon and Claire talked casually, the latter being able to see that her former partner was struggling inwardly but did not want to lose face. This situation went on for a few weeks, meeting in the same place at the same time every second Saturday. In the meantime, however, Claire had become friendly with an older woman, who seemed to be able to read her like a book. Clementine, known as Clemmy to everyone else, was twelve years older than Claire and it seemed she was going through an extramarital period of excitement herself.

Claire detected a strain on her parents due to the unusual situation, and needing to rid herself of the friction, wanted out. Consequently she decided to rent a house in the Aireborough suburb of Moorfield and moved in with both Tanya and Marc. She had been in court a few days earlier, after Milton, her father, had persuaded her to divorce Sharon. The family attorney had had a private detective watching Sharon and reported that she was living with Eric in a tiny bedsit in Tullminster while she worked evenings as a barmaid in a local bistro. Claire's solicitor argued that it was not a suitable place to rear a young boy as his mum was sleeping in a single bed with a man who had been her neighbor, and the man appeared to be of dubious character. When Sharon was advised of this by her lawyer, she decided to relinquish her rights to Marc and granted full custody of both children to Claire. The magistrate read her letter of admission in court giving 'William' custody. Sharon's letter appeared to be a legal device confirming that she had given up all rights of custody, and this was the main reason why Claire had decided to move out of her parents' home to find alternative accommodation. Clemmy said she would live with Claire and the children and look after them as their aunty, and to make sure they attended school. But would the situation last?

Again Sharon requested a meeting over a cup of coffee in Tullminster, during which Sharon admitted that she was not happy away from her children and would like to make a new start. Claire agreed to this suggestion and they took the children away for a weekend in the Yorkshire Dales. *A bit of fresh air*, she thought might be the best approach.

The weekend was rather strained for both of them and on the drive back into Aireborough Claire asked Sharon if she would like to take both children, despite the letter she had given the court. She said that she would like both children with her and looked quite relieved at the suggestion. By then Eric's wife Marney had left him to live with her sister in Dalton. So Sharon moved into Eric's original house in Wetherton, with Tanya and Marc – and Eric's children too at weekends.

Claire was now left on her own to make new decisions.

35

A Sucker

Sharon taking both children and moving into her lover's house after his wife and children had moved out convinced Claire that maybe now was the time in her life to effect a full change of gender and she began to make enquiries. Her endeavors, however, were short lived, as within a few days Sharon rang her for another meeting and they agreed to take Tanya and Marc down by the weir under the bridge in Wetherton. It was lovely down by the River Wharfe where the children could feed the ducks and play in the shallow water if they wanted. When they met, Sharon looked very upset and Claire wanted to know why she had changed her mind yet again.

It transpired that after they had returned from their weekend in the Yorkshire Dales National Park, Eric had told her that if she left him, he would commit suicide. Sharon did not want that on her conscience so she said she would live with him in his place in Wetherton. But then, just as Claire was beginning to plan her gender change, Sharon was having serious doubts about her own future. Eric was dangling the proverbial *sword of Damocles* over her head and she didn't like it. Sharon admitted that she preferred to be with Claire and the children as a family again and had made up her mind to leave Eric despite his seemingly idol threats. Claire wondered if behind it all was Sharon's eventual realization that Eric was of unstable character after all, having threatened to kill himself a number of times previously.

So Claire, caught in a cleft stick, rarely one who overturned the proverbial applecart, went along with Sharon's wishes for the sake of the children and agreed that she should move into the leased semi-detached house in Moorfield. Clemmy said she would move out, even though her husband had by this time cut her out of his life. Clemmy found a flat to move into in Headingley and Sharon moved into the semi in Moorfield with Claire, Tanya and Marc.

A few days later, Sharon had a phone call from the police. She was requested to go to the morgue at Harrogate hospital to identify Eric's body. He had, it appeared, carried out his threat and committed suicide at Brougham Rocks. Sharon was shaking like a leaf as she arrived at the morgue at the same time as Eric's wife, Marney. The latter told Sharon that she wasn't surprised. Her husband had done what he had always threatened to do – take his own life. He had been consulting a psychiatrist over a number of years with little effect to show for it.

Sharon blamed herself for Eric's death and was totally irreconcilable. She stayed in bed for two weeks, not eating anything, crying constantly. Eventually, Claire got through to her that according to Marney, Eric had been dating various women over recent years and in the end, all he wanted was an excuse to bow out of society. Sharon merely happened to be the latest scapegoat. She could not blame herself as he had threatened suicide a number of times, a fact with which she was well aware. Eventually however, Sharon's stability was restored and Claire suggested they buy a house in a new private housing estate in Harrogate.

Claire took Sharon, Tanya and Marc to look at the show houses of Bignall Homes (Harrogate) Ltd and decided to buy one of those under construction on the estate. Some weeks later they moved in, and over the next two years made the house into a home. Claire built a bookcase for her growing number of books; a long fireplace surround to the hole in the wall, which housed a small gas fire; new double doors to the kitchen; and wardrobe units to the room that Tanya had preferred over the garage. Claire laid out the back garden in a fan shape, with a fish pond and arbor in the far corner. All seemed hunky dory.

In business, Claire had resigned from the architectural practice she had been working with for some time as she had been offered a partnership with a former colleague Gerald Robinson, in Henry Worthing's practice in Aireborough. Claire was shown the financial accounts and put them to Milton, her dad, for his business advice. He said they looked good and 'William' would be a fool not to take up the offer of a partnership with Gerald. Claire's dad even offered to loan her some deeds to a holiday chalet he owned near Scarborough, to be used as collateral for a loan from the Westminster Bank in Park Row. Consequently, Gerald and 'William' formed a new partnership. It was to be known as the Blenheim Design Partnership. On Gerald''s suggestion they met his bank manager in Park Row and it was agreed that they should commence the new partnership with a small overdraft. With the bank loan paid into the new partnership account, Gerald purchased for himself a new Citroën to replace the old car he had been driving since 1952. He suggested that Claire buy a new car too, to replace the Škoda she so loved. Claire chose a Datsun 180B.

Claire's contribution to the new practice was to bring in new commissions and in that she was quite successful, even though they may not have been so lucrative at first. Gerald said he had some clients already in place that had been on the books of the former Henry Worthing practice. All looked fine.

But trouble started early for the partnership. Within a few weeks Claire was advised that one of the staff members, Simon Harley, who had been befriending a particular housing developer for a few years, was accused of fraudulent dealings. He had told his client that he was an architect, when in fact he was not. In actual fact he had never done a day's architectural study in his life, merely filling his working week as an architect's assistant. To add to that lie he had told them he had obtained planning permission for a large housing estate near Warkfield. This was also a lie and Simon had been living on a financial tightrope. The developer Mainline Construction PLC, was going to sue him, as Henry Worthing had apparently made him a partner. Even though Gerald and Claire didn't accept Mainline's claim, the builders decided to sue the successors of the old practice, which meant the two partners of the Blenheim Design Partnership. The only saving grace on Claire's part was that she had not accepted liability for the debts of the former practice. Nevertheless, she still had to take legal advice.

Within a few short months after the debacle, another blow was thrown in Claire's face when her very capable secretary Sally Donnelly came into her office after the lunch break one afternoon and closed the door. Walking over to Claire's desk she sat down and explained that she had something very serious to tell her. "What is it Sally?"

"In a nutshell William, Mr Robinson has been doing the dirty on you."

"What?" Claire was dumbfounded. "Go on Sally."

"Well, he has been doing drawings in the office for one particular client and getting paid privately at home."

"Thank you Sally, that's all I need to know. Could you ask him to come in here to see me please?" Sally walked out leaving Claire's office door slightly ajar.

She could hear Sally speaking to Gerald through the connecting door between the secretarial office and Gerald's room. She told him that 'William' would like to see him in 'his' office but he suggested his partner should go and see him instead. Claire cut this conversation short by walking through to Sally's office and standing at the door she very sternly asked Gerald to come into her office. So doing, she went back and stood by the window, which looked over the back yard and the end gable walls of 'the Blenheims'. Rows of terrace houses built in the previous century.

Gerald poked his head around the door: "You wanted to discuss something William?"

"Yes Gerald, please close the door and sit down, would you please."

"No, it's alright. I'll stay standing if you don't mind William."

"No Gerald, I would prefer you to be seated with what I have to say." Gerald sat while Claire remained standing. This gave her the superiority she needed to say what she was about to say. Looking down on him she started: "Gerald, it has come to my notice that you have been preparing drawings in the office while the proceeds have been paid into your own private bank account."

"Who told you?" he asked

"Never mind who told me Gerald, I just know, okay?"

"Well, I was going to pay the amount into the practice account."

"I don't believe you Gerald, not for one minute or you would have done something about it before now. Paying the proceeds of a practice project into your own personal account shows a gross disdain for our partnership. I am not happy Gerald. Not happy at all."

Gerald was silent. So Claire went on as she had had the upper hand in the conversation and had to make quick decisions. "As a result of this stupid action of yours our partnership is now at an end. I cannot trust you ever again." There was silence as the two of them stared at each other intently. "I want you to repay the money into the practice account immediately and then to move out of your office. I will take over the lease of the building." Gerald blushed crimson and vowed to make things good again if Claire would give him a second chance. "I'm sorry Gerald but as I see things, I have bought into a practice that is fraudulent. Firstly with Simon, and now with you it seems. I will not be a party to fraud under any circumstances, or in any shape or form. There is no second chance. You must have known about Simon's antics when you presented the practice to me last year and now this." Claire was getting more and more annoyed over the situation. "Just go Gerald, go." She waved her hand in a gesture of dismissal as she had to remain strong and resolute. Claire returned to looking out of the window at the terrace houses in the back street, as Gerald slumped out of her office with his tail between his legs. No doubt his face was red with shame.

Over the next week Gerald moved out of his office lock, stock and barrel and Claire sublet the room to a scaffolding company, whom she knew were very successful in business and her landlord would have no fear of losing money.

But the writing was on the wall that things were not looking good. Claire decided to lay off the drafting staff on the upper floor and sublet those rooms too and turned Sally's work into a private company called *Secretarial Services Unlimited* (SSU). It did not take long for Claire to calculate that the work on which she had been commissioned, was not enough to support even her own rent on the one room and so she sublet that too, making Sally a director of the letting company. Claire then moved her drawing board and other equipment to her garage in Harrogate. Her only chance was to work from home until she had cleared the debt she owed to the bank for buying into the practice. She was determined to have her father's deeds on his coastal chalet returned to him after she had paid her debt to the bank.

But while all the uproar was going on, her office was broken into and important design reports she had completed for her previous employer were stolen. Claire knew instinctively who had taken them but she could not prove it. She was convinced that a rival colleague in the previous practice, who she knew was friendly with Simon Harley, had been tipped off, and unknown to Claire he had a duplicate set of keys to each room. That being so, Claire's former colleague had apparently looked through her library and extracted the reports she had published. It appears that Claire was faced with treachery. In all this, her gender dysphoria found itself at the bottom of the pile. She was faced with other huge decisions which affected her future in a different way.

Claire's time working at home in Harrogate had been productive as far as non-business activities were concerned as she had joined the local branch of the Liberal Party. But her period with them came to a head when it was suggested that her name be put forward to represent them as a candidate in the local elections. The day came when she had to front a panel of selectors. Sitting next to her waiting to be interviewed was a tall well-built man wearing a pale gray shiny suit. He turned to her and asked if he could borrow her new slim silver ballpoint pen to fill in part of his form. This somewhat unsavory character was a car salesman in Harrogate, and very pompous. Claire could not imagine him being a local councilor, so she took an instant dislike to his overbearing attitude. But by the end of the day he had managed to soft-soap the selection committee and they nominated him as the local Liberal candidate. Claire hated him more when he walked off with her silver ball-point pen. She would never trust a politician or car salesman ever again. That was her personal threat to society.

But even working in her converted garage, Claire was getting worried about the family finances. She could not support Sharon and the children on the fees that she was earning. Architecture was a difficult game at the best of times when so many clients dragged out the paying of her already low fees for months. She still owed the bank her share of the partnership's establishment and this was crippling.

Not knowing what to do, her mind was made up for her one day when Bertram Sherborn, her new attorney asked to see her. He had been doing some confidential research and told Claire that he had heard on the grapevine that Mainline Construction PLC had finally decided to sue the Blenheim Design Partnership (in succession to Henry Worthing FRIBA) for fraud caused in the first place by Simon Harley, but conjoined with Henry Worthing and Gerald Robinson. Claire was to be included as an accessory, even though she was in Australia when the fraud had been committed and had not bought into the debts of the practice. She went hot and cold rapidly on hearing this news but had been ready for something like this. "Well, what would you suggest Bertie?"

"Unfortunately, we have a problem William. You being here in England is a problem. No matter whether you can prove your innocence or not, you will have to pay for your legal defense, and it is going to be expensive." Claire sat there racking her brain. Bertie went on after a short pause: "William, I will be totally honest with you. Is there anywhere you can go that gets you out of the way while the court case progresses?"

Claire smiled as she said, "I thought you might say that," as she put her hand inside her coat. "In actual fact, Bertie I am an Australian and can go back to Australia out of the way." On saying this she took out her Australian passport from the inside pocket of her coat.

"I thought as much William," he suggested, "I have known that for some time and suggest you leave the UK as soon as possible." Claire thanked Bertram and assured him that she would heed his advice.

That evening back home in Harrogate, Claire told Sharon that they should go back to Australia. "How are we going to do that William, we have no money?" It was true, there was no money for the airfare and other arrangements would have to be made. But, as luck would have it, Claire had seen an advertisement in the *Architect's Journal* for the position of Chief Architect to the Zambian Government and forwarded a letter in application.

Three weeks later Claire attended an interview in London, where she was scrutinized by a committee of three men, one Zambian and two white British colonials. She was told that the position of Chief Architect she had applied for had already been appointed, but would she be interested in the position of Regional Architect in one of the provinces? Things were slowly working in her favor. "Yes, I could be interested if a position was offered to me." Inwardly Claire was jubilant that the world seemed to be opening up. One member of the panel advised her that the position had a house to go with it. The news was getting better by the second and so without much hesitation Claire accepted the offer. Back home in Harrogate, upon hearing the good news, Sharon was highly delighted that at last 'her husband' was being recognized for 'his' skills.

In preparation for taking up the post, Claire (as 'William') and Sharon had to attend briefing sessions over a weekend in a large mansion somewhere in the southern English countryside. They were taught about living in Zambia, using the Zambian currency based on one hundred *ngwee* to one *Kwacha*, their customs and so on. Soon after that the Wilsons put their furniture and possessions into storage and flew out to Zambia.

They were met off the flight at Lusaka International Airport by a young man sporting a rather scruffy beard, but appearing to have the bearing of authority. He took one of their bags as they walked out to the airport car park. The man introduced himself as Danny Walker and they piled into his VW tourer. On the drive into Lusaka city center Claire asked Danny which region she was to take charge of. Danny laughed: "Oh, another sucker. Sorry William, but things here are not what you may have been told at your interview. What did they say to you in London?"

"Oh! That I was to be a regional architect and a house was waiting for us to occupy in one of the provinces." Danny laughed loudly.

"Sorry," he apologized, "as I said before, you're just another sucker. There are no regional architects and certainly no spare houses."

Claire gulped and Sharon sitting behind her gasped in alarm. Tanya started to cry and Sharon put her arm around her to quieten her.

"You will, in actual fact, be my assistant," Danny admitted, "working under my direction in our offices in Buildings Branch in the Government compound."

"What about the accommodation we were promised?" Claire asked wondering what other nasty surprises were to follow.

"Well, I am taking you now to the Lusaka Hotel where you will stay until a house becomes available, if at all."

"And how long is that likely to be?" she queried.

"To be honest William, we've had people work their two years without ever being allotted any housing. Most people get offered what we call expatriot housing for a few weeks at a time, so you might like to consider that."

Claire was dumbfounded. She really had been duped. She had been a sucker to fall for the partnership deal with Gerald Robinson, and now this. That night Sharon cried openly and would not speak to Claire. She blamed her for being taken in by these people. Claire would have cried too but she had to put on a brave face to hide the huge amount of turmoil which was piling up alongside her gender dysphoria problems.

In Lusaka, the country's capital city, Claire and Sharon registered Tanya at the International School and Marc into its kindergarten. Of course, 'William' was busy in 'his'" new job as assistant to Danny Walker. Poor Sharon was bored to tears sitting in the Lusaka Hotel all day knitting or doing some embroidery. The pair may not have minded their stay there if the food had been good, but it was anything but palatable. More than often the starter was cabbage soup and the main meal consisted of *Nshima* (a sort of mealy meal cooked into a mashed potato consistency), with a tiny piece of meat of whatever variety was available; or some bacon, and some carrots, tinned peas or cabbage. Dessert was almost always an apricot, peach or guava. This became quite monotonous and the family really hoped they could be given a house as soon as possible.

One morning Claire was advised by another expatriot in her office that a house had come available and that she should put in a requisition for it pretty quick. Immediately Claire went into overdrive, completed an application form and took it personally to the housing department. At lunchtime the next day she decided to drive past the house only to see an Indian family moving in. It was obvious what had happened. The Indian community in Lusaka, obviously with many connections, had pulled a fast one and had one of their own countrymen placed at the top of the list. It had been a foregone conclusion that while European expatriots were regarded as second class citizens, even though they appeared to do most of the work there, citizens of the subcontinent had precedence in everything. Once again corruption appeared to raise its ugly head.

36

The Unveiling

Late one particular morning Danny came into the drawing office and looking at Claire first, addressed his staff: "Can anyone design monuments?"

"Yes, I can Danny." Claire immediately offered her skills as she was bored with the rest of the rather mundane work.

"Right William, take a notepad and pen and get over to the chief's office immediately." Claire dashed over to the main administration building and told the orderly outside that she was reporting to the meeting. He showed her into the boardroom. The chairman looked at her and asked: "Are you the specialist?"

"Yes sir," was Claire's blurted reply.

"Well, take a seat over there and start taking notes." He pointed to a row of vacant chairs near the window.

"Yes sir." Claire's ears were well pinned back, waiting for some action.

Claire sat down as the conference participants at the huge conference table turned to look at the 'specialist' who had arrived. She gathered that the meeting was to discuss the forthcoming visit of the frontline presidents to witness President Kaunda open the newly completed Chinese railway from Kpiri Mposhi in the north of Zambia to Dar es Salaam in Tanzania. Claire had already been informed through expatriot whispers that the Canadian Government had built a railway for the Zambians a number of years previously. She was told that the work of the Canadians had fallen into bad repair as most of the time the Zambian train drivers were drunk and the track was not maintained properly. As a result of this the Peoples Republic of China had stepped in and not only made good the railway track and equipment but built new stations at various points on the line too, albeit designed and built like the ones in China, using Chinese personnel.

Claire's job was to design, prepare drawings for, and arrange for the production of a monument and have it erected in time for the opening of the railway station at Kpiri Mposhi, the terminus on the Zambian section of the line. The problem was that while there was enough time to design and detail the monument, it was an impossibility to procure marble for the monument, make it and erect it within the time scheduled. What the committee had done was to book all the frontline presidents to come on a particular date without any consideration as to the length of time it would take to manufacture a monument. Politics ruled, rather than pragmatism.

That afternoon Claire had to drive over to ZBC, the Zambian Broadcasting Corporation, to meet their production director who had originated a sketch of the proposed monument. In her view hardly a suitable professional to design a monument, except that he was the guy whose task it had been to create the initial idea. His name was Humphrey Mwale, a really nice friendly man. Claire took to him immediately.

Claire and Humph, he preferred the shortened name, really did get on very well. He was very friendly and not puffed up with his own pride like so many of his fellow Zambians. Despite this, all Humph had done was to provide a rough felt-pen sketch, without any idea as to how such an idea could be put into production, including who was able to manufacture it. Claire's job was to take Humph's sketch in hand and within a short space of time, like yesterday of course, produced detail drawings of a marble monument. These had then to be presented to the Works Department for approval and scheduling. This process completed, their answer came back pretty quick as the director had been at the previous meeting and acutely aware of the shortage of time available to manufacture the edifice. The answer was simple – there was no way that the Works Department could procure the marble and manufacture each section of the monument in the time available. The problem was now back in Claire's hands.

She discussed the problem with the works director further and their solution was to make a wooden monument, but with the final carved marble plaques of the participants' names, all of which could be added to the base of the temporary structure. Having put her case to the Director of Building for approval, the result was that the proposed temporary monument had to be started, with the final marble structure commenced as soon as the marble could be obtained. The latter had then to be scheduled for erection some time following the unveiling of the temporary structure.

That being agreed, Claire set to and produced some drawings of the temporary monument which was to be made in plywood, incorporating spaces for the photographs of the presidents of Zambia, Tanzania and China fitted in recesses toward the top of the monument. Claire had to admit, it did look spectacular on paper with the pinnacle, sprayed in gold paint, providing the finishing touch. Claire, the director, and his production foreman assumed the committee would approve their plans. Thankfully, they did and Claire obtained the written approval of the committee for the manufacture of the temporary monument, the date of the unveiling being confirmed too.

Visiting the Works Department during the manufacture of the temporary monument, Claire became friendly with one or two of their personnel, especially the foreman and supervisor. She also engaged a marble tombstone manufacturer to make the plaques with the names of the presidents on them. It was the Italian owner of that company she dealt with, Enrico Pitzobaldi, and she was pleased to be able to brush up her Italian language skills with him and learn some new phrases in the process.

In addition to the manufacture of the temporary monument, Claire had to consider, design and organize an unveiling shroud. Not a problem for our seamstress as she could sew herself, and was able to give directions to the company she had chosen to make it, Raja Patel & Co. The design was to be like a wigwam, each of the three sides in the colors of the respective national flags of the two countries through which the railway passed, Zambia and Tanzania, plus its benefactor China. Claire had designed it to open from one of the seams at the top of the 'wigwam' where a few strands of upholstery cotton were to be threaded through a set of eyelets from the base to the top. Then she had to devise a system which would cut the cotton causing the shroud to open up lengthwise and fall to the ground for the unveiling ceremony.

For this, she took matters into her own hands and cut a piece of sharp-edged tin from a can of peas, fixed to an orange rope. All being well, when tugged, it would pull against a single strand of cotton threaded through eyelets around the top of the unveiling cloth, above the gold-colored pinnacle. The pulling rope was to be long enough for President Kaunda to hold while standing a little way back from the base.

The day before the unveiling arrived and Humph drove the two of them to the railway station at Kpiri Mposhi. The monument was following behind them, strapped into the back of a Works Department truck. The plinth on which it was to be mounted had already been laid in concrete. Claire and Humph had to supervise the fitting together of the parts of the monument upon their arrival. The delivery team thankfully had thought to bring a step ladder with them as this was an essential item with which to assemble not only the monument itself but the shroud too. The latter, its delicate intricacies needed steady hands like those of Claire. It was very fiddly to assemble but by the end of the afternoon it was accomplished. Humph and Claire stood back to admire their joint effort.

The pair were told that they had to see the station master about some accommodation for the night, and to obtain some food too as they had not eaten all day. They searched and found him in the bar of a local hotel, and having been advised of their needs, he provided them with a newspaper each, two candles and a box of matches – a curious combination. The newspaper was apparently to stick onto the glass at the windows of the Chinese-built worker's house they had been allotted for the night, and the candles and matches for illumination as there was no electricity in the two-bedroom cottage. There was no kitchen either, as all cooking by rural Zambians was generally done on the ground outside. However, in the cottage at least there was a bathroom and cold running water.

Their personal items safely locked inside the house, the pair wandered back to the bar for something to eat. The station master had given each of them a printed meal ticket to be presented to the chef in the back room of the bar. The problem was that the only food available was a somewhat dubious meat pie, a dollop of *Nshima*, and some rather squelchy processed peas. But at least it was food. After consuming this Claire and Humph went back through to the front bar and the station master bought each of them a glass of draught Castle Ale. They had almost consumed their beer when the station master returned to ask them a highly personal question. "Would you like a local girl for the night?" *What! Was this guy serious?* Claire could imagine Humph blushing under his dark skin and she certainly did herself at the horrid thought. They slowly and purposefully declined the station master's invitation, explaining that they were really very tired and needed sleep before the big day.

Back in the cottage, after chatting for the remainder of the evening, shouting comments to each other from adjacent rooms, they didn't get much sleep. Humph was up first, however, and peeled a piece of the newspaper off his window. For a modicum of privacy they had the previous evening each wetted one side of some sheets of the *Times of Zambia* and stuck them onto the glass of the windows. Humph shouted through the doorway, "Hey William we have to get over there quick, someone is messing about with the unveiling cloth."

Claire looked through the window and froze. Humping around under the fabric was someone or something, judging by the moving bulges. *Was it human or animal*, she wondered. They quickly dressed and scooted over to the monument. Lifting the back of the fabric slightly, Claire commanded: "Come out of there whoever you are."

Before she could poke a stick at anything, a tall Zambian security officer emerged, holding a threatening rifle and asked: "Who are you?"

"I am the designer of the monument and you should come out right now as this cloth is very fragile and it is likely to fall down. What are you doing under there anyway?"

"I am checking to see if there are any bombs or explosives."

"Well, I can assure you *Sir* that there aren't any as my colleague Humphrey and I have been sleeping in that house over there and we have seen no one suspicious hanging around." Claire pointed across to the cottage in which they had slept.

"You stay with us." The uniformed officer commanded and at that very moment a tall similarly attired man appeared. Claire saw an opportunity to allay her fears of something going wrong.

"Okay you guys." She thought she would treat them as human beings instead of official guards. "What I would like you to do when the Presidents arrive is to station yourselves at each corner of the back of this unveiling cloth. When President Kaunda starts pulling the rope at the front of the monument, I want you to count 1, 2, and 3 and if the cloth doesn't start falling by then, I want you to step forward and give a tug on each of these seams here." Claire pointed to where she wanted them to stand and what to do if the shroud didn't fall as planned. They stepped over to the places she had shown them, made indications as to what was required, and they indicated that they understood.

Just then two tall gray-suited men arrived and grabbed each of Claire's elbows. "Are you in charge here?"

"Yes sir, I am the designer."

"Good, you will come with us." Claire flushed and expected to be arrested for speaking to their colleagues as she had done, but all they did was to take her around to the front of the monument and stand with her, one at each elbow. "Tell us what you have just told those other men."

So Claire related her instructions, adding: "and the President will take this orange rope here and pull. The tug will cut some cotton at the top and it wall fall. If there is a slight delay in it falling, I have instructed your colleagues on the other side to step forward and pull on the cloth, but I don't think it will be necessary."

A large crowd had been assembling while all this palaver had been going on and just then there was an almighty roar from them. A white helicopter flew overhead and landed directly in front of the station's main entrance steps. President Kaunda alighted from the side door of the airplane and was immediately surrounded by his bodyguard. They looked over to a marquee on the grass where the other dignitaries had been sheltering out of the already sweltering sun. They now started emerging from the tent unto the bright light. The President and his guests walked across to the monument and within what seemed like only a few seconds Claire was surrounded by the frontline Presidents and their wives and retinue. By this time she was still standing between the two gray-suited guards, one at each elbow. President Kaunda spoke to one of them asking what he should do and Claire was nudged by the guard. She spoke: "Excellency, you take this rope here and give it a tug to release the unveiling cloth."

To her left, the guard was standing just slightly behind her elbow; the tall President of Zaire, Mobutu Sese Seko, was to his left and past the official at her right elbow was Hastings Banda Karma, President of Malawi. In front, to the left of President Kenneth Kaunda of Zambia was President Julius Nyerere of Tanzania and on President Kaunda's right was the representative of Chairman Mao of the Chinese People's Republic. Claire felt as though she was in a dream. It had to be a dream as this sort of thing didn't happen to her – ever. Not ever! Where was her gender dysphoria right at this minute? A good question!

President Kaunda made a short speech and gently pulled on the rope. Nothing happened. At least that is what Claire thought as she felt she was about to faint on the spot. He then tugged on the rope and this time and slowly the cloth started to fall around the base of the monument. The guards at the rear helped to rest the shroud on the concrete plinth and President Kaunda waved his crisp white handkerchief in the air and started singing *Nkosi sikelele Africa* which brought tears to Claire's eyes. It was such a beautiful song.

Behind the official party there was a line of musicians with their marimbas and drums, and as President Kaunda started singing, they started playing and everyone joined in the singing. Slowly the party moved away from the monument back toward the marquee and from there up the steps to the railway station entrance doors.

Claire was still in a trance and stood there on her own trying to take in what had just happened. She could hardly believe it. She had been there with all these famous people and could not move. Would anyone else understand the enormity of what she had witnessed? Indeed, had been part of. Would they believe her? When she arrived back in Australia, they probably would not. Most likely, folk would think she was making it all up. But she hadn't, as everything she remembered was true.

The official party climbed aboard the train which would take them down the line for their lunch. The crowd of onlookers which had experienced the event was already dispersing, many starting the long walk back to the surrounding villages. The musicians had disbanded and were driving away in a truck.

Claire walked over to the station steps to see Humph sitting there in an agitated manner. "C'mon William where's your invitation to board the train? You will have to be quick as it is about to leave the station."

Claire took out an envelope from the side pocket of the safari suit she had been wearing. Inside was an official invitation which read: "President Kaunda invites William and Mrs Wilson to join him and his guests on the first journey of the Kpiri Mposhi to Dar Es Salaam railway."

"Where's your invitation?" Claire asked him.

"I didn't get one."

"Well, my dear friend, as we are both in this together, if you can't go, then I am not going."

"No, you go William, I don't mind, really I don't. You go quickly."

Claire sat down beside him and put her arm over his shoulders. "No my dear friend, if you don't go then I am not going. That's final. Come on let's see what we can get for lunch." The pair was in this together. In her mind they had become a couple, and if truth be known, she was falling in love with Humph.

Just then the station master arrived with two small cardboard lunch boxes. He handed one to each of them and walked away without another word. Claire opened the flip top of her box to discover a fast-drying sandwich and a piece of fruit. Humph had the same, so they sat there quietly on the station steps and ate their lunch. That effort completed, they smiled at each other and then walked across the grass to the cottage where they had spent the previous night. They packed their bags, loaded up Humphrey's Land Rover and off they went, leaving Kpiri Mposhi behind them as they sped back south to Lusaka. That was the end of an adventure neither of them would ever forget. Ever!

Another of Claire's projects was to design an extension to the Zambian Law Courts. The existing building had been erected by the British in the old colonial days and consisted of a Palladian-style colonnade and pediment with the main two-story building set behind it. Her design respected the original building by leaving it as it had originally been built. That decision out of the way, she designed a modern building to be sited to the left of the main building. This was to house the judges, magistrates and barristers offices at the first floor level behind a wide-columned overhang. The courts were in the center of the building but accessed at ground floor level with a corridor around them giving access to interview rooms, access stairs and toilet facilities. It worked well as a functional design and Claire believed it would be a fitting extension to the historic main building, even though its attachment to the new wing was simply a glass-walled corridor.

A few days later she received a call from the office of the Chief Justice of Zambia, His Excellency Jacob Kasunga. His secretary said he would like to see her in his chambers the following afternoon. Claire was mortified, wondering what mischief she had inadvertently gotten herself into. It was possible in Zambia at this time in its history to be accused of something quite out of the ordinary, not knowing what one might have done to deserve it. There were too many rivalries and jealousies in government departments and anyone could make up a story, merely to get an expatriate into trouble.

So Claire duly arrived at the chambers of the Chief Justice the next afternoon and was ushered into his hallowed sanctum, her heart turning summersaults with trepidation. As it turned out however, she need not have worried. His Excellency, or whatever form of address he was used to, stood up from his desk and after shaking her hand, led her over to some easy chairs and bade her be seated. He asked her how she was enjoying living in Zambia and working in Buildings Branch. As she was enjoying her stay in his country very much, Claire was honest enough to disclose this fact. Then he led the conversation into the designs she had been preparing for the High Court extension. She was waiting for the punch line, but it didn't come. Instead he mentioned her friend August Kafundu, whom she had spoken to on the phone before leaving England. Her Syrian friend Zakka Homil had introduced her to August initially, and unbeknown to her, he in turn had given her a good word or two in front of the Chief Justice.

A side door opened and a man in uniform carrying a tray set it down on the low table in front of them. Afternoon tea was to be served using what appeared to be an expensive china tea service. There were cakes and pastries too and Claire was suitably impressed. If truth be known, she was absolutely amazed at the opulence of her surroundings. As the afternoon played out, her visit to the offices of the Chief Justice of Zambia had been a real pleasure, drinking a good quality tea from real bone China cups. It was not until afterward that she once again realized that she had been in an enviable situation. How could she explain back in Australia, or anywhere else for that matter, that she had had afternoon tea with His Excellency the Chief Justice of Zambia in his private chambers? No one would believe her.

37

The Escape

Claire's life in Zambia seemed to be full of extraordinary events. Shortly after she had arrived there, in fact no less than the following day and the first in her new office surroundings, her department head, Danny Walker had come through their connecting door. "Hey William, I am impressed. You've only been here for virtually a few hours and now there is a personal call for you from no less than a former cabinet minister." Danny jerked his head as though inviting Claire to follow him. She walked through to Danny's room and picked up the phone.

"Hello?"

"William? It's August – August Kafundu. You remember we spoke on the phone before you left Aireborough. We were introduced by your friend Zakka."

"Oh yeah, right. Hi Mr Kafundu."

"No William, it's August to you. Listen, would you and your good lady like to come over to my place for a party at the weekend?"

"Oh right. Thank you August; that would be cool.

August then suggested that as she would not have had time to buy a car yet, he would pick them up at the Lusaka Hotel. As far as the children were concerned they had another hotel guest listen at the door to their room for any sound coming from Tanya and Marcus while the couple were out. Claire could hardly remember what went on at the party but she was most certainly introduced to a few of August's colleagues and met Elizabeth, his Aireborough-born wife. The party had been organized by August to test his guests' taste buds on some new fruit products that were being produced in Zambia. They were offered dried fruits and drank some lovely sweet wines, but Sharon became quite tipsy on what at first glance appeared to be non-alcoholic beverages. They turned out to be very toxic, in the same way fortified wines and liqueurs can be very toxic to a great number of people. As a result, Sharon fell asleep in one of the comfy armchairs, and had to be woken up to guide her out to the waiting car. Another guest and his wife had volunteered to drop them back at the Lusaka Hotel.

Another experience for Claire, and indeed a scary one for the family, was when she had to drive to a project some kilometers away from Lusaka to carry out an inspection on a building which had recently been completed. As it was a lovely day and the outing she thought might give Sharon and the children some experience of the varied Zambian countryside, she took them along for the drive. There were no outstanding problems with the building she had to inspect and therefore the report she had been asked to produce was very simple. However, on the way back to Lusaka, driving her tiny Fiat Uno, they saw a soldier or policeman standing at the side of the road holding a rifle in what to them appeared to be a menacing manner. Waving for them to stop, they all panicked and feared what was to happen. Sharon wound down her passenger window and Claire leaned over and asked, "Yes officer. How can we help you?"

"Are you driving to Lusaka?" he asked.

"Yes we are."

"Could I beg a lift from you please?"

"Sure, hop in." Claire said.

Sharon climbed out and folding the front passenger seat down she clambered into the back seat with the children. Their 'guest' folded his long legs into the void in front of the passenger seat and managed to wedge himself into position with his rifle between his legs.

As Claire pulled back onto the road to continue their drive back to Lusaka, she asked "Have you been on an important mission out here?"

"Yes sir, I have. My section commander had me driven out here this morning to investigate a robbery last night, and they had not allowed for transport back to headquarters."

"I'm sorry to hear that. You must be very tired."

"Yes I am, but it has mainly been boring as I could do very little on my own."

The ice was broken and the policeman opened up and told them about his family and all-in-all the trip back into Lusaka seemed to take no time at all. Sharon and Tanya asked him various questions to allay their fears at having a policeman sitting in the car. His friendly replies were interesting and he had the family in stitches with some of his escapades.

Part of Claire's workload was to oversee alterations being carried out in the Parliament complex. To oversee this work, she had been given a special pass to affix to the windscreen of her Fiat and this allowed her easy access into the grounds of Parliament House at any time. When that work was completed she was asked to follow it up with supervision of the new Speakers Lodge in the same grounds. This had been designed by a local architect but as an officer of Buildings Branch it was her job to make sure that the work was completed according to the approved drawings.

While Claire was supervising the erection of government buildings, however, she had the distinct feeling that she might be under surveillance and suspicion. It came to a head early one morning when a bomb had exploded on the steps of the High Court. The chief architect of Buildings Branch, Henry Mwandabe, appeared to have decided that as Claire was the architect responsible for the design of the extensions, she had to be the prime suspect. It was Danny, her immediate boss, who alerted her to the precarious situation. Mr Mwandabe, in addition to being chief architect was also a member of the para-military, often coming to the office in his blue uniform carrying a rifle. That particular morning he was wearing his colorful outfit and everyone was on their best behavior, especially Claire.

Another of her duties was to organize the turning of the first grass sod at a site where a motel was to be built for provincial members of parliament. Good organizer that she was; all matters had been arranged and she expected no trouble. The event was to take place a week hence and so she arranged for a mechanical grader to be scheduled to level out the bumps at ten o'clock that particular morning. She had previously had someone from the works department lay some turf in a particular spot and to water it every day until the day of the unveiling arrived. The area was to be fenced off and guarded. But late one morning Danny walked through to Claire's desk and told her to get over to the boss's office "pronto" he said, as she was in big trouble. Now what had she done?

Claire knocked on Mr Mwandabe's office door, responded by his usual "Come!" He was sitting with his back to the door, the window shades down and wearing a pair of dark sunglasses. This seemed very odd. Claire felt something sinister was about to happen.

"You wanted to see me sir."

"Yes, I certainly did Wilson." There was a short pause. "This morning you made me look like a complete fool."

"Me sir? No sir, I would never do that."

"Yes, you did! I visited the site of the new motel for our out-of-town Members of Parliament only to find that nothing is happening."

"But sir…"

"Don't interrupt me Wilson," he shouted at her, banging on his desk with a clenched fist. "So I arranged for a truck to collect some people from the nearby village to come with their tools to level the area near where the first grass sod is to be turned. But after a half an hour a large grader arrived and the people shouted at me that the machine could do their work in a few minutes and could they go back to their village?"

"Well, sir…"

"Wilson, will you stop interrupting me when I am talking! The villagers blamed me for their predicament and I had to explain that I was not aware that a grader was coming. So you embarrassed me in front of the people. I am not very happy with you Wilson; I will watch everything you do from now on."

"Sir, I had everything arranged for the ceremony and if you had consulted me I would have saved you the embarrassment."

"Go! I will remember this day," was Mr Mwandabe's reply.

Claire was duly dismissed, not being allowed to explain the situation, and she decided that her life in Zambia was becoming very problematical. She decided to end her contract – but how to go about it?

After quietly speaking to several of her loyal friends about the situation, they all agreed that perhaps it may be the time to move on to Australia. Getting out of Zambia was certain to be the real problem. But, there were means and ways.

As Claire had already accrued some holiday, she decided that this might be a good excuse as any to escape. In order to build up a small nest-egg from which to buy their tickets back to Australia, she decided to sell lots of clothes, and even her damaged guitar. Her Fiat Uno was regularly parked under the awning across the road from the office and she decided that it would be easy to sell the items directly from the car's rear hatch door. She passed the word around the various sections at their offices via one of the Zambian girls that on a certain lunch time she would be selling various items. This seemed to go well and did not alert any suspicion. Through this, she managed to sell everything; clothes, household items and ornaments. The proceeds from the sale were put toward the cost of their air tickets.

Under the terms of the contract she had signed in London, Sharon, Tanya and Marcus were allowed to return to their place of last residence, which was England. She completed the appropriate application form and a week later received a check for their air fares from the finance department. After cashing it, she then went into a travel agency and booked their flights to Mauritius, as though they were going on vacation. They were to travel Zambian Airways to Mauritius, and from there to board a Qantas Airways flight to complete their journey back to Sydney. While the travel agent in Lusaka could arrange their flight to Mauritius, he assured Claire that there was a scheduled Qantas flight to Australia.

As the family had been living in expatriate housing, their 'escape' was timed to coincide with the end of the period they had been living in a house owned by the Belgian Embassy. On the last evening the Wilsons invited the ambassador and his wife over for evening drinks and supper.

They were talking about life in Zambia and Claire made the comment that they would like to explain to people back home in Australia what life was really like in Zambia. The ambassador's wife was shaking her head. "I would not recommend you do that," she said, "our son did the very same when he went back to Belgium from one of the poor South American republics and our friends shunned him. It seems that people don't really want to hear the truth. So William, I would not recommend you say anything at all about Zambia and its political struggles." Claire received the message loud and clear.

The next morning Claire's colleague Tony Golightly collected them in his Renault and took them to Lusaka Airport. Tony had eyes everywhere, as he had left the office early to collect the Wilsons, and was worried about spies watching what they were doing. He told Claire that they would be safe once they were moving up the escalator toward the departure gates. He said he would stand back and watch from a distance.

Claire checked in their baggage and then walked over to the immigration desk to get her passport stamped. She pretended that she was returning to Zambia, and when the officer asked her for her work permit, she handed it over, together with an approval to travel to Mauritius on vacation. The man was reading the *Times of Zambia* at his side, the main article of which was about the government's budget provisions announced the previous day. He took the Wilson passports, Claire's work permit and the signed approval to go on holiday to Mauritius, offering them merely a cursory glance. He looked up once but then went back to his newspaper. "You coming back?" he asked, as he stared at the article in the paper.

"Yes sir, I'm coming back in two weeks." With that he stamped the passports and handed Claire's documents back to her. The family then proceeded to the escalator as planned, and turning around, with her hand shielded partly by the flap of her raincoat, she gave Tony the "thumbs up" sign. He smiled and, turning around, left the building.

It was stinking hot in Mauritius and extremely humid. They had been booked into a really nice hotel by the travel agent as their connecting Qantas flight to Sydney was not due for another two days. The surf looked so inviting and so they all changed into swimming gear and stepped into the frothing white surf which fringed a vivid turquoise sea. The Wilsons had never experienced such a sight and wallowed in it.

The next morning Claire hired a Morris Mini and drove the family across the island to the travel agents in Port Louis. She had to reorganize their travel plans to make sure that Sharon and the children's travel destination was changed from London to Sydney. But there were problems.

Claire soon discovered that the travel agent in Lusaka had not told her the truth, and had only booked them to Mauritius. The Zambian travel agent had not scheduled the family to connect to any ongoing flight or flights. To add to their woes, Claire was advised that there were no Qantas flights from Mauritius at all, they just didn't exist. So having been told lies back in Lusaka, Claire had to start over – to book flights for all of them to Sydney. But even that was not as easy as it might have sounded. The earliest flight they could join was a South African Airways (SAA) flight leaving in five days time. This posed a serious major problem: the free accommodation in their hotel only lasted for another day and Claire did not have enough money to stay there until the SAA flight left Mauritius. Having no alternative but to accept passages on the SAA flight she had to do so. Fortunately, the payment for a flight to London had gone through the travel agent's system, and the cost of changing the destination to Sydney was not very high. That left the other problem of where to stay after the last day/night in their hotel expired.

The answer was that Claire had to find some cheaper accommodation pretty darned quick. It was obvious that accommodation was cheaper on the Indian part of the island so the next day they set out to find a cheap place to stay until the SAA flight was to leave.

Auberge de la Mer sat by the waterside of a small smelly inlet – and the Wilsons had no choice but to accept what they were offered. The auberge was run by a French restaurateur who spoke both French and English, and he traded with Australia in shells. But the Wilsons soon discovered that the only room available to them was unfortunately crawling with cockroaches. Sharon took one look, screamed, and refused to stay even for one night. Claire reminded her that they had no choice. They had no money to stay at a more expensive hotel, and no spare cash left over for any tourist souvenirs either. Eventually, Sharon buckled under and with reluctance put up with the cockroaches. They bought some insect-repellent candles to burn while they were asleep and hoped that they would keep the insects at bay while they slept.

While the Wilsons were in Mauritius they knew they just had to visit the Pamplemouse Gardens where there was a pool on which floated the world's largest water lily leaves in the world. The problem was that it started raining like the proverbial cats and dogs. So the family had to view the scene from under their umbrellas, steaming in the humid atmosphere, munching on some large slices of fresh pineapple for their lunch. Another day they visited an Indian bazaar but shortly were glad to be flying home to Sydney via SAA. It was to be the completion of yet another interesting saga in their lives. In Claire's case just one of too many. Too many by far, for one lifetime.

38

Sydney Again

Back in Sydney, the Wilsons stayed with some friends in Winston Hills for a few days while they found a house to lease in Castle Hill. The next day Sharon booked Tanya and Marcus into St Bernard's school while Claire went looking for a job. This was a lot harder than she had imagined. It seemed that she was now overqualified for everything for which she applied. Calling in to the local social security office she was offered unemployment benefit for a few weeks, which she greatly appreciated and accepted it with thanks. Then a break came when she was taken on as an architectural sales person with *Pacific Homes Australia* in the suburb of Auburn. As a member of a sales force of eight, Claire's task was to service a number of potential clients who had answered the advertisements of *Pacific Homes* and to turn the enquiries into sales. For Claire, endowed with *the gift of the gab*, as her mother often commented, she actually found this quite easy. She wondered if she had inherited some of her skills from some mysterious Irish ancestor, but in addition, she had a great imagination. Claire didn't know it at the time but the Irish connection proved to be factual when she discovered her roots, a number of years later.

The sales manager of the company at the time was an English Liverpudlian called Sam Birtley. He knew nothing much about building as he had been working for Walton's department store previously, but he seemed to be a good marketing manager. Seeing some potential in 'William' he decided to put his 'salesman' on a special *Pahlman-Tack* training course in North Sydney. Claire had to attend each day from 8.30 am to 6 pm for the sales training sessions and on the Saturday and Sunday from 9.30 am to 4.30 pm for a condensed marketing course. As she loved learning she took to this like a duck to water and soaked up as much information and role-playing as she could. All this without pay so she made sure that she listened to what she was being taught. She had to make up for the time lost learning.

The following Monday back at *Pacific Homes*, Claire was handed her usual list of potential clients and set about her work with real enthusiasm. Consequently, by the end of that month she found that she had converted ten of her presentations into firm orders. By so doing, she had apparently broken the company's monthly sales targets and marketing manager Sam Birtley was proud of the decision he had made to have Claire trained.

After lunch one Friday he called 'William' into his office and presented 'him' with a small black and white television. He said he realized that as 'he' was out most evenings, Sharon might be bored and a television might be very welcome. The family was understandably overjoyed, and it proved to Claire that the company was pleased with her hard work and achievements. Walking through the front door of their leased home in Castle Hill late that afternoon, Sharon and the children were not so much as overjoyed as amazed that the company could think so highly of 'William', Sharon was still trying to get to grips with her father-in-law's attitude that 'her husband' was absolutely useless. Due to them having to move around so much, she was beginning to wonder. There was an underlying reason for all this of course, but at the time Sharon was completely unaware of 'William's' struggles with gender dysphoria. This was to take a few more years to be exposed.

The Wilson's life in Castle Hill was not what they really wanted. They would have liked to have built their own house further north, but could not get a mortgage due to the fact that the income Claire earned was based on a low basic wage plus commission. So it was paramount that she had to get another job, a permanent one which paid her a salary. Fortunately, it did not take long to find such a job as there were a number advertised in the *Sydney Morning Herald* that week.

Claire rang one of the advertisers and was asked to attend an interview in Parramatta with Ian Smithers of *Civic Manage-*

ment Pty Ltd, the building wing of the *Parkway Corporation*. Had she not been as successful as she had been at *Pacific Homes*, maybe she would not have gotten the job, and of course the Pahlman-Tack training course she had completed was the icing on the cake. Ian Smithers set her on as a marketing executive working in the industrial division, but she was really worried as she knew next to nothing of that field. However, she was fortunate enough to quickly win a contract to design and build a large extension to an existing warehouse owned by a Swedish company. As a result she had proved herself in the eyes of her boss and her future seemed secure.

Claire approached the Bank of New South Wales for a mortgage and based on the details of her new position with *Civic Management*, it was approved. This gave Sharon and Claire the opportunity to look around for opportunities and they selected a piece of land in a new subdivision in the northern suburb of Arcadia. The piece of land was covered in trees and some of these had to be cleared, but Claire set to this task with gusto. Her gender problem had taken a back seat in all this while she had other serious considerations on her mind. She bought a chain saw and cut down only as many trees as were necessary for the erection of their new house. She worked like a Trojan and dug the trenches for the foundations and laid the steel reinforcement ready for concrete to be poured. On the following Saturday, the revolving drum of concrete spun the slurry into the trenches via its rear chute and in no time at all, building work could commence in earnest.

In St Bernard's parish Claire had become friendly with a young contractor called Mick Donnelly who gave her a price on the drawings she presented to him, and they agreed on a figure and signed a contract. Mick had suggested he make the windows himself out of cedar and Claire agreed as the builder was also a qualified and experienced carpenter and joiner. In addition he knew enough about building contracting to work with Claire in subcontracting various tradesmen. In no time at all, the house rose above the foundations.

One humorous situation centered on Mick's suggestion for a bricklayer. Harry Birkhall was his name, and he turned up each morning in his slippers, together with his faithful old bull terrier. In the lounge room, Claire had designed an arched brick fireplace as the main feature, and when the time came for this to be built, she did wonder if she was capable of building it herself. Harry, however, would have none of it and threatened to walk off the job if she as much as laid one brick. Claire was duly threatened and respected Harry's trade skills.

Claire had become somewhat of an expert in the design of fireplaces, due to devouring a book by Vrest Orton called *Observations on the Forgotten Art of Building a Good Fireplace*. This had been the story of Sir Benjamin Thompson, Count Rumford, and his fireplace designs that had remained unchanged since 1795. Thompson was described as an American genius and as Claire had used his principles on a number of fireplaces previously, she knew that she was on to a winner. She had purchased the eleventh printing of the first edition of the book in 1969 published by Yankee Books of Dublin, New Hampshire, and treasured the book ever since.

The day came when Harry was to build the fireplace. Planks had been laid over the floor joists and Claire had made two cast concrete lintels of the shape required to create the throating to effectively suck the smoke up the chimney. She gave Harry the detail drawing of the fireplace but he thrust it back into her hands: "Look William, don't show me your detailed drawing, just tell me where to lay each brick, will you?" So they started. As Claire laid out the base with the bricks she had purposefully cut, Harry dutifully did what he was told and laid the bricks.

By the end of the afternoon, the brickwork Harry had laid actually looked like a fireplace, ready to take the cast concrete lintels when the mortar had set. For that process they allowed one week to make sure all was well. The working arrangement between bricklayer and architect to produce an outstanding fireplace continued the following Saturday.

The chimney stack was easy taking account of all the detailed work Claire had produced. The house slowly grew up above the ground floor with the chimney stack surmounted by twin chimney pots, rising through the surrounding trees. The surrounding roof of the house was to be covered with cedar shakes and Claire decided to lay them herself with the help of a couple of friends Kurt Kolman and Don Mackenzie. Kurt was married to Laura and they had been neighbors of the Wilsons when they lived in Winston Hills a number of years ago, and of course Don was the husband of Claire's dear cousin Debbie.

In no time at all, the roof covering progressed and Claire finished the ridge capping by nailing two shakes together like a tent, before nailing it to the upper battens. But as she was finishing the ridge capping the skies opened and although she had been wearing a pair of hiking boots, thinking that they were the best for the job, she found herself slipping. Panicking, she twisted her body to stay upright and then began sliding down the roof as the soles of the boots had no grip. With hindsight it would have been better to have worn sneakers. But this was no consolation to Claire as she slid down the roof heading for an almighty crash on the ground below. In those few split seconds, she knew she was plunging to her death, or at best to become a critical hospital patient, possibly maimed for the rest of her life.

Claire screamed in fright and stuck out her left arm, which fortunately caught against one of the studs which supported the second story, as yet unclad. With the force of her fall her arm wrapped around the stud and she was saved, shocked, but alive. A man passing on the street called up. "You okay mate?"

"Yes, thanks, I stopped myself just in time."

"Yeah well, I thought you were a goner."

"Yeah, so did I." Claire gulped, "So did I."

The family moved into the Arcadia house before it was finished as Claire ran out of money. Burning smelly coils against the unceasing attack of night-time mosquitoes was a necessity, but they survived. For the next couple of weeks she nailed cheap fluted plywood onto some of the walls and engaged a plasterer to nail and set the dry walling in the living room and upper floor. Claire bought all the gyprock sheets and the blue adhesive needed to glue the sheets to the studs and she paid the plasterer $200 in advance to secure his services. But, after the first day on the site, the plasterer vanished. Not only did he not turn up the following day to carry out the work, but when Claire visited his home in Blacktown at the end of the week and spoke to his wife, she said she hadn't seen him. Claire had been defrauded out of money she could ill afford to squander.

Hardly ever sticking fast in any given situation, she was told of a couple of young Russian plasterers, recommended to her by a man in the next street. She engaged them immediately and they advised that it was not necessary to pay them until the job was finished to her satisfaction. Now that was what she expected – honest and trustworthy. The two Russians actually finished all the work in one day, a Saturday, and Claire had taken time out to help them where necessary. The job completed by late afternoon, she produced a pack of beers for them and paid them what had been agreed. No more, no less. Their job was first class and her faith in tradesmen returned.

Even the tiler, a Dutchman, said he didn't want any money from her until she was satisfied with his work. Things were looking up by this time and her trust in certain tradesmen, especially those born in Europe, improved. The European tradesmen appeared to be a cut above the average blue-singlet-clad Ocker, a colloquial name for an Australian.

The following year Claire was moved from the Parramatta office of *Civic Management* to their offices in Pitt Street in the Sydney 'Central Business District', known to Australians as the CBD. Her new position was a marketing executive in the Leisure division. Her new job turned out to be very boring until, after a few weeks, she was asked to accompany another executive to attend a meeting with one of his clients, a Roman Catholic parish committee. A much older man than herself, Geoff Burlington had been nurturing the parish priest for a while after he had been made aware that the parish wanted to build a new church. Geoff had heard on the grapevine that Claire knew the documents of the Second Vatican Council like the back of her hand, especially as it applied to the new English Mass. Geoff reasoned that if he produced someone with specialist knowledge on Catholic Church architecture, then the committee may be persuaded that *Civic Management* was the right company with whom to enter a contract for their new church building.

At the meeting, Geoff introduced Claire as a colleague who was a specialist in church matters. After a while their parish priest Fr Garry Spinner realized that she really did know the *Documents of Vatican II (Flannery Edition)* inside and out as Geoff had claimed. As a result, he felt that the parish could work with Geoff's company if Claire was added to the team. On inspecting the contract which Geoff presented to him, the manager of the Commercial Division Alan Speight, was highly delighted and said he would select an architect for the project. Claire's face fell, as she had mistakenly thought she might be asked to design the new church, being a qualified architect herself, and having designed churches previously.

A few days later Alan called Claire into his glass-walled office and introduced her to a couple of men. Arnold Craven was a white-haired smooth skinned rather effeminate looking older man, and Jon Harker was his young partner. Claire thought Jon might have been the effeminate one in reality as he carried a round leather handbag, hardly the attire of a typical Aussie male. The architects were duly commissioned by Alan, who then produced a bottle of *Château Tanunda* as a celebration. Claire was however dismissed to go back to her desk in the outer office, leaving the three men happily supping the red nectar.

Craven & Harker produced their initial design drawings six weeks later but the work had not yet been priced and needed to be within the parish's budget. Claire handed a set of the architects' drawings to her department estimator Ralph Greenway to work his magic. Four days later the estimate was ready and Fr Spinner was called into the office. He was highly delighted with the design but constantly interrupted with: "How much does it all cost?"

Claire using her tactical experience, continued to deflect Fr Spinner's question until Craven & Harker had completed the explanation of their design. Then she turned to Ralph with: "C'mon Ralph, now it's your turn." To Ralph's credit he laboriously explained what he had included in his estimate but Fr Spinner was getting impatient. Claire stepped into Ralph's cost presentation and asked him to let them know the bottom line.

Ralph gulped, but when he announced the figure Fr Spinner's face quickly turned a shade of dark beetroot and Claire thought he was going to pass out. He looked across at her and told her in no uncertain words that she had failed him. He started to get up out of his chair. "Obviously we are wasting our time here" he muttered to his curate. Perhaps he believed in miracles, or was out of touch with the real world, in Claire's mind so typical of priests. Claire said that this was only the first run through, and that costs could invariably change based on many factors in the design.

Claire forced herself to walk with the priest and his curate to the elevator lobby and touched Fr Spinner's arm. He turned toward her, with mist still in his eyes. Claire appealed to him: "Father, do you trust me?" The priest stared at her as though she should not be asking such a question. She repeated the question. "Father, I said I would get the project within your budget and I am asking you if you trust me to keep my word."

"Yes William, I trust you but you are stymied by your company. Maybe they cannot build me a church for my budget."

"Father, I want you to trust me to deliver you a design of your liking to a budget that suits the purse strings of the parish. Will you please trust me to do this for you? I promise you it can be done." Claire stared into his eyes to make eye contact.

"Yes William I trust you to deliver on your promise. Let me know when you are ready for another meeting." And with this he entered the elevator car which by this time had arrived.

Claire walked back to her waiting colleagues. "What did he say?" Ralph asked.

"I asked him if he trusted me to deliver a church in line with his budget and he said that he did, although not without some persuasion."

Alan gave vent to his personal thoughts: "In my opinion you have taken too much upon your shoulders, and I think Fr Spinner could become a difficult client." There was a short pause as he stared at Claire. "So what are you going to do?" Alan asked.

"I am going to redesign the church to bring it into budget."

"No you're not!" He nervously answered back. "You can't do that. I have appointed Craven and Harker as the architects and it is up to them to re-shape the design."

"No." Claire rapped back at her boss: "I don't think they are capable of doing it as they are not familiar with our costing process. Don't forget Alan I am a fully qualified architect myself and am quite capable of changing their design so that it can be built within their budget."

"Okay," he said, "be it on your own head. I will give you over the weekend to come up with a solution." With that he stormed off into his office and closed the door behind him.

She looked at Ralph and smiled. "Don't worry Ralph, I am used to this. I do know what I am doing. I want you to trust me too."

Claire went home early and told Sharon and the children not to disturb her as she worked over the weekend on her ideas. When Monday saw the light of day, she was still not happy with everything but was beginning to see the proverbial light between the trees. By that evening she believed she may have solved the design problems and then worked through most of the night on the revised drawings.

Claire rang Cheryl, their department secretary at nine o'clock Tuesday morning for her to tell Alan that a revised scheme had been produced, and it looked as though it would work, and be cheaper than the original design. Claire told Cheryl to tell Ralph to clear the decks after lunch. She caught the train into the CBD and on the sixth floor walked straight to Ralph's desk and laid the drawing down. "There you are Ralph. Do your best mate," and walked back to her own desk and laid her head in her hands.

Barry, who lived at the desk behind her asked: "Are you okay William?"

"Yeah, just a little tired and apprehensive I guess."

Claire explained the situation to Barry and all he could say was: "Best of luck mate. I think you're gonna need it." Then he looked over the top of his spectacles and rather pointedly said: "You know why Alan is against you getting involved with the design don't you" Claire shook her head from side to side. "He gets a kick-back from every designer he appoints." He added, almost as a last resort, "Sorry William, I shouldn't have said that." Barry winked at his colleague and then turned his head to look out of the window into Australia Square.

On Thursday morning Ralph walked around to Claire's desk at ten o'clock. She looked into his eyes and saw nothing, and immediately became alarmed. "What's the verdict?" she asked him.

"I think you had better sit down for this," he said. She sat down as he sank into the chair opposite.

"Well?" Claire nervously asked as he leaned across the desk top toward her as though he was going to whisper a secret.

"How'd you do it?" he said with a grin spreading across his rather cute round face.

"You mean we did it?" Claire questioned.

"Yes, YOU did it." Ralph started to go through the costings but she stopped him.

"Look, just let me ring Fr Spinner. She reached for the phone. Fr Spinner came on the line. "Father, it's William." She could hear him sigh. "I promised you we could do it and we have. I need to see you this afternoon, say at 4 O'clock. Is that okay?"

Father Spinner confirmed the time and that he would be there. At the due hour a black-suited priest small in stature with a somewhat rotund but very red-face appeared in reception. Claire met him and together they walked through to Alan's office as her boss wanted to take charge again. She seated everyone and opened the roll showing the revised design. Claire explained what she had done and looked at Fr Spinner for his reaction. Alan was doing the very same, looking at the priest's face. He then turned to Ralph and asked what the final cost was for the revised design. Ralph went through his costings, the priest looking closely at his face. Then the final sum was announced and everyone switched their gaze to that of the priest. Fr Spinner turned to Claire and softly muttered: "Thank you William for your hard work, I like it."

At that, Alan breathed a sigh of relief and ignoring Claire, turned to his estimator: "Well done Ralph". In Claire's boss's mind it was Ralph who had won the day and the project had been saved.

"It was all due to William's clever design," said Ralph, giving Claire the credit she was due.

"Yes well, had you not brought the cost within budget, we would not have a project," came back Alan's quip.

"No Alan, all I did was price up William's design; it is he who deserves the praise."

"Well we will have to see whether Craven & Harker will accept the task of re-doing the working drawings. They are the official architects. William is only a marketing executive."

Claire walked Fr Spinner back to the elevator lobby and pressed one of the buttons. The priest turned to her "Your boss doesn't seem to have much of regard for your talents William. Have you annoyed him in any way?"

"No Father. I know why he ignores me, but I cannot tell you the reason." The elevator car arrived and the two said their goodbyes.

Back in Alan's office, she and Ralph were dismissed with Alan's usual wave of the hand. He chose to ring his friend Arnold Craven. How he described Claire, she was never to find out, but she assumed it was derogatory as she had taken matters into her own hands in the matter of the re-design. Nevertheless, she had won the day.

Over the next few weeks Craven & Harker, much to their annoyance, created a new set of drawings based on Claire's changes and quoted an increased fee to Alan which he accepted reluctantly, secretly blaming Claire. The problem was that the appointed architects very noticeably objected to her re-designing their 'brilliant' design.

But officially the project had started in earnest and Claire had saved the day. Two weeks later, Alan's boss Ernest O'Mahony asked that Claire see him in his office two floors below. Claire entered Mr O'Mahony's huge office on the fourth floor wondering what she had done wrong. He asked his secretary to fetch them both a cup of coffee as he drew up a chair for Claire across from his. He asked her how she was settling into head office and she answered as truthfully as she could. But then he changed the subject and told her that his old friend Fr Garry Spinner had asked if it were possible for her to be appointed as the project manager for his new church in North Rocks. "What do you think William? Can you do it?"

"Well sir, I am a qualified architect and have run projects before, so I guess I am capable of doing the job."

"Well that's just great, as I have a lot of faith in you as does Fr Spinner. You will now be classed as a project manager in addition to your work as a marketing executive and there will of course be a salary increase too. And I think I can bring forward your application for a company car."

Claire was over the moon and when she told Sharon that evening, the latter realized once again that all the hard work 'her husband' was putting into 'his' job was paying off. Tanya threw her arms around Claire's neck and whispered words of love. In an almost heartbreaking choke, Claire answered: "I love you too sweetie – very much."

Of course, Claire didn't realize just how much she really loved her beautiful daughter. But in Tanya she saw herself as she should have been many years ago, had her father not intervened and arranged for her mutilation.

Claire's position as a project manager with *Civic Management* was not without problems, however. Fr Spinner changed so many things, and the cost shot through his cherished budget. He selected a far more expensive carpet for a start, and then one item after another was upgraded. However, once he was made to understand why the cost was higher, he settled down and admitted that the parish could afford it. On one occasion, after Claire had been invited to share a cooked lunch with him in his presbytery, he said he had to go out that afternoon to gather some more money. She apparently looked puzzled, so he put his hand into his left trouser pocket and produced a huge roll of dollar notes. There must have been simply thousands and thousands of dollars in his hand.

"This is what I am going out to add to William, some more money to finish the job." It was later Claire learned that Fr Spinner had been allocated the parish by the archbishop as he was good at squeezing money out of the pockets of his parishioners. In reality he was a businessman as well as being a priest.

The church was ultimately finished. The architects who had prepared the drawings on Claire's revised design received all the praise, their name being placed on the plaque in the entrance foyer. Her name didn't appear anywhere. Her company, as project manager, was praised for their insight into cost management and she then found herself being moved back to the Parramatta office to handle community projects for Western New South Wales. In one way it was a promotion but in another way it was literally moving her sideways. Claire's problem as always was that her mind often wandered off the task in hand. What diverted her attention need not be a question that the reader might ask, knowing the way she was born. Constantly, although her mind was inevitably on the task in front of her, part of her brain was elsewhere. One might say that she lived part of the time in the real world, and the rest of the time in her dream time. Claire remembered that at high school the head had made a comment that she was a dreamer. Little did they all know or understand.

Looking back on those years from her current advantage point, she guessed she was living a life that she found hard to describe. It was a life that others could not under any circumstances understand.

39

To the Back O'Beyond

Living in Arcadia was in many ways a blessing. Both Claire and Sharon had good jobs and they were able to pay off their mortgage quicker than they might have done otherwise. Sharon had obtained a position as secretary to a Roman Catholic primary school over in Riverdene. After Claire had departed for work early morning, she was free to see the children off to their respective schools. The parish school where she worked was run by a small community of Lebanese priests assisted by nuns from the convent next door. Her interesting and valued work gave her an outside interest from the home which Claire thought she needed. Sharon was extremely efficient at her job and her work at the parish school and was greatly appreciated. But one evening, after Tanya and Marcus had gone to bed Sharon said she wanted to ask something. Claire was puzzled. "Okay fire away," she said, taking a mouthful of hot chocolate.

"Well, I have been invited to have a coffee after school with one of the teachers."

"That sounds fine by me, what's her name?"

"That's the thing, it isn't one of the female teachers, but the only male teacher we have on the staff."

Claire listened intently, getting quite anxious over the issue. "Tell me more," she asked Sharon.

"Well, his name is Richard and he said he would like to get to know me better."

"Are you serious?" Claire probed. "I mean, you are a married woman who has been asked out on a date by an unattached male teacher who says he wants to get to know you. That means he wants to date you, don't you see? Have you told him you are married?" Claire stared into Sharon's eyes.

"Well, not exactly." Sharon replied.

"Get serious Sharon. I think you should nip this affair in the bud right now."

Sharon went quiet for a moment, while staring at the floor, before adding, "I suppose you're right William, it's just that I thought you wouldn't mind."

"Damned right I mind Sharon. I can just imagine Tanya and Marcus coming home from school to find you not at home but dating a male teacher from the school where you work. Can you imagine what they would think of you if they found out? Let's face it Sharon, you did this before to me and the kids over in the UK a few years ago didn't you? Look what happened to that guy!"

"Well, looking at it that way I suppose I should cancel the date."

"By heck Sharon, you mean you have already told him you would like to have a coffee with him?"

"Well, not exactly like that," she answered beginning to blush.

"I suppose you have been sitting with him during the lunch breaks too, have you?"

"Yes," she said sheepishly, averting her eyes downward.

"Okay, if that's what you want to do Sharon, you are a free agent. I suppose you'll do what you want to do anyway like you did before." Claire stormed off to leave her contemplating what had been said.

Three weeks later the same discussion was opened with Sharon telling 'William' that she didn't see the teacher again as he had accepted a teaching position in Townsville. In other words, Sharon had not had to make a decision, as the teacher in question had made the decision, letting her off the hook, so to speak. Claire's reaction was one of alarm, as Sharon had not in fact put an end to the affair, Richard had.

Claire began to see that there might be a problem in their relationship and Sharon seemed to want out. Claire did wonder if Sharon somehow knew of her enigma, her gender dysphoria, and saw that as a danger lurking in the shadows. Many years later Sharon did admit that she knew there was something strange about her husband and that 'William' had feminine instincts, but more of that later.

Throwing many painstaking hours into developing the land around their two-story house in Arcadia, it began to look like a garden at long last. Claire had laid a sloping driveway down to and including the floor of the carport in recycled bricks and laid a compacted earth path with some log steps down to the front door, the sides also bordered by logs. Then she made a path leading toward a small chicken run. From there she laid a path along the side of the creek toward the open area under the family room and kitchen. The land at the side of this path she laid out with raised beds bordered by some of the smaller tree trunks which were left over from the original site clearance. It was all looking extremely nice and Claire was pleased with her handiwork, assisted from time to time by Marcus.

The Wilsons had befriended a woman across a couple of paddocks who had a small herd of goats and Marcus and Claire had volunteered to clean out the goat shed if they could have the droppings as manure. This suggestion was greeted with pleasure by their friend.

One Saturday afternoon, therefore, Claire and Marcus drove around to the smallholding in their Ford Fairmont station wagon. In preparation for the smelly load they folded down the rear seats and covered the whole of the back with heavy-duty plastic. Cleaning out the goat shed was hot and very smelly, as might be expected. However, they persevered as the manure was needed for the new vegetable beds as the soil was not very productive. Back at home they unloaded their prize, the smell of which seemed to permeate everything. On completion they cleaned out the station wagon and both took well-earned showers.

But always the talk of showers reminded Claire of another more serious situation which had happened previously. One Saturday morning Claire had taken a breather from spreading top soil from a pile she had had delivered the previous day from a local builder's merchant. The pile of soil was heaped on the unpaved sidewalk and she had been removing its rich contents from one side of the earthy pile to barrow down the slope to where it was needed.

During the mid-morning break Sharon and Claire were in the family room supping mugs of hot coffee when the latter happened to look out through the open front door. What she saw startled her senses so much that she shot out of the door like a speeding bullet. Marcus had been playing next to the pile of topsoil with one of his Tonka trucks, digging into the side of the pile. But at that moment all Claire could see was a pair of boy's legs shaking in the air from the side of the heap. Racing across the garden beds she knelt down and started digging to free Marcus after fruitlessly trying to pull him out by his legs. Claire was crying and shouting for help in her frustration but continued digging. Sharon stood at the front door watching. After what seemed like a few minutes, but in fact was less than a minute, Claire had freed her son and picking him up as a dead weight, rushed past Sharon back into the house and ran upstairs to the second shower room.

Stepping into the shower, both of them fully clothed and still holding Marcus, she turned the cold tap full on and started washing the soil from Marc's eyes, nostrils and mouth. The boy showed no signs of life and Claire was getting frantic, still crying. Gradually, however, Marcus opened his eyes and started crying too. Not only was Claire relieved that she had saved his life but in her own tears she hugged her son with so much love and protection. Sharon stood outside the door asking: "What's matter with him? Why are you both in the shower with your clothes on? What's happened?" It was as though Sharon had sailed through the incident like an observer sitting on a balcony. It was really weird and later, with hindsight, Claire wondered what thoughts had been going through Sharon's brain, because they certainly were not in the present.

Claire didn't have the energy to answer Sharon's questions as the former was slowly coming to her normal senses. These had been surpassed by the adrenalin that had risen when Claire saw Marcus's plight. She hugged him tightly at that moment as she stood under the shower still holding him in her arms, kissing his face. She loved him so much. The strange thing was that Marcus had no memory of what had happened. When the soil had begun to fall over his head he had partially covered his eyes and nose with his hands and then blacked out. It was that which had saved him, plus Claire's swift action in rescuing him from the abyss in which he had been falling.

The next summer the Wilson's crop of tomatoes, lettuce, radishes, sweet corn, cabbages and potatoes were a sight for sore eyes and the abundance of the produce was worth all the hard work Marcus and Claire had put into the plot. The manure from their own chickens became a standby fertilizer, as they spread and dug it into their various vegetable beds.

Then there was the morning when Sharon screamed as she looked out of the glass doors onto their bedroom balcony. She was pointing at one of the hanging baskets. "Look – a snake!"

Claire followed her pointing finger and sure enough there was a green snake, which was curled up asleep in one of the hanging baskets. Nervously, Claire went outside and sprayed the snake with what she seemed to remember was fly spray, which she had taken from under the kitchen sink. No one makes 'snake spray', so fly spray had to do. Slowly the slithery critter raised its head and started to unwind. It cannot have liked the perfume of the spray as it slowly slid along the beam from which the basket was hanging and worked its way down the nearest post to the ground. Claire and Sharon stood behind the glass doors to the balcony watching, as the long green shape slithered its way across the earth toward the creek. They saw it no more. Panic over!

It was 1978 and having earned the Wood Badge for Scout leaders Claire had been given charge as "assistant" scout leader of the Arcadia Scout troop. The group leader and leader of the Venture Scouts, Rob Charlesworth, a single man who had been with the scouts and cubs for many years, refused to relinquish his title as 'scout leader'. He allowed 'William' to become his official assistant. Nevertheless, it was Claire who led the boys, not Rob.

It was Anzac Day and Claire and her scouts were standing outside the meeting hall waiting to line up for the annual parade to the war memorial. By this time she had another leader with her. John Barker was standing nearby talking to some other scouts, but glancing back at Claire. Suddenly he appeared in front of her, smiling, and with his hand on his hip in a somewhat effeminate manner made the comment: "Do you always stand like that?" pointing at her hips.

"Like what?" Claire asked.

"Like this," he added, emphasizing how he was standing by flaring one of his hands out. "Are you a poofter or something?" he asked.

Claire blushed crimson and slowly realized what was happening. She had let her guard drop and was standing normally with her hand on her hip. Claire had to admit it might have looked feminine to John. In fact, Claire was standing like a normal woman, and had not been paying attention to how men stood, as distinct from women. She could have kicked herself. Quickly she put her hands in the pockets of her shorts and trying to lower her voice a little, told him that the way she had been standing was nothing. John walked away smiling to himself, scratching his head as though he really was confused. Claire doubted it as John could obviously detect something odd in her and she had to be more careful in future.

But as the years progressed, her gender problem was getting more and more difficult to control. She remembered trying on Sharon's things quite often when the latter had gone downstairs to prepare breakfast. On one occasion Claire remembered even putting mascara on her eyelashes hoping that no one would notice. Another time she painted her nails with a clear varnish, hoping that no one would notice. But eaten up with her enigma and thinking that others might easily notice, she spent the rest of the day clenching her fists so that people would not stare at her shiny nails. The next morning she removed the glaze with some of Sharon's varnish remover, hoping the smell would vanish quickly.

After completing the building of the church in North Rocks as project manager, Claire was moved back to the Parramatta office of *Civic Management* with a new title as marketing manager for the Western NSW Community Division. Her immediate boss was the new Western NSW general manager Phil Burton, not that he seemed to know much about marketing as he had been a carpenter previously. Her new appointment was a feather in Claire's cap as she had more responsibility. But it was going to be harder for her to put packages together out in the west of the state, from her base in North Parramatta. Nevertheless, she planned trips by road and by air to distant towns and cities to meet people who might be in a position to help her build up a portfolio of potential projects.

One of her trips was to fly out to Cobar, which she had visited many years earlier for *Elder Smith Goldsborough Mort*, their name later changed to *Elders GM* and today simply known as *Elders*. Previously, working for an architectural practice in Parramatta she had designed and organized a new stock and station office for *Elders* in the main street. That had been a strange experience before the current airport had been built. That particular day Claire had flown to Cobar from Sydney and the small airplane landed on an oiled-sandy airstrip. Alighting from the aircraft she was to discover that there was no one there to meet her. Finding an antiquated wall-mounted phone on the back wall of the arrival shed, she wound the handle a few times to get the operator, as she had watched cowboys do in Wild West movies. She asked the operator to connect her to the office of *Elder Smith*. It had previously been arranged by their office in Sydney that their branch manager would meet her off the morning flight.

"Oh, I forgot you were coming today. I'll be out in the Ute to pick you up, in a few minutes when I've finished my lunch," was his casual answer to her plight. He didn't seem at all concerned.

An hour later the manager arrived and driving back into town dropped her in the main street as she needed to buy some food for her own belated lunch. Wondering if one of the hotel bars sold meat pies, she walked through the swinging doors of the nearest one and strode up to the bar. As she, a stranger to the locals, entered the saloon, all the guys leaning on the bar turned toward her in unison as though they had been programmed alike. Yes, they sold pies, so she bought one and was glad to be back outside.

Cobar was a real strange town. No longer did the hotel patrons tether their horses outside the hotels but the line of rear-parked utility vehicles, *Utes,* short for Utility Vehicles, to Australians, bore testimony to the fact that really nothing much had changed over the years.

But now on this later occasion, Claire hired a car at the airport and drove into town to book herself a room for a couple of nights. The motel manager was apparently the president of the local Rotary Club and after he had quizzed his new guest who she was and why she was in town, asked if she, seen as 'William', would be the guest speaker at a men's business fellowship the following evening. Claire agreed and felt a sense of achievement already. Then, she walked to the offices of the local newspaper for some news as to what was happening in town. She was again greeted warmly and invited to write an article for publication in the next issue, which was to be published at the end of the week. That evening Claire wrote the article in her motel room before climbing into bed.

After calling into the newspaper offices the next day to hand over the article, Claire called on the president of the local hospital auxiliary. He was also the local meteorological officer and Claire was invited to visit him later at the weather station up on the nearest hill. During the ensuing conversation, it appeared that there might be a possibility for the design and build of a new nurses' home. So far so good, she thought.

About ten O'clock the next morning, Claire decided to call on the local Roman Catholic parish priest to see what plans the parish might have in their building program. She found his flat-roofed presbytery a lot more modern than his traditional Gothic-inspired red brick church across the road. As an architect, Claire thought the modern presbytery looked somewhat out of place in this outback town. Obviously it had been designed in Sydney.

There was no reply when Claire knocked on the front door, but as she stood there wondering what to do next, the door opened to expose a gap of about ten centimeters. Peering through the space was a rather bedraggled and bleary red-eyed face, with a noticeable growth on its chin. Claire explained that she wanted to interview the parish priest and his reply gave her the impression that the apparition she was speaking to was his. He suggested that she meet him in his corner in the pub at midday.

A few minutes before the appointed time Claire went into the hotel and asked the barman where Father Moran usually sat when he came in. "Are you here for confession?" he asked with a smirk across his face, telling her that Father Moran heard confessions in the pub more than in the church.

"No, but he asked me to meet him here at noon."

The barman pointed to a table over in the far corner: "He always sits over there for confessions," he told her.

This place was getting more and more weird. Claire could not remember the ensuing conversation with Father Moran, but it can't have been of any value or interest as nothing came of it. That being so, in the afternoon Claire decided to call on the Anglican rector who seemed to be more welcoming than the Catholic priest. They chatted about possibilities quite amicably over afternoon tea sitting under a tree in his front garden. *Very English*, she thought.

The third day of her trip to Cobar, Claire drove her hire car back to the Avis office at the airport and boarded the return flight to Sydney. She was happy, feeling that she had accomplished a great deal with a potential new order for her company. Back in the office the following day, Phil Burton, her immediate boss, queried her achievements. Basically he didn't see how 'William' could fly out to Cobar and in three days fly back with a potential order. So Phil suggested he fly to Cobar with Claire to meet the people she had been chatting to. Maybe he thought she might then back down from her claim and be exposed as a fraud. In her mind this reaction of Phil's registered as a veiled attempt to check up on her; he thinking she was simply boasting to make herself out to be a brilliant marketer. A week later Phil and Claire flew out to Cobar and thankfully everyone she had met confirmed what she had told him earlier. Later that day, Phil admitted that he had engendered doubts that she had effectively achieved so much in so short a time and had to finally admit that she was good at her job.

But Claire's time in the Parramatta office of *Civic Management* was numbered. It was time for a change as Sharon was getting restless again and the children didn't like their schools. More to the point was that Claire had decided to open an architectural practice again and to move up to northern NSW. Claire had previously driven up there with Sharon, Tanya and Marcus one long weekend, and they had looked at a 290-hectare piece of land just outside the Elgindale town boundary. It seemed too good to be true and arranged to buy the leasehold. As there was no house on the property, the Wilsons then found rented accommodation in nearby Merryland Street and agreed terms on that too.

Claire had passed on a lead to a marketing colleague in the Newcastle office of *Civic Management* of a Roman Catholic parish in Gunnedah that wanted a church and school built, and in return her colleague offered her a lead in Invergordon. He told her that it would be an uphill struggle though, as the local parish priest hated architects.

With that knowledge in mind she rang the priest: "Gerday Father, you don't know me but apparently you hate my sort." He laughed and asked why. Claire told him truthfully that she was a Catholic architect and was planning to open up her own practice in Elgindale and would love to meet him. As a result she was invited to meet him and his committee and yes it was true, they were looking to build a new church.

Settling Sharon, Tanya and Marcus in their new leased house in Elgindale, Claire took her family with her to the meeting at the presbytery in Invergordon. On arrival Sharon, Tanya and Marcus were escorted by the housekeeper to a lounge for some refreshment. Claire found herself seated in front of the parish priest and his committee, ready to receive a grilling from them. As always though, Claire was well prepared as she had previously given them an outline of what she could do for them – to identify their needs and desires.

One of the many questions they had lined up to ask her was whether she had designed and built a church before, to which she answered in the affirmative, albeit over in Yorkshire, but she then mentioned her success in North Rocks, Sydney. They also grilled her about her knowledge of the Catholic Church's revised rules for the design of churches, and of course she could answer that question and subsequent queries positively. The questions being over, Claire was then asked to wait outside the door while they considered her submission. Not long after, she was called back in front of the committee and was overjoyed to be offered the commission to design their new church.

Sharon, Tanya, Marcus and Claire were then invited to join the parish priest and his committee for lunch. Knowing that Claire and her family were Catholics, the priest invited Tanya to say grace for them before starting the meal. Poor Tanya started crying as she had never said it in her life and was extremely scared. Tanya had chosen to attend Elgindale's Presbyterian Ladies College rather than St Michael's Catholic High School, and Protestant grace was totally different to Catholic grace. Claire saved the day for Tanya and after making apologies for her, said Catholic grace.

Back in Parramatta later in the week, Claire went in to see the office manager Kurt Brederer to hand in her notice. It appeared that he had been told by head office in Sydney to get rid of eight people as a cost-cutting measure and he suggested that if Claire would let him lay her off instead of her resigning, she would be entitled to $3000 compensation to start her off in her new venture. This was great. Opportunities were beginning to slot into place.

Claire sold the house in Arcadia and drove up to Elgindale with new hopes. On the land they had leased on a ninety-nine year term, Marcus and she built a basic shed that would function as an architectural office. Claire even hired a young architect to work with her on her new projects.

Behind the office the construction of their new home slowly took shape. When it was finished, she moved it up toward the other sheds Marcus and she had built, to be used as a farm office. Claire then opened an architect's office in March Street in Elgindale as she had won another church project in the meantime. Her former colleague in the Newcastle office of *Civic Management* had lost the lead she had given him in Gunnedah; instead the parish priest invited her to discuss designing them a new church. It appeared that he had been speaking to the parish priest in Invergordon and had been told that they were highly impressed with 'William' and 'his' ideas. Things were looking up for Claire, not realizing that the priests of various parishes exchanged their views quite often when they played golf together. From this second project she then won a commission to re-design the interior of the Roman Catholic church in Timberton, this included a new marble altar and pulpit. Following that commission, she then received a phone call from yet another priest, this time from Warburton further west, who wanted some advice.

Claire spent lots of time with this new client, but it seemed that after weeks of design sketches and talks to his parishioners, he was not intending to pay her. Later she found this attitude typical of Roman Catholic priests, with one or two exceptions like Fr Bernie MacDuff of Invergordon, who unfortunately passed away before the building work was completed. The Gunnedah parish priest she won over with her skills in management and arbitration and she received her full fees from him, which was unusual to say the least. He was the exception to the rule. The priest from Warburton, however, was to prove troublesome and ultimately was to change her attitude to religion.

40

Disowned Again

But at this point we have to back-track a little on the Wilsons relocation from Arcadia to Elgindale. The reason is that some problems have not exactly been made clear. It might appear that Claire's enigma was in recess, and this was very far from the truth. The separation from Sharon, Tanya and Marcus for a few weeks led her to live a more closeted life for a while.

Everything packed up for their move to Elgindale, and having fixed a date with a removalist, the day had finally come for their move. The furniture mover did not arrive however, and no amount of telephone calls allowed Claire to unfold what had gone wrong. So almost in panic she opted to ring a smaller operator down the highway in Dural. Fortunately, it was a Friday and the guy she spoke to was able to get a mate of his to help. Subsequently, the new removalist turned up later in the afternoon to load up his van. The Wilsons, in their Ford Fairmont, followed by the removalists van, set off up the Putty Road and then the New England Highway for Elgindale.

It was a long hard drive but eventually, after midnight, they arrived at their new leased home. After a brief snack, they bedded themselves down on the floor to try to get some sleep. At about 6 am, however, they were awakened by the noise of a van trying to reverse up the driveway. Their belongings had arrived and their secret fears that the guys might have driven off with their possessions, melted away into the dawn.

After unloading, Sharon made the guys some breakfast to warm their stomachs for their long drive back down south. Waving them off on their journey the Wilsons returned to the house for their own breakfast. After settling the family down in their new abode, Claire stayed a few days with them to get the children into high school. Tanya took a dislike to her school immediately and after a number of weeks of crying bouts, Claire and Sharon moved her to Elgindale Presbyterian Ladies College, which she seemed to prefer. Marcus was enrolled at St Michael's Catholic High School run by a religious order known as the Christian Brothers.

Prior to moving up to Elgindale, Claire had been able to stay in their house in Arcadia while it was being sold and had set about designing the new Invergordon church in her little studio off the living room. But her evenings were fraught with the usual gender problems. While drawing at the board she was in the habit of painting her nails, which in her mind was yet another sign that she was female, and not the male that others perceived.

She had borrowed a foam mattress from her cousin Deborah and her husband Don, and laid it on the bedroom floor. But spending evenings on her own, in an empty house, didn't take long for Claire to buy her first set of underwear, nightie and negligée, a skirt and blouse, and some make up. She felt that she should be true to her innermost feelings.

The first Saturday on her own, 'William' had gone into the David Jones store near the bridge in North Parramatta, telling an assistant that 'he' wished to buy 'his' wife a beautiful set of undies and could she help 'him'. It was later on that afternoon that Claire tried everything on. *Ooh,* she was in another world. This was what she had been dreaming of for so many years, since she had worn her Mum's things. She had also bought a black nightie and negligée from the old F. W. Woolworth's store in Church Street and slept every night in ecstasy. The only fly in the proverbial ointment was that she knew her actions were limited, and that once the house was sold, she would have to get rid of everything and return to her false identity as 'William'.

Each evening and some Saturday afternoons, when she didn't expect anyone to call, Claire dressed up as the real person she knew she was in her actual gender and she felt so special. She had bought herself some new shoes and some strappy heeled sandals too.

But one evening there was a knock on the door. Claire panicked and quickly wiped off her lipstick and donned a raincoat to see who it was. It was their next-door-but-one neighbor Roddy who asked if she had seen anyone prowling around.

"No, I haven't, I have been in the studio drawing. Why?"

"Well mate, I think we have a prowler. I've rung the police and they are sending someone out. But if I catch anyone, it will be God help them."

Roderick told her that the police suggested that if he saw the prowler first he should call them to set their process in motion. When Roddy knocked on her door again, this time closer to midnight, he told her that the guy had been caught running down Old Northern Road. Roddy had pounced on him and held him on the ground to wait for the police to arrive. Apparently when they did, the senior of the two officers asked Roddy if he would like to do anything to the guy while they turned their backs. To Claire's mind this was hardly an ethical way of conducting a police arrest. Being given the official nod to do what he wanted, Roddy smashed his fist across the man's face so hard, he thought he might have killed him. The police then took the man away to charge him. So Roderick was back reporting to Claire what he had done, feeling rather pleased with himself.

Claire slept very warily that night, wondering who might be looking through her windows. This was to become a permanent worry for her until she let her guard down many years later, living in a small community in Prince Edward Island, Canada. On that occasion, she was told by a distant cousin who had moved there from Yorkshire that she had a *Peeping Tom* nearby. In reality, it was to be *Peeping Tomelina*, a local female liability whom everyone knew.

Just after the 1979 Christmas festivities had subsided, Claire had received a long-distance telephone call from her sister-in-law Veronica, to advise that her mum had been killed. The shock did not sink in at first and she asked what had happened. Dad had explained to Gerry and Veronica that he and Olivia had driven to Collingsby for their customary evening drink and parked in their usual place behind the shops opposite the Old Mill Inn. They had walked through the gap between the shops toward the guard-rail that protected children from running out and into Wetherton Road, and her mum was killed crossing the road at that spot. Claire was devastated. She became silent for a few seconds before Veronica gave her the next piece of news: "Your dad wants you over here for the funeral."

"Oh no!" Claire answered, her body going from hot to cold alternatively. She told her sister-in-law that she had no money for a flight as it was expensive. Then Claire had a brainwave as she spoke. She thought she might ask Don Mackenzie, the husband of her cousin Debbie, who ran a news agency in Blacktown, if he could loan her the money. "But I think I can borrow the money somehow, so I will be there. When does dad want me over there?"

"The funeral is planned for Tuesday next week," she said. "You can stay with us if you like, and maybe Danny and Elspeth would like you over in Tullminster too. So, accommodation is no problem once you get here. If you let me know when you can get to Aireborough Station, I will pick you up from there."

Claire rang off with the feeling that her insides had been squashed into a lump. She rang Don immediately and he was sympathetic and told her to call over the next day and he would give her some cash for the air fare. She could pay him back when she was able. Debby sent her condolences too.

Claire flew over to London a few days later and from Kings Cross railway station took a train up to Aireborough. Veronica met her in her bright red sports car and took her to their house in Oakhill. Gerry was his usual self, as though butter wouldn't melt in his mouth, but nevertheless full of his own importance. Milton was there too and Claire gave him a hug, only to feel him pushing her away. It was most disturbing and she wondered if he was still bearing the shock of the situation, or his mind had traveled back to her birth as a hermaphrodite. It wasn't until a few years later that she realized that her dad still harbored a rejection of her, and had done so from the day she was born.

The following day Claire was collected by Danny and taken to their home, a detached house in a modern estate in Tullminster. Their daughters had been doubled up in each other's bedrooms so that 'Uncle William' could have a room to 'himself'. One evening, one of Claire's Australian cousins, although he would have described himself as British, collected her to take her out for a drink to their Uncle Leopold's pub in the village of Chapel Minton.

The public bar was smoke-filled and somewhat rowdy, and Uncle Leo and Aunt Katarina looked bleary eyed serving behind the bar. Claire was told that nanna Levine was in the living room out at the back, and without a formal invitation she walked toward the door and opened it. Claire found her dear nanna with eyes wet from crying. Her mum had been nanna's third eldest daughter who had died, although to Claire she was beginning to see her mum's death as murder.

Milton had told 'William' that he and mum had been ready to cross the road at Collingsby when his wife was thrown up into the air by a passing car. Danny had raised his eyebrows at that story, as he had serious doubts about the whole affair. Putting two and two together, Danny and Claire worked out that their dad must have crossed the road first and, standing on the other side he would have told their mum to cross over. Knowing her dad from many previous occasions, especially when her parents were out together, she imagined him to have shouted at her using typical words such as: *Come on you silly bitch, stop dithering and come across now.* Olivia might have hesitated and Milton is likely to have added: *Look I can see the road clearly you silly cow, come on!*

Why Olivia stayed with Milton when he constantly pulled her to pieces she would never know. It was Aunt Irma, Olivia's youngest sister, who commented to Claire a few years later in Australia that her mum should have left her husband as he was so cruel, both verbally and physically. On that occasion Claire told Aunt Irma that her mum was not the kind of woman to walk out of a Catholic marriage as she regarded it as sacred – not to be broken. "What God joined together let no man separate" or similar words Claire recalled. Such was the influence of the Roman Catholic religion.

So as her mum stepped off the kerb that fateful evening, a car apparently came from nowhere at high speed, even though it was in a twenty mile an hour restricted zone. According to one of her dad's stories, her mum had been tossed into the air. Traveling in the first car of the funeral cortège a few days later, approaching the cemetery gates Claire's dad spoke aloud: "She was thrown up in the air like a rag doll."

To Claire this seemed somewhat strange because had the car been coming at the regulatory twenty miles an hour she would not have been thrown up like that. A normal motorist, on seeing a person crossing the road in the bright lights, would have braked hard and the person merely knocked over and perhaps dragged under the car, or whatever vehicle it happened to be. To make matters worse in Claire's mind, she reckoned that if her dad had crossed to the other side of the road, he would have been able to see all the vehicles that were approaching. One version in Claire's mind might have had her dad encouraging her mum to step off the kerb at that precise moment. The driver of the car, together with her dad, would then have been guilty of premeditated murder. It was all too much to take in and she needed to really think out the situation. Claire vowed to get to the bottom of her mum's murder at some stage in the future, but it was to take her forty years to finally complete the process.

The morning of the funeral came around and 'William' was told to sit in the first funeral car behind the hearse. So Claire had to sit on the inner side with Nanna Levine sitting between herself and her father on the outer side. The latter spoke to the air in front of him in statements, as was his wont: "It should have been this one here that was killed, the useless piece of flesh that she is." He pointed his finger at Marjory Levine.

"Dad, don't say such nasty things," Claire said in a subdued voice. Her nanna could not help hearing her dad's hurtful words.

"Well, your mummy didn't deserve to die. She was just thrown up in the air and landed on the road behind the car in a heap."

By this time Claire was trying, once again, to build up a picture in her mind of what actually happened. She wondered if her dad was, as he usually did, romanticize to make himself out as an innocent bystander, which of course he was not. Unknown to Claire at the time, he had told his sister in the USA a totally different story.

After Olivia had been buried in the Roman Catholic section of Wetherton Cemetery, the guests were driven back to the family home in Rigton for the wake. Claire was still in a state of shock, trying to take everything in, as one relative after another came up to her to offer their condolences. She hardly ate or drank at the wake.

Soon, however, people started to leave and Danny indicated that they should leave also to get 'William' to Aireborough Station to catch the train to Kings Cross. Claire said her goodbye's to everyone who seemed to have no intention of leaving just yet. She didn't know when she might see them all again, especially her dear nanna. Claire gave her a big hug and then went out to Danny's car in the driveway. Gerry and Milton came out too and climbed into the car, Gerry in the front next to Danny who was driving, and Claire's dad next to her in the back.

She tried to hold a sensible conversation with them all as they drove along Wetherton Road into the city center. Arriving in the station forecourt her dad handed her an envelope in which there was a check. Milton explained specifically that he had not paid for her trip over to England, as the money had been taken from his wife's private account. Then he started his tirade: "You are going back to Australia without my blessing," he said. But then added, "When you first went to Australia I said I disowned you as a traitor and I repeat that now. England is the best country in the world by far and Australia is to us a land of convicts. Your Uncle Jeremy is one of them. He would have been in jail if he had stayed here but he got out of it and escaped to Australia. So in my eyes you are just the same as him. You could never make a go of things here in your own country. So I repeat again, you are not my son and never will be, as you are a traitor to England, deserting this land in disgrace. Go now before I say anything else." His words left Claire staring blankly into space.

She didn't think Danny and Gerry were expecting their dad's outburst to be so cruel and hurtful. Gerry had never loved 'William' as a brother, being jealous of what 'he' had achieved. He had constantly shown his jealousy over the years and seemed to see himself as superior. Danny took Claire's case out of the trunk of his car and looking her in the eyes said: "Forgive him if you can, he has become so bitter and nothing will change him, other than time."

Danny gave her a hug and while saying his goodbye, Milton wound down the back window of the car: "Come on Danny, we're wasting time. There's plenty to be done back at 'the works'."

Who would have thought their mum had just been buried? Danny winked at Claire as she moved toward the station entrance and the last she saw of them was their car speeding under the columned side portico of the Queen's Hotel into City Square. She was in more shock than ever by now and like an automaton walked to her designated platform.

As the train left Aireborough station Claire started to cry. *Oh why was Dad so cruel,* she thought? *Why does he have to be so bigoted all the time?*

Claire dosed fitfully as the train sped on its way down to London. At Heathrow Airport, she took her bag to the check-in desk, received her boarding card and walked away to make her way to the departure gates. She then thought she heard her name announced over the *Tanoy* system. But by this time she was quite a distance away from the desk at which she might have had to report, so she shrugged her shoulders and walked to the departure gate to fly home to Australia. Claire was sadder than ever, but pleased to be leaving England.

Arriving back home in Arcadia, Claire was inundated with bunches of flowers that kind people had sent her, expressing their condolences. How nice some people were! The parish priest, Father Gabriel Fattorini, OSB came around the next day to offer his condolences too. She didn't particularly like this priest as he was too gushing and full of his own importance, but she put on a brave face to receive him. Putting on 'a brave face' seemed to have become a normal way of dealing with other people and events. Her enigma, her gender dysphoria, was as powerful and mysterious as ever.

41

More Problems

Having established an architectural practice in Elgindale two years earlier, Claire spent a couple of years designing a number of buildings and seeing them built. But 1983 was to see her struggling for new commissions. She had terminated a lease she had taken on three first-floor rooms in Meriwether Street, and then back at home she tried to work on a drawing board in what used to be the entrance lobby of the first building she had erected at their property re-named as *Ripley Park*. It was a struggle to earn enough money to live on, but Claire was able to manage until certain events began to affect her daily life. Her future, however, took on the character of a huge question mark. She knew without a shadow of doubt that her gender problem was getting worse.

It happened that the wife of one of her rather awkward clients had taken a dislike to her, mainly because those particular clients had defaulted on their building contract by running out of money. This resulted in her architect's stage payment certificates being dishonored by the clients' bank, and the builder not being paid. The impasse went to arbitration and as Claire's clients had broken the contract, she had to stand aside from both the builder and the client to act as a quasi-arbitrator.

As she sat in a lawyer's office in Elgindale, with the builder Rick Bookman on her left and client Patrick Kirk on the right, Claire could only state the truth of the matter. Patrick didn't like that and said in a low breath: "But you should be defending me against the 'F…ing' builder, not acting as though you are an 'F…ing' fly on the F…ing wall." Claire detested his use of foul language and ignored him.

The attorney tut-tutted at him, adding: "Mr Kirk, I will continue to remind you that you have defaulted under the terms of the contract and taken possession of a property which is still contractually under the management of the builder. Until you pay him the amount owing, and move back out of the house, you are in default."

"Well, it's all wrong. It is my 'F...ing' house he has been building and I have a right to live in it."

At this the lawyer stepped in again and repeated his previous statement. He came to Claire's defense by saying that under the terms of the contract, she had conducted herself correctly, and it was he who had defaulted and not the builder. Patrick was not going to have any of this. "You're all bloody 'F...ing' mad. It's my house and I am staying put. I will get a decent builder to finish it off."

The attorney lost his cool: "Mr Kirk! Patrick! You still have not understood the seriousness of your situation. You cannot get another builder to finish the work as you are in default to Mr Bookman. No other builder will touch your house, as they will be breaking the law if they do."

Patrick stood up and stormed out like a spoiled child. The remaining three sat there looking at each other, shrugging their shoulders.

"He will have to go to another bank to borrow some more money I think as the other builders in town already know of his money problems and I doubt if they will take on such a project" Claire commented.

Three weeks later, Patrick rang her to say he had gotten some more money and would pay Rick Bookman what he owed him providing he went back to finish the work. Claire breathed a sigh of relief, as this was what should have happened in the first place. A few weeks later the house was duly completed and the snagging items sorted. But Mr & Mrs Kirk's default was turning into a fester. Patrick's wife Daphne was on the Roman Catholic school board and had the ear of the Catholic Bishop of Elgindale, the Most Rev Bernard Mulherrin. Unknown to Claire, Daphne had been spreading lies about her to the other board members and in the hearing of Bishop Mulherrin. Subsequently, Claire heard on the Catholic grape vine that her name was mud and she would not be awarded further commissions from the diocese. Unfortunately for Claire, Daphne's lies had spread further than Elgindale.

One lunch time the Catholic priest and his curate from the outback town of Warburton walked into Claire's office and demanded all the original sketches she had ever done for him, for which she had never been paid. Then he demanded the original drawings he had loaned her, from which to prepare her sketches. Thrusting all these into the outstretched arms of his curate, he flung a check into the air with the words: "And there's your bloody money."

With that he stormed out of the office slamming the door so hard Claire thought the glass panel would shatter. The priest's check lay on the floor where he had let it fall. Sharon, who had been at her typewriter listening to the priest's outburst, gave a disgruntled huff with the words, "What a nasty, nasty man – and he calls himself a priest." She looked across at Claire. The latter was shaking like a leaf.

Over the next few weeks Claire had to decide what to do. There was virtually no money coming into the practice and she needed desperately to find work. The couple had talked at length about the situation and Sharon asked if it would be better if they went back to England, where 'William' could get a job. Claire considered this option and it was very tempting. The problem was however more immediate and she needed to earn some money quickly. She decided to write to one of her old employers, Tan Petruski of *Pacific Homes Australia*. Tan actually rang her after he received the letter and offered her a job as one of their sales reps. But Claire had to find accommodation down in Sydney pretty darned quick, and Sharon had to stay at Ripley Park while their property was on the market to be sold. Being an active member of the local Anglican parish, Claire discussed her predicament with the vicar, Reverend Paul Winterton. His solution was to ask her: "Would you mind staying at the rectory in Carringbah, just south of Sydney?" Claire asked what the deal might be and Paul admitted that the rector was a friend of his and it would only be a temporary measure of course until their Elgindale property was sold.

"I have no problems with that, as I don't anticipate *Ripley Park* taking long to sell." Claire remarked.

"Well William, I am sure you would be made most welcome as the Wintertons are a nice family."

Sure enough it worked and Claire drove down to the rectory in Carringbah where she was offered a small bedroom at a nominal rent, for whatever period she needed. But living as a guest at the rectory was unfortunately yet another expansion of Claire's problems relating to her gender dysphoria.

She started at *Pacific Homes* the following Monday morning and, as she already knew everyone in the office, she was fed a batch of enquiries from potential customers, each of which was interested in having an extension designed on their home. Claire was in her element as she had been previously trained in sales and marketing and within the next couple of weeks had a string of confirmed orders to hand over to the drawing office. Tan Petruski, her boss, was highly delighted with her immediate progress as it confirmed his faith in her skills. It did not take long for him to re-offer her the post of marketing manager. Claire wished she had not been considered for that position and had to come clean with her plans for moving back to the UK. But, in order to soften the blow to him, she twisted the story slightly by saying that it was in reality Sharon who wanted to go back. Tan was very disappointed but eventually settled down to accept the fact that he was to lose one of the best employees he had ever engaged.

Back at the rectory Claire had bought a small desk to work on which fitted under the window in her room and she had purchased a tiny A3-size drawing board to use for her sketches. But the privacy she experienced, after everyone else had gone to bed each night, was too good to be true. For the second time in her life, she bought herself a set of female undies, a pair of red high heels, an oatmeal-colored two piece, a wig, and some make-up. So when she took her leave from the rector and his wife each evening, retiring to her room, she dressed as what she considered her real self, and sat down to design. Unfortunately she became too blasé, and during the day even wore panties, slip and bra. The repercussions of this really were to shake her to her painted toenails.

The first time was after Holy Communion one Sunday at which the rector had presided. Members of the congregation were hanging around the back of the church drinking cups of coffee and tea, when one of the younger men in the choir approached her sporting a wide grin. That day Claire was wearing a lacy bolero top under her white shirt, over which she was wearing a gray cardigan. The guy started chatting to her and without a by-your-leave reached forward and parted her cardigan with his right index finger: "I have a shirt like that," he stated.

To Claire, all men's shirts looked the same, so she could not understand how the guy could identify the one she was wearing, until she realized that he appeared to be staring through it. She blushed, as he might have been able to see the outline of the lacy top underneath. Claire mumbled something to him and said she had to go. Obviously, the young man may be on the brink of discovering her secret. Back in her room Claire stood in front of the mirror and gasped. She could see her lacy top through the shirt, so obviously could the guy who made the comment. What a fool she had been.

The other incident was that one particular day she had gone into the office of *Pacific Homes* and was called into Angus McCann's room. Angus had been a foreman for a number of years and when Claire had originally turned down the first offer to be their marketing manager, he had been chosen to fill the position. But Angus felt out of his depth and wanted to sound her out as to whether she would be interested in taking over from him. As she walked into his tiny office he put his hand on her shoulder, and kept it there for a few seconds. Claire winced with embarrassment as while the shirt was a dark colored one with a vertical stripe, underneath she was wearing a bra and slip. She just knew he could feel the shoulder straps, and realized that maybe he knew what she was. Her world, while looking into the future back in England, was crumbling apart in Australia.

Claire drove back to Elgindale for Christmas and discarded the women's apparel she had lovely bought and worn for a few weeks, into a charity bin in Scone on the New England Highway. She was slowly sinking into depression again, having to return to the world in which she felt she didn't really fit. It was becoming very noticeable to her that her real gender was showing and she had to try to suppress it somehow in order to allay any fears others might harbor.

A few weeks later, the Wilsons traveled back to England together. Milton, her dad, was in his element showing off to all and sundry that 'his son William' and 'his family' had chosen to return to 'God's own country – England'. Claire and Sharon were offered the use of her parents' holiday bungalow on the coast at Seamer, and were grateful for the offer. Claire bought an old *Austin A40* to get them there and after a few days searching, she was offered a job with one of her former assistants in a small architectural practice in Harrogate. Henry Brown had decided to use her skills as he remembered working with her in Aireborough a few years previous. Knowing Claire as his former superior in the Aireborough practice, he knew she was a good designer and illustrator. So Claire had a job, demeaning though it may be, but it was a job and she realized that she should look for somewhere to live closer to Harrogate, instead of having to travel to and from Seamer each day. All she could find however was a ground floor rental apartment in the city of Ripon, to the north.

It was while they lived in Ripon that daughter Tanya had her former boyfriend Fergus, over from Australia. He had been so shattered when Tanya had left Australia, and was so much in love with her, that he just had to follow her across the oceans. How could Claire and Sharon turn this young man away from their door, much as they might have liked to do so? Tanya seemed besotted with Fergus and Claire could do nothing about the situation, except grim and bear it.

After a few weeks, however, they realized they had to ask him to leave, explaining that they were to move down to Hampsthwaite and had not enough room in the cottage they had found.

It was during this period that Tanya fell out with Fergus. He finally accepted her decision and flew back to Australia to start a new life for himself. It would be many years later, Claire saw on an Australian news program that Fergus had joined the police force and had been shot by a drug dealer. So sad! It was so very sad for such a well-meaning young man.

In the meantime Claire had left Henry Brown's practice as she was being paid a pittance for all the work she was doing in designing a new outdoor leisure park in Lancashire. She had seen an advertisement in the *Yorkshire Post* for sales professionals to work in Insurance and it was tempting. The job on offer was in York and she was given the opportunity to train with them. Unfortunately, this job didn't exactly work out the way that the company had outlined, and she found herself looking at another Insurance company from the south of England, although working from their Warkfield office. Again this did not work out as she reckoned she was not very good at selling insurance.

Her next job was to work for a company in the Valley Trading Estate near Walton, as a member of their door-knocking group. Claire was interviewed by their marketing manager Guido Favorini, a 'Spiv' if there ever was one in her opinion. But the compensation was that the company's commission rate was good, and as Sharon and Claire had moved to Hampsthwaite, it was a relatively easy drive to Walton. But the boss of the company James MacAlister soon saw her skills in art and design and suggested she work full time in the office instead of with the door-knocking team. Her new job was to act as marketing manager, while at the same time preparing design schemes for people's homes that the door-knocking team could sell. The skills she had developed working with *Pacific Homes Australia* were paying off.

Although Claire was still being paid a pittance for all the hours she put into her work, she really enjoyed it and put every effort into it. Mr MacAlister saw her potential in marketing and asked if she could obtain samples of Scottish, Welsh and Cumbrian slate from which he could make molds. His idea was to make artificial slate at a much cheaper price than the natural product.

It did not take Claire long to source suitable quarries, and as an architect she could request samples of the slates on the grounds that she would be interested in specifying them.

Mr MacAlister made some great copies of the natural slates but then sold the patent to give himself maximum profit at a personal level. Claire had written the specifications for each of the products and designed sales brochures, but received nothing from James MacAlister in payment. He was indeed a tight-fisted Scotsman, true to his reputation, and Claire felt she was upsetting his apple cart by complaining. So she left his company and answered an advert to work as architect with an Aireborough practice.

But at Gamble and Partners she found herself no higher up the ladder. Her work was extensive but her pay was minimal. As usual she found it so hard to eke out a living as an architect. Claire was to spend about nine months with this practice but left to take up a position on trial with a young practice of architects in Newton Arncliffe, Co. Durham. But again, oh why did this always happen to her, producing valuable work with pay that was always described as minuscule?

While living in Hampsthwaite, Tanya and Marcus managed to find work for themselves and paid Claire and Sharon a small contribution toward their keep. This helped the family finances a little. Tanya worked as a waitress in a small restaurant in Harrogate and Marcus during the day worked for an engineering company welding frames for pig pens, and in the evening as a sous-chef with one of the local hotels.

One evening, however, when Sharon had gone out to attend an evening meeting of the Women's Institute, Tanya having since gotten married and Marcus working at his hotel, Claire decided to have a nice leisurely bath. She placed a bath bomb in the water and soaked for a while before alighting, drying herself and wandering back into her bedroom. She had decided that this evening all was clear to engage her gender dysphoria by dressing up. The big trouble however was that, true to form, something had to go wrong. She had applied make-up and before dressing, she heard a key being thrust into the lock on the front door below. Claire froze as she thought Sharon had returned and she was to be unmasked.

There were footsteps on the stairs: "Dad, are you in there?" It was Marcus's voice outside the door and he tried to turn the knob to enter.

"Don't come in Marcus I have no clothes on," Claire really didn't want him to see her. That was blatantly obvious.

"But I need to see you, I need to borrow the car to go somewhere," came his somewhat irate request.

"Sorry Marcus, but your mum has the car and she has gone to a Women's Institute meeting over in Birstwith."

"Drat," he said, raising his voice in disgust.

Claire heard him running down the stairs and back out of the front door. A car door opened and closed and drove off. By this time her mind was in a spin. She had been extremely foolish and assumed that Sharon could return at any moment. Albeit earlier than she had thought. Weighing up her options, Claire decided to clean herself up, put things back where they belonged and climb into bed. What had started out as a 'freedom' evening had turned into a loathsome nightmare.

Sharon and Claire then decided to move from Hampsthwaite to upgrade a dirty little end terrace in a tiny village near Ripon. The cottage had belonged to the brother of a man who lived across the other side of the main street and he was pleased to have gotten rid of the old end terrace. So much so, that the elderly couple offered for Claire and Sharon to stay with them while the builders were in their cottage. This was very welcome and showed their apparent friendliness, as long as it lasted. Eventually however, having almost completed the restoration work, Claire decided to move into their cottage to avoid further friction between themselves and their hosts.

Sharon had been told that at some stage in the past someone had lived in the cottage that had repaired boots and shoes. Persuaded by this knowledge, true or false, they decided to change the name from Jasmine Cottage to *Shoemaker's Cottage*. Claire arranged for a new concrete floor to be laid in the sitting room as the original wooden floor was rotten, and she redesigned and rebuilt the fireplace in that room too. In the dining room their old Yorkshire farmhouse table fitted perfectly and in the kitchen she replaced all the cupboards with new doors and a more serviceable worktop. The rotted floor joists from the living room, after being treated for worm infestation, were screwed to the kitchen ceiling to give the effect of exposed ceiling joists. Their new home was developing a real old-world charm about it.

Another problem they discovered after living in the house for some months was that during periods of heavy rain, it blew in the back door. So the next job was to progressively build a stone-faced porch, prior to replacing all the windows in the house with new timber windows, each one with Georgian glazing bars. These Claire produced herself using a router which she had specifically bought for the purpose. The following year she added a stone-built garage, and of course by this time the cottage was looking really lovely.

She then complemented the side of the house by changing the vegetable garden into a lawn and dug out a huge pond. This was a draw for much wildlife too. In the corner, looking over the pond she built a pergola and it was a pleasure to sit there and admire her handiwork. Claire had been successful in pushing her gender issues to the back of her mind most days and thought that hard work was the way to fight the problem. Could she continue that for the rest of her life?

But the inevitable dispute arose with some neighbors who had been allowed to build a stone house adjacent to the Wilson's field gate, now the main driveway. The neighbors constantly left their car in the middle of the access drive which led to the Wilson's gate. Claire and Sharon were the legal owners of the driveway and needed it clear at all times, giving clear access to their gateway. Technically while the Wilsons owned the access lane, they had to allow common use of it to the houses at each side of it. The people from the detached house to which this story refers, while constantly leaving their car in the middle of the driveway, objected to Claire asking them to move their car each time she or Sharon wanted to drive out. It was so simple for the neighbors to place their car three more meters away outside their back door, but they just couldn't be bothered. This friction made them *the neighbors from Hell* in Claire and Sharon's minds.

Having secured a position as architect working for a practice of architects in Middlesborough, it was a longer drive to get to work than Claire had intended, and she really didn't want to move again. But the practice founder started appointing young graduates to senior positions over her and she saw the writing on the wall. The result was that once again Claire decided to open her own practice, this time in Durham.

Having won a great opportunity to design a shopping complex in a town in Lancashire, and even though her fees were whittled down by the builder to half of what they should be, she decided to accept the commission. In order to carry out the extensive design and detail work however, Claire had to employ staff and that brought with it more headaches, especially when she discovered that two of them were designing their own private projects on the practice computers, in office time too. Had it not been for the fact that Claire occasionally checked their computers when they had gone for the day, she would not have discovered this. There was only one solution as she hated disloyalty – she had to sack the individuals immediately.

During the period in which she ran the practice in Durham, Claire and Sharon decided to sell the cottage near Ripon to realize their tied up capital. After buying a two-story house in a small village in southern County Durham, she quickly improved it and then sold that for a profit too. It was the only way Claire could exist, buying properties, restoring them and then selling them on at a higher price, as the fees she received as an architect barely kept the proverbial wolf from the door.

But things never seemed to run smoothly for her and Sharon had decided that she wanted to live in the high country to be away from troublesome neighbors. So, one weekend they decided to search the 'for sale' boards in the shop windows of various real estate agents in the region centered on Haltwhistle. It was immediately successful as they discovered a large farm in Cumbria on which there were a number of derelict houses, and two of them were for sale.

After producing drawings for restoring one of the derelict farm houses, together with alterations and an extension, the Town Planners in Haltwhistle finally gave permission for her to go ahead. The only fly in the ointment was that the town planner in charge insisted on the use of timber windows and doors. As the building was in a very exposed position, facing the full blast of winter snow and ice, Claire knew that she would have continual problems. She had had enough experience of wooden windows sticking and having to paint them outside every year or two. Her solution therefore was to use uPVC windows. The local planning officer objected to this decision and instructed that she use wooden windows. The particular officer in Claire's opinion was merely an amateur as far as design was concerned as he had no qualifications to back up his perceived authority. Nevertheless, the planner dug in his heels over the issue. In the end Claire won as she refused to accept the planner's tantrums. She simply ignored his threats to stop the job and her argument won the day.

The next issue was that she was told that the stone slates on the original roof had to be matched as like-for-like. In other words, she was told to replace the 50-mm-thick slabs of stone back on the roof and find a supplier of thin slabs of matching color. This was a total nonsense as far as Claire was concerned as there were alternatives which looked almost the same. She therefore decided to cover the roof with artificial stone slates, made in South Yorkshire, instead of reusing the original thick stone slabs. Once again she was threatened by the planning officer, this time in writing. But again she won the argument and the finished house looked beautiful in its hillside setting.

The first winter in the house was to prove her judgment correct in the use of uPVC windows and doors and artificial stone roof tiles. On one occasion the ice was so thick on the front of the finished house that Claire had to use some de-icer from her car to melt the ice which covered the lock on the front door. Yes, the conditions were extremely harsh in this valley. She considered that the planning officer, who was from the south of England, knew nothing of local weather conditions and she had been right to fight against his silly ruling on materials used in the restoration. He had even insisted that she use wooden roof gutters and cast-iron down pipes, similar to those that the house might have had 150 years previously. What he didn't know was that Claire had sourced some plastic PVC gutters molded to match the ancient wooden gutters, and after they and the downpipes had been painted with a black bituminous paint, they were indistinguishable from the original products. *What a clever girl I am*, Claire thought.

42

Truth at Long Last

Claire's mind was in complete turmoil. While she wanted to complete the remodeling of the farmhouse as economically as possible and to the best of her ability, she was struggling hard with her gender dysphoria. It was now developing at an alarming rate. The enigma had always been with her since childhood, and she constantly thought it could be defeated. But she was beginning to realize that her future would be fraught with constant struggles and, in reality; could she cope with them, while getting older by the year?

She had accepted a commission from Irwins Shopfitters of Warkfield to provide them with working drawings and details for many of their projects. Her work in this field took her from Glasgow to just south of the Yorkshire border. But as some of the fit-outs were for women's clothing shops and one large department store, Claire was experiencing huge psychological problems. Being exposed to working with other women she easily saw herself as the woman that she knew she was, but her physical appearance said otherwise. How was she going to cope? Was this going to be a constant question for her in the future?

It was during one of their many holiday periods in Scotland, that Claire fully intended to tell Sharon about her lifetime secret, but the occasion just didn't seem right. Every so often, whether they were on a moorland track or walking by the coast, she intended opening up the subject but she didn't know how to broach it. There were no guidelines as she knew that her news, which would be absolutely devastating to Sharon, was considered a public joke by so many. While on vacation Claire was thinking about her enigma most of time, but on the way home, driving down the A689 from Brampton and the A7, Sharon casually said: "You're very quiet!" Claire could not suddenly tell her why she was quiet and remained silent, almost tongue-tied.

Sharon persisted in her question and after another short period of silence Claire finally replied, "I'll tell you when we get home."

They were not all that far from their turn off and Claire was now getting rather anxious about telling Sharon. In fact, Sharon was equally anxious as to what it was she was about to hear from 'William'. Quite understandable under the circumstances.

Back at home, they sat down over a cup of tea after their evening meal and Sharon, fearing the worst scenario, opened up first. "Come on William, out with it. What did you want to tell me?"

She sat down at 'William's' feet dreading the worst. Claire gulped air into her lungs praying for courage in what she was about to relate. But it could not be held in any longer. Claire was petrified. "I am sorry to have to tell you love, but I have a lifelong secret to tell you."

"Oh?" Sharon murmured, looking up at 'her husband', eye to eye.

"I know it will be hard for you to believe, but I have always known I was a woman." There. It was out. The words had been said.

Sharon was quiet for a few seconds: "What do you mean?"

"Well, since I was little I have always known that I was female and not male." Claire went on, "Mum knew of my problem and tried a number of times to get me to open up about it, but I was so scared of my dad that I dare not say anything. You see I have always known that when I was born, I had two genders and Dr Kelly arranged for me to be seen by doctors at Aireborough Infirmary. It was there that they did something to me to suppress my female parts and give prominence to the male parts. As I grew older I knew without a shadow of doubt that I was a girl and not a boy. The male parts I had were disgusting to me and over the years I have many times tried to emasculate myself. Each time, however, I backed off, scared of the consequences. In a nutshell, love, I need specialist help. I need help from the right people."

Sharon was dumbfounded, and without saying anything at all, stood up and after donning her coat left the house by the front door. Later she said she had walked across the fell and cried her eyes out. Claire supposed she also would have done exactly the same had she been in the same predicament. Sharon came back late and by then Claire had tidied up and gone up to bed.

Claire could not remember Sharon's words when she returned, but the next morning she said she wanted to discuss the situation with Tanya and Marcus. Unknown to Claire, while she had been working in the studio, Sharon had also telephoned someone who lived over by the coast who claimed to be a 'specialist' in such matters. It transpired that the man belonged to a religious cult that believed gender dysphoria to be an illness inflicted by Satan. The man told Sharon that her husband needed their 'expert' help to turn away from 'his' affliction and to pray with them for guidance. The man told Sharon that 'William' could be cured, but had to give 'himself' to Jesus Christ unreservedly. Not knowing that Claire had tried this technique over many years previously, Sharon revolted at this suggestion as she really didn't see what God had to do with such condition. Claire told Sharon that a few months previous, when she had been in London on a business trip; she had visited a clinical nurse who had medical experience in gender dysphoria. After having had Claire complete her answers to a long list of a hundred questions, the clinician declared that Claire was indeed female.

Sharon admitted later, that when 'William' told her that 'he' had something to tell her, she thought her husband was seeing another woman. Claire wondered if such an admission may have been less of a shock for Sharon. However, together they visited a private clinic in Manchester attached to a transsexual shop, at which a supposed 'medical practitioner' was available for consultation. All at a price of course! The health professional asked 'William' simple questions like, "If you had a choice to wear a skirt or jeans, what would you choose?"

"A skirt," was Claire's reply.

The other questions were of a similar ilk and then 'the medical specialist' made the pronouncement that Claire was not transsexual but a transvestite. Claire knew that she wasn't, as her problem had been with her all of her life. On that occasion Claire had not gone across to Manchester dressed as a woman, and when she saw some of the queer characters in the waiting room, many dressed as women and made-up to the nines, she was appalled. Claire knew without a shadow of doubt that she was nothing like them whatsoever. Seeing those characters shocked Sharon too and she became even more agitated.

Believing the verdict of the so-called medical 'expert' who declared that 'William' was a transvestite, Sharon made a decision. She thought that if her husband was one of those, she would with much reluctance allow 'him' to dress up as a woman for a time, in the privacy of their own home, until the effects wore off. Allowing this to happen for a few weeks, Sharon came to realize that 'William' was easily passable as a woman. She was adamant however, that 'her husband' should not go out of the house in case anyone saw 'him', thereby ridiculing both of them.

Claire then sought guidance from *The Gender Center* in London and they recommended she speak to their representative in the North of England. Consequently, a visit was arranged to meet with the representative. So one evening, dressed as only she knew how, as a normal woman, Claire drove across to Gateshead. Before calling on the representative she dropped into a branch of the *British Home Stores* in Gateshead and bought herself a new winter coat. As this was the first time she had been out in public dressed as a normal woman, she was interested in other people's reactions to her presence. Not observing any untoward comments or looks, she made her purchase and then drove across town to the representative's house.

When the front door was opened, Claire was shocked to see a man dressed as a woman, and a real woman standing behind 'him/her', of a much smaller stature than the tall individual. The meeting progressed over cups of coffee in the couple's lounge room, and Claire had been asked to explain her life's problem.

At the end of her narrative, 'the representative', who Claire referred to as 'Beatrice', told her that she showed all the classic signs of transsexualism. She was told that hermaphrodites were a rarity as most of them died in their childhood or teens, but that she really ought to see a specialist in London, who had advised all the famous *Trannies*, including Jan Morris, the travel writer.

A couple of weeks later Claire took Sharon to see 'Beatrice' and 'his/her' wife. While they dined over some baked beans and slices of tinned corned beef, Sharon felt trapped in a situation that she did not like. Driving home, she admitted that she had felt filthy during the evening and that it was all wrong. Claire had to admit that she felt very uneasy too. But Claire was of the opinion that Sharon might be coming around to see her in a different light. That particular evening Beatrice had appeared from her bedroom dressed in a flimsy short dress and it was pretty obvious that 'he/she' was a man. It was indeed all wrong. Claire felt as though she was experiencing a nightmare. Sharon, however, subconsciously was able to compare Beatrice with 'William' as Claire. There was a difference and it needed to be opened up. So upon 'William' obtaining an appointment in London with the gender specialist Beatrice had recommended, Sharon eventually agreed that the two of them should travel to London together.

Claire was seen by Dr Bartholomew Padgett, a gender specialist at the Thames Institute in the December of that year. He listened to her story and declared that, because he had also read the questionnaire she had submitted through the clinical nurse at the same Institute, he was of the opinion that she was totally genuine. For Claire, at the tender stage she was at, it was such a relief to hear this from Dr Padgett. She asked if he would mind telling Sharon who had been patiently sitting in reception during their discussion, and had probably bitten off all her fingernails with worry. He agreed and so Claire took her into Dr Padgett's office. Sitting Sharon down opposite him, he carefully and sympathetically explained that, as a specialist in gender dysphoria, he was fully aware of Claire's problem and the classic signs were that she was genuine. He told her that in his professional opinion she was indeed a woman and her history, dating back to her childhood, confirmed his views. In other words, Claire fitted the textbook cases so far investigated worldwide.

This was not what Sharon wanted to hear and she was in total shock. She had thought Dr Padgett might have said it was all a fantasy and that 'William' needed psychiatric shock treatment. But Dr Padgett was a gender psychiatrist and his medical opinion was all so dramatically real. What Claire had told Sharon about her past were the classic symptoms of gender dysphoria or gender identity disorder, and this specialist psychological practitioner was confirming what she had been told. Leaving London to return to the North of England, Sharon and Claire collected their Honda Accord from the supermarket car park where they had left it and finding their way out of suburban London, they drove back up to the north in silence. They did not stop until they arrived home in Cumbria.

Dr Padgett had given Claire a medical prescription and so the next day she visited a pharmacy away from the nearest town where they lived. Upon opening the medications prescribed, Claire discovered that one was an anti-androgen and the other a chemically produced estrogen. Back at home Claire found Sharon still in shock. Sharon had decided to raise the matter with Tanya and Marcus at a Christmas Day party in Tanya's home. Marcus and his girlfriend Lorna were there too and as the discussion heated up, Claire found herself attacked on all sides as a freak. They declared unanimously that it was all wrong and that if she went ahead with the medications prescribed, then she could say goodbye to them. This was their ultimatum. Shocked by everyone's bigotry, if she was to proceed with the treatment for her dysphoria, Claire was destined to become a recluse.

While her family was not interested in trying to understand her medical diagnosis, their threat was for Claire to gradually let her dysphoria twist her physically and mentally into total madness simply to please them. This was so that they could continue to see and experience 'the man' they had been accustomed to seeing over the years. The alternative was for Claire to go ahead with whatever medical treatment offered and in the process lose her family. Those were the only two choices offered by Sharon, Tanya and Marcus. But rather than dampen everyone's Christmas activities by making an announcement there and then, Claire reserved her decision until after the end of year festivities.

Unknown to her, Sharon had rung Claire's brother Gerry and his wife Veronica and the latter showed no immediate sign of shock. *These things happen,* may have been Veronica's words. Claire's stepmother, however, was not as kind, declaring that 'William' had always been weird and it was obviously some fetish through which 'he' wanted to be noticed by other men. She wanted nothing to do with it and told Sharon to keep 'William' away from Milton if "he wanted to dress like a woman" she added. At the time, Milton was in hospital for observation. In the meantime Claire had been to see her medical practitioner in Haltwhistle and he was very understanding. She broke down and cried when he said he would apply for some funds from the National Health Service for her treatment. Her medical practitioner was to become a great support to her.

Claire continued with her prescribed oral medication and at the beginning of the following January changed her name by Statutory Declaration in front of a Notary Public. She presented herself to him as a female and he was very understanding, declaring that she was a beautiful young woman. *How nice of him,* she thought. Her new name, Joan Claire Porterhouse, her new family name was to use her grandmother's middle name. But in her world it would have meant that when she was younger she would have been Joan Claire Wilson instead of James William Wilson. She had eventually hoped to have her birth certificate changed, but knew that the British Government was antagonistic to those diagnosed with gender dysphoria. In fact, the British in general seemed to be against anyone who was in their estimation – not 'normal', which meant 'queer', and in her dad's brain 'a poofter'. It appeared nevertheless that she had been one all of her life, but had always tried to hide it.

The attitudes Claire was to experience from this time forward stemmed from ignorance of the medical facts coupled with the rejection of anything that was out of the ordinary. Today such bigotry appears to be slowly changing due to British society incorporating people from various cultures. But there is still a misconception that people with gender problems are sick and are often treated with contempt. If Claire was to go ahead with medical treatment, then she had to tread very carefully as very few would understand. Apart from Sharon, Tanya and Marcus and their children had deserted her. Her brothers tolerated her but kept their distance.

As Claire had changed her name, one major obstacle was to raise its unsightly head – the loss of income. Having been producing working drawings and details for Irwins of Warkfield, a large shop-fitting and building construction company, she had been working on a very large project, a four-story department store in Blackpool. Her work had been to prepare working drawings on her computer from the sketch drawings issued by a famous London-based interior design company. In this she was very successful and she timed her change to coincide with the completion of her work for Irwins, although she still had to appear on site as 'William'. In this role Claire often arrived home as an absolute psychological wreck after working on site during the week. On many such occasions Sharon would find Claire hunched up in a fetal position in a corner of their bedroom crying her eyes out. When this first started happening, Sharon told 'her husband' to get dressed for dinner and 'be a man'. Hardly the right command under the circumstances, indicating that Sharon still didn't understand, or perhaps never would. However, it soon became apparent that dressing up as a man and having to live a man's existence on a building site, was having a really bad psychological effect upon Claire. Sharon changed her attitude accordingly and encouraged Claire to dress in her normal women's clothes and to go down to dinner. This turned out to be the only sensible thing to do under the circumstances.

Claire started to advise her clients that she had been born a hermaphrodite and had now changed to her female side. Within days, the marketing manager of Irwins, Kevin Thompson, wrote back to her saying that as a result of her stupid decision, there would be no more work from them. The inference was that 'William' had gone mad. The loss of the interior design work for Irwins comprised the bulk of Claire's income and she dreaded what was to come from other clients.

As anticipated, it came soon enough. A builder from Bishop Auckland told her that there would be no more interior design work from him either. A new client, to whom she had only recently been introduced, reversed her earlier decision to commission Claire to design a new house as she had decided to look elsewhere for an architect. This left Claire with two other builders for whom she had been carrying out designs, and an existing client in Newcastle, for whom she had converted part of his house into an office. This latter client ran short of money and decided to sue Claire for errors in her detail work. Knowing that her work was error-free, Claire visited the client's builder, who turned out to be honest thankfully. He told her that the client had changed her design in two places, and when there were problems with the changes, they decided to blame Claire. She thanked the builder and rang her indemnity insurance company to advise that one client was fraudulently trying to claim that she had designed a feature which he had 'designed' himself after her work was terminated. The client wanted to blame her for it so that he could claim compensation. Consequently, Claire won against his claim.

Two of her clients were very nice and accepted her but on completion of the building work for them, there was no more work forthcoming. Claire put all this lack of work down to discrimination as previously she had had a constant stream of design work throughout the whole of the north of England. Yes, she had picked up one or two small projects from those who were sympathetic, but the total income she had been in the habit of receiving annually, dropped dramatically due mainly to the Warkfield shop fitters. She managed for the rest of the year and into the next, but could see the writing on the wall. Bigotry and discrimination had set in with a vengeance.

In one instance, Claire had received a negative response from one of her regular builder clients in Chester-le-Street, and decided to visit their estimator, who had previously been quite friendly. They had agreed to have a pub lunch together and she was to meet him at his company's office at noon. Being early for most of her appointments as usual she was asked to wait in reception while the estimator finished a phone call. Just then the managing director of the company, accompanied by his wife and daughter walked into the lobby before going out for lunch. The director had met 'William' on many occasions previously, especially on building contracts. This time he approached Claire: "May I help you young lady?" He said, looking her directly in the face.

"Thank you but no, I am waiting for your estimator to take me to lunch."

"Good." The director said, "enjoy your lunch," and walked out of the doors into the street with his wife and daughter.

During Claire's lunch date, she suggested to the estimator that he should tell his boss that he met the former 'William' in reception before he went to lunch himself. She added that maybe he was just another bigot, trying to imagine a male dressed as a female. By seeing her in the flesh, it might have registered with him that she was nothing like his imagination. Nevertheless, he didn't follow up the meeting with any more commissions.

43

The Penultimate Year

Before Claire embarked upon her final year struggling with her enigma, described medically as gender dysphoria, she was to see herself in a different light. The only problem was that Sharon didn't share the same thoughts and somehow seemed to assume that 'William' would not go ahead with 'his' intention to go the whole hog. She seemed to be mocking her husband half of the time, appearing to go along with what she seemed to think was a fantasy dream-world in "his" obviously sick mind.

In order to acquaint herself with the broader issue, Claire decided to join others experiencing gender problems at a conference held in the Civic Center in Gateshead. This was to be held over a weekend, with talks on gender issues being presented during both days. Claire dressed in her 'Sunday best', so to speak, as this was a function at which she could be her real self. Not knowing anyone else there she sat alone at the first couple of sessions in the council chamber. Gateshead City Council had opened its doors to the gender issue and lectures were held listening to what each of the guest speakers had to say. Because she knew that every speaker was transsexual, apart from a policeman who spoke about safety issues, Claire saw them in a somewhat different light to herself. There was no indication that any of them had been born with two genders like she had been.

There was a lawyer who was undergoing transformation, speaking with apparent knowledge of the law but looking like a man dressed up. The black bobbed wig the solicitor was wearing looked totally wrong and obviously, while the speaker might have known the legal situation inside out, 'she' knew nothing about how women dressed and presented themselves. Another session was led by a pair of male to female transsexuals, who while looking feminine to some degree, their voices were very deep. Obviously, they had learned nothing about how women speak differently to men and Claire was unnerved by this.

At the end of the first afternoon, Claire had been prepared for everyone to dine together, but she had not been ready for the 'official' banquet provided by the staff of the civic center catering department. Also she had not realized that delegates had been expected to dress up for the occasion. That being understood by others, Claire was surprised to find herself surrounded by a motley-looking crowd, some even looking like drag queens, heavily made-up and wearing slinky gowns. Claire was still wearing her gray two-piece suit, comprising fitted jacket and medium length skirt. Her make-up was normal by contrast to many of the others.

After the first course, there was a variety act performing on a small dais in front of the dining area. The artist was herself a transsexual but very accomplished as a magician, dressed in top and tails. Claire did not stay for the complete duration of the meal as she had suggested to Sharon that she may not stay and drive home early instead. So with that thought in mind she drove back to Fell House, only to find that Sharon had gone to bed already. As Claire undressed for bed Sharon pretended she had just woken up, and asked how the talks went. Her attitude was matter-of-fact and so Claire answered in similar fashion. Sharon was obviously not really interested.

The next morning Claire left early to attend the remaining sessions. One of the transsexuals who had apparently stayed over in a local hotel appeared to be having problems with his/her car so Claire stopped to see if she could be of assistance, not that she knew anything about cars. He/she asked Claire why she was at the conference: "Are you a newspaper reporter?" He/she asked. Claire assured the questioner that she was not and he/she looked perplexed. "So why are here? Are you a specialist or a nurse or maybe a doctor or psychiatrist?"

"No I am not actually."

"Well why are you here?" came back the questioner. It appeared that he or she thought Claire was a normal woman attending the conference to possibly learn something with which she might help perhaps a transsexual client of hers.

"If you must know, I was born a hermaphrodite, now known as intersex and have had to live my previous life as a male." It was strange and somewhat baffling that he/she could not see any maleness in Claire at all and had had to live a life contrary to the way now appeared in public.

"Oh I am so sorry to ask so many questions but you don't look like the rest of us. You look really lovely." The person attached him/herself to Claire and the latter found it difficult to break away from the assumed friendship. So much so that when four o'clock came around, and all attendees drove off to their respected corners in the North of England, Claire helped Dorothy, the name he/she used, to start the car using some borrowed jump leads. Dorothy wanted to keep in touch and announced that it was his/her birthday the following Sunday.

Back home Claire told Sharon that she had invited a transsexual called Dorothy to join them for lunch as it was her birthday and she felt sorry for her all alone on such a special day in the back room of her father's shop in Penrith. Sharon reluctantly went along with the invitation and the table was set accordingly. Sunday lunchtime came around and there was no Dorothy at the appointed time.

About half-an-hour had elapsed when a figure appeared at the front door. It was Dorothy. She explained that traveling to Fell House, on icy roads she had skidded off the road in the snow, and had walked the last mile to advise of her plight. So Claire drove Dorothy back to her car in the four-wheel-drive and called on a local farmer to see if he could pull Dorothy's car out of the ditch with his tractor. That done, the local farmer asked Claire if she was a visitor. When she told him that she lived in Fell House, and that she was an architect, his attitude changed toward her. He had apparently heard rumors in the local bars about an architect who lived on the fell who had changed gender. Obviously, Claire fitted the description but as she didn't match the already formed image he had in his mind as how she might look, he could not take it all in and quickly vanished.

By this time Sharon was getting used to Claire living full-time as a woman and they decided to take a few more vacations in Scotland. They booked their vacation cottages through an agency called McKay's, but one particular time they had booked a cottage, it unfortunately coincided with Claire's attendance at a conference in Stirling. She had been President of the Northumbrian chapter of the Society of Architects and Surveyors and received payment from her local committee to represent them at the conference. She had changed gender while she was in office as President and thankfully not one member, or the staff in head office in London, blinked at her change. Thankfully she was easily accepted. So much so, that her voluntary workload for the Society increased, instead of decreasing.

On the Friday evening at the conference an opening dinner was held and delegates had been asked to wear something 'Scottish'. Thankfully, with her paternal ancestry emanating from Caithness, in the far north of Scotland, she was fairly authentic in wearing her Gunn clan tartan. The Wilsons as a 'sept' had been part of Clan Gunn. Claire borrowed a mid-blue skirt from Sharon, and wore this with a white blouse. Her Clan sash she hung over her right shoulder draping to her waist, and she wore her clan broach too. Dressed appropriately she fitted the part as 'a Scottish Lassie' and was mightily proud of herself. She noticed that many members of the Society, who had traveled up from the south of England, had made no attempt to dress appropriately in Scotland. It later transpired that a great number of the members were opposed to having any meetings or events outside their precious south of England. Claire was told by one delegate that if this was the price they had to pay for electing a Scotsman as their President, then it would be the last time anyone who was not English would be elected. The bigotry against Scotland by the southern English astounded her.

But there just had to be a proverbial fly in the ointment didn't there? Something had to go wrong. During the second day's sessions, Sharon had joined a bus tour arranged for the spouses of delegates. But of all the people she happened to meet was a former high school friend of hers, Wendy, whose husband was manning a display stand, of his company's products, at the conference. The two friends, who had been neighbors growing up in the next street to each other in their teens, caught up on their respective past histories until her friend remarked: "Oh of course, I remember, William was an architect wasn't he? So is he here at the conference?"

The floor of the coach opened up and was about swallow Sharon, or so it seemed to her. Well it had to be told, and Sharon could not hold in the news.

"William isn't here" Sharon stated nervously.

"Oh I am so sorry Sharon, did he pass away?"

"Not exactly Wendy. You see William is now called Claire. He was diagnosed last year with gender dysphoria and has changed gender."

"Oh Sharon, I am so sorry for you. It must be awful having to live with a man dressing as a woman."

"Well, it isn't like that exactly Wendy, as Claire is very presentable. The specialist explained to me that William has had it since childhood and it had been getting worse over the years. So I had no choice but to go along with the charade."

"Oh but you will not stay together will you. I mean it would be very awkward for you living with a man dressed as a woman."

"Well, it does get easier I'll admit, but I am prepared to go along with the situation for now. I mean he might not go ahead with any surgery. In fact I hope he comes to his senses and abandoned the whole silly idea." By this time tears were forming in Sharon's eyes and her friend put her hand on her arm in assurance.

At that point the coach arrived back at the hotel and conference center where the event was being held. Sharon asked if Wendy and George would like to join Claire and her for afternoon tea so that they could all meet before the evening ball. The question in Sharon's mind was would her old school friend accept Claire, as both of them had attended her school friend's wedding a few years earlier?

The Wilsons went to the hotel's cafeteria for afternoon tea and Sharon directed Claire over to meet her old school friend. Claire recognized Wendy Manor instantly. Her husband George was standing behind her talking to one of his colleagues and then turned toward the ladies. Wendy whispered in his ear: "You have met Claire before you know".

"Have I?" George questioned, obviously not detecting any hint of Claire's former persona as 'William Wilson'.

"Yes, they both came to our wedding."

The penny dropped and George simply stared at Claire. Wendy broke him off by suggesting the four of them find a vacant table and order afternoon tea. The ice had been broken and they all chatted amicably over tea and scones. However, the big test was to come at the ball that evening.

Claire had made herself a ball gown of midnight blue satin, with a high neck to the front edged with a silver and dark blue braid, and a low back with a huge bow at the waist. She had bought a new pair of strappy sandals and carried a small sequined bag, which she still has to this day. Her hands and arms were covered in some stretch evening gloves up to her elbows, and the picture she believed she portrayed was of elegance. Even Sharon was impressed with Claire's outfit. For a couple of weeks Claire had had hair extensions added to her natural dark brown hair and she really did feel very special. For the first time in her life she actually felt really glamorous.

In the hotel's ballroom Claire and Sharon were shown to a table which they were to share with other delegates from the north of England together with their partners. She particularly was pleased to be asked to dance by the representative from Lancashire, Harry Wells. It was obvious that Harry was not a particularly good dancer as Claire's feet had been trodden on so many times by him. She suggested they change to a modern dance, which was her main forte, but he bowed out of that suggestion.

After everyone had finished their main course, the Scottish president of the institute stood up and calmly walked over to Claire. Everyone was staring as Stuart MacDonald who arrived at her table. "Claire, would you do me the honor of drawing the first ticket from the raffle barrel?"

"Och, Stuart, no! Why can't the lady provost do that for you?"

"Because I prefer you to do it please, if you would be so kind."

So Stuart took Claire's hand and calmly led her across the floor to the head table. She duly spun the barrel and removed a ticket, handing it to him to be read.

"Thank you Claire," he announced into the microphone. Ladies and gentlemen, Claire Wilson is the first and only lady president of one of our regional committees. She heads up the Northumbrian branch and is doing a great job there. She also assists head office with book reviews and the assessment of government white papers. Thank you Claire for all your hard work."

Everyone clapped as the lady of the moment trotted back across the dance floor in her strappy sandals, blushing a deep shade of pink.

The following day, a Sunday, the conference finished with an address by President Stuart in the late morning, following which Sharon and Claire were able to drive off to take up residence in the cottage they had booked for the ongoing two weeks in Dalmally.

That same year Claire had also to represent the Northumbrian Chapter of the Society at its head office in London. She had decided to take the train down to London to attend the function on her own as it was a daytime meeting. Unfortunately, her train was slightly late due to a bomb hoax outside Doncaster, but she arrived not too long after the commencement of the meeting. One of the girls in head office knew Claire and ushered her into the gigantic meeting room.

Henry Golding, the chief executive officer, upon seeing her at the door, dashed down the back of the line of chairs to greet her and led her to an allocated seat. He pulled out a chair for her and asked her quietly if she would like coffee or tea. This was so nice, as Henry knew of her change and it had not bothered him one iota.

The last meeting she had to attend, as president of the Northumbria branch, was accompanied by Shirley Jopling, the honorary secretary. The two of them had arrived in Newcastle together and took their places in a meeting room at the City Council offices before the other delegates arrived. The door opened and in came a bunch of men chatting to each other. The men promptly sat down at one end of the large conference table and ignored Shirley and Claire. A piece of paper was handed around on which they had to identify themselves and sign. At least they were expected at the meeting as their names were on the list. But as the meeting progressed, the rudeness of the men was unnerving. One of the motions presented was the launch of an exhibition of opportunities for the Youth of Newcastle and the chair of the meeting was discussing a suitable name for the launch. The guest speaker for the function was the captain of Newcastle United, but the men could not agree on a suitable name for the opening event.

It appeared that the guest footballer was to cut a red ribbon across a doorway into the exhibition room, so Claire put up her hand to make a comment. The chair of the meeting looked at her aghast. *How dare a woman interfere in what was a man's discussion?*

"May I suggest you call it the kick-off?" She calmly announced.

Everyone turned toward her and stared.

"Did you say something?" The chairman asked, rather rudely.

"Yes, I suggested that as the guest is a football player, you may like to call the opening the 'kick-off'".

The man turned to his colleagues and said, ignoring Shirley and Claire at the end of the table.

"Oh! A woman has spoken. Maybe I should have asked my wife to look in her handbag to see if she might have a suitable name in there." The committee members laughed and they ignored Claire's comment. Because a woman had made a sensible and somewhat obvious suggestion, the men not wanting to be outdone by a woman, changed the subject. Claire had been belittled because she was a woman. This was the first time she was to experience a put-down simply because she was female. She saw red and Shirley noticed that she was put out.

"Just ignore them Claire. They're not worth it."

A while later the meeting broke for morning coffee and Claire suggested to Shirley that it was a wasted morning as their presence was totally ignored by the men on the committee. However, before walking away to drive back across to Haltwhistle, Claire approached the chairman.

"As the official representatives of the Society of Architects and Surveyors, our views have obviously being ignored, so we are leaving the meeting. The matter will be reported to head office in London as you obviously don't want women at the meeting."

Claire turned about and walked away from the guy, leaving him staring at the two of them.

The next day Claire wrote to the City Council and advised them that she was disgusted at the attitude of the committee, accusing them of misogyny. She received no reply from the council.

44

Acceptance

At home in Fell House, Sharon, unknown to Claire, had been discussing the situation with neighbors. Sharon was surprised that, while one of them was at first somewhat skeptical, all in all they were supportive of 'William'. In fact, Sharon told Claire later that Judy, the woman in the house on the upper side of the slope, was convinced that 'William' was naturally female. Judy came to this conclusion when one day Sharon and Claire were returning from one of their customary walks on the fell. Judy had looked out of the window and brought her husband's attention to the way 'William' walked, and Jack admitted that, although he hadn't noticed previously, 'he' definitely walked like a woman.

Prior to Claire's transition, the couple were well known to a number of other residents on the fells and there had been many gatherings over suppers at various houses. Sharon went out of her way to spread the word of 'William's' change of gender, hoping in her heart of hearts that there would be rejection and she could use it to thwart Claire's plans. But except one self-opinionated woman, Claire was accepted by everyone and the entertaining between friends continued without a hitch or recrimination. In fact, things went so well that Claire and Sharon received more invitations, not less.

As a result of this success, Sharon gradually gained confidence that her partner's change did not really affect her, except that she was losing 'her husband', to use her own words, and everyone agreed that her feelings were completely understandable.

During this period, Claire began attending sessions at the Freeman Hospital in Newcastle, where a group of transsexuals met in the Speech Therapy Department under the guidance of Sheila Capewell. 'William' had visited Sheila prior to the change, to have 'his' voice checked, and was pleasantly surprised that it was not a man's voice but the lowest of the women's voices. The next time Claire presented herself to Sheila, she was in her real gender, that of an attractive woman. Sheila was pleased that Claire had already transitioned, and invited her to attend regular meetings of the group. Claire was fast becoming a role model for the transsexuals who attended.

There were a number of unusual characters in the group, certainly most of them experiencing big problems. Their circumstances were extremely varied and it was difficult to generalize, although the common problem appeared to be that their families and work colleagues were antagonistic, even discriminatory against them. Not surprisingly, this was fast becoming Claire's case too, and so she found empathy with a few of the participants.

Of the folk who attended the meetings, Claire particularly remembered three of them. The first was a young, leather-jacketed male who constantly belched. Claire found this very uncouth and rude into the bargain, and she was thrown into doubt as to whether anyone could help this young man. She was not aware from his/her conversation whether or not he/she was transitioning from male to female or female to male.

Another character appeared to be a middle-aged woman who had been diagnosed with not XY or XX chromosomes, but somewhere in between. She was a caterer by trade and often took samples of her catering talents, in the form of cakes and sandwiches. The problem was, as Claire found among so many over the ensuing years, this woman seemed to consider herself unique in the world, without considering that there may be others with her particular chromosomal affliction. In later years, Claire was to discover lots of research data which confirmed that the designations XX and XY were no longer determining factors in categorizing those people suffering with gender dysphoria. Due to ongoing research in many countries, the general opinion of the specialists was that an individual's self-identity was of far more importance. Some saw themselves in the opposite gender to that which they appeared to have been born, whereas some flitted between genders with ease. Claire was to discover one person in this latter category in Scotland many years later.

The third person that Claire remembered in the Newcastle group was a rather subdued young man, who hailed from actor Rowan Atkinson's village south of the River Tyne. Claire always spoke of this 'young man' as *Candice*, as she assessed his or her real gender to be female and not the male that Candice's father insisted upon. In fact s/he almost always arrived in tears, dressed as a young man and in conversation with him/her; it appeared that his father was extremely cruel, not accepting that there was such a medical condition as gender dysphoria. Candice latched onto Claire and quite often the latter put her arms around Candice's shoulder to give her sisterly and psychological support. Nevertheless, Candice was stuck in a family that was very prejudiced. Claire was not to know at the time that she herself would experience a lot of rejection, especially from her expanded family and potential clients.

In time, Candice lost her job as one of her workmates found out that she was transsexual, and to crown it all, her father refused to let her stay at home. She was to seek help from a sympathetic friend who took her in and let her be herself. But, as happens with so many people suffering with gender dysphoria, many commit suicide or self-harm, or are institutionalized, when they cannot become their true selves, Candice was to end her days in an asylum, committed to such place by her father.

As for Claire, she continued seeing Dr Padgett in London every month costing her sixty pounds sterling each time, and during the sessions she related many of her problems over past years. Among the situations was the predicament she was facing with her family.

On one occasion she was waiting in the reception lounge to see Dr Padgett when members of a television crew entered, filming a young man and his mother. It appeared that they were from BBC Bristol and they were building up a program on transsexuals and the particular young man was planning to change gender. His mother looked across at Claire and smiled: "Is my son likely to turn out as nice as you have done my dear?"

"Thank you for the compliment but every case is different as gender dysphoria affects everyone in different ways," Claire advised.

The woman blushed and apologized for her intrusion but that it was all so worrying. Claire explained that in her situation she was born a hermaphrodite, referred to nowadays as intersex. The woman nodded in affirmation but by the look on her face, she obviously didn't understand. More likely she had never even heard of the term.

Throughout 1997 Claire gradually became more confident in her real self and Sharon agreed that she was quite passable. In fact she told her that she quite liked going out shopping with her into Newcastle or Gateshead, as though Claire was her sister. They really enjoyed themselves shopping in Newcastle-up-on-Tyne and this helped Claire enormously. One of their favorite venues was the unique fish and chip restaurant known as *Harry Ramsden's*, which had started its life many years ago in Yeadon, near Aireborough. The restaurant chain had subsequently opened branches in various other towns and cities throughout the UK.

Claire and Sharon really enjoyed having their early Friday evening supper at *Harry Ramsden's* in Gateshead after they had been on a weekly shopping spree at a nearby supermarket. In the restaurant, every customer was treated like royalty, having to wait to be shown to a table by a *Maitre d'* dressed in black tie and tails. Soft background music flew from a grand piano sited on a raised dais and brought back memories of times long gone by. The restaurant tables were arranged formally, surrounded by lots of potted palm trees, and the arrangement appeared to be very pleasing to their clientele – completing a scene of sophistication. A waitress, dressed in a traditional black and white uniform brought a menu and after taking their order, would then arrive with plates of bread and butter and a pot of tea each, together with individual tiny jugs of milk. When cooked, their fish and chip supper was laid before them, complete with a small pot of mushy peas. This was indeed sophistication.

As the year progressed, Sharon agreed to have neighbors to their 'Northumbrian Long House' for an evening meal from time to time, and Claire was always accepted readily by them too. Being the quiet talk of the fells, they were almost always invited back to other people's homes.

Quite often the problem was what to wear, unless neighbors advised them whether the evening was to be formal or informal. On one occasion Claire and Sharon had assumed that the evening was 'formal', only to find their hosts wearing tea-shirt and jeans. On another occasion they wore casual clothes only to find that their hosts were well attired in evening dress, all 'dolled up' to the eyebrows. On another occasion a male neighbor even decided to wear his somewhat well-worn Buchanan ancestral kilt, with sporran of course. Had Claire been advised beforehand, she could have worn her Scottish plaid too. All in all, their life on the fells and in the valleys became very pleasurable.

Later in the year Dr Padgett made an appointment for Claire to consult a surgeon in Hove, and in the meantime she had to obtain a second opinion. Sheila Capewell had suggested Claire might consult the main gender specialist at the Freeman, Dr John Mulherrin. He was an Irish psychiatrist and Claire's case apparently fascinated him. So much so that he asked if she would mind if a female student was present at her interview with him. Of course she didn't mind, the more people knew of gender dysphoria, and in her case intersex, the better.

The subsequent interview with Dr Mulherrin lasted for over an hour and Claire was advised by others waiting outside, that she must have been a special case. The usual length of a consultation was only half an hour. As it transpired, she heard on the proverbial grapevine that Dr Mulherrin considered she was not a transsexual in the normal accepted sense, but that her diagnosis was closer to what she claimed, having been born intersex. Dr Mulherrin was an absolute gentleman and treated her as a very special lady. It was not until a few days had transpired that Sheila Capewell told her he had discussed the case with her in one of their weekly discussion sessions, not knowing that Claire had become a friend of hers. He admitted that she was not like the usual cases he saw, some of whom were really border-line. To Dr Mulherrin, Claire was very convincing as a woman and Sheila was highly delighted.

Back at Fell House, it was while Claire was chatting to Sharon over a glass of red wine in the kitchen one evening early in the year, that she asked Sharon if she would mind if she cooked the occasional meal for the two of them. The agreement had been that while Claire was working in the studio, Sharon would cook and clean. By that time Claire was even composing and typing her own letters. She had been getting somewhat exasperated that Sharon's typing was not careful enough, with lots of mistakes being made. The latter didn't like to be reminded of this either, and so Claire brought an old computer she had almost mothballed, back to life by having *Clarisworks* installed on it by a man who lived up the valley toward Nenthead. He was willing to set up the program for her in exchange for some thick stone slabs off the roof of the old farmhouse. The exchange meant that in addition to having a mainframe computer for her design work, she could swivel her chair around and type her own letters or spreadsheets on another machine. However, when Claire asked Sharon if she would allow her to cook the occasional meal, the latter seemed rather put out but said she would allow her to cook a Sunday meal from time to time.

After a few weekends during which Sharon experienced Claire's cooking skills, she admitted that she could not understand how her partner could prepare a meal without a recipe. She explained that while she had to constantly refer to one of her cookery books, Claire appeared to simply put various ingredients into a wok and every time the meal turned out brilliantly – without a recipe. Claire explained that just as an artist was able to mix colors together to obtain the right result, it was the same with her cooking. She just seemed to know what went together and how it would all taste. To Claire it all seemed so natural.

So Claire lived through 1997 completely as a woman, apart from one occasion when she had to wear what she referred to as 'male drag'. The particular occasion was to visit her father in hospital. Her stepmother, being extremely antagonistic toward her change of gender, had forbidden her to see her father. Ignoring this half-baked command, Claire donned male attire and with Sharon drove down to a hospital in Aireborough where her father was recovering from an illness. She explained that she was his 'eldest son' and that they had traveled down from Northumberland to see Mr Wilson. Claire did wonder if her stepmother had left word with the hospital not to admit her but there was no objection made by the hospital staff to her visit. Unfortunately, her father looked as though he was at death's door. He looked so old and kept falling asleep. An orderly brought him a meal of fish and chips while 'William' and Sharon were visiting and Claire tried to get her dad to eat some of it. Instead, he kept falling asleep and Claire was so upset. However, her father was to improve and so this was not the last time she would see him.

That particular year was an exciting period for Claire as she did not have to pretend any more. At last she could be the woman she always knew she was. One situation fascinated her however, that of seeing and experiencing her breasts enlarge. It was exciting to feel buds develop behind her nipples and slowly the Hormone Replacement Therapy tablets she had been prescribed helped her breasts to rise like small hills from her chest.

Sharon noticed more and more that Claire was female and could not really understand how someone could change from one gender to another. She remarked one day that Claire even threw stones like a girl and not like a boy. All Claire could say as a way of explanation was to state that most of her previous life had been pretence. In order to stop her dad from making fun of her, she had had to practice throwing a ball like a boy. In fact Milton had suddenly noticed her throwing a ball with her brothers and berated her. He then went out of his way to specifically show her how to throw a ball like a boy. Claire certainly had to carefully watch how boys and men dealt with things and copy them, or train her brain to react differently to her normal and natural reaction as a girl.

The biggest hurdle for her was how Tanya and Marcus reacted to her change. Tanya simply refused to have anything to do with her and Claire was forced to sit in the car outside Tanya's house or go for a walk for a couple of hours when Sharon wanted to visit their daughter and grandchildren. Claire was so sad, merely sitting in the driver's seat of their car around the corner on a cold frosty day, while Sharon sat in Tanya's warm living room drinking a cup of tea and enjoying cakes with Tanya and her little children. Claire found Tanya's attitude to her very hurtful and in spite of Sharon repeating that Claire was totally acceptable, Tanya's refusal to see Claire was ruthlessly defended. Tanya simply imagined her dad dressed in women's clothes and she didn't like it one little bit.

Later in life, Claire was to discover this was one of the biggest problems with family acceptance. Those who had known her previously, could not imagine her in any other way than as an obvious man who dressed up as a woman. In Australia, many years later, after having been a legal woman for such a long time, quite a number of her relatives simply refused to include her in family gatherings because they were not prepared to accept 'a man dressed up as a woman' in their perception. In those instances, Sharon was to make the comment that Claire could only be accepted accompanied by her, not by herself. Such was people's bigotry.

But while Tanya held her attitude hard and fast, Marcus agreed to meet Claire, although he was extremely cold in his approach. When she learned from him fifteen or so years later that he suffered from gender dysphoria too, she could understand his attitude. Subconsciously, he wondered if he would become a younger version of her, except that his large body frame and general looks were quite masculine. In this, Claire was convinced that gender dysphoria ran in families, through the genes they inherited from one parent or another.

But patience eventually prevailed and at last Sharon was able to persuade Tanya to meet Claire. It was timed to coincide with her boys Martin and Joseph arriving home from school. Joseph was the younger and was already home from primary school. Poor boy just stared at Claire, not recognizing her at all. Not long afterward Martin arrived home from High School and, knowing already that Claire would be there, walked in the door, flung down his school satchel and ran over to her and flung his arms around her shoulders.

"I've missed you Martin." Claire whispered in his ear.

"I've missed you too Claire."

They both sat there for a few minutes holding each other, before he swung away, "Mum, have you got anything to eat, I'm starving." The ice had truly been broken by Martin. *Out of the mouths of babes*, Claire thought.

45

The Good Times

The reader might be under the impression that Claire may have been morose and sad on many occasions, and this could be construed as a fair assessment of her gender dysphoria. But there were many times when she found happiness, even with Sharon. Claire was no stranger to the great outdoors and her love of fresh air and the bleakness of the Cumbrian and Northumbrian fells and Scottish moorland was to be a great attraction for her in future years. In fact, she thrived so much on fresh air and being at one with Mother Nature. Wherever she and Sharon had lived, she thought constantly of donning her hiking boots and jeans, packing a lunch of sorts into her backpack, and allowing for wet weather, off they would drive to some remote spot or other. Fell House was situated, as the name might imply, on the side of a Cumbrian fell on the invisible border with Northumberland. It was their restored home, looking very much like a traditional 'Northumbrian Long House', and from the house they could walk in many directions to their heart's content.

Even before Claire 'transitioned', she and Sharon had trekked throughout Scotland, walked through the Black Forest, the Austrian Tyrol, parts of France, Slovenia and Croatia. But Scotland was Claire's favorite country and it was here that she felt at home all the time. One time they had driven up to Fort William and turned off the A82 along the A830 on the north side of Lock Eil. On reaching Kinlocheil, instead of carrying on that road they had turned south and after driving along the south side of Loch Eil they headed south to Lochaline. They crossed the Sound of Mull on the car ferry and on the other side had driven up to Tobermory. That time they had stayed in a cottage in which they could hardly stand up in the first floor bedroom, nevertheless, they enjoyed two weeks of lovely weather during which they hiked up hill and down dale enjoying the breezy atmosphere of the Isle of Mull.

Another time they had turned off the A82 at Invergarry and sped along toward the new bridge and onto the Isle of Skye. That was the time they leased a small cottage in the tiny village of Elgol, which has been mentioned in a previous chapter. Here they walked on many of the well-known routes, their friendship becoming strained at the time, due to Claire's worrying thoughts as to how to tell Sharon her secret.

But once that period had been overcome, they continued their Scottish adventures and Sharon allowed Claire to dress as a woman instead of pretending to be a man. On one of these occasions, they had driven up beyond Perth and up the A9 to Pitlochry. Their destination that time was not far beyond, but they had to aim for Blair Atholl and over the Bridge of Tilt. While Claire navigated the road, which became narrower every kilometer, Sharon read the instruction. They had almost given up hope when in the distance they espied a tiny cottage, looking as though someone had dropped it there from out of the sky. It was totally deserted but the key was where the instructions said it would be, and the door creaked open when it was inserted and turned.

Being able to be herself once again, Claire looked forward to the isolation with relish. For two whole weeks the pair of them walked up the moors and down to the burns below, carrying their food and wet-weather gear. The smell of fresh air was breathtaking but trouble was lurking and was to unfold. One day Claire decided to fill up her Suzuki Sierra with petrol at a service station on the new bypass road. It was quite crowded and as she stood in line to pay the cashier, she looked around to see the men in the line sniggering while glancing at her sideways. It appears that, as Claire had not all that long been taking hormones, she had to rely on make-up to disguise the remains of minor male facial features. It was very embarrassing and she vowed that in the future she had to take great care over her appearance.

Another day they had been in Blair Atholl shopping when Sharon noticed some people looking at her. It seemed that using the personal names for each other, prefaced with 'darling', some of the other shoppers were staring at them. Claire assumed that the onlookers either saw the two of them as lesbians or that one of them was transsexual. The incident made them wary of how they spoke to each other in public.

Then there was the time they had driven away from the conference at which Claire had to represent the Northumbrian Chapter of the Society of Architects and Surveyors in Stirling. Leaving the conference venue after the provided Sunday lunch, they had driven toward Callander and up the A85 on to Crianlarich. Driving along Glen Lochy they arrived in Dalmally about tea time. The cottage they had arranged to lease for the rest of their two-week holiday was situated across the river toward the tiny village of Stronmilchan. It was owned by the elderly couple who lived next door and they were very welcoming. That holiday was filled with taking in many of the local castles and stately homes. The old folk next door even invited them into their own home for tea and scones one afternoon, such was their friendliness. By this time Claire was easily passable and there were no recognition problems.

One of the best vacations that Claire remembered was the time they had driven further up Scotland and into the Highlands. Their cottage was again quite remote and it was accessed from Ardgay, just south of Bonar Bridge. The instructions were quite specific and it was just as well as they could easily have thought that they were heading into oblivion for at least twenty kilometers or more. Eventually they arrived at a low building, which comprised a cottage at the western end and a barn to the east. It was here that Claire experienced deer snacking on the grass verge outside their bedroom window during the night, when the noise had awakened her. The afternoons had been peaceful, sitting out the back on some folding chairs; both of them spending time at their respective embroideries, and watching the newly born lambs frolic together in the paddock next door.

It was during this period that Claire wanted to follow up her father's ancestral roots. So one morning they set off to drive north through Lairg, up the A836 toward Tongue. Here they wandered around stretching their legs a while and then decided to have lunch in one of the local cafés. Claire's intention in the afternoon was to drive across to Thurso, and then down the A9 to Latherton. She had been tracing her Scottish roots through the Gunn clan, as her family name of Wilson was one of the names associated with that particular clan. But, being unfamiliar with the weather in the north east, Claire had not bargained for a thick mist that had come in from the North Sea. This slowed their driving speed and it took them four times as long to get down to Latherton, where she hoped to find the Clan Museum. Eventually they arrived, and as luck would have it, they found the old parish kirk which housed the museum exhibits. It was closed.

But the mist was getting thicker and they decided to drive south to Helmsdale where some of her ancestors may have lived, after they had apparently arrived from Norway according to her dad. But there was no time to look at anything else, as the sky was looking quite threatening. The weather did break out into a steady drizzle a while later, but at least Claire had discovered where some of her kin-folk may have come from. That was the end of a lovely vacation period in her developing life as a woman.

Prior to taking hormone replacement therapy, known as HRT, there were times when Claire wondered if Sharon was out to scare her. While shopping in Bonar Bridge one day, Sharon told Claire that a couple of young boys had pointed to her behind her back and described her as 'a man-woman'. On another occasion, they had been in a branch of the Scottish Woolen Shop and Sharon said that she overheard a customer describe Claire as a man. But times would change as this was before Claire had been prescribed hormones.

During the period between 1996 and 1997 Claire's life was changing fast; too fast if truth be known. But the next few years were to prove that her life was to alter beyond all recognition. Thankfully, her previous male facial features altered naturally and no longer did folk make silly comments. Nevertheless, she had to be prepared and looked forward to exciting times ahead. She had been advised that many things in her appearance would change, although some were too subtle for her to take much notice.

Sharon made fun of Claire spending over an hour to apply make-up before they went out, but she was somewhat of a perfectionist and was never happy with her appearance until she decided, and not before. Many years later, she was to smile to herself as she took only a few minutes to make her face presentable. No longer did she need to apply a foundation and powder, a little tinted moisturizer being sufficient to balance out her soft facial skin. Her eyes were a different matter as they were, in her opinion, her main feature. *Didn't everyone look into each other's eyes?*

Claire's taste in clothes was developing too. She had been guided by Sharon at first but some of the comments she received from others was that she looked 'too frumpish'. So gradually she changed her personal style, letting her natural eye for fashion dictate her looks. Sharon didn't like this and she often told Claire to dress for her age instead of younger. Claire took no notice as she felt much better when she made her own choice, not being assessed all the time by others.

46
The End of the Enigma?

Early in 1998 Claire was booked to attend an interview with the local gender panel at the Freeman Hospital, which investigated *National Health Service* (NHS) cases for gender reassignment surgery. Sheila Capewell, the speech therapist Claire had previously consulted, was a member of the committee, as was Dr Mulherrin, the specialist psychiatrist who had interviewed her in depth. On the day of the interview it was he who entered the waiting area to collect Claire to lead her to the interview room. Inside the meeting room, he pulled out a chair for Claire to sit on and then bent down and whispered in her ear: "You'll be just fine Claire. Relax my dear."

Did he know something that she didn't, she wondered?

The panel consisted of two lawyers and various medical specialists. Their task was to meet Claire and assess her case as to whether or not she was genuine and whether the £60,000 already allotted by the NHS for her treatment, through her local general medical practitioner was adequate. As might naturally be expected on such an occasion that could affect her whole future, Claire was very nervous, despite Dr Mulherrin's comforting words. Sharon had traveled with her and was waiting back in the corridor outside the conference room. But inside the huge paneled room, sitting to one side of the table, Claire felt alone in front of such a gathering. The questions that each and every member of the panel asked her were thorough and she breathed a sigh of relief when the interview was over. Not knowing when she would be advised of the result of her 'interrogation'.

Claire and Sharon left the building by the rear doors and walked back to their Suzuki Sierra. Their shoes scrunching on the gravel surface toward the vehicle they heard the sound of running feet on the tiny stones behind them.

"Claire, wait!"

Turning around they saw Sheila Capewell calling as she headed for the two of them. As she arrived, trying to catch her breath. "I hoped that you hadn't left as the news is all good." Claire smiled from ear to ear but Sharon didn't.

Claire looked at Sheila with anticipation: "Well?" was all she could ask.

"The vote was one hundred per cent in your favor Claire. You were brilliant and everything will be taken care of as soon as possible."

"What do you mean?" asked Sharon, who had been expecting a rejection of Claire's case.

Looking at Sharon directly Sheila told her without mincing words: "Claire's interview was a total success and the decision of the panel was completely overwhelming, not one of them raising any objection whatsoever. On behalf of the NHS, the panel pronounced her to be one of the most genuine and worthy cases they had ever seen, and that surgery should be carried out as soon as possible.

Sharon wasn't expecting this and felt as though she might pass out. She was totally shocked. Secretly she had hoped that 'William' would have been rejected as a fraud. As a result, it was to take Sharon a few days to recover from the shock, noticing in the meantime that Claire was more confident than ever.

The letter from the NHS gender panel arrived a few days later. It confirmed everything Sheila had excitedly stated in the car park that particular afternoon a few days previously. It mentioned that a letter had been sent to Claire's private consultant Dr Bartholomew Padgett and her local general practitioner Dr Simon Simpson together with a copy of their report. In a nutshell, Claire's surgical correction was to be carried out as soon as possible.

Watching Sharon closely for a few days after the receipt of the letter, Claire had the distinct impression that Sharon had been hoping that something would go wrong. To her it was a nightmare. It appeared that she was secretly hoping that someone in the NHS would negate the decision of the committee and things could go back to normal. But this was not to be.

Two weeks later, Claire received a phone call from the secretary of a urological surgeon in Hove on the south coast of England, requesting that she attend an interview the following week. Consequently, Sharon and Claire drove down to the south coast and in a rear room adjacent to his office, the surgeon, Mr Nigel Waters, inspected Claire's genital region as she lay on the consulting couch.

"You can get dressed now Claire," Mr Waters told her. "Then come back into my office when you are ready."

Unknown to Claire however, while she was getting dressed, he had asked Sharon if she was prepared for her partner to go through the whole operation that had been approved by the National Health Service. Full funding was being provided under the government scheme. Not understanding his question she asked what he meant.

"Well Sharon, under the law as it stands, if the patient for Gender Reassignment Surgery is still married, under the law the approval of their spouse has to be obtained prior to surgery being carried out."

Sharon realized that this was what she had been waiting for. "You mean the final decision is up to me, whether my husband has the operation or not?" Mr Waters was about to continue when Sharon started again. "At last somebody is listening to me. I knew there would be something to stop this whole charade and take my side of the story for a change." She was ranting on, spouting her secret thoughts.

"I'm sorry Mrs Wilson, but you seem to have misunderstood."

"Oh, I understand alright Mr Waters; it is those of us who suffer the loss of a breadwinner who now have the final say in all this tom-foolery."

"No Mrs Wilson, you have misunderstood. If you would allow me to continue with what I started to tell you…" Sharon was taken back a peg and was now silent and listening.

"What I am trying to tell you is that if you intend to stay living together as a married couple, under the terms of the NHS your husband can receive the basic treatment or the full treatment. The basic treatment is simply removal of the penis and scrotum, what we refer to medically as a penectomy and orchidectomy, and the creation of a pseudo labia, known as labiaplasty. That is all. If she is to get the full treatment, then I have authority from the NHS to create a vaginal passage too by using a skin inversion of the penis. But if you intend to remain married, then you have the right under current government legislation to refuse permission. The decision is yours to agree to the latter of the two procedures or for me to carry out the basic cosmetic procedure."

A smile spread across Sharon's face. "Okay," she said thoughtfully and with a hint of treachery in her eyes. "Just do the basic procedure as I'm sure that will suffice. I don't want to lose my husband and my livelihood as well. Is that clear?"

In reality, Sharon did not want 'William' to have any surgery at all. So if she was to be the final arbiter, she could stop 'him' having the full operation. Claire was not aware of this conversation until Sharon told her later in the year. Had Claire known this, she would have objected to Sharon having so much authority to dictate what surgical procedures Claire was to undergo.

The NHS, according to Dr Simpson, Claire's doctor in Haltwhistle, had approved in writing the sum of £60,000 for the full procedure, not a partial one. The gender panel at the Freeman had agreed that she should have the full operation carried out as soon as possible. This was to complete the total feminization of Claire's body to equate it with her brain. But now Sharon had the upper hand and would teach 'her husband' a lesson for his foolishness. She had been most annoyed that the Gender Panel had not called her in to meet them and to ask her opinion. She believed that to have been an injustice. Here she was having been married to a man for God-knows how many years, who thought he might be a woman, and no one asked her opinion. At least now she could get her own back and put a 'spanner in the works'.

So in a nutshell, and what Claire had not known at the time, Sharon had suggested that the NHS did not need to spend all the allocated money as she didn't want 'her husband' to have the full procedure. She had objected to 'William' having a vagina created out of what 'he' claimed might have remained there from childhood. All she wanted 'William' to have done was a penectomy and labiaplasty, just for the look of things, nothing else. Her revengeful decision was to cost Claire dearly in later years, at one time almost losing her life.

Three weeks later Claire was booked into the Nuffield Private Hospital in Brighton, in the south of England. Having flown by airplane from Teesside Airport in the North, she had boarded a train in London's Waterloo Station and then taken a local bus to the hospital. After waiting only a little time in reception, she was shown to a room at the end of a short corridor on the first floor. On the outside of the door to the room was a sign which bore her name – *Mrs Claire Porterhouse*. Apparently, it was the room used by all the patients of Mr Waters, the surgeon to whom she had been introduced, and who was to perform her surgical procedure. Claire supposed she was simply just another number on his books.

Claire put her clothes away in the drawers and closet, took out her knitting and was sitting crossed legged on a corner seat, listening to a classical concert on the radio, when a head bobbed around the door, "Oh I'm so sorry!" the head mumbled, and vanished.

Strange! Claire thought. *Maybe she had the wrong room.*

Five minutes later the same woman came back and poked her face around the slightly open door. "I'm so sorry to disturb you dear, are you Mrs Porterhouse? Mrs Claire Porterhouse?

"Yes, I am," Claire answered and the woman entered the room, closing the door behind her.

This was apparently one of the administrators among the medical staff, and she was just checking to see if her charge had settled in to the room. Claire asked why she had looked in on the room a few moments earlier and then vanished. Her answer was amazing: "Well, you see this room is reserved for the patients of Mr Waters and to be quite honest Claire, they all look like men dressed as women. When I saw you sitting there knitting, you came over as a normal woman and I automatically thought I had the wrong room, or that you were in the wrong room."

"I'm sorry sister but I am not the average transsexual. I was born a hermaphrodite you see and since I was finally diagnosed as female, I appear to have simply taken on my real female gender as though it is so natural to me."

"I am so pleased for you Claire, because you would be shocked to see the ones who come here, especially, transsexuals from Canada. How they think they are passable as women I don't know, because to me they have serious problems of self-perception. But then there is an extraordinary high suicide rate among transsexuals, and I guess so many discover eventually that they are not successful, and never will be."

"I know what you mean sister and indeed they do have serious problems, as much in their perception of themselves as women, but also in the trauma of gender dysphoria itself. They cannot help themselves and try their damndest to fit in, even if very badly. Even I have had problems, but mainly with members of my family. Many of them refuse to accept the medical diagnosis, preferring to see me as I previously appeared to them. With new people I meet, I have no problems whatsoever."

"Well Claire, I am pleased that you understand the problem. I think you will be a great success in whatever you do in the future."

The administrator ticked boxes on a variety of forms; had Claire sign each one; and then left her to her knitting.

Claire was puzzled. It had become plainly obvious to her that the transsexuals who visited the hospital were placed in this room waiting for an operation to turn them into women, as if that were possible. Claire tried to imagine a man being turned into a woman and seeing in her mind's eye some brawny figure of a man with hairy legs, a hairy chest, and needing a facial shave. What she had succumbed to was the popular misconception of 'change of gender'. The general public only saw what they could see with their eyes: men who looked like those they saw around them, some even looking like powerful rugby players. In the case of female to male cases the public wondered how a 'week and feeble' woman could possibly become a bearded, pot-bellied man. Such characters were the public's image of gender reassignment as portrayed by the media. The actual situation was far different to this and many men had become successful women and many women had become what appeared to be normal men.

Claire erupted in a coughing fit. The mind boggled. How was it possible? To most people you were either one or the other from birth. Religionists claimed that what God had made, man should leave well alone. But Claire was aware that she had been born differently to most girls knowing she wasn't 'a man' in the normal sense – *God forbid! Yuk, what a horrid thought! Who would want to be a man?*

In bed, after she had eaten the French onion soup she had been served, Mr Waters visited her. He was wearing a pin-striped suit, looking more like a lawyer or a politician than a surgeon. He asked her if she had any questions. Yes she did: "I would like to make it clear that I am not like some of your other patients, according to the descriptions other members of the staff have given me. I am a woman, not one of the men you normally deal with. As I told you at our previous meeting in your office, according to my mom I was born a hermaphrodite. I always knew that I was a girl but my parents had treated me as a boy and I was so frustrated. So later, I would like you to tell me later what parts I might have remaining down there." She pointed to her lower region.

Mr Waters merely nodded his head in acquiescence, albeit with a smirk on his face. He walked toward the door and commented: "I will visit you again Claire, later on tomorrow. You are on first in the morning so you will have lots of time to recover."

Early the next morning, Claire remembered being given what the nurse called 'a pre-med' at 5.30 am. She started feeling 'woozy' and then she became aware that the bed was being wheeled down a corridor with fluorescent lights passing by overhead. She was wheeled into a large elevator car and then out of that to an operating room on another floor. Claire felt herself chatting to the male nurses wheeling her along. She was trying to hide her nervousness.

Later, she could remember the anesthetist telling her to breathe normally, and then she blacked out. This was a serious operation and she would finally be the woman she always knew she was, when she awoke – or would she?

I hope you enjoyed reading *The Enigma* but it is only part of the full story. Claire's life becomes fulfilled in so many ways and in the next volume *The Nymph* she continues her life's battles. The next periods in Claire's eventful life take on new meanings, even walking through many of her childhood dreams. Stepping with her through her many escapades and experiences is as interesting as any thriller. In the next saga, Claire blossoms into the butterfly she was to be described as, by one of her ongoing college tutors.

Bella Waxman

The first chapter of the sequel follows as a taste of how Claire copes with her new life.

The Nymph

The continuing story of a very remarkable woman who gradually overcame gender problems she had experienced from childhood and throughout her developing years to achieve what she had always wanted in life.

This book takes us through the second period of her life from her mid-fifties to her senior years, seeing how she coped with all the problems with which she was faced every so often.

Prologue
Escaping Bigotry

Claire awoke slowly but then fell asleep again and dreamed of walking across a Northumbrian fell listening to the skylarks above her and watching a kite or buzzard fly a little way off, looking down for its prey. It was a glorious day and she was happy just being alive and out hiking. She didn't know how long she had slept but, "Are you awake dear? Would you like a cup of tea?" She was awakened by someone asking. It was afternoon already but she was so sleepy, and after shaking her head in response to the question, she was left alone and drifted off again.

Claire's dreams were so lovely. She had never in her whole life had dreams like this. Certainly not like some of the dreams she had had over the years wondering who she was. She knew she was a girl, now a woman she hoped, but who had she really been previously? What was her real history? How come she was here in this room? Claire constantly asked herself so many questions in her dreamy state. In fact, all she wanted to do was to dream of nice things and float through whatever one floated through in happy dreamland.

Claire didn't feel like doing anything much but sleep. But this was the first time she had been in a hospital for an operation and, *oh yes*, she remembered – she had had an operation many years ago. What for? Why had she been sent here, by whom and for what? So many questions she had to answer, and she drifted off again.

Later, before the sky went dark on the other side of the window, a nurse came into her room. "How are you feeling Claire?" The nurse fiddled about taking her temperature and checking the drip in her arm. Claire asked the nurse for a painkiller and when she opened her eyes again, the nurse was offering her a small plastic container in which was a couple of tablets. Another hand was holding a glass of water for her. When the nurse had gone Claire let herself float up among the clouds again, which was quite comforting as she knew instinctively that she didn't have to get up to do anything. At least she didn't right then, except she realized at some stage she would have to visit the bathroom. But in that regard she was aware that it might be a problem due to all the bulky dressings she felt she had on her lower parts.

Awake again for a few moments, she glanced down the side of the bed and saw a thin pipe in which she assumed urine was escaping from her lower region. It oozed out of her without effort somehow and into a plastic bag of some sort on the floor at the side of the bed. *Good, so now I don't need to go to the bathroom.* Claire's private parts were no longer private. The surgeon had done something to her to get rid of 'the disgusting bits of flesh' that she had had to put up with for many years. Now she felt content. She was very happy. Yes she was very happy indeed and so peaceful.

Claire drifted into the mysterious Land of Nod again in her new surroundings and thought about her birth and wondered what had really happened when she was born. Her mum had told her that she was a girl. With tears in her eyes, she said that she wanted to call her Claire. So why didn't she? Claire remembered on one occasion she had taken a friend home to Rigton, to a large house that her parents had moved to in her early twenties. Diane had gone through to the living room to speak to Milton, Claire's dad. Her mother touched her arm as she was about to follow, and asked: "Would you like me to tell her what you are?"

Claire must have spluttered "No" as her mum shrugged her shoulders and walked away from her. So what was she? It was then that Claire really started to come to grips with who she was. Diane loved her to put her make-up on for her and went into dreamy rapture when she applied her lipstick for her. Well one would, wouldn't one? Claire too went into a dreamlike state sometimes when she applied lipstick, especially if it was bright red – so sexy!

Gradually, coming out of the anesthetic, Claire found herself crying. At long last the male parts that nature had presumably bestowed upon her had been taken away or somehow altered. So her tears were not of sadness as in the past, but this time of happiness. She was now free to be her real self. But this was to be a hard-won freedom. Little did Claire know that the trauma she had experienced over the years was to continue, this time in a different form! Bigotry and rejection by family and those who used to know her, even friends, were to be the reactions with which she was to endure. Was it any wonder why so many transsexuals could not cope and ultimately committed suicide? In many ways the bigotry and discrimination she was to experience were to become far worse than the ridicule she had been subjected to by her father and brothers over the years. Adding to this form of discrimination as she grew older, she was to experience ageism, a form of bigotry by the younger generation that virtually told those over sixty that they were not wanted any more. Claire was now to enter the next phase of her life.

It wasn't until later in the day, that someone came into her room and offered her some chicken soup and a small bread roll. She ate it but then drifted off to sleep again.

The following day was a Sunday and as Claire opened her eyes, it was to see the ward sister staring down at her, "And how do you feel today Claire?"

Oh, this is me she is speaking to. I am really me. Wow! I am me, really me. Claire was slowly coming into the real world. "I still feel tired sister, but I am hungry and looking forward to having a wash."

"Well, we'll give you a wash later but first, I just want to know if you would like to receive Communion when the vicar comes around."

"Oh, yes please."

This was wonderful. She was being treated as a normal woman and yes she really would like to receive communion. *In God's eyes that would make me normal wouldn't it?* After a lifetime of feeling abnormal, it was good to know that the enigma had vanished. At least she hoped it had, as it had affected her thoughts constantly throughout the whole of her previous life.

The vicar came in only a half hour after the ward sister had left and he administered communion. '*Administered*' Claire thought. Was it a chore for him or was he really pleased to offer her the little wafer and a sip of wine out of a mini-chalice? Did she really believe that they represented a man who had apparently died almost two millennia ago? So many questions she had to ask herself.

After the vicar had departed to 'administer' communion to other hospital patients, Claire was asked to pull herself up into a sitting position while she was served some cereal and tea. Apparently she had to be careful eating solids straight away and was to be introduced to them gradually.

Later, as she drifted off to sleep again, she had been thinking about Sharon's comment that at last someone was on her side, namely Claire's surgeon Mr Waters. Sharon had told him that she didn't want 'her husband' to have the full operation. This thought began to niggle her, and she would have loved to know what he had actually done. If the NHS had earmarked the full £60,000 for a full operation, then surely that was what had been carried out, wasn't it? What Claire did not know at the time was that Sharon had told the surgeon that the National Health Service did not need to spend all that money on her as she didn't want 'her husband' to have the full procedure. She had objected to 'William' having a vagina created out of what was already there from childhood. All she wanted 'William' to have done was an orchidectomy and penectomy and then basic labiaplasty, just for the look of things, nothing else. From Sharon's point of view, her attitude was a rearguard reaction to losing the husband she had possessed for many years, before 'he' told her the truth about 'his' real gender. It was to be Sharon who was to have the last laugh.

On Sunday afternoon Mr Waters, the surgeon, called in to see his patient and to see how she was faring after the surgery. He sat on the side of the bed and looked down at her, appearing to be sympathetic. Claire asked him point blank what he had found during surgery and what procedures he had carried out. But Mr Waters was non-committal, not disclosing what he had done, only telling her that he had done what he had been paid to do. He was so cagey that it was slowly confirmed in Claire's mind that the full operation may have not been carried out. She was annoyed, as the NHS had insisted that she have the full surgery, not just a partial procedure. It was slowly dawning on her too that it had been Sharon who had been the one to make the choice, not herself as the patient. It was not until the swelling receded over the next couple of weeks or so, that Claire was to discover that things were not what she had been led to expect. She learned that only £9,000 had been spent on the surgery and wondered why. Her doctor had been paid some of the money that the NHS had laid aside for the operation, but the full amount allotted for her treatment had obviously not been spent. Sharon had gotten her own back on 'her husband' and objected to 'him' not having the full operation. But then Claire had to look at things from Sharon's point of view. In order to view the mess, she had to try to look into Sharon's mind.

These thoughts were paramount on leaving the hospital to catch a bus and train into London and a flight back to Teesside Airport. One of the sights to cause Claire to temporarily forget her deepest thoughts was the apparition of the highly exotic Brighton Pavilion as the bus passed by. Then later Claire had to concentrate on which airport terminal to head for when she arrived at Heathrow.

Back in the north east, Sharon was waiting to collect her from the flight. She drove them home to Fell House near Alston.

One evening, during the next few days, Claire was having a relaxing warm bath when Sharon entered their en suite bathroom to clean her teeth. She looked down at 'her husband' soaking in the tub. "I suppose you're happy now, not having what you term 'a disgusting thing' between your legs?"

Claire stared at her. *Was this all it was to her, that I needed to have my penis removed?* Maybe that was why Sharon refused permission for Claire to have a re-constructed vagina? Maybe in her mind, that would have completed the feminizing effect on 'her husband', and which she felt she could not cope with. *Was she being selfish or was it me who was to blame?*

As Claire took in her condition, she could feel how different her genitals were, and certainly felt relief that the horrid male appendage and its bits and bobs had gone. But there were still problems. She could definitely tell that she did not have a vagina and could not understand why. One evening Claire broached the subject with Sharon and it was with the red-face of embarrassment, that the latter explained the choice she had been offered by Mr Waters. The choice was to agree or not to 'her husband' having the full surgery, or only partial *cosmetic* surgery. She explained that she had not wanted to lose 'William' completely, and had told the surgeon that she objected to 'him' having a vagina as that would just about complete the transformation. Claire was mortified. How could British Law allow someone else, no matter who they were, to make a decision on her behalf, without her consent, and without asking her? Claire began to see Sharon in a different light after this. Sharon had possessed 'her husband', despite the fact that she had walked out on 'him' twenty-five years previously, and with the backing of the law as it stood, she legally had every right to make the decision she had made. To Claire this was selfish.

To Sharon, Claire was the selfish one, wanting to live her life as she wanted and not as others wanted her to be. Sharon could lead the life she wanted, using the money 'her husband' had earned to make her life easy. Claire couldn't. She had had to live a secret life; a life that tore her to pieces; a life that was not her own.

The next few years were to see Claire being accused of many things and being forced, to live a life away from her family, not by choice, but because they didn't want her any longer. Sharon was to walk out on 'her husband' a second time after finding someone new to provide her with a living. The family that she and 'William' had nurtured together was to walk away from what they saw as an embarrassment. Claire was to become a pariah, according to one new member of her family. Sharon chose to divorce 'her husband' to marry a real man. She was the one wanting normality. In her eyes Claire was abnormal.

One particular relative, a man, was to tell her that she should have been drowned at birth like they drown unwanted kittens. So maybe she was after all the selfish one. Sharon had the right to live a normal life with a husband and children. Claire could accept this but at the same time she knew she had a right to expect a happy life too. It would have been so nice to have a husband to provide the financial side of things, to have a lovely home and a family around. But Claire had now lost all hope of this type of happiness, if she really did want it. Sharon obviously did. But then, that was normal wasn't it? To have a husband who provided for you and who could share a family with you was normal. That was what society expected and in ninety-nine per cent of cases achieved.

Apart from being disowned again by her family, once people were told of her past life, Claire was to be shunned as though she was an untouchable. As a result, she was told by one of her friends that she should not disclose her former identity to anyone. Claire's friend told her that no one could tell by looking at her. That way she could exist as a normal woman.

Physically she now looked female, apart from three more hospital visits in the future, and even guys she was to date could not tell the difference. So, at long last she was to be free of the enigma and trauma she had lived with, in her earlier life. In a nutshell, she was free of gender dysphoria at last. At least she hoped so.

But what Claire was to experience instead, was the attitude of men toward women. Women were fair game for men's sexual domination and very often their deviation. Over the next few years, Claire was to be raped and treated as inferior simply because she was a woman. Indeed, her life as a woman was to share her fate with other women who were seen as sexual fodder by much of male society. Men who needed a body with a vagina to satisfy their sexual cravings. Just like animals.

The author

The author Bella Waxman was born in February 1940, in Leeds, Yorkshire. In her professional life she has worked as Architect, Building Industry Sales & Management, and Real Estate Secretary. She remains Single. Her favorite activities are writing, painting, embroidery, and walking. She has special skills in design, writing, problem solving, and management. She has written many professional reports and studies, magazine articles. She is the editor of various publications, book reviews, and academic papers. She is a short story writer and on-line magazine editor. Her previous publications were all non-fiction. Bella has spent a lifetime writing. From her first crime thriller at age 14 she went on to write many short stories for women's magazines and had six of her plays produced. Having been an actor and studied dialogue, she now turns her skills to writing her third novel. Bella now lives in Caithness, Highland and is a member of her local writers group.

novum 🕮 PUBLISHER FOR NEW AUTHORS

The publisher

> **Whoever stops getting better, will in time stop being good.**

This is the motto of novum publishing, and our focus is on finding new manuscripts, publishing them and offering long-term support to the authors.
Our publishing house was founded in 1997, and since then it has become THE expert for new authors and has won numerous awards.

Our editorial team will peruse each manuscript within a few weeks free of charge and without obligation.

You will find more information about
novum publishing and our books on the internet:

w w w . n o v u m - p u b l i s h i n g . c o . u k

novum PUBLISHER FOR NEW AUTHORS

Rate this book on our website!

www.novum-publishing.co.uk